DEMON

The face was the worst thing of all. The vessels in the eyes were hideous. And the eyes themselves. Oh, God they were shiny, glowing with a reflection of insanity. There was no nose to speak of other than two holes above the mouth. And his teeth—long, jagged spikes dripping with spittle.

Jose had watched him kill a young girl, had watched him take her fingers, had watched him mutilate the rest of her body as though he hated her. And while the killer was doing it, carving her soft, creamy flesh with a dagger, those jagged teeth had been exposed in a smile, or something resembling a smile. Jose felt his blood curdling in his veins as he realized for the first time that the killer had been enjoying himself!

Other Leisure books by Dana Reed:

SISTER SATAN
DEATHBRINGER
THE GATEKEEPER

DANA REED

Demon Within

To
James Colaneri and Mary Lee Gaylor,
who were forever encouraging me to write
a love story.
And to John Berkman,
my love.

Book Margins, Inc.

A BMI Edition

Published by special arrangement with Dorchester
Publishing Co., Inc.

Printed in the United States of America.

PROLOGUE

Gail Lindman opened the front door and hesitated. The overhead light in the foyer was barely noticeable, probably another ten-watter. The real estate agency managing this building was notoriously cheap, that was for sure. But at this point they'd outdone themselves.

She surveyed the foyer and beyond, and felt herself weaken; the area around the elevator was encased in darkness. As for the elevator itself, *if* it was there on ground level, there were no interior lights in the damn thing. She thought about taking the stairs, then decided six flights was too much, even for someone as young as she.

She shook her handbag, trying to locate her door keys before entering the elevator. The lights in the hall outside her apartment were just as bad as this. But her palms were sweaty; she lost her grip and the handbag dropped to the floor, making a loud noise that seemed to echo forever in the stillness around her.

She stooped to retrieve it; her legs were ready to buckle. Something was going on inside of her head, something that shouldn't have been there. She'd only moved in the week before and almost never read the papers—she didn't have time. And hell, everyone should've kept it to themselves. But the other tenants were trying to be helpful by recounting those stories. They had only her best interests in mind when they tried to warn her about . . .

The murders.

The mutilations.

She stuck her handbag under her arm and steadied herself. Those rumors were about to be shoved from her mind. This was hardly the time to dwell on them, and rumors they were. She was sure of it.

The heels of her shoes made a loud clacking noise, emphasizing her solitude: there was no one else in the hall. And for some reason, everything seemed louder than it should've. Perhaps that was only a reflection of her fear, and the thought made her realize that she was being ridiculous. Just because it was dark in the hall was no reason to carry on so. And certainly not reason enough to let her imagination run wild, to start remembering those rumors again . . .

All of those girls had been around her age.

All had been in their early twenties.

And all had been strangers to New York, foreign to the ways of the city.

She, herself, had come from Nebraska to find fame and fortune in New York. She smiled at that, because fame and fortune somehow passed her by, and now she was a secretary for The Garrett Lang Corporation, Inc., and just a face in the crowd at the office.

She walked the length of the darkened hall,

trying not to think about the even darker corridor she had to pass to get to the elevator. It was to her right, and led to the alleyway out back where the garbage cans were stored.

Three of the victims had been found in that corridor, she thought, and shoved the memory to the back of her mind along with the others.

Anyway, Gail almost never used it. She couldn't: it was ten times darker than the hall, even in broad daylight. No, she avoided that corridor, taking her trash the long way around. Of course, it meant leaving the building entirely, then walking half a block to the corner and then turning and walking half a block further, but it was safer . . .

Safer than finding another body.

Safer than becoming another victim.

Something grabbed the hem of her dress. She froze and prayed that it wasn't a hand. . . . She reached down and knew she'd die if she felt flesh touching hers. But the culprit seemed to be a thin piece of metal. Damn it! It was so dark in there and a loose wire had been . . . what . . . hanging in midair?

To make matters worse, the wire seemed to be firmly attached to something in the corridor. She tried to pull her dress free, but it wouldn't budge. Was this a trap, she wondered? Had someone deliberately tried to ensnare her?

No! She was acting silly, she reasoned. But it took more of an effort to convince herself for the second time in less than a minute. She leaned over and grabbed the wire, determined to trace it to its source, and heard the elevator, only a few feet away, hum and go into motion.

The car had been on the main floor, damn it!

She could've just hopped on and would've been safe inside her apartment in no time. Now she'd missed it because she was playing games with a stupid piece of wire some damn fool had left lying around. But the elevator only rose as far as the second floor and started back down.

Good, she thought, now all she had to do was free her dress without tearing it and hop on the elevator when it returned to the main floor. But the wire was snagged in such a way that she might have to carry the entire piece up to her apartment where the lighting was better and where she could see what she was doing.

But to accomplish that, first she had to find out what the wire was attached to. She'd have to walk into the darkness of that corridor and feel her way along. Oh God, it was so dark she couldn't see beyond the entrance. She dreaded going in, but she had no choice unless she planned on spending the night down there.

Thankfully, whatever the wire was attached to, it was close because she kept tugging at it and kept feeling more resistance as she progressed into the darkness. That meant she would soon be free.

When the elevator came to a sudden jarring halt behind her, she stood still for a moment and listened as someone stepped off. Maybe it was someone she knew, someone who could help. But the footsteps she heard had stopped too quickly . . . That was odd, she thought. Someone was standing just outside the elevator.

Giggling!

Gail put her back against the wall and felt her body go limp. According to those rumors she'd heard, the killer giggled a lot, and for no sane reason. And although no one had ever seen him face to face, it was rumored that he wore a cape. A cape, she'd thought at the time? Who wears capes these days? The killer, she told herself, and wished she hadn't answered her own question.

Maybe it was Jose! But no, he grunted a lot; she never remembered him giggling.

She stood on her toes and tried to walk ahead without her heels touching the ground. If she made a noise, the stranger behind her would know where she was. She was afraid of him, and that fear led to a more urgent need to be free from that damned wire. She didn't enjoy feeling this helpless. She wanted to be able to run, if necessary, without tearing her dress. It was expensive and it was new—

Her foot bumped against a solid object on the ground. A cold slab of fear iced her spine. Something was there, and it was blocking her path. She sucked in her breath, reached down and felt something cold and stiff. It felt like a face.

Oh, God! It couldn't be a face, she told herself. It was something else, only it *felt* like a face because she was nervous and scared and her mind was playing games. She glanced toward the head of the corridor and wished there was more light so she could see the object lying at her feet.

She also wished whoever was standing by the elevator would just leave.

Visions of mutilated bodies flooded her mind. The bodies of those young girls had been ceremoniously mutilated. The police, she'd been told, had first assumed it was the work of a maniac, until they discovered the truth: it was the trademark of a cultist member, the signature of a fervent follower of . . .

She couldn't finish the thought. Not now, not when she was alone and helpless in the dark, and her dress was snagged on an object she couldn't see. Not now when she'd tried to free her hem and her hand had come in contact with a face! And the face had been cold. That meant *death*. Oh, God! Please help me! She reached to touch the face again. She had to be sure. It could've been her imagination. After all, she was doing a right proper job of scaring herself—

It was a face all right! There was a nose, and a mouth! The mouth was open . . . Oh, God, this person had been trying to scream for help, like Gail felt she should be doing right now. But who was there to help?

The blood in her veins congealed when she realized her only source of light had been severed as though sliced through with a razor. Someone was standing at the entrance to the corridor, blocking her only escape route. The door behind her, the one leading to the back alleys, was locked at night. She was trapped like an animal in a cage. Someone was standing there . . . Oh yes . . . Someone wearing a cape.

But no, it wasn't a cape: it was a shroud, the kind used to wrap dead people in for burial, and it had a hood. And that hood was covering a head she couldn't see . . . And the person under the hood was giggling—

1

Samantha Croft saw him standing by the side of the boat and wondered if it would start from the beginning again. Would he wave at her and pretend they'd never met? If he did, then Samantha would be forced to play his game of 'getting to know one another' before their love could be consumated. She was torn at this point.

She wanted him badly and she wanted their relationship to last. After all, she had searched long and hard to find him, and once found, she would never let him go. And if that was what it took to please him, she'd have to play along.

But, after the first few times the game grew boring and she'd tried to rush him to the point where his gaze alone would warm her flesh, and his strong intelligent hands would tenderly explore her body. But it never worked; he still took his time. So she played the game rather than chance offending him. He waved at her and smiled, and his smile said, 'Hey, baby. I don't know you yet, but I'd like to.'

She sighed wearily and waved back, trying to

13

remember what his name had been the last time. It differed from one meeting to the next: another confusing detail. But that part of it had been her idea: it kept the mystery alive and added dimension to their affairs. Dirk? Had it been Dirk? Or was it Lance? "Hello," she called to him, leaving out his name. Besides, she wasn't supposed to know it yet. He'd tell it to her eventually.

"Why hello yourself," he said and narrowed his gaze on her face, her body. "My, what a beautiful baby. And just running around loose . . . Would you like a ride on my boat?"

She started to say yes, but didn't want to appear anxious. He loved it when she was coy. "I'm waiting for a friend."

"You been waiting for your friend for an hour now. I've been watching you. Somehow I don't believe your friend intends to show up. A short ride around the bay won't hurt."

His voice was deep and husky; his body long and muscular. And yet, it was the eyes she felt mostly attracted to. He had hazel eyes and they never seemed to blend with the rest of him. His skin was too dark, too finely tanned; his hair too brown, despite the slight hint of gray at the temples. No, they didn't blend. But she realized then, as always, that his eyes attracted her *because* they didn't fit.

"Well, are you coming? Or are you still thinking about it?" he asked. But he didn't have to; her answer was generally the same, as if written from a script.

She was right on cue when she said, "Okay. But just around the bay." She reached for his hand and felt her heart lurch with excitement. It wouldn't be long now and she'd be in his arms again. If all went smoothly, he'd try to kiss her, gently of course and with the utmost respect, while passionately asking for more. Samantha, in turn, would fight his advances. She had to, otherwise he'd lose interest. He hated aggressive women.

Oh, Lord, she prayed, hurry him up, make him try to kiss me now. But it was a foolish request. He was only just beginning to start the motor, while maneuvering the boat out into deeper water. They had a long way to go and she knew it. She peered down into the cabin and tried to see the bed. What color were the sheets, she wondered? What color would his eyes be when he took her? For they changed and kind of blended in with the tint of the pillowcases, the sheets.

Hazel eyes played chameleon-like tricks with background colors.

"Are you hungry?" he asked, heading for the channel and open water. "It's getting near lunch time. I know this great little place where we can bring the boat right into the dock—"

"I thought this was supposed to be just a ride around the bay," she said, feigning anger. She had to, it was part of the script. Still, her heart was fluttering wildly because he was moving faster this time. The noon meal preceeded their love making.

"Their house specialty is surf and turf—lobster and filet mignon," he said, continuing as though he hadn't heard a word she said.

"No thank you. I usually limit myself to tuna and minute steaks. When you live on a bud—"

"Then The Captain's Table it is. Come on up front here and help me navigate the boat."

She didn't move, not at first. But then, this was part of it too. He had to ask her again, he had to sort of force her into his arms. And oh, it was worth the wait. The scent of his cologne, and the warmth of his body drove her to distraction, especially since she already knew what was coming next.

"What's your name, beautiful baby?" he asked softly, his voice a passionate whisper as his lips brushed her neck.

"Samantha."

"Ummm, Samantha. Old fashioned and stately. Lovely name . . . for a lovely lady. Tell me, is it Sam for short?"

She turned to look at him and heard a buzzer sounding somewhere in the distance. *Kiss me*, she wanted to scream, *make love to me now!* But there was no time left. The buzzer was blaring! It wasn't fair, this was awful. She'd taken too long getting into it. The dream had taken too long to materialize, and now she was waking up to the annoying tune of her alarm clock.

But it wasn't her fault. Her sleep had been rudely interrupted by those awful screams—

Samantha was drinking coffee in the breakfast nook when Morgan Housner, her roommate, came stumbling in. Morgan looked nearly as bad as Samantha felt. There were dark circles under her eyes and her face was pale. "Morning, Samantha," she said, peeking over Samantha's head with one half-opened eye to see what time it was. "Oh, no. Is it eight already?" She was wide awake now.

Samantha smiled. "It's eight all right. Don't tell me you've got a date at eight in the morning?"

16

"What makes you ask?" Morgan poured coffee and directed her gaze on Samantha, her long, angular face creasing into a smile.

"Because you only panic when you figure you're about to keep some man waiting." Samantha got up to get another cup of coffee and realized it wouldn't help. She was really tired; they both were.

"I can see if he's got a friend," Morgan offered lightly.

"No thanks!"

"Come on, Samantha. It's time you got with it." Morgan's tone was serious now. "You should date once in a while. Christ, I don't even remember the last time—"

"My career comes first."

"Bullshit. You're just too fussy. Everytime you meet someone nice, you look for an excuse to pick him apart, to find something wrong with him. Either he's too short, or he's too fat, or his eyes are the wrong color. Samantha, you have to stop this. Nobody's perfect."

"Who's the date with?" Samantha asked, anxious to change the subject. "Anybody I know?"

"Just my old friend, Charlie. He called last night. You remember him, don't you?" Charlie was fat and bald. But Charlie owned a yacht, and Charlie knew how to treat a woman. "He's taking me to Bermuda."

"Bermuda?" This was awful. She'd be gone for a week or more. Samantha's mind raced in circles. She was thinking about the murders, the mutilations, and trying hard not to.

"Yes, Bermuda." Morgan toyed nervously with a strand of platinum hair hanging over her

17

shoulder. "You'll be all right here alone, won't you?"

Samantha wasn't sure; especially not after last night. "Oh, yes. I'll be just fine." She shifted in her chair and tried not to remember the sound of that poor woman screaming last night. "So. When're you leaving?"

"In a little while. Charlie wants to get an early start."

Samantha suddenly had a mental image of what it would be like to be alone in this great, big apartment at night. There were so many hiding places, so many closets. And the high ceilings made it dark. Then too, she was aware of the stone gargoyles on the outer ledge of the building.

"Can I borrow your yellow shorts?" Morgan wanted to know. "I just bought a white blouse with yellow print. It'll go great with the shorts."

Samantha nodded silently, then surveyed Morgan's thin frame and wondered if the shorts would fit. Morgan had always been slight in build, but lately she was almost anorexic in appearance, due to her poor eating habits. If she wasn't starving herself, she was binging and purging. Samantha wanted to say something about it, but decided to mind her own business. Morgan could be testy when she wanted to be, and she generally wanted to be when someone stuck their nose in where it didn't belong.

Morgan was making a list now, writing on a napkin with a pencil. She was meticulous about the way she dressed: everything had to match. "Are you going into the office today?" she mumbled absently, then looked up when Samantha didn't answer. "Maybe you oughta stay home and rest. I mean, after last night . . ."

Samantha excused herself and left the room. She didn't want any reminders about last night. And she sure as hell had no intentions of staying home and dwelling on the murder . . . She was about to step into the shower, but the word *murder* disturbed her. Just because they heard someone screaming last night was no indication there had been another murder . . . or another mutilation.

She remembered hearing screams during the night, screams that were horrible enough to wake her from a deep sleep, make her get up, and run from her bedroom to the living room. To her surprise, Morgan was already standing near the front door of the apartment with a cleaver in one hand. Morgan wanted to help whoever was screaming.

Samantha was frightened, but she went along with Morgan's wishes. After releasing the sliding bolt on the police lock, they stepped outside to find out where the screaming was coming from. It was louder out there in the hall, but not loud enough to be coming from their floor.

They both knew it had to be coming from downstairs, from the corridor near the elevator, the place where most of the other bodies had been found. Samantha remembered looking at Morgan and wondering if they should go down and see. But the screaming stopped then and they knew it was over.

At that moment, Samantha grabbed Morgan and held on until those awful recurring chills left her body. It happened whenever she suspected another murder had taken place: a deathly cold feeling would start at the base of her spine and wind its way up to her brain, causing epileptic-like spasms.

But she should have been used to the idea of murder. There were mutilated bodies before . . . Wasn't that why she left home?

Voices of the other neighbors, speaking in loud, excited tones, began to drift eerily up through the elevator shaft. Morgan knew there was nothing more they could do, so she suggested they go back inside and try to sleep. Samantha tried, but then the police cars came with their terrible revolving lights, the ones that funneled their way up the side of the building and lit up the features of the gargoyles.

The huge one . . . Last night his wings moved, didn't they?

Drifting back to the present, she steadied herself and knew she had to stop thinking like this, especially since Morgan was going away and she would be alone there at night. But the gargoyles were still there. Whoever had dreamed of putting those gargoyles on this building for decorative purposes had to be an idiot! The idea was absurd.

And then to stick the damn things on a ledge directly outside of her apartment so she would stay awake nights and stare at them and wonder when they'd come to life—that was the worst idea of all.

They were so damned hideous: large winged creatures, they had scaly, reptilian bodies and stood on two legs, like a man. And their faces were gruesome caricatures of humans. The big one, the one who stood a full head above the rest of the stone statues, was the one who frightened her most—

"Samantha? Are you all right?" Morgan had come into the bathroom.

"Uh . . . Yes . . . I'm just trying to decide what I

should wear to the office today."

"I won't go if you're afraid—"

"Don't be silly. Hey, I'm a grown woman. You go on ahead and get ready and have a good time."

"You're sure?"

"Yes. Now go!" She watched Morgan leave, and realized she was suddenly afraid to take a shower. All of those damn horror movies with their gut-wretching shower scenes were finally taking their toll.

"Aunt Mona. There were *two* murders last night."

"How many times do I hafta tell you, it's *Ramona*. Like the song. I don't like being called Mona."

Ramona Blattfield had already promised not to do this, but after criticizing the boy, she shuddered in spite of herself. Two murders this time! And what the hell were the police doing? Nothing! "They oughta throw a dragnet around this building." She sipped her morning tea and shifted in her seat, reaching for the tray of home-made miniature pastries in front of her.

Sweets were as soothing to her as a pacifier was to a baby. She lifted one to her mouth and frowned. If she had't been raised this way, having a goodie shoved into her face every time the world mistreated her, she might not have a weight problem now. She put it back. "How do you know, Jeffrey? How do you know there was more than one murder?"

"Well, you're not gonna like this . . . But I went downstairs when I heard a woman screaming—"

"You could've been killed yourself! What a

stupid thing to do. You're just a boy!''

"But Aunt Mona, I'm already dead.''

That was true, she thought, and closed her eyes as if to erase it from her mind. But it didn't work. He was dead, and nothing could erase the memory. Jeffrey was, or rather had been, her sister's only child. And what a beautiful boy he'd been, with his dark hair and olive skin. And sensitive, oh God, yes he was sensitive . . .

He died after a long illness when he was barely eighteen. Ramona had been in her thirties at the time. She opened her eyes and looked at him, wondering what he saw when he looked back. The last twenty years had made their mark on her, but had spared the boy. He looked the same now as he did the day he died. The heavy aroma of spices and herbs hung in the air around her. She took a deep breath and tried to find comfort in the familiar.

"Did anyone see you?'' she asked. "Or were they too taken with the bodies?''

"You're the only one who can really see me. I'm just a puff of smoke to everyone else. Anyway, the police came and said these were numbers five and six. Then they tagged the toes.''

"Five and six. Oh, I see. Now there's been enough to keep a body count, just like in the war. But the police won't do anything to stop this. They just let it go on . . .'' Her voice trailed off as she wondered if she would be next. So far, the killer had limited himself to younger women, those in their mid-twenties. And Ramona was not so young anymore. She was close to fifty now, which meant she was safe for the time being; at least until he ran out of choice victims.

"One of the detectives . . . Wheatley I think his

name was . . . He said they were gonna do a stake-out. You know, have a police woman walk the halls at night disguised as a tenant.''

"The killer will still do as he wants. He's smart." Ramona tapped the side of her head for emphasis. "Otherwise, they would've caught him by now. He's one jump ahead of the police."

"I hope not," Jeffrey said, "I hope they stop the killing. It's really awful being dead."

There were chalk marks drawn on the hall floor, clumsily sketched across the tile, when Morgan Housner passed the corridor leading to the alley where the garbage cans were stored. She knew she should have kept going, should have ignored those marks, but the killer only struck at night, so she felt safe about stopping to peer into the semi-darkness to study them. As a child, all of her drawings of people resembled these. They were not quite human forms—the lines were spaced too far apart, the angles of the joints were too rigid.

She walked to the entrance of the corridor and counted two chalked forms, which meant the killer had outdone himself: he'd killed two women instead of the usual one. She stared down at the drawings and realized there was an arm missing on one of the bodies. The police officers must have been in a hurry and just didn't bother to sketch it in. What a sloppy thing to do.

Because if they didn't forget to sketch in the arm, then the killer took it!

Ridiculous! They just forgot; they had to, because the other drawing depicted a corpse with no *head* . . . Her stomach turned.

What would any normal person want with an arm and a head? Then again, this killer was far from normal. And this wasn't the first time a body had been found with missing parts. On the contrary. The sicko who was doing this usually helped himself to something: a few fingers, some toes—small stuff mainly. He'd never taken anything as large as an arm or a head before—

"You ready, Morgan?"

The harshness of the tone startled her. Was she ready? For what? To die like this? To become another victim? She turned and saw Charlie—bald head and fat stomach—standing in the frame of the door leading to the sidewalk out front. She composed herself as quickly as she could and managed a smile for his sake. "Yes. I'm ready." Then she rushed to be near him, to feel the comfort of his presence. "Let's go," she said, hurrying him along. She was anxious to get out of there and away from the chalky tell-tale memory of those bodies.

"Okay, skinny," he said and smiled. "Let's go do Bermuda!"

Samantha managed to take a shower and get dressed, even though she was frightened half out of her wits the whole time. First there had been the incident in the shower when her head was full of shampoo and her eyes were closed and her mind had played tricks on her. She heard heavy breathing near the glass doors and then someone fidgeted with the doors themselves: not really trying to open them, just sort of letting her know he was there.

At the time, she wondered if it were really happening, or if those sounds were the product of an active imagination. She remembered a television program she had seen on occult phenomena the week before. A few psychics, some exorcists, and a few demonologists were present, discussing their latest investigations.

One of them had made a statement that stuck with her. He was a priest, and he claimed that most of his investigations yielded nothing; they were a waste of time. According to him, a lot of people imagined they were going to either see or hear something unusual when they were alone. And, like Samantha, they had a reason to fear being alone. Therefore, the fear of hearing or of seeing the unusual was enough to stimulate the brain into action, and thus set the scene for these people to hallucinate.

So those noises she heard, those scratches on the glass doors, were all in her head. She had been afraid of hearing something, so her stimulated mind provided the sound track. But she was still scared, enough to half-rinse her head and grab for a towel while shuddering over what was coming next. She had to walk into her closet to get a dress and since the closet was so big as a small room, anyone could be hiding in there.

She recalled the first time she had seen it, when Morgan had been showing her around the apartment as a prospective roommate. The closet had been impressive then. The clothing racks covered three walls and were two deep. So she was able to picture scads of clothing all hung neatly in rows, not smashed together as they normally would have been in standard closets.

But then, soon after she agreed to move in and share expenses, the murders started. And now she viewed the closet differently. It was a good hiding place for anyone who didn't belong there—

"Good morning, Samantha."

She had her key in the front door, ready to lock up the apartment and wondered if she should run back inside. She was afraid to turn and see who it was who had spoken her name. And yet, the voice belonged to a female, one that she knew quite well.

"Morning, Ramona."

"On your way to work? You look so beautiful today."

Ramona had a knack for asking a question, to which she expected no answer, followed by a statement. "Thank you, Ramona."

"You're such a pretty girl, Samantha. Some man's gonna get lucky one of these days."

Ramona had her apartment door open, and Samantha was able to get a good whiff of the pleasant odors emanating from within: cinnamon, ginger, purple jade. The woman's place was a veritable conglomeration of herbs and spices. "You know," Ramona said with a dreamy expression on her face. "I was pretty once. Not beautiful like you. God, you have such a gorgeous figure. And your hair, so nice and long." She cupped her chin pensively. "Mine was about the same color before I went gray. Auburn . . . yes, it was auburn."

Samantha felt herself growing impatient to leave, and yet Ramona was the kind of person she just couldn't be abrupt with. The older woman was motherly and considerate; always giving the impression she was interested in your well-being. There weren't enough people like her around. "How are you feeling?" Samantha asked, not really wanting to change the subject. But according to what Morgan had said earlier in the week, Ramona had been quite ill.

"Oh," Ramona said, waving a hand a
dismiss her illness. "I'm fine now. I just sl
some herbs together and took care of it mys

Samantha smiled. "It never fails to amaze ine.
You seem to know so much about . . . what?
Medicine?" The smile faded from her lips when
she caught a glimpse of something moving behind
Ramona. There was a puff of smoke, white and
thick, swaying back and forth in the foyer. Since
Ramona did not believe in using drugs and
considered cigarettes to be on the same level as
valium, Samantha knew she was not looking at
cigarette smoke.

And if not, then what was it? It had substance
and form. And Samantha could have sworn there
was a *pair of eyes* in the center of it staring at her
with an intense curiosity.

Ramona followed her gaze into the apartment
and suddenly became anxious to end their
conversation. "Well, I gotta go," she said with a
nervous inflection in her voice. "I got so much
cleaning to do. See ya later."

Then she rudely closed the door in Samantha's
face. That was odd, Samantha thought. She never
pictured Ramona doing such a thing. Oh well, she
imagined everyone had their days. And Ramona
was nice in every other way, so it was hard to
take offense at anything she did. Still, it was
puzzling how upset she became over a mere puff
of smoke.

But it had eyes, didn't it? And it stared at
Samantha with those same eyes, didn't it?

No, she thought, *no eyes!* She was not about to
add another fear to her list. She had enough to be
fearful about, with the murderer striking at least
once a week. And to think he picked this building

27

every time. But why? What was the attraction?

Samantha turned and faced the elevator, hesitant to ride it down to the main floor. Of course, if she were on it alone and it went straight down without stopping once, that would be fine. But what if it stopped in between and someone she didn't know, the killer perhaps, got on. She shuddered and glanced towards the exit door: there *was* an alternative, she could walk down. And maybe meet the killer on the stairs . . .

She pressed the buzzer and noticed that the car was on the main floor. She hoped it would be empty when it came up.

To her relief it arrived empty and it went straight down without stopping. Samantha reasoned that her fears over meeting the killer in the building on her way to work were groundless since he usually struck at night, when it was easier to go undetected in the shadows of darkness.

The elevator groaned to a halt and hesitated a moment before the doors opened. Samantha was about to step off, but her heart caught in her throat when she saw a man standing in front of her. He was a huge man with long arms that hung well below the hips. She could not see his face because his body was outlined by the sun streaming through the door behind him. He grunted at her, then stepped onto the elevator.

Her body went limp when she realized it was Jose Torres, the building superintendent. Jose was a deaf mute who grunted a lot, but only if he liked you. Otherwise, he made no sounds at all. She smiled at him and got off just as the doors were beginning to close.

She was so embarrassed: he must have noticed the look of terror on her face. And since he couldn't hear, it would've been impossible to explain why she'd been so scared. There was something else involved here too. Samantha knew she'd have to find a way to deal with her fear, even though she wasn't just being hysterical, even though there was a good reason for it. Otherwise she might wind up giving herself a heart attack and doing the killer's job for him.

2

Ron Wheatley had witnessed the autopsies, not because he wanted to, but because he had to. He was a homicide detective, and getting the facts straight was part of his job. Each and every gory detail of the mutilations had to be noted for the record, just in case that maniac was caught, because this was evidence—the killer's signature. And it sickened him.

There were two this time: two gorgeous young women whose lives had been snuffed out in their prime. He recalled hearing an old song once, something about having a lot of living to do. Well, their living was over, and they had no more songs or anything else to look forward to. He got into his car and headed for the Queens Midtown Tunnel. No way could he sit behind a desk after what he'd seen. He was going home.

But home to what? To face what? More misery? More guilt?

Still, going home meant suffering through a different kind of guilt. It wasn't quite the same as the torture he experienced each time a body was found, knowing it would go on until he caught the bastard and had him locked away someplace. And yet, at the same time, realizing that finding the killer was next to impossible. He'd tried. God, how he'd tried.

He'd already gone over the list of known crazies on file with the department, but unfortunately none of them matched. One or two of them had been strong possibilities: they'd served time for having mutilated bodies also, but their signatures were different. They'd never been known to steal body parts, and especially not an arm or a head as the killer had done the night before. So he had to release them.

Jose Torres, the building superintendent, had been a prime suspect for a while because his apartment was so close to the spot where many of the bodies had been found. And yet, there was something about the man that spelled out 'victim of tragedy' rather than 'murderer.' Jose was extremely introverted, afraid of people, a mouse looking for a hole to crawl into. Ron had a gut feeling about Jose and about his innocence. He told his people to keep an eye on Jose, and at the same time warned them not to hassle him.

He stopped at the toll plaza and snapped on the radio while he waited in line. Then he quickly turned it off when a love song blared through the speakers. There was no love left in his life, none whatsoever. His wife was incapable of showing love.

Maybe this was the reason he'd taken the murders as hard as he had. To think of those wonderfully firm young bodies wasted in death; their sexual organs violated with a knife, their breasts carved in layers. And damn it, he could've had any one of them, if he'd been so inclined. He was still a nice-looking man with a healthy sexual appetite. Women were still attracted to him.

He thought of the blonde hooker who'd knocked off her pimp and had slid her hand beneath the desk to fondle him while he was booking her. She wanted him, she had eyes for him. But he let it go, told her to drop dead, told her he wasn't available because he had a wife.

What a joke! Sure he had a wife. And that was about where it ended: in name only. Still, to set the record straight in his head, he had to admit that Debbie never slighted him in the area of sex before he hurt her, before her put her out of commission. It was his fault!

He pulled off at the next exit—108th and Main Street on the Expressway, and made a u-turn. He couldn't go home, not now, not when he had a maniac to catch. And especially not now when the guilt of facing Debbie would've been far worse than the guilt of not being able to bag a killer!

The wind swept her hair straight out, and the taste of salt water brushed against her lips; the boat was going full speed now with Dirk or Lance, or whatever his name was today, at the wheel. She was on his yacht this time instead of the cabin cruiser. It was small, but it was a yacht nonetheless. "Where are we headed?" she asked, and listened while he whispered the location in her ear, his voice barely audible over the sound of the wind.

"Bermuda! Oh! How wonderful!" Samantha had always wanted to go to Bermuda. "Do I need a passport?" she wondered aloud, her face blushing coyly when he laughed. Oh, but he was so handsome with his dark, finely tanned skin and those dreamy hazel eyes. She could almost feel the touch of his lips—forceful yet gentle—against hers, the touch of his hands roaming her body with skillful determination—

Somewhere in the distance she heard rattling, something metallic rattling against a flat surface, and it was enough to bring her thoughts back to the present.

June DeSoto, one of her co-workers, was sitting on the edge of her desk, smiling because Samantha's mind had been so very far away. "Welcome back to the here and now," June said and Samantha heard the rattling noise again. She looked down and saw that June was wearing a charm bracelet, some of the charms were scraping against the top of the desk.

"Hi, June. I'm sorry I wasn't paying attention."

"Hey, kid. No need to apologize. I read the papers this morning. There were two murders in your building last night. Hell, I'd be kinda out of it too at this point."

Two murders! Samantha could hardly bring herself to believe there had been one! She could still hear that poor woman screaming. And now to find he'd murdered two young women . . . She sat very still and tried to listen while June scratched the side of her face with an overly long red fingernail, then continued. "What I don't understand is why you stay there. Why don't you move?"

Samantha couldn't understand it herself at times, even though there were a few good reasons why she didn't move. For one, she couldn't afford to. Sharing expenses with Morgan was the only way she could afford to exist, with rents being what they were in New York. The second reason was a stupid one, but hell, she was used to being stalked by a murderer.

Hadn't one raped her?

"I don't know, June. Where do you run to? I mean, I read the papers every day the same as you. At least we know there're problems in my building. What if I were to move elsewhere and there's some guy living in my new building who's on the edge and he decides to wig out? Then I might get to be the first victim next time. And with no warning."

"Samantha, that's ridiculous and you know it."

So was the amount of make-up June was wearing. June was in her forties and trying hard to look as though she were still in her twenties. "Well, ridiculous or not," Samantha said, "It's where I call home."

"What does your roommate think of all this? I'll bet she's scared."

Terrified was actually a better word, Samantha thought to herself. And now she was beginning to feel uneasy again because June had mentioned Morgan, and by doing so had reminded her of Morgan's trip to Bermuda. Samantha would be alone in the apartment tonight.

"Has Morgan said anything about moving?"

"She really can't afford to either. Don't forget, there's a lot of expense involved. There's the first month's rent, the security, and a broker's fee if you want to find a better place to live." Morgan had been barely making it on her own before Samantha came along, and that was puzzling. Morgan's parents were wealthy upper-class people, and although her mother was dead, her father was still alive. And yet, if it hadn't been for her friends and their generous donations, Morgan would've been living on skid row.

"I don't know where the answer lies," June said "But if I were you, I'd think of something. Maybe you could go home and stay with your parents for a while, at least until this maniac's in jail."

Samantha smiled. Home was no safer than this. "I'd rather stick it out and see what happens."

"I do have to admire your spunk," she said, rising from the edge of the desk. "Anyway, we have some calls to make. Right, kid? Gotta shake up those people out there and make them appointments. Gotta keep those commissions rolling in."

Samantha watched her walk to her desk. Her dress was both too tight and too short. 'Go home where it's safe,' June had said, and that made Samantha smile. Before she came to New York and started selling insurance for a large firm, her father had told her something similar, only it was the reverse of what June had said, and for different reasons.

"Go the hell to New York," he'd said. "Go live with the muggers and the drug addicts and the rest of the animals. Go live where your life's on the line every minute of the day."

"But, Dad," she'd argued, "it's not safe here either." At that point her father stopped quarreling because he knew she was telling the truth.

Someone had stalked the woods near her home; that beautiful, calming place where Samantha often went to air out her problems when she'd been nothing more than a sensitive teenager. That place where oak and maple grew wild, and their branches were long and heavily burdened with leaves. That place where birds nested in those trees and had babies.

Someone came there and hid until a young girl went by . . .

There were rapes, murders, flaming bodies . . .

Home wasn't safe. But it wasn't safe here either.

She had no place to run to, no place to hide.

Beginning at the top of a list of prospective clients, she lifted the receiver of the phone and began to dial the first of many numbers. June had been right about one thing: Samantha had to make those calls, had to book those appointments. Otherwise there would be no income next month and she'd have to move. Out of necessity, rather than fear.

Ramona Blattfield had been ready to take her morning nap when the noise made her sit up in bed and convince herself she wasn't a bit tired. Of course, it wasn't a loud noise. On the contrary, it was barely noticeable. But it was there and she heard it—a banging sound, a thumping, as though someone was in the process of nailing something together. Then she thought of coffins and how the lids were sealed before leaving the funeral home, and she knew she had to get up.

Jeffrey was in the kitchen just hovering around when she went in to make some tea. "Can't sleep?" he asked.

"No. There was some noise. I decided to get up." She stared into her cupboard, at the large selection of herbal teas she generally kept on hand, and wound up taking the one flavored with rind of oranges and sweet spice.

"Good choice," Jeffrey said.

"How do you know?" she asked. "You've never even tasted it."

"Well, it smells good. I like the aroma."

She put her hands on her hips and felt her annoyance growing. "Jeffrey, will you *please* come down off that damn ceiling? You're making me nervous."

He floated down and settled into a chair at the table. "I don't mean to be disrespectful—"

"But you will be." She looked at him, at those dark, almond shaped eyes and felt a smile replacing her annoyance. "Go ahead. What is it?"

"All I'm try'na say is, I wouldn't be in the way or making you nervous if you sent me back."

Ramona plopped herself down wearily and felt she couldn't answer. The truth was, she couldn't send him back. She'd tried many times, but for some reason the reverse chant wasn't working. And now, how could she tell this to the boy while he was looking at her with those sad eyes and she was, in turn, staring at that wonderful face of his?

"Do you really want to go back? Is it so great there you wanna leave Aunt Ramona and go live with strangers?" She heard the banging noise again and decided to ignore it this time.

Jeffrey didn't answer right away, and his silence disturbed her, made her feel guilty for having summoned him up without really knowing how to send him back. But then he spoke to her and what he said smoothed things over between them. "No. I don't think it's such a good idea to send me back. Although it really isn't such a terrible place. There's sunshine and trees . . . But Aunt Mona, you're right about one thing. It's awful depressing to be living among strangers."

Ramona felt a lot better because of what he'd

said and she tried to enjoy the feeling, tried to make it last. After all, Jeffrey had been the first one to be called forth, so to speak, and there were bound to be mix-ups. But she couldn't relax, that damned banging noise was driving her nuts. "What is that?" she snapped, getting to her feet.

"There's a big, ugly man mopping the hall."

"Oh, jeez. I forgot. Jose does the hall every two days." She sat down again and tried to compose herself, but it was too late. She'd already lost what little was left of her happy disposition. "You know, Jeffrey, this murder thing has got us all going crazy. I mean, I should've recognized those noises. The damn halls are mopped three times a week, so it's not as if I never heard it before." The thumping noises occurred whenever the metallic base of the mop came in contact with something solid like the bottom of a door or the moulding along the walls.

"It's okay to be scared. Everyone else is. You're only human, you know." He sat there and studied her for a moment before speaking again. "What's wrong with Jose? The woman down the hall said hello and he didn't answer. He kept his back turned as if he didn't hear her. She went up and tapped him on the shoulder to let him know she was there. And boy, did he jump. Then he got angry and grunted at her."

He *jumped?* Jose Torres actually *jumped* when someone touched him. A big man like that? Ramona knew he had to be scared, along with everyone else, otherwise he wouldn't have reacted as he did. "He's a deaf mute, Jeffrey. He can't talk and he can't hear. So he grunts when you say hello."

"Gee, what a shame. To be a deaf mute and so

ugly on top of it."

Jeffrey had a point there. Jose was ugly, a real double bagger. However, unlike most ugly people, he lacked a pleasant personality, which made him appear to be twice as ugly—a horror actually. Then something important came to Ramona's mind and she forgot Jose for the moment. Jeffrey had been outside in the hall again. She sighed and tried to find the right words so he wouldn't think she was scolding him.

"Jeffrey. I know you're a young boy and you're naturally curious. You like to roam and look around and see things. But, honey, nobody's supposed to know you're here. People would be frightened of you if they found out. So please, for Aunt Ramona's sake, try to stay inside the apartment."

"Uh huh. And watch television all day."

"We have no choice, now do we?"

"No. But it does get boring."

The tea pot whistled but she ignored it. Speaking to Jeffrey was more important. "Is it as boring as living among strangers?"

"No. You're right. I'll stay here where I belong."

The sadness in his voice was like a knife through her heart. She loved the boy so much, more so now than when he'd been alive. And somewhere, she knew, there was a solution to the problem of his loneliness, and to his boredom as well. And she intended to find it; she'd damned well find it for Jeffrey's sake.

Jose Torres couldn't hear the mop thumping when it hit the wall, just as he hadn't been able to hear the old lady when she came up behind him a while back. And, Jesus Lord, this was a curse: he couldn't talk, couldn't hear. And somehow he'd never felt the need for speech and hearing as much as he did now, when he had something important to say and couldn't say it.

He couldn't even tell the old woman why she'd scared him so badly, sneaking up on him that way. Then again, if he hadn't seen the killer with his own two useless eyes, he wouldn't have been so afraid. It was a curse all right, seeing something and not being able to warn someone. But then, if he could talk, who would he tell? Who would believe him when he described that monster? For surely he hadn't been looking at anything human!

He stopped mopping and straightened his back to give it a rest. There had been no reason to jump when the old lady touched him: it was daytime, they were all safe for now. But how safe, he wondered, when up against an inhuman beast? Oh Lord, he closed his useless eyes and tried to blot out the memory, but it wouldn't go away. He alone had seen the killer and he couldn't erase it from his mind.

The beast had no skin. Jose had seen his vessels and his arteries pumping blood. At least it had been true of those parts of the body that weren't covered by the cape he wore. And his face . . . *Madre, Dios!* Jose thought he'd fallen asleep and was having a nightmare. The face was the worst thing of all. The vessels in the eyes were hideous. And the eyes themselves. Oh, God they were shiny, glowing with a reflection of insanity. There was no nose to speak of other than two holes above the mouth. And his teeth—long, jagged spikes dripping with spittle.

Jose had watched him kill a young girl, had

41

watched him take her fingers, had watched him mutilate the rest of her body as though he hated her! And while the killer was doing it, carving her soft, creamy flesh with a dagger, those jagged teeth had been exposed in a smile, or something resembling a smile. Jose felt his blood curdling in his veins as he realized for the first time that the killer had been enjoying himself!

And he had to tell someone, had to!

Then again, what if the killer were to somehow find out Jose had seen him? He'd kill Jose next! And it would be horrible to be mutilated, to have your body cut and sliced by a maniac!

But still, even realizing what he did, knowing his life would be in danger, Jose couldn't go on this way. He could hardly eat, couldn't sleep, hadn't been able to do much of anything except mop the halls and tend to the garbage since he'd seen the killer's face. He had to alert the authorities . . .

But the police scared him. They'd done terrible things to him back in Puerto Rico. So he couldn't go to the police for help.

Once again he considered keeping quiet and saying nothing. But if he did and the killer was allowed to continue—three women had already died since Jose had seen him—then each future death would be on his conscience, and he couldn't live with so much guilt eating away at his insides.

Garrett Lang had already heard the bad news: one of his secretaries had been killed, along with another woman, the night before. And it made him think about death and dying, a subject he'd been dealing with quite often these past few weeks. So it was only natural for him to have been responsive when Samantha Croft called and asked to speak to him about insurance.

Of course, the young girl from the typing pool, the one filling in for the late Gail Lindman, hadn't been aware of his feelings. Therefore, when he spoke to her over the intercom and sensed her reluctance to put the call through, he couldn't blame her one bit. But he wanted the call, wanted it badly. As the working founder of The Garrett Lang Corporation, Inc., he'd acquired a vast fortune and, being single, he had to make sure his wealth didn't fall into the wrong pockets after he was dead.

This Ms. Croft had mentioned reviewing Corporate Wills, Estates and Trusts, and Key Man Insurance for Garrett as well as for the other top executives, whose deaths would cause a temporary, yet costly, halt in the operations of his corporation. His lawyer had been asking him to sit down and discuss this subject for a long time now. In fact, Ms. Croft wanted to see both Garrett and his attorney. Garrett, however, decided to see her alone first, then call in his attorney if she seemed knowledgeable enough to handle his affairs.

And although he'd made an appointment, Garrett felt it was odd that she'd picked this time to call. Especially since he'd been thinking about death quite a bit these past few weeks and hardly needed the news about Gail to set him off. But it was only because his life was so full of uncertainty due to the way he'd acquired his wealth and the deals he'd made. And now he was afraid time was growing short, his cards would be called in and they'd send someone after him . . .

He rose from his desk and leaned against the

frame of the window behind him. In his reflection he saw nothing but torment in the hazel of his eyes. Then he considered doing what he normally did when things really got to him, he considered taking his yacht out for a spin, or maybe just lounging on deck and catching another layer of tan, except he was already as brown as a berry.

He noted the gray flaring at his temples and felt old and spent, even though he'd barely reached the age of thirty-six. He suddenly turned and hit the buzzer on his intercom and listened while a nervous, young, voice responded.

"Yes, Mr. Lang."

"When is that Croft woman supposed to get here tomorrow? Is it before or after lunch?"

"Before, sir."

He sighed. That wouldn't give him much time. "Call her back," he said, amazed as always at the deepness of his own voice. "Tell her to make it around one o'clock. I'm taking the yacht out. I won't be back until then."

3

When the call came, Samantha had gotten a knot in her stomach. Garrett Lang was canceling out; she just knew it! But to her relief, his secretary was only calling to change the time of the appointment. She smiled and felt she'd done well.

She heard deep-throated giggling coming from a desk nearby and recognized June DeSoto's voice. While she wasn't crazy about June, she just had to tell someone: she'd actually managed to pin down the elusive Garrett Lang, a feat nobody in this office had ever been able to pull off. Which was a good sign. He was probably ready to sit down and get serious about his insurance.

But June was speaking to one of the male agents. He was sitting on her desk and she was leaning close to him, close enough to allow one of her buxom breasts to brush lightly against his arm. "And I'd kiss your fingers and your toes,' he said to me. And I said, 'Only my fingers and my toes? What about . . .' " Then June whispered in the other agent's ear, and they both laughed while he rolled his eyes in agreement.

Samantha decided to stay put and go over her list of prospective clients again, searching for a good hopeful, one she may have missed the first time around. But June was speaking in a normal tone again, and while Samantha tried not to listen, June's voice carried over to her desk. The other agents in the room were obviously listening too, while pretending they weren't.

" 'But I'd have to tie you up first,' he said, 'to make it more enjoyable.' " June was laughing so hard she couldn't finish.

Samantha felt her stomach turn. Rapists tied people up.

She didn't want to hear any more, but if she got up and left for no reason at all, everyone would know the truth: she'd overheard June's conversation and that kind of talk went against her morals. And then what a time of it she'd have around the office. As it was, everyone called her a prude because she didn't care for dirty jokes and never laughed when someone used smutty words. No, she couldn't leave. So she sat where she was and tried to block out the sound of their voices.

" 'Have you ever been tied to a bed post?' he wanted to know. And I said, 'Hell no, I've never been tied to anything. Not even to some bum in marriage.' So then he told me, 'There's a first time for everything and I shouldn't knock it 'till I've tried it.' "

Samantha looked at her watch and realized it was getting late. It was nearly time to go home. And yet, home was the last place she wanted to be now, since Morgan was away. She turned back to the list on her desk. Maybe she'd work harder than usual; tire herself to the point where sleep would come easily once she was home in her apartment. That way, she wouldn't spend the night wondering about the killer, wondering when her turn would come, or wondering about the gargoyles . . . and when they'd come alive.

"Hey, kid. Are you ready to knock off yet?" Samantha heard June's voice, only it was louder this time. She glanced up and saw June standing in front of her desk. The man she'd been speaking to was just leaving the office. "I said, are you ready to knock off yet?" June asked again.

"Almost. Why?"

"Because I thought we'd go grab a bite to eat. You and me." June was smiling now. And while Samantha didn't really want to go, there was something pathetic about that smile, a hidden loneliness, so she just had to say yes.

"It'll take me a second to clean off my desk." She swept a handful of papers into her top drawer and saw a notation about Garrett Lang on one of them. But she didn't mention him or the appointment because June would probably turn it into something lewd by asking her if she'd go to bed with Garrett Lang if he asked her. And the answer was no.

Jose Torres was downstairs in his apartment when he first heard the noises, which was impossible because he was deaf, and had been since birth. It seemed to him there were shuffling noises coming from somewhere inside of his head. And so he covered his ears and tried to block them out because those were the same noises his body must've made when he'd been hanging from a rope in jail, his tortured form brushing against a cold, concrete wall.

He didn't want to think about that and tried to cover the vision with more pleasant memories: his childhood in Puerto Rico when everything around him was beautiful; the sky, the fields, the water, and he could see and smell good things, so it didn't matter if he could talk or hear.

Then again, it did matter. It mattered a whole lot to the others—the villagers, those pious peasants who called his handicap a curse from God and who called him a walking abomination. . . .

Jose was sitting on the bed in his one-room apartment, eating chicken and rice; the same thing he'd been eating for days now. But he'd made so much; he'd cooked two chickens and a couple of cups of rice, had thrown some beans in. And it was too good to waste. Still, he resented sharing it with roaches, so he sprayed the place first, before eating, although it hadn't actually helped. There were roaches running across the top of his television set, and it caused him to wonder when the beans on his plate would get up and run too. Some of them looked like roaches.

His stomach did flips and he knew he couldn't continue, so he scraped the rest of his food into the garbage and stared down into the bag until the rice turned black with roaches. This was good, he thought, they were trapped. He grabbed a can of spray off the grimy sink behind him. And as he sprayed he watched them run, watched them scurrying around trying to escape the deadly fumes.

But he soon tired of that and went back to sit on his bed, wondering when one of the tenants in the building would discard a chair so he'd have something decent to sit on. The chair he had now, the one he shared with the roaches that lived in

48

the stuffing, he'd gotten the same way: a tenant had thrown it out. It was still in good condition when he got it, just a few holes here and a few stains there, but otherwise it'd suited him fine. Only now the springs were beginning to come through, so it was shot.

He brushed a few roaches off his pillow and laid down. If only sleep would come, as it had before he'd seen the killer. Now that was a walking abomination! Then he smiled and wondered if the villagers back in Puerto Rico would've been as afraid of the monster as they'd been of him. He raised a hand and stared at the thick, black, tufts of hair on his fingers. Monkey beast they'd called him, said he wasn't normal, said he was too big and too ugly to have come from God.

Jose couldn't hear them at the time. And yet, hearing them wasn't necessary when he could see their faces; their contempt, their fear, their anger. And all had treated him equally as bad when he'd been a confused heartbroken little boy who'd grunted a lot because he couldn't talk and had grown to be a larger version of the same. All except Louisa.

He closed his eyes and thought of Louisa, of her dark auburn hair and dark eyes, her long legs. Samantha Croft reminded him of Louisa: her body was similar, but Miss Croft's skin wasn't olive like Louisa's. And she didn't have the same carefree expression on her face as Louisa did, like the whole world was a playground and nothing was ugly and untouchable, including him.

He'd grown up with Louisa, had spent his child-hood working side by side with her in the fields, picking somebody else's crops to help put food on his family's table. Once in a while, they'd both reach for the same piece of sugar cane and his hand would brush up against hers, and something, some emotion he knew nothing about at the time would make his stomach flutter. Then he'd turn and look deeply into those dark, honey-brown eyes of hers and he'd catch her smiling.

At first, when he was a kid, he didn't understand his emotions. But when he got older, and had grown to be big and ugly, he knew what they meant: he wanted Louisa with the same passions as any normal man, who had eyes to look upon her loveliness, and a nose to smell the sweet scent of her body. And the villagers ruined it! He balled his hand into a fist: they ruined everything!

The shuffling noises echoed in his head again, but he refused to listen, refused to acknowledge the sound his body must've made when it had been dangling from the end of a rope. He also sensed something odd in the room around him and chose to ignore that too by keeping his eyes closed. Too many times in the past few weeks—since he'd seen the killer—he'd allowed fear to dominate his senses, and he jumped at every odd sensation.

Jose might've been a deaf mute, but his other senses were sharp and had grown beyond their normal limits due to his handicap. For instance, he could generally tell when someone was near. He could smell the sweat on a laborer's body from fifty paces away. He could pick up the body heat from tenants before they knocked on the door to his apartment, and he could almost hear someone coming up behind him on the street.

And all of those senses were alive now and he felt he should open his eyes.

But he also felt he needed some sleep, and it

would surely come if he kept his eyes closed long enough. He brushed a roach off his cheek and smiled to himself. The roach had probably been the odd thing he'd sensed near his body and now the roach was gone so his senses should've relaxed. But they didn't. He sensed body heat. Someone was in the room.

Without looking, he reached for the grimy blanket heaped in a ball near his feet and covered his body up to the neck. He was suddenly cold, as he usually got whenever he was afraid. And fear had been a constant companion these past few weeks, as had his alarmingly acute sensations. Only, those sensations had been going wild lately, making him sense things that weren't there.

How often had he felt someone coming up behind him since he'd seen the killer's face, and had turned to find he was alone on the street or in the halls of the building? How often had he sensed another presence right here in this room and had been so scared he couldn't look? Then, thinking perhaps it was the killer, he'd sit up in bed and allow his eyes to become accustomed to the dark, and he'd scan the room to find he was alone.

Seeing the killer had done this to him, had caused him to react in such a way as to prove his former neighbors, the villagers, correct in their assumptions: he was a senseless idiot!

But this time, things would be different! He vowed to ignore his senses, the same way he ignored them when he sensed the old woman coming up behind him in the hall today. Yes, he vowed to ignore them, vowed to ignore the face he felt looking down into his, vowed to ignore the hot, stale taste of someone else's breath on his lips . . .

He needed sleep, he had to sleep. Louisa came to him in his sleep, and he was able to see her and to feel her without the ugliness associated with their romance. He could feel her body beneath him in bed; her soft, buxom, breasts pressed against his chest; her long, shapely, legs wrapped around his. And he could almost hear the sweet, breathy, sound of her moaning as she raised her lower torso in ecstasy—

But they were caught by her father, and Jose was carted off to jail. Louisa was two years younger than he, and since he was eighteen at the time, she was considered underage. What he had done was statutory rape! Only it wasn't, as he tried to tell all who would listen, all who would read his hastily scribbled notes. They were in love, he and Louisa, and what they had done had been merely a consumation of their love and nothing else.

But he couldn't talk beyond a grunt and he was a freak besides. So no one listened and no one cared. And no one cared either when the guards took him from his cell at night and hung him from a beam with a rope tied under his arms and did awful things to his naked body. And no one cared that now, because of the things they did to him, he was less than a man.

He recalled that while he was still in jail, his mother came to him with news of Louisa. She'd been sent to a convent as punishment for her sin because she'd dared take as her lover a man who was a physical and mental abomination in the eyes of God. Louisa had a baby there, a boy. Word had it that the child had been stillborn. But there were other rumors, as told by those who had direct access to the convent. The nuns

52

suffocated the child because it resembled him!

There was an old familiar knot in the pit of his stomach and he knew he couldn't sleep; but it wasn't because of the killer this time. Rather, it was because of the way his life had turned out since. Louisa had married another man about ten years ago, he'd heard, and had borne him six children, all healthy, beautiful, and acceptable in the eyes of the church.

He felt pressure on his bed, on the side of it, as though someone had just sat down. But that was impossible. He lived alone. Still, the bed was down on one side, a weight was pressed against it. He kept his eyes closed and tried to feign sleep. He'd read in the newspapers that this was a good defense if your apartment was broken into and you were home in bed: pretend you're asleep and that you've heard nothing. Otherwise, the offender would kill you just to eliminate a witness.

Jose's heart leaped to his throat when he felt a hand brush against his. He had the sensation of being touched by a stiff, cold, chunk of flesh with a jelly-like texture. And he thought of the killer and how the killer had no skin on his body, at least not on those parts he'd been able to see. And now he tried to imagine how a skinless body would feel: jelly-like—

He wanted to cry, wanted to scream, but he had no voice to do either. And he tried to calm himself by reasoning this out. The killer went after young girls. Jose wasn't a young girl, although he wasn't all man anymore, not after what those guards had done to him in jail. Still, why would the killer be after him?

"Because you saw me."

A soft, gentle voice—hardly what one would expect from a killer. Then he was amazed as well as frightened because the voice had been inside of his head. The killer had been able to penetrate his brain, to shoot words into his conscious mind. Then he wondered if the killer would further mutilate his body, finish the job the guards had started.

"Only after you're dead."

Only after you're dead, he repeated to himself. And again his mind spoke to the killer as a helpless, sinking sensation filled him with dread at the thought of his own death, his own murder. He wondered if the women had been so lucky. Had the killer taken those body parts before or after they were dead?

"Sometimes before. Sometimes after. It depended on how hard they fought me."

Then, before opening his eyes, two final questions came to mind and they had to be answered. How did the killer know Jose had seen him? And why had he waited this long to kill him?

"I am legion! I know all things. You will die because you are ready and willing to tell someone. You will not keep the vision of my countenance a secret."

Jose opened his eyes then, not because he wanted to, but because he felt compelled to. He had to see if the vision had been accurate: nobody could live without skin on their body! He opened them and saw that it was so, there were a myriad number of vessels, some blue, some red, pumping inside of the face he was looking into. The eyes were hideous, there was no nose, and oh, God, those teeth—

* * *

J. J. Holiman turned on the table lamp next to an aging, over-stuffed chair and sat down. He'd read about it in the papers today: two more murders to add to the growing list. He raised a hand to fondle the skull lying next to the lamp and wondered if this poor creature's death had been as violent. Then he wondered if his hand had been shaking because he was old or was it because he was scared.

There was a definite abnormality connected with this murderer and he was still trying to figure out which way it ran. Either the killer was insane or he knew what he was doing and needed the body parts for a ceremony. J.J. scanned the library of books he'd collected over the years, those dealing mainly with the occult world, and knew he'd have to turn to those books for help. Five rows of shelves ran from wall to wall and ceiling to floor. He had most of the important works, and they'd generally given him the answers he'd needed in the past.

But he was stumped this time and didn't know where to begin looking. If the killer were truly insane and human, he'd start with 'Abnormal Psychology,' and work his way up to something like 'Demon Possessed.' But he wasn't sure about the human part of it. He'd come across something like this before, and the killer had been demonic in nature, a little, tooth-sucking horror.

Then he laughed. What a time he'd had of it: trying to explain that to the police, trying to make them understand what route they had to follow to apprehend the killer. If those detectives hadn't mocked him, the exorcist would've been called in right away, and the case solved a whole lot sooner.

And as always, J.J. had been correct in his assumptions: the killer was a demon, one of the foulest he'd ever crossed paths with. He rose and selected a book from the third shelf, the one dealing with Demons and Satanic Ceremonies. If he was going to New York, he had to carry some ammunition along, some proof that he wasn't crazy. And this book would do it.

"Katie," he called, hoping his housekeeper would hear. He watched the knob of the heavy oak door leading into the room turn soundlessly and readied himself with a smile. Katie was hard to fool, and if anyone would try to discourage him from investigating those murders, she would. She stood before him, aging and gray, like the years that had passed between them. "Would you throw some things into a suitcase for me? I'm taking a trip to New York."

She didn't smile back. "I knew it. Soon as I read about those murders in the newspaper I knew you'd be running off to New York to stick your nose in."

"It's not what you think," he lied wondering if she'd fall for it this time. Katie and he had been together for over thirty years, so she knew him better than anyone. She was silent now, silent and angry: he was supposed to be retired. He studied her face, overrun with lines of aging, a shriveled mouth. Did he look that old? Would those people in New York believe him or consider him to be just another senile senior citizen who thought he had all the answers?

"It's not what you think," he repeated. "Garrett is forever asking me to come and visit for a while. So, now I'm taking him up on his offer."

"I'll pack your bags." Her voice was a sigh of

defeat. She turned and started to leave the room without saying anything more. But he knew her as well as she knew him. She had to have the last word, no matter how sarcastic, just to prove he hadn't fooled her. "Don't forget your books. They might come in handy when you start your investigation."

Ramona Blattfield might've been relieved had she known what Ron Wheatley had in mind. Jeffrey had tried to tell her, but since Jeffrey wasn't sure of what he'd overheard, Ramona dismissed it from her mind.

Police Officer Janice Clark, dressed as a civilian, entered the lobby of Bridge Gate Court and proceeded to let herself be used as a decoy. She opened her blouse a bit to check on the hidden mike, just to be sure it was functioning properly, and walked toward the elevator. According to the coroner's report, this was approximately the same time of night that three of the victims had been killed, giving her a fifty percent chance of running into the killer.

Her only hope now was that those two detectives in the car down the block weren't goofing off. If and when she needed their help, she wanted to be sure they were listening and would come running.

But would they run fast enough?

Or would she be dead when they got here?

The sound of her heels clicking against the tile floor was a bit unnerving. The noise they made was loud enough to alert the killer if he was in the area, true, but she wondered if the noise was too loud: would it muffle his footsteps as well? Would she hear him coming before he struck? Then, despite her attempts not to, she began thinking about the descriptions of the bodies and how each had been mutilated.

One hand shot up involuntarily to clutch at a breast: she could almost feel the sharpened edge of a blade slicing through. Her gun was in her handbag and she allowed her hand to slide from her breast until it was safely nestled against the silk lining of her purse. She didn't want to appear obvious because it might frighten the killer away, but she wasn't anxious to become a statistic.

And Detective Ron Wheatley had told her to keep the weapon handy, which was precisely what she was doing. So what if the killer saw her walking toward the elevator with her hand in her purse? Why would he automatically assume she had a gun? She was as young as the other women he'd killed, and she was dressed similarly.

She decided to keep her hand on the thirty-eight and take her chances. If he ran from the building, so what? There were enough cops stationed around the area in addition to the two in the car down the block; somebody would catch him. Why put herself at risk? Then she realized she was being hysterical, which was a mistake. She was a police woman. She wasn't allowed the luxury of showing the same emotions as anyone else. Therefore, she had to stiffen her upper lip and proceed with this decoy routine.

She heard grunting noises coming from the corridor leading to the alleyway out back. That was the spot where most of the bodies had been discovered. She took her revolver out and released the safety. No more decoy act. Either the killer was hiding back in the darkness or he'd already nailed another victim. And since he giggled a lot, but had never been known to grunt, she felt it was the latter; he'd done it again, had attacked and mutilated some poor soul. This time, though, it sounded like they'd gotten lucky, the victim was still alive and might be able to identify the murderous bastard.

Officer Clark stepped in front of the corridor and peered into the darkness ahead. She was tempted to call in on her hidden mike, to let the others know what was happening. Then she decided not to. If the killer was still hanging around, it would only alert him to the fact that she was a cop. Then, instead of running outside where he'd get caught, he might find a hole somewhere and hide. There were plenty of places to hide down here, and they'd never catch him.

The grunting noises were faint. They seemed to be coming from the rear of the corridor. She reached into her handbag and extracted a flashlight. No way was she going in there without being able to see. She scanned the area with a strong beam of light, but there was nothing to be found, no mutilated body, no sign of movement, just nothing.

She started to walk the length of the corridor and noticed that the grunting noises were growing stronger. They were definitely coming from the other side of the door leading to the alleyway. The superintendent's apartment was beyond.

She knew his name was Jose Torres, and that he was a Spanish deaf mute. And because of his close proximity to the murder scene, he was a prime suspect and was being watched. She heard the grunting noises again and recognized the sound of pain in those noises. She hadn't been a cop for eight years without being able to pick up on pain.

Her heart was pounding heavily when she approached the door to the alleyway. In her mind she was confident that Jose, if he was the killer, had slipped up this time. He'd gotten stupid enough to bring the body to his apartment, probably to finish the job. She knew she'd have to move fast before the victim died.

She clutched her gun, ready to fire, and opened the door with the same hand holding the flashlight. It was a clumsy maneuver on her part, but it was dark outside. She had no way of knowing if there was an overhead light in the alleyway, or if she'd be stepping out into complete darkness.

Jose's apartment was off to one side, near a row of garbage cans. The door was open; the grunting sounds were coming from inside. She scanned the alley with her flashlight to make sure Jose wasn't hiding in the darkness waiting for another victim.

Once she was sure it was safe, she pocketed her flashlight and gripped her revolver with both hands. She was ready to kill him if he resisted arrest. Standing flat against the wall, she counted to three, then moved in front of the door to his apartment, assuming the stance they'd taught her at the academy when she was still a rookie. Knees bent, gun poised in both hands, she blinked once or twice, her eyes partially blinded by the glare of a single bulb over the bed.

It would've been better had she been unable to see. Jose was lying half-naked on the bed, blood pouring from numerous holes and slashes in his flesh.

He was the one who'd been grunting in pain.

His body had been mutilated with a knife, a sharp one . . .

"Oh, God!" Bile rose in her throat; she felt nauseous. Eight years on the force were wasted at this point. Nothing—none of the atrocities she'd seen so far were as bad as this. Jose looked at her and raised a hand to wave her off. "I'll help you," she said, knowing he was deaf and might not understand. Maybe he was afraid she'd hurt him too because when he waved at her a second time his gestures were almost frantic.

"No. Wait. I'm a police officer." she explained, stepping inside, mouthing the words in case he read lips.

Jose grunted even louder, his eyes wrought with fear. Janice was frustrated. She opened her blouse at the top and started to speak into the mike when the door slammed behind her. It wasn't until then that the truth became evident. Jose wasn't waving her away because he was frightened of her. He was doing it to warn her!

She heard movement back near the door and caught the sound of someone giggling. She turned, her hand still on the button of the mike, and screamed and screamed and screamed.

4

He leaned against the side of a building, his throat constricting, his lungs heaving for a breath of air. He looked down at his chest and watched the violent rhythm of his heart. All for nothing! A wasted trip this time. He'd gotten nothing usuable from the Puerto Rican, other than the chance to deliver a highly satisfying dose of torture. And even at that, he hadn't been the first to mark the mute's body with a knife. Someone, prior to him, had mutilated his genitals.

Then the woman came. Another useless effort. She had excellent body parts, but she screamed into an instrument and some men came running out of nowhere. He barely had time to make the kill and escape unseen.

The heaving motions of his chest were starting to die down. He waited a moment longer and thought about the perilous journey home, perilous because he was different: his body, his face, just didn't conform. Like the mute he'd killed, he was unable to remain anonymous in a crowd. People stared and grew frightened, horrified at the sight of his skinless body, making him want to kill, to destroy the single-minded inferiors.

For that's what they were: single-minded inferiors who through evolution had lost the ability to utilize their brains to the extent of complete control.

He thought back to the time when things were different, when the human animal was in the early stages of development, when the brain was a source of wonder, when the sub-conscious mind was recognized as the key to all! That part of the brain controlled the energies of the universe, gave off tremendously important psychic forces. Man was able to see and foresee, to foretell his destiny, to guide his future by using his sub-conscious mind: for therein was the sixth sense, the third eye, the power force of the body.

DaVinci used it, as did Nostradamus. They looked into their sub-conscious minds and foresaw many things. DaVinci, for example, saw the future of air and space travel. Nostradamus saw the rise of evil: the war leaders who, centuries later, would seek to gain control of the world through battles. They utilized their brains to the fullest, as did other great men of their time, with the realization that the brain was on the same level as a well-functioning computer.

But these modern fools lost it, gave it up in the name of technology. As man evolved into the present, he invented machines to do his thinking for him. And the brain, in retaliation, allowed itself to weaken until the mystical forces of the sub-conscious mind were gone.

But he hadn't lost it. He was animal, with the abilities to look into and live in his sub-conscious and utilize the forces therein. He was all things, he was invincible!

He stood directly across from Bridge Gate Court, his body heavily veiled by the shadows of night and watched the men who'd chased him run in circles. Wild-eyed and angry, they were yelling back and forth about having let him escape. He smiled. If those men had the ability to scan their brains, to dig into their subconscious minds, they would've been able to sense him standing across the street watching them.

But then, they were ony human, as he was, by a small fraction . . . There were times when the human counterpart of his existence took control: when he'd killed and maimed until frenzied exhaustion swept over him. Then the human side of him took over. He smiled at that because while he was aware of a split in his personality, his human half wasn't really sure.

Of course the human suspected something was wrong, mainly due to the blackouts; those long periods when his mind was a blank, when he'd awaken as if from a dream and know he hadn't been dreaming. And it was for him, the human in his soul, that the beast roamed at night and killed and stole body parts. The human knew there was a crack of sorts in his id, the only thing lately it seemed he knew for certain. Body parts had to be gathered for use in complicated ceremonies to set his mind straight, to rid himself of the beast he suspected was a part of him.

And the beast cooperated by gathering the necessary flesh to aid in his own destruction. Another joke. The beast was stronger and would survive the human. However, this quest for flesh afforded the beast a chance to satisfy his primal urges: a chance to kill and mutilate.

The beast pulled back on the hood of his shroud and allowed his gaze to wander over the facade of Bridge Gate Court. From all outward appearances it was a grand dame of a building with its fading gray brick exterior, its tall windows trimmed in black wrought iron, its eaves of hand-carved stone. Inside there were apartments with high ceilings and spacious rooms and real oak trim. Then his gaze rested on the gargoyles and he smiled.

They thought they had him fooled. Took him for an imbecile. Well, he was the smart one. They might've been able to change the look of the place by removing the stained glass windows, but they slipped up when they left the gargoyles on the upper ledges to stand guard.

The gargoyles let him know the truth: this was once a church, a house of worship, and as far as he knew, it still was. His nerves throbbed with his anger. He wasn't stupid. Why treat him so? Everyone knew that in medieval times churches were heavily decorated with stone gargoyles and other winged horrors to keep evil spirits from entering. It was like using applied psychology: employ evil to keep evil out.

Obviously Bridge Gate Court had holy beginnings, was a place of worship where so-called men of God practiced the art of brain-washing. A place where pious priests layed the nuns and then spoke of the evils of the human flesh. A place where those same priests greedily counted the gold coins from their collection plates in private, and gave a scant tithing of it to the poor. He clenched his fists and stared down at his heart. It was beating heavily again. But only because he was angry at the church for trying to fool him.

In all outward appearances, Bridge Gate Court was, at present, a normal building, as the church wanted him to believe. But they made the mistake of loading it with soft-breasted nuns with smooth thighs for the satisfaction of the priests. And those bitches had to die. Screwing with those holy men, pulling their joints and singing hosannas in the name of God. And it wasn't even his God, it was theirs! His god had more integrity; they didn't hide the truth of his existence. However, as every good plan has its flaws, the deception of the church was flawed by the gargoyles. They left the gargoyles. The fools! And he alone knew that Bridge Gate Court was a church.

He wanted to murder them all, each and every occupant, to turn their warm, soft, human flesh into festering masses of bloody horror as he had with the women and the mute he'd killed. Then he smiled because he'd lied to the mute, told him he'd only mutilate his body after he was dead. But he did it while the mute was still alive and it felt so good to hear the fool gurgle because he couldn't scream; it felt so good to scan his naked body and see that he was no longer a man—

Dagger-sharp pains came into his head, familiar pains. He felt faint. His stomach crawled with nausea. His human counterpart wanted out; wanted to be the dominate factor in the partnership, for a while at least. Well, it was good. The beast was tired and needed rest. He grabbed his head and staggered down the street, trying to stay in the shadows, trying to hold onto consciousness for a while longer. Once he was home he could lie down and succumb to the pain, and let his mind go wherever it went whenever he yielded control to the human.

Samantha was walking home along Central Park West when her mind began to drift. It was spring, and during the day the park was a thing of beauty, a place where trees grew and birds nested, where mothers pushed their babies in strollers. But it was different at night. Once the sun fell from the sky, the park became heavily shadowed and eerie. She stopped for a moment to stare at a tree growing so high it was frightening; the branches resembling the gnarled hands of an old hag reaching for her in the darkness. She shuddered and started to walk again, only faster this time.

The park had two faces, two sides, just like her beloved woods back home. It used to be safe there also, especially during the day. Then someone came and violated the sanctity of those woods. A maniac came and that maniac hid until a young girl went by. The maniac got her best friend, then he got her—

There were police cars outside Bridge Gate Court. She stopped in the shadows, knowing she shouldn't have, and wondered if it were safe to go inside, to go upstairs to her apartment where she'd be alone, where there were so many hiding places. But then something came to mind and she continued on down the street. Maybe, just maybe, the police were here because they'd caught the killer. She was near the entrance of the building when a tall, good-looking man approached her. He had sandy blonde hair and strong features.

"Excuse me, Miss. Do you have business in this building?"

"I live here. Who are you?"

"Detective Wheatley. I'd appreciate it if you'd go directly up to your apartment. We're in the middle of a police investigation."

Samantha felt those old spasmodic chills starting at the base of her spine. What he'd said in short was there had been another murder and it wasn't safe to stand around. But it wasn't safe to go upstairs either.

"Please, lady?" he asked, sounding slightly annoyed.

Samantha's mouth tightened. He was being rude and obnoxious to the wrong person. She wasn't the killer. She strode briskly through the front door and approached the elevator. Two uniformed officers were standing near the corridor leading to the back alleys. Oh, God, she thought, they were guarding the body. Her legs started to buckle.

"You all right, Miss?" one of them asked.

"Yes. I'm fine." But she wasn't. She was about as well as could be expected under the circumstances. The murders were still going on; they had followed her to New York City. She couldn't escape the horror, it seemed. She turned her back on the officers and waited for the elevator. She didn't dare take the chance of looking in their direction because then she'd probably see the chalk marks, and not the same ones from this morning. The killer had been busy.

"For what it's worth, Miss, we contacted the owners of this building. They're installing new lighting sometime this week."

She looked back at the officer who'd spoken and managed a smile. "It's about time. Thank you." The elevator came to a jarring halt in front of her and her heart lurched along with it. She just couldn't get on it alone, or go up to her apartment alone. But she had no choice.

"Good night," she said and listened while the officers echoed her words, although she wanted to say more. She wanted to ask them how long they'd be there, and if she needed help, would they come?

The elevator ride up was uneventful and she thanked God. This was awful. An hour before she'd been brave enough to turn down June DeSoto when June offered to spend the night with her. But June didn't really have her heart in the offer; Samantha knew it from her expression and the way she asked. Still, had Samantha known about this new murder, she would've ignored June's reluctance and said yes.

When the elevator stopped on the seventh floor, she got off and quickly inserted her key in the lock. Once inside, she turned on the overhead lights instead of the small table lamps she and Morgan used at night. Something mentioned by one of the uniformed officers had stuck with her. The owners of the building were installing new lighting, which meant that so far the killer had been doing his thing in semi-darkness. Perhaps if the lights were on good and bright he'd stay away and she'd be safe, for the night at least.

Samantha kicked off her shoes and laid her purse on the sofa in front of the television. Morgan would've had a fit had she known, but this was where Samantha intended to sleep—on the sofa. It was too awful to even dream of sleeping in her bedroom with so many wonderful hiding places in there, especially in the closet.

She went into the kitchen to make herself a

70

soothing cup of tea. It was close to eleven and this was part of her nightly ritual: sipping tea and watching the news. She tried to keep her movements casual and pretend she wasn't scared to death. But her eyes kept drifting to the door separating her from the living room. If someone came through that door, she had to be ready, to have a weapon handy. Her gaze rested on the set of chef's knives Morgan kept over the stove. The sight of a cleaver made her feel secure.

Still, what good were knives against stone gargoyles? What if they suddenly came to life? A cleaver would fix a killer, sure, but what about them?

Oh, God, she'd done it again. She'd managed to recall the one thing that scared her most about being in this apartment alone—the gargoyles. Her hands were trembling when she poured her tea. She was trying not to think about it, but what if one of those gargoyles was the killer? No, Samantha, she told herself, you're being ridiculous. They're statues, made of stone. Period!

But it didn't help. Her hands were still trembling when she sat down and used the remote control to snap on the television. She tried to keep her attention focused on the set, and yet it was hard to concentrate on anything other than those gargoyes. It was also hard to watch the screen and keep an eye on the window behind her. But they were out there, on the ledge, and she had to be ready—

There was a shadow on the window, the shadow of a man wearing a cape.

A cape!

Her nerves burned under the skin: her gaze was

frozen on that cape.

How long had it been there? Was it the killer?

Oh yes, she answered herself and wished she hadn't. The killer wore a cape. . . .

Her heart was a congested mass of nerves.

She couldn't move, but she had to, had to force herself to get up and run to the door. If she was lucky those uniformed officers were still downstairs. All she had to do was scream and they'd come running.

But would they get there in time?

She got to her feet, never taking her eyes off the window, or the shadowed cape, and eased her way back toward the door. She was almost there when a sound shattered the stillness around her and she had to fight to keep from fainting. It was the telephone. Her first thoughts were to ignore it and keep going. But then what if she couldn't make it to the outside hall; what if the killer stopped her? And what if she made it and those officers were gone? At least the person on the other end of the line could call for help.

She slowly edged her way back to the sofa, to the phone on the coffee table, and picked it up, keeping her eyes fixed on the window and that cape. It was odd though that the cape never moved. The killer was standing so still . . .

''Hello.''

''Yes . . . Hello. Who's this? Samantha?''

She didn't recognize the voice. ''Who's calling?'' she asked, then cursed herself for being so stubborn when her life was in danger. Her mother had warned her as a child: never give your name first when someone calls; you never know who you're speaking to. But hell, this wasn't the time—

"This is Phil Housner. Morgan's father. Is she home?" He was abrupt, business-like.

"No. She's on her way to Bermuda—"

"Bermuda! Who with?"

"Charlie. He's a friend—"

"Oh, I see. That little bitch is still playing her games. Well, tell her I called!"

Then he was gone, and with him her hope of telling him about the caped killer outside her window. She held onto the receiver for a moment, then pressed the disconnect button and dialed a three-digit police emergency number. After a long wait, a recorded voice told her that the police lines were busy. She was told to hang on; someone would be with her shortly. The sound of canned music rang in her ears and she knew she'd been placed on hold.

That single act infuriated her. This was ridiculous. Her life was in danger and the police had placed her on hold . . .

And the cape was moving. Or was it the fluttering motions of the curtains that made it seem so—

The doorbell rang. She dropped the phone and wheeled to stare at the door. Oh, God, help was here. She ran to the door and started to open it, then hesitated when the thought struck her that this might be a trick. What if the killer had left his cape dangling on a hook outside of her window? She glanced back over her shoulder and saw that the cape was still there and realized she could've been right.

When the doorbell rang a second time, she began to cry. This was more than she could take. The killer had singled her out for death this time, and he wasn't about to give up the hunt. It reminded her of the killer in the woods back home. He was, or rather had been, just as persistent—

"Samantha Croft!" A voice called on the other side of the door. He knew her name! But how? And yet it didn't matter if he knew his victims' names or not. He still intended to kill her. "Samantha Croft! Hello in there. Would you please open the door? I'd like to speak to you."

"Not on your life," she raged, but the words sounded choked and strained. He had to know she was scared. Still, she wasn't about to let him in so he could kill her. She wasn't crazy.

"Miss Croft. I'm Detective Wheatley. I'm investigating the murders that have occurred in this building."

She recognized his voice from downstairs. Oh God, thank you. Help was here in the form of a cop. Samantha released the bolt on the police lock and opened the door. "He's here," she cried, pointing to the window and the shadow of the cape. "See him?"

Ron Wheatley pushed her inside, motioning for her to stand near the door while he pulled a gun from a holster under his jacket. As she watched, he approached the window with such determination she had to admire him. Cop or no cop, gun or no gun, she would've been frightened herself under the circumstances. And yet, he acted as though this was a part of his everyday life. Then she realized that for him, it was. But still, he was so brave, so handsome.

She watched him flatten his body to the wall beside the window. He stood there for a moment, then assumed a stance with his gun in both hands, blocking her view of the cape. "This's the police. I want you to drop any weapons you may have, open the window and come inside.''

After receiving no answer, he repeated the phrase, but still there was no response from the killer. Curiosity must've gotten the better of him, Samantha figured, because while she watched he got up real close to the window and peered out. Then she saw him stiffen as though someone was out there on the ledge. But immediately afterward his body went limp and he leaned his head against the frame of the window. ''There's nothing outside but stone statues. The one closest to the window . . . His wings were the cape you saw.''

Ron Wheatley was a gorgeous hunk of a man. Samantha had a better chance to get a good look at him as he sat across from her drinking the coffee she'd made minutes before. Although she wasn't prone to inviting strangers in to sit at her table, she owed him for scaring him half to death over a mere shadow on her window.

His eyes, she noticed, were a hazy blue, as if they'd started out to be another color and had wound up this way. His hair was sandy blonde, close cropped and curly. He could almost be taken for a Greek. And while he didn't have the tan her dream man did, his body was athletic enough to make her stomach flutter. Even with a suit on, the knotted muscles of his arms showed through.

''. . . and your name as well,'' he was saying. But she hadn't been paying attention, so she asked him to repeat the thought. He sighed impatiently and began from the beginning. ''Jose was still alive when we reached him. Our police woman, unfortunately, wasn't as lucky. I asked Jose if he could write down a description of the killer. We propped him up and gave him a pad. He said, in writing, that he just wanted to die in peace so that he could spend an eternity dreaming about his Louisa. Then he wrote something down about his Louisa . . . He said she was as beautiful as Samantha Croft.''

He stopped speaking then and concentrated on Samantha, on her dark, honey brown eyes, her full, sensual mouth. ''He was right about one thing. If Louisa looked anything like you, she was beautiful.''

Samantha felt her heart lurch with fear. She'd welcomed this man into her home and had trusted him with her life. Now he was making advances. He was as bad as the rapist. ''It's getting late. What say we call it a night?''

Ron studied her expression, his face the mask of blankness that came with practice; a real cop never showed his emotions. ''I'm sorry if I made you feel uncomfortable. I just wanted to enjoy the company of a beautiful woman for a change. It's a release; there's been so damned much tension. I really didn't mean any harm.''

Samantha listened to his words and realized how foolishly she'd been acting. The man was a cop, hardly the type to rape her. Besides, hadn't she been admiring his face and his body only moments before? Maybe he saw her and caught something in her expression, like a come-on, for instance. But he didn't know that she was a fraud: that she could admire a man with a good body because of a yearning hunger deep inside, and fear him at the same time because of the rape. ''I'm sorry, too,'' she said. ''I misunderstood.

And Jose never did describe the killer, you say?"

"No. It seemed as though Jose was scared of us. His eyes were crazy with fear and he kept gurgling like he was afraid we were gonna finish the job the killer started."

She heard the sound of defeat in his voice and felt pity for him. He was in some tough position: trying to stop an insane killer who was smart and shrewd ehough to escape every time.

"I just wish," he continued, "that I had time to look into Jose's past. The killer wasn't the first to mutilate his body." Samantha gasped. Ron responded by reaching across the table and laying his hand on hers. "Oh geez . . . Sometimes I talk out of turn. I tend to forget I'm not always rapping with another cop. I didn't mean to shock you. Besides, these are things I shouldn't even be telling you. These are details that are supposed to be kept under wraps."

While she listened his hand enfolded hers with a forceful determination. She felt strength in his touch, and yet there was warmth too, reminding her of her dream man. "It's okay," she said and listened to the tone of her own voice. It sounded different, not efficient and business-like as it usually did. And that puzzled her. Of course she wanted nothing more at the moment other than to be able to respond as any normal woman would, given the same circumstances: she wanted to turn her hand and allow the warmth of their palms to mingle. She wanted to let him know she was human and felt something in his touch. Then she thought of the rape and withdrew her hand from beneath his.

Again his face was a mask of nothing. "I'm sorry. I only meant to comfort you. Please,

Samantha. Don't mistake my intentions. I think you're lovely and appealing. And to tell the truth, while I'd like to get to know you better, I'm not about to jump your bones.''

She smiled and noticed a wedge in his mask: he was smiling back. ''I'm acting like a silly school girl. I'm sorry, too.''

''Oh, no. Please don't apologize. I should be the only one doing the apologies. I mean, here it is, late at night and you probably have to get up early for work. And I'm keeping you awake with my gory stories . . .'' His voice ended in mid-thought and again he concentrated on her. ''It's just that you're so damned easy to talk to. You seem to be intelligent enough to understand what I'm going through. I can see it in your face.''

''I do understand.'' Her own voice was soft again, she noticed. For some reason she was beginning to sound like a woman attracted to the man she was with. ''I guess finding Jose alive gave you false hope. And then when he only wanted to talk, or rather, write about Louisa it blew your hopes to hell. He didn't say anything else before he died?''

Ron stifled a yawn and smiled as though he were embarrassed. ''No, he didn't. He died saying nothing more. Well, I better be going. I guess I'm more tired than I imagined.''

''Before you leave . . . Call it curiosity or what-ever, there's one more thing I have to ask. When you said that Jose never did describe the killer, you made it sound as though this would've been a big breakthrough in the case. And yet, it's rumored that the killer wears a cape. How do you know if no one's ever seen him?''

Samantha wasn't positive, but at this point she

could've sworn Ron's face blanced white. He muttered an answer that was barely audible. "I've seen him. Only from behind of course, but I know he wears a cape." He rose quickly then and she got up to follow him to the front door where he turned to take one final look at her. "Thanks for the coffee, Samantha. You know, we really should get to know one another better." He smiled broadly this time, his rugged features softening around the edges. "Would you like to have lunch with me tomorrow?"

Without thinking twice, she started to say yes. However, she quickly remembered her appointment with Garrett Lang at one in the afternoon. "I really can't. I have this meeting coming up right after lunch and I have to be prepared for it. I ordered computerized print-outs on a client, and if I don't take a look at them, the man will think I don't know what I'm talking about."

Ron never said a word the whole time she'd been speaking, and now she realized how phony her excuse sounded. Maybe he thought she was telling him, in a nice way, to get lost. "Could we make it some other time?" she asked, then quickly added. "Like in a day or so."

"Sure," he said. "No problem. As long as I know you're sincere, I'll call. Good night, Samantha."

He started to open the door, but turned at the last minute and brushed her cheek with his lips. His breath was hot and soft against her face, again reminding her of her dream man. After he'd gone, she thought about him long and hard, deciding that perhaps it was time to take Morgan's advice and try dating. Ron Wheatley was a stunning man, and he was interested in her. This was hardly the time to fall back on memories of the rape if she wanted to get on with the rest of her life.

She was standing at the wheel, her love behind her, his arms wrapped around her body. She was on his yacht, headed for Bermuda. Oh, God, this was wonderful. To be completely at ease with Ron, for his name was Ron this time, not Dirk or Lance. And somehow the color of his hair had changed, and his eyes as well.

His hair was no longer dark brown wth a hint of gray at the temples, and his eyes weren't hazel. Rather, he was a sandy-haired, blue eyed, Greek god of a man, with sweet, hot breath and a yearning in his gaze. He wanted her, there was no doubting that. And he made his intentions known with the touch of his body against hers. Samantha was at peace. She had everything a woman could ask for and more.

"How about lunch, beautiful baby?" he whispered in her ear and gently cupped one of her breasts with determination. Her body shuddered with desire, and small goose bumps raised on her flesh when his lips brushed against her neck. She felt the swell of his manhood and knew he was ready. "I brought some sandwiches and wine coolers. It takes too long to get waited on at The Captain's Table. We could eat below and spend some time together."

She wanted to shout her answer, to scream yes, because he was moving faster this time. He seemed as anxious to get on with their love-making as she. However, she had to act coy or risk spoiling the mood. "What do you mean when you say we should 'spend some time together?' " she asked, trying not to smile.

"I want to rip your clothes off and jump your bones!"

Samantha felt her stomach turn. It wasn't a smooth, husky voice full of passion that she was listening to now. Rather, it was the hateful, raspy voice of the rapist. She turned and saw him: a huge man wearing a ski mask, his eyes through the holes were full of insanity. "Kiss me, bitch!" he bellowed and trapped her against the wheel with his body, his strong hurtful erection digging into her lower torso.

She started to scream and heard that scream echo inside of her head as though there was more than one sound, more than one cry of agony in the night.

She sat straight up in bed, her sweat-drenched body going through those awful spasms again. She heard the sound of her own screams and covered her ears to drown them out. But it was no good, she could still hear her own pitiful wailing. Then she realized it was the phone. The phone was ringing, that was the sound echoing in her head, magnifying her misery.

"Hello."

"Yes. This is Phil Housner again."

But it wasn't, she told herself. Oh, it was the same voice she'd previously heard when she'd been frightened by the shadow of the gargoyles on her window. But how could it be Phil Housner when it sounded exactly like the rapist? And she'd been so alarmed the first time she hadn't noticed the resemblance.

"Do me a favor," he rasped. "Tell Morgan she'd better call me when she gets back from Bermuda with her pig boyfriend. I'm through playing games with her!"

81

Then he was gone, and Samantha was left alone to spend the rest of the night wondering about him and why he treated his daughter so badly, and why Morgan wasn't allowed to share in his wealth. And also why he sounded so much like the rapist in her past. Then something else came to mind and all else was forgotten: Samantha began to wonder about the killer, whether or not he was finished with his killing for the night. And the gargoyles, were they part of it? And if so, when would they come to life?

June DeSoto ordered another scotch and wished she'd left with Samantha. The restaurant was beginning to thin out, along with the bar section she was sitting in. Lately it seemed there was just no action at this time of night. Then too, she was competing with a lot of younger women: women who were also single and available.

She glanced at her reflection in the mirror over the bar and felt disgusted enough to forget her boredom. She looked like a clown,like her make-up had been put on with a brush and a gallon of paint. But then, in her own defense, it was because she was over forty now, and time was taking its toll, wrinkles were replacing the freckles. And damn, if only there weren't so many younger women doing the same thing she was doing, hanging around bars trying to get lucky, she wouldn't have to resort to trickery just to stay in the game.

This was some helluva way to wind up, she thought, and quickly downed her scotch. Hell, at her age she should be sitting around a comfortable living room, knitting, with her hubby beside her, dozing in an overstuffed chair, waiting for the arrival of their first grandchild. She should've been married years before. And if she hadn't been so stubborn and greedy, she would've been. And now, all she had left to spend the night with was a gold bracelet full of charms that told the story of her life.

She was like an old fighter pilot, the ones who had those tiny planes hand-painted on the sides of their own planes to show how many they'd shot down. Well, she'd shot down a lot of men in her life, only now she was the victim, the casualty, rather than the victor.

She remembered the very first time she'd been given a charm to add to the bracelet her parents had given her for Christmas. The only thing she couldn't recall was the name of the boy who'd given it to her. It was sort of a pre-engagement present. That was a laugh. He'd given her the charm along with his heart, and June had rejected him, but she kept the charm.

And why? Why did she take his present and turn him down and crush his delicate ego? The answer was obvious: June had a dream; she was going to set the world on fire, she was going to marry a man who went places! Oh yeah, a man who had the world by the short hairs. She dreamt of wealth, and position and power. And throughout her life she'd gathered many charms, all proposals of marriage that she'd refused after coldly evaluating the man's ability to make something of himself.

Now, here she was, forty and unmarried, baggy and wrinkled, hanging around bars trying to get lucky—

She was still looking in the mirror and something she saw over her shoulder caught her eye. The man she'd been laughing about today in the office, the one who wanted to tie her to a bed-post and make love to her, had just walked in. And while he'd been a pure joke earlier in the day, at this point she was desperate enough to leave with him, if and when he asked her.

She lit a cigarette and ordered another drink, her gaze carefully trained on nothing in particular; the word here was casual. She had to make it appear as though she was just sitting around having a leisurely drink before going home, and if luck was with her—

"Hello, June . . . It is June, isn't it?"

She turned and cringed. While his voice was soft and soothing, his appearance was anything but. He was a tall thin man with deep-set eyes and the pallor of an undertaker. He was wearing his usual hat and cape-like coat, reminding her of the Phantom of the Opera. People just didn't dress like this nowadays. "Yes, it's June," she said, not sure she wanted to leave with him. He was so spooky, but she was desperate for a man.

"Did you think about my suggestion?" he wanted to know.

June was angered and had to fight hard not to show it. He could've at least offered to buy her a drink first. Hell, she wasn't used to this. She was used to being wined and dined. But then, he was holding the cards. "Yes. I thought about it."

"And?"

"It sounds like a great idea."

He smiled, or at least his face creased into a contortion that could pass for one. "Let's go. I have plenty of scotch at home."

She grabbed her bag and followed behind him, wondering if she'd wind up with another charm to add to her collection.

5

Ron Wheatley was almost home by this time. He was driving down a road in Queens, trying to keep his mind on his job. He couldn't walk into the house and face Debbie while his thoughts were on Samantha. Debbie was smart: she'd know he'd found himself another woman. And what a woman at that. Tall and leggy and beautiful.

Samantha was a dream come true. And, tonight, if he was lucky enough, he'd dream about her and not the beast who'd haunted him of late. It was odd, the beast started coming to him in the night around the time the murders began. In the beginning, he thought nothing of it. Now he was sure there was a connection.

Tonight, for instance, when Jose Torres was being mutilated and Police Officer Janice Clark was being killed, Ron had been dreaming of the beast. Ron had been stationed in an adjacent alleyway waiting for something to happen when he'd somehow fallen asleep. That didn't surprise him much, since he'd been practically working around the clock trying to catch the killer. And he'd been dreaming while the horror was going on.

In those dreams he saw Jose—

No. He couldn't allow himself to think back on the nightmare, couldn't allow himself to admit that it seemed at times as though he and the beast were one because he was able to view the murders, in his sleep, with alarming accuracy.

He drove up to the front of his house and tried to clear his head. Debbie was an invalid, and that was his fault. He couldn't do anything to upset her. If he seemed troubled and she noticed, she'd automatically assume it was because of her and her present physical condition. But it wasn't, not entirely, and so he had to compose himself. He had to forget Samantha for the time being, along with the nightmares, and the sound of Janice Clark screaming while she was being slaughtered by the beast.

Then again, he had a gut feeling that that part of it would be with him for a long time: Janice Clark's voice was the first thing he heard when the nightmare became too much for him and he woke up. And it stayed with him. Even while he'd been enjoying Samantha's company, he was somehow able to hear her voice echoing in the subconscious area of his brain.

Debbie was in bed, where she normally spent her time. "That you, Ron?" she called out to him. "Yes. I'll be right in." He went straight to the kitchen for a beer, amazed as always at the calmness in her voice. If he, himself, were confined to bed and alone most of the time with a killer on the loose, he'd be damned scared. But Debbie never showed a sign of fear. Probably because the killer always struck in Bridge Gate Court. So she felt safe. And perhaps she was.

And that was a pity, he thought at first, before shame overtook him for feeling that way. But he had to admit there was a valid reason for wanting her dead. Debbie was useless, thanks to him, and if she became a victim, it would relieve a lot of people—namely him—of a helluva lot of pressure. But the killer was smart: he took prime meat, took those lovely, young, voluptuous women with those dynamite bodies and slaughtered them, while women like Debbie were left to linger, left to be a burden to their families, financially and otherwise.

He'd gotten a letter from the state only days before, answering his question about medical aid concerning Debbie. The answer had been a terse, "No." He'd have to use his own resources first: deplete his savings account, sell his house and everything he'd ever worked for before the state would come up with any sort of help. And that meant one thing: the housekeeper had to be kept on a part-time basis. Debbie had to be left alone for the better part of the day.

Sometimes he wished she was dead; wished she had died the day he shot her. If only the bullet had entered her heart instead of a delicate spot in her spinal column. But that wasn't fair and he knew it. She didn't ask to be shot. She didn't even want to be where she was when he shot her, he forced her to go. And now the guilt was eating at him a piece at a time, day by day, until at times he wished he was dead along with her.

Debbie was sitting up in bed, propped on pillows, when he finally got the courage to go in and face her. "Hello, darling," she said in her sexiest voice. He smiled at that, because she was incapable of having sex. And yet her eyes were aglow, and her cheeks flushed, which meant only one thing: she'd been reading those romance novels again.

He went over to the side of the bed and glanced at the cover of the book lying next to her. It was an x-rated novel this time, nothing like the usual love and perfect couple melodramas she generally read. "Who bought it?" he asked.

"I've had it for a long time. Ever since we first got married. It used to help put me in the mood before you came home."

"And all this time I thought it was you. That you were just a hot little number." He threw the book down and started to go into the bathroom when she called him back. He turned and saw her give him that look. She was ready. But how? She had no feelings down there. How could she want him so badly? Unless she was just doing this for his benefit, faking her emotions as she'd sometimes faked orgasm. And if this was true, he wasn't about to question her motives. He needed a woman badly: had almost been tempted to jump Samantha.

"Come here, darling," she said softly, and he went to her, removing his clothes along the way.

It was a beautiful night. Garrett Lang stood on the balcony of his penthouse and looked out over the lights illuminating the city. New York was alive and well, a city that never slept. And like the city, he was alive and fired up. But it was late, too late in the night to be so hyper, so full of everything that he couldn't get back to sleep.

He turned from the view and scanned his apart-

ment, then tried to imagine himself a stranger
here, a visitor. And what would a visitor think of
the man who owned the entire penthouse suite of
a luxury condo? Well, he thought, from just seeing
the evidences of his vast wealth, the stranger
might assume Garrett had it all. And how wrong
that would've made him, because Garrett lacked
a lot of things in life that didn't cost anything.
Peace of mind, for example.

Oh, he was fired up and all that, but not because
of any real sense of happiness. Rather, it was
because he'd long ago trained his mind to accept
what he had and to discard the rest. So he was
able to feel a false sort of euphoria and enjoy his
material holdings. He had a yacht and a jet and
several homes scattered throughout the world.
Hell, Garrett boy, he told himself at times, considering the statistics on poverty in the United
States, you're a lucky guy.

Then he poured himself a glass of sherry and got
ready for the downfall. His mind could hold onto
its sense of well-being for only so long, before
crashing to the depths of despair. He would wake
up soon and see the truth, 'smell the coffee
burning,' to quote Ann Landers. The truth was
that his life was a failure. Everything around him,
the goods he'd acquired, all were ill gotten gains,
the result of his careless dealings and deal
making . . .

Garrett was now beginning to lose his grip on
the fantasies he'd created with his own superior
sub-conscious mind, and the realities were
coming home. Garrett had been born poor, in a
broken-down house on the outskirts of a town in
upper Westchester County. Oh, the house wasn't
a complete disaster: they had lights and running

water and indoor plumbing. But that's where the luxuries of modern civilization ended and left him with memories of badly soiled furniture and shabby linoleum.

Hand-me-down clothing was the only kind he knew until he grew up and his world changed—when he changed it. He remembered the idea for this change came about one scorching summer afternoon when he was around ten. He'd gone into town to hang out at the five and ten cent store with his friends. There wasn't much of anything else for a young boy to do on a long Saturday afternoon when the chores were done. So into town he went. And it was funny, he'd been doing the same exact thing for a year or so, but on this particular day something happened to change his way of thinking, and that something eventually changed the entire course of his life.

Garrett was, or at least had been, a country boy, reared in the same rural frame of mind as his Pa. Garrett, when old enough, would run the family farm. He would till the soil and plant the seeds and hope that something grew. He'd watch his crops get eaten alive by bugs, be scorched by the sun and drenched into oblivion by heavy rains. And through it all, he'd keep the faith and hope he'd wind up with something half-way decent to take to market.

This was his dream until this particular Saturday when those rich tourists came to town: the ones with the air-conditioned Mercedes with the push button windows and the body chrome that glared hard in his face when it caught the reflection of the sun. Of course he'd seen others—rich tourists with big cars and fat wallets. But this time it was different. Maybe because he was getting older and maturing and was looking at the world through the eyes of a boy approaching puberty.

Whatever it was, he noticed a change in himself, a change in his own small-minded, small town personality. He no longer viewed his take-over of the farm as a rightful inheritance; he viewed it as a death sentence. No way was he about to spend the rest of his life trapped in poverty, struggling against the odds and the worst forces of nature to bring in a halfway decent crop and get shit money in return. Hell no. Especially when there was another world outside; when it didn't have to be this way.

That's when his so-called campaign to get out became the leading obsession in his life. And it could only be accomplished through book learning. The man with the Mercedes and the money to burn talked real good—he was obviously well-educated. And Garrett, even though he was only ten, managed to equate the two: education had a lot to do with making it in this world, and he wanted to make it.

Prior to that his attitude about school had been a poor one. Like most of his kind, he only needed to learn enough about spelling to be able to read the instructions on his seed packages. And as far as arithmetic went, if he could add so he wouldn't get screwed at the market, his education would be complete. But after seeing what life could be, that it wasn't meant to be hard and he wasn't meant to be perenially holes-in-the-shoes poor, he changed his ways. He became studious, buckled down with his books, and shocked the ass off his teachers. And he made it. All the way through college.

With little or no help from his parents.

His Pa thought he'd gone mad, spending so much time with books. Garrett then made the biggest mistake in his life, he tried to explain how it was to his old man. And his old man promptly disowned him, told Garrett he was dead as far as he was concerned for not wanting to follow in his footsteps, for not wanting to resign himself to a life of poverty.

That was around the time Garrett started college and left home for the first time ever; around the time he was able to escape the boundaries created by poverty and use the mind God had given him to win a scholarship to a small, private school of higher learning about thirty miles from home.

The mind God had given him . . .

He repeated the thought and smiled. He hadn't given God credit for much these past twenty years.

It was odd that he should remember his Christian upbringing now, when it was almost too late.

And the more he thought about his past, the more he realized that a lot of credit for his present belonged to none other than J.J. Holiman, his old professor, now Professor Emeritus at William J. Hunt University. J.J. Holiman took Garrett under his wing and taught him the things he had to know in order to fulfill his quest for wealth and power. He taught Garrett about the world of economics and business management and corporate structure.

Then, after hours, the ancient, graying professor invited Garrett to his ancient, graying library where he taught Garrett about corporate power struggles and take-overs, until Garrett knew enough about the real world of business to go out on his own and conquer his past.

He defeated his poverty, gained wealth and power, and broke J.J. Holiman's heart . . .

But he wanted to forget that part of it, and felt he should do something to occupy his mind. Earlier in the day he'd wanted to take the yacht out, but most of his time spent on the yacht was lonely and boring. There was no one in his life to share the spoils of his wealth, no one to take for a ride out into the deeper water and teach to fish, or to just lounge on deck with. No one to make love to, except for an occasional spoiled bitch from the aristocratic upper-world of which he was now a member.

He stepped out onto the balcony and listened to a clock chiming, the noise coming from somewhere inside the vast apartment. And as it chimed, he counted until it stopped at three. Garrett sipped his sherry and thought about going back to bed where sleep would come and his mind would rest for a while. But then he remembered the nightmares that haunted his dreams of late. In fact he'd fallen asleep earlier in the evening only to be awakened by the worst one yet.

He decided to wait until he'd drank enough sherry to knock himself out so that he wouldn't dream, wouldn't see the horrors buried in his sub-conscious in such vivid detail.

J.J. Holiman was another whose mind was on fire, but it was late at night, too late to call Garrett. He'd arrived in the city around midnight and had taken a cab to a hotel in midtown Manhattan. Of course, he knew Garrett would be offended when

he called him in the morning and told him he'd
spent the night in a hotel, but J.J. didn't want to be
a bother.

Then again, there was a bond of sorts between
him and Garrett, or at least there had been years
before when he and Garrett had spent many
hours studying in the library of J.J.'s home. So
maybe he should've called Garrett; maybe Garrett
wouldn't have been angry about coming out late
at night to pick his old professor up at the train
station.

J.J. had unpacked his bags; had neatly placed
his underwear and socks and shirts in the huge
double dresser opposite the bed; had neatly hung
his suits in the closet with the louvre doors. And
now that it was over and done with, he had
nothing to do except glance through his books and
think about the murders. Unless of course he
wanted to allow his thoughts to wander back to
the past, to the disappointments he'd suffered
when Garrett left for the big city to make his
fortune.

He decided on the books and propped himself
up in bed with a few pillows. But it was no use.
He'd read those damn books so damned many
times they couldn't hold his interest; not even
when he tried to force the issue. His mind kept
wandering back to the past and Garrett.

He remembered the first time they'd met on
campus. Garrett was standing in the middle of the
square, staring at the various buildings around
him with such awe in his expression he reminded
J.J. of the fabled tourists in New York City. The
only thing missing was the camera around
Garrett's neck. And J.J. knew from just looking at
the lad that he was a hick facing the big time for

the first time in his life. At that point, J.J. decided to take the boy under his wing to make the transition less painful.

Garrett, he later learned, wanted to study economics, hard economics. He desired the necessary knowledge to really make it in this world. But J.J. had other ideas for the lad's future. Although he was one of the country's leading professors in the theory of economics, he was also a leader in studies dealing with the occult world. And that's where he wanted Garrett to succeed.

Hell, any fool, given the right training, could make money. He could've done it himself—could've made a fortune—had he been inclined to apply his knowledge in the outside world. But that wasn't his bag, so to speak. It was the occult world with all of its mysteries and strange powers that captured his attention and kept it these many years. And he tried to pass the banner to Garrett, but Garrett wasn't having any of it.

J.J. could now recall the first time he'd introduced Garrett to his books and suggested he read some of them. It was a dark moonless night and they were comfortably seated in front of the fireplace in his library listening to the howl of the wind and the thrust of the rain through the trees outside. J.J. stopped to wonder for a moment if that's what scared the boy so badly: the terrible force of the elements coupled with some of the treasures he kept in his library. The skulls and severed body parts, the hands and fingers taken by fervent Satanists from unwary victims. Then too, there were the books themselves.

Garrett was listening to his old professor interpret some of the mysteries contained in

the phenomena of the occult world while leafing
through a text. The pictures of the demons in that
text were what caught the boy's attention more
than anything, and yet horrified him at the same
time. He pointed to some of them and laughed at
the idea of beasts with human features and beasts
with animal/reptile body parts: heads of dogs,
arms shaped like fins and alligator-like tails.

The boy stopped laughing though when J.J. told
him he'd seen some of these creatures with his
own two eyes. There was more to them than the
vivid imagination of an artist: they were real, had
substance, walked the streets at night, hid in the
shadows of darkness. J.J. had to stop at one point
for the wind to die down, for such was the force of
it that the boy had trouble hearing him. The wind
enhanced the horror. And instead of Garrett being
interested enough to want to be J.J.'s protege, he
withdrew and became sullen, but only to hide his
fears.

J.J. now felt that perhaps he should've dropped
the subject right then and there. But he was old,
had never married, and there was no one who
would rightly inherit his wealth of knowledge on
the occult world. Someone had to take over when
J.J. became too old and weak to fight the forces of
evil. Those demon bastards just couldn't be
allowed to run wild with no check on their activi-
ties.

Therefore it became a game of blackmail
between the old professor and his unwilling
student: J.J. would teach Garrett everything he
knew about the world of finance, providing half of
their study time be spent learning how to defeat
the demons of darkness. Garrett consented but it
was a forced consent. J.J. was sure that Garrett

would soon forget about acquiring a fortune once he became fascinated by the mysteries of the occult world.

But it backfired. When Garrett's financial training was complete, he left and never looked back and never cared that an old man's heart was broken because he'd lost the son he'd never had.

J.J. glanced at his watch and saw that it was now three in the morning: the bewitching hour. The forces of darkness were about to begin their stuff, their night roaming, their hauntings. He decided to try to get some sleep since he was too old and weak to fight should a night beast happen into his hotel room. At least if he was asleep when it attacked, he would mercifully die at rest.

Ramona Blattfield was sitting in her living room staring at the television, not particularly paying attention to the old movie on the screen in front of her, when Jeffrey floated in. He could tell from the expression on her face that she was upset. Well, more than upset. She was horrified because there'd been two more murders, too horrified to sleep.

Jeffrey could sympathize with her, but not because she was his aunt. No, it went deeper than that. Jeffrey was well acquainted with being terrorized. But only Uncle Max was aware of how much he'd suffered. And now Uncle Max was dead. So there was no one alive and breathing who understood him or how he was able to understand how Aunt Mona felt.

Then, for a moment or so, he stopped to wonder why he hadn't seen Uncle Max recently. After all, Uncle Max had expired long before Jeffrey and yet Jeffrey never ran into him in that place where dead people dwelt, the place with trees, and grass and sunshine, the place where good people went. Uncle Max was a good man before he died. Jeffrey really hoped he hadn't been sent down below by mistake—

"What's on your mind, Jeffrey!"

The boy was startled when she spoke. And it wasn't because he'd been so deeply involved with thoughts of Uncle Max. It was because of her tone: she was angry and he hoped it wasn't due to something he'd done. "Nothing. I just came in to see if you're okay."

"Well I'm fine. So you can go back to bed."

"I . . . I don't really sleep, Aunt Mona."

"Oh, yes. Excuse me." She turned and looked straight into his face and he cringed. Her eyes were cold and indifferent. "And, Jeffrey, for the last time, it's Ramona. My name is Ramona. Like the song that was written for me."

She'd always claimed that: that the song had been written for her. But Jeffrey figured she'd made it up because she was in her fifties and the song was probably written years before she was born. But he wasn't about to argue the point, not when she was this angry. "I'm sorry, Aunt Ramona. But I've been calling you Aunt Mona since I was a kid. Remember? I couldn't pronounce it right so I shortened it?"

She half-smiled then and he was able to relax. She was coming around. "It's okay. I'm just being picky because I'm tense. And scared."

The last part was spoken as she stared off into space again. Jeffrey felt bad and suddenly angry. That damned murderer was upsetting his aunt and she was such a kind, loving person; she didn't deserve this. Rather, she deserved peace and happiness for the compassion and deep love she'd been giving to others all her life. He floated down next to her and put his arms around her neck. Then he wondered if she felt anything: any sensation from his touch since he was nothing more than a wisp of air.

As if in answer to his question, she turned and clumsily planted a kiss on his lips, her face blending with the vapors, but hitting nothing solid. Still, he in turn felt warm because of her gesture, her show of emotions. Then he wondered why he'd kept his past from her, why he'd shared everything with just Uncle Max. She would've understood.

"I know how you feel inside," he began in an attempt to rectify matters, to tell Aunt Mona about the things he'd kept hidden up to this point. "A few days ago I told you it was awful being dead. Well, it was awful being alive, too."

She moved from his embrace and trained her attention on his face. She was angry again. "What're you saying? You had a good life. Your mother, my sister, God rest her soul, was the best there was. And your father—"

"It had nothing to do with my parents." He felt now that maybe he shouldn't have been so overtaken with her fears as to want to share his own; to tell her the secrets he'd recounted to Uncle Max. "Look, I was a young Jewish boy growing up in a religiously mixed area in Long Island. Jews in those days were jokes. They weren't too well thought of."

Her face softened and he relaxed once again. She understood. "That was over twenty years ago, and things haven't changed all that much. Go on, tell me what happened to make your past memories so bad.''

"Well, I had these friends . . . They weren't really my friends but they pretended they were and I believed them. Uncle Max used to listen to me—''

"You shared this with Uncle Max and not with me?'

"I didn't even tell Momma and Papa. I was afraid it would break your hearts. We faced the same things back home before we moved to America. I was afraid to tell you.''

She clutched at his hand, hers settling on thin air. He smiled because while his bodily features were plainly visible to her and her alone, he still was composed of nothing more than a vaporous kind of material resembling gas. "Go on, honey. I'm sorry. You were being kind not to tell us.''

"Well, these friends used to play tricks on me.'' He stopped for a moment as the horror from his past overtook him.

"What kind of tricks?''

"They gave me candy one time. It tasted awful, but they were being nice to me then so I trusted them and ate it. After a few minutes I got sick. My head felt swollen and my whole body seemed to be floating. I still don't know what it was except it had to contain a drug of some kind—''

"LSD. I read about it in the papers. Even today children are giving their friends candy coated with this. It causes hallucinations, terrible ones.''

"Yes, I saw strange things in front of me. And it seemed I was asleep, only somehow I knew I was still awake. And voices, I heard voices that sounded like my friends telling me things and then I'd see those things they spoke of.''

"Like hypnotic suggestions," she said. "I've read about those too. Go on."

"Well, they kept telling me I was in Germany, in a concentration camp called Dachau. I mean, I've never been to Germany, although I've heard of the camps. But a strange thing happened, I was suddenly transported back in time to the war and to that camp. I was a Jew in bondage, suffering through the tragedies that Momma told me some of our relatives did. It was awful. I was beaten and starved. Someone operated on my body, a doctor. He did terrible things and I was awake . . . He cut me open and removed vital organs. Then I died in a gas chamber, and it was so real that afterwards, when the drug had worn off, I lay in bed at home and cried the whole night long from the memories. And I never forgot what they did to me."

"Oh, God, Jeffrey. How you must've suffered."

Her face was contorted with grief. She had a protective air about her and never wanted anyone close to her to know pain, physical or otherwise. Jeffrey hugged her again. "It's all right, Aunt Mona. It was a long time ago and it's over." There was more, but somehow, seeing her reaction, he couldn't go on. Uncle Max had been stronger. "I just told you to show I understand how you feel. I know what it's like to be scared. And now, if you want to go to bed, I'll stand guard. I'll watch that no one gets in here and harms you."

She half-smiled again. "With an offer like that, how could I refuse?" Then she rose and started to leave the room. "Listen, big protector, do me a favor and wake me up at around nine. I have some errands to run and I don't wanna oversleep.

Good night, love.''

"Night, Aunt Mona.''

After she'd left the room, he felt relieved at having revealed part of his past. It was enough to let her know how he felt, and at the same time show her he'd grown up the hard way and was capable of defending her. Otherwise she never would've gone to bed. With this in mind, he reached for the remote control for the television and switched stations until he found an old James Cagney movie. As long as he was unable to sleep, he might as well be watching something he liked.

6

Samantha had tried very hard to stay awake, to be alert to the dangers around her. But she'd fallen asleep sometime during the night, after her eyes had grown raw from watching the shadows for movement and she'd exhausted herself by mulling through the maze of possibilities of becoming a victim of the killer. And this time, she was able to dream of Ron Wheatley without any interference.

She'd dreamt of being on his yacht, headed for Bermuda, and she dreamt of having lunch below decks, and she dreamt of their love-making. When at last it was over, and she was awakened by the phone, there was an old familiar wetness in the area of her crotch and she knew it had been good.

"Hello," she sang into the receiver, not expecting anyone in particular.

"Hello, yourself."

The voice was familiar and wonderful to hear. "Morgan! Oh, God, it's you."

"Of course. Who else would be calling at this time of the morning?"

"Your father." Samantha heard nothing for a few seconds more. She thought the line had gone dead; Morgan was never quiet for long. But Morgan was still there.

"My father called? Did he say anything about me? About me going to Bermuda?"

Morgan's voice had changed then, she sounded hostile. "He didn't have much to say," Samantha lied.

"Oh, never mind. Screw him! So, how the hell are you?" Morgan had gone from angry to happy-go-lucky, had scanned a cornucopia of emotions in seconds flat.

"I'm fine. But we'd better not talk for long. This must be costing a lot of money." Samantha didn't really want the conversation to come to an end. Hearing Morgan's voice was like taking a sedative.

"Charlie's paying for the call. He said it was okay to talk, meaning money is no object." She hesitated then. There was something she either wanted to say or ask, but she was struggling with the words. Samantha kept quiet, knowing Morgan would say whatever it was in a sudden outburst as usual, and she did. "Were there any more murders?" she wanted to know.

"Yes. Two."

"Shit! I shouldn't have left you alone. Oh, Samantha, I'm sorry."

"Don't be. I wanted you to go as much as you wanted to go. Besides, it's not as bad as you think. I met a really gorgeous man—"

"And he asked you out but you said no. You just wanted to remain friends, right?"

Samantha wished she were face to face with Morgan just to see her expression. "I said yes."

"Am I hearing right? We must have an awful connection. You told him yes?"

Samantha could imagine Morgan with those bright, blue eyes of hers all shiny and alert. "He said he'd call in a day or so. And he will. We had coffee together last night, here in the apartment."

"You had him there, alone with you? He must be pretty trustworthy." She was laughing now.

"He's a cop." Morgan gasped but Samantha continued on. "He's the detective investigating the murders."

"Really? What does he look like?"

"He's gorgeous, as I've already told you. But why describe him? Just wait till you get back and you can meet him in person."

"Okay. Listen, I better go. Charlie just stuck his head in the door. I think he wants to go sight-seeing again. Anyway, you take care of yourself and get some birth control pills. I mean, if you're gonna become sexually active—"

"I didn't mention sex. I didn't say anything about hopping into bed with him." Samantha noticed the annoyance in her own tone and knew she'd messed up. Here she'd been trying to convince Morgan that she was ready for a healthy relationship, but her attitude betrayed her.

"Oh, grow up! That's what men and women do when they're attracted to one another, and it's gonna happen to you. So you'd better get some pills. Okay?"

"Okay." She was quiet now, subdued. She didn't really mean it—that she might go to bed with Ron—but Morgan would've settled for nothing less than a positive answer.

"And I'll see you when I get back."

After she'd hung up, Samantha laid back down and thought about going to bed with Ron Wheatley, really going to bed with him, not as in her dreams. Would it be as perfect in real life? Or would he turn into a pervert and make unreasonable demands on her, ask her to do unnatural things? After all, he'd been around the block a few times as far as life went, she could tell. And she hadn't.

And would he leave her once they'd slept together? Samantha had hoped for more than a one-night stand, provided she was able to find the courage to love him while she was still awake.

One phrase stuck in Morgan's head: that's what men and women do when they're attracted to one another. She let it roll around in her head a few times and then tried to forget it, but it was too late; Charlie had noticed there was something wrong. And when it came to forcing an issue, Charlie had her beat ten ways to hell and back.

"We've been friends for a long time now," he insisted. "And I've always felt there was something you were keeping from me. Whatever it is, skinny, it's tormenting you."

They were sitting up on deck by this time, in beach chairs, the sun drenching their bodies in warmth. Morgan should've felt good inside. She was on a yacht with a really swell man, despite his girth, in the middle of the Atlantic Ocean, drinking pina coladas, surrounded by a group of islands that brought her about as close to paradise as she was ever going to get. She should've been happy, but she wasn't.

Samantha had told her that Phil called. Her

father was still hanging on; he'd never let her be completely free.

"Come on, babes, tell old Charlie what it is. Then, maybe once we understand each other, our relationship will progress as it should."

Morgan heard his words and somehow they sounded like a threat: either tell all or it's over. She looked at him, straight into his pudgy face and tried to decide if she wanted their so-called relationship to progress. After a moment or so, she realized he was the best of the worst. He wanted her because she was terrific in bed, and yet there was more. He also desired her as a person. "It concerns my father. It isn't easy to tell anyone what happened between me and my father after Mom died. I never knew my mother . . . You probably won't believe me."

"Try me! I mean, Morgan, I love you. I've been thinking about us getting married. But this thing with your father comes between us at times."

"In what way?" She couldn't believe she was hearing this. She'd tried with everything in her to forget the past, to live her life in the present. And now Charlie was telling her she hadn't succeeded. This was news to her. "In what way?" she repeated.

"Well, it's nothing you could point to directly and say here it is . . . Sometimes when we're together in bed, you act as though you're just doing it—going to bed with me—to prove a point. I don't feel the emotion coming from you that I should."

"You picked that up, did you?"

"Yes." He diverted his gaze and nervously ran one finger along the outside of his drink, making designs in the frost on the glass. "I knew there was another man and that there was something about him that troubled you. What I didn't know till now was that it was your father.''

She felt foolish. Charlie was right, he didn't know the truth. Had she been thinking ahead, she could've made up a lie. She could've told him a story about an old flame or something on that order. Now she had no choice. She'd mentioned Phil and, painful or not, she had to go on with it, to tell Charlie why her father haunted her and tormented her and kept his money to himself.

Garrett Lang laid down the phone and stared at it, his trembling hand still clutching the receiver. J.J. Holiman was in town. J.J. had just called and Garrett's severed link with the past was no more. J.J. had come to visit.

And what bothered Garrett and made him feel like a fool was that J.J. was only doing what Garrett had urged him to do years before: he'd come to New York City to see his prize student. But at the time of the offer, Garrett still felt he had a past worth remembering. Only now things had changed, and he wanted to forget. After all, J.J. had been a friend and nothing more, no blood relation. Garrett's parents didn't even try to contact him, not since he'd gone away to college years before . . .

The worst part of it was, this wasn't just a normal visit—how do you do, I love your house, and all that. No. J.J. wanted to get involved in the mutilator murder case; he wanted to help solve the crimes, find the killer's identity and stop the killings. And, as he told Garrett, he felt certain the killer wasn't human, at least not entirely. Oh, there may've been times when he was able to hide in a crowd, but he still wasn't completely human.

He, J.J., wanted Garrett to help solve the murders using the knowledge Garrett had gained from him.

Garrett couldn't do this: couldn't go back to the past and start with that demon shit again. It scared him, badly.

And yet, he'd fooled with it once . . .

And now he wanted to forget that also.

The buzzer on the intercom sounded, shattering the air around him. He hit the response button. "Yes."

"Miss Croft is here to see you."

"Oh, for Christ's sake," he mumbled under his breath. He wasn't in the mood to listen to some broad expound on the virtues of insurance, trying to sell him something he didn't care about at the moment. However, he'd asked her to come, asked her partly because Gail Lindman, his secretary, had been killed by the so-called demon. And that reminded him again of J.J. and the reason behind his visit. But he didn't want to go back to thinking about J.J. again. Miss Croft would be a diversion. "Send her in," he barked.

Samantha heard that old familiar sound in his voice: the one that said he was sorry he'd made the appointment. She should've been used to this by now, but she wasn't, not really. Damn it! These people listened to her on the phone and were hot to make appointments. But then by the time she got to see them in person they'd changed their minds and she was the enemy, the intruder. They were so damn sure that Samantha was about to wrestle them to the floor and force them to sign on the dotted line, and then they'd be stuck paying for a policy they neither really wanted or needed for the rest of their lives.

"Should I leave?" she asked the secretary, a nervous young thing who was obviously caught in the middle. The secretary shook her head and motioned for Samantha to wait. When Garrett Lang ordered her in, she got a tight grip on her folder full of projections and followed the secretary, hoping he wasn't as harsh as he sounded.

Garrett Lang was seated behind his desk at first. But when Samantha came in he rose and extended his hand. Samantha looked at him, at his hazel eyes and his hair—brown with gray flaring at the temples—and went into shock. She reached for his hand and dropped her projections, her gaze locking onto his. Sparks, yes, she was sure of it, there were sparks flying in all directions. This was her dream man in the flesh. And all the time she'd felt she made him up.

"Miss Croft? Are you all right?"

His voice was deep and husky, the same one she'd heard in her dreams a thousand times or more. She wanted to kiss him, to go to lunch, for that would proceed their love-making. But no. This wasn't a dream, this was real, and he wasn't playing their little game by pretending not to know her. He really didn't know her, had never seen her before and she was making a fool of herself.

"Would you care for a glass of water?" he asked.

I want more than that, I want you, she started to say, then caught herself in time. "Uh, no . . . I just felt a bit dizzy. I'm fine." She bent to retrieve her papers and looked up in time to see him pull back his extended hand. Damn, she cursed inwardly, you've blown it this time. And not just the sale. The man you've been waiting for all your life probably thinks you're an idiot by now.

"I'm sorry," she murmured.

"Won't you sit down?" he asked and remained standing until she was seated opposite him. "Now then. You mentioned bringing some projections."

"Yes . . . I have them here." She stared down at the computerized projections that had been neatly stuffed into a folder, giving them and her a look of professionalism. But, when she dropped them they'd fallen out of sequence, and that sequence was important in proving the need for the vast amount of insurance she'd proposed for Garrett Lang as well as the officers of his corporation. "Uh . . . I'll fix them in order."

"Never mind. Just leave the projections and I'll look them over."

Samantha's heart climbed to her throat. He wanted her to leave them, wouldn't even give her the chance to discuss them, wouldn't give her the chance to get to know him. What about lunch, she wanted to ask but stopped before making an even bigger fool of herself. "I wanted to explain—"

"No explanations are necessary. I'll have my attorney go over the projections after I examine them. I'm much too busy today to spend time on this." He rose then in a polite attempt to dismiss her.

She felt tears welling up inside. This wasn't fair. He knew nothing about the dreams and about the time she'd spent with him, being intimate, and had he known, he probably would've treated her differently. But how could she make him aware when he was practically throwing her out without a second thought? "I'll call you in a few days, at your convenience. When is the best time to call?"

"I'll get back to you," he said in an impersonal tone, his attention focused on the proposals on his desk. "Is your number here?"

"Yes," she said, her voice full of defeat. She'd finally met her dream man, only from his attitude she knew it would be the last time. Then she saw herself, crestfallen and bitter, stationed outside of this building nightly just waiting for a chance to look at him, to see his face, to add a touch of reality to her dreams.

He looked directly at her and hesitated, something different in his expression, while she felt a stirring deep inside. This was the way he generally gazed at her when he was ready. "Look, I'm sorry. This isn't fair. You've obviously spent a lot of time preparing for this meeting. And it's true, I'm extremely busy. Why don't we have dinner together this evening? I'll bring the proposals and we'll discuss them then."

Samantha felt warm all over. Lunch usually proceeded their love-making. But it didn't have to stay that way: it could be dinner this time. She automatically put on her coy routine. "Only if I pick up the tab."

"What!"

He was indignant. Oh, God, she'd blown it again! Think, girl, think, she told herself. "Well, it's to my advantage to have dinner with you. I mean, it's not your fault that you're busy. I should at least pay—"

"I won't hear of it." His voice softened, despite the huskiness of its tone, and then he smiled. Samantha was still in the game. "Give me your address. I'll pick you up around eight."

"That'll be fine." Oh, Lord, I did it, she wanted to scream. I made an impression on my dream man. "I live at Bridge Gate Court. Do you know where it is?" She couldn't be certain afterwards, but at the mention of Bridge Gate Court his face became pale in spite of his heavy tan. "On the seventh floor."

He smiled again, but it was a weak attempt. "I'll see you then, Samantha."

She stared at the bruises on her body, at the rope burns on her ankles and wrists. Then she shifted in her seat because of a raw wound on her inner thigh and wondered if the end result had been worth the pain. But then, it was. Once the masochism stopped and the bastard got on with his intended purpose, he drove her to such fits of ecstasy she wanted to scream. They made love until early morning.

Then he took her back to the bar where he'd picked her up and dumped her—flat!

June was sitting at that same bar now drinking and giving thought to her past and to her future as well. Her make-up, she noticed in the mirror opposite, was hideously smeared in some spots, and completely missing in others. The mascara on her eye lashes had run down both cheeks when she'd been crying, when he'd bitten her on the neck so hard she was sure her jugular vein had popped. And screaming did no good, since he lived in a small private house in the upper Bronx surrounded by abandoned buildings.

What she couldn't figure out at this point was why? Why did that man brutalize her so badly once she was tied to the bedposts and helpless and then turn right around and make such sweet love to her that even now she yearned for more? It just didn't make sense, along with most of the other events in her life. Like when both of her parents had heart attacks and died within hours of each other. At least one of the two should've hung on there for her sake. Instead, they chose to die together.

She lifted her glass and took a hefty swallow of scotch, the charm bracelet rattling incessantly from the motions of her arm, the tinkling noises it made reminding her that she'd let a man get away without acquiring the usual trophy—another charm. Then she thought about it some more, about what sort of charm that brutal, sadistic, tender lout would've bought her. Something with tiny whips and chains perhaps?

She laughed at that, then quickly downed the rest of her drink. She was, after all, a messy looking, beat up old drunk, who was sitting alone having a high time by herself. Only crazy people and bums laughed at nothing that was visible to the rest of the world. Then again, she could get away with it: she was sloppy enough at the moment to pass for a bum or a bag woman.

After throwing a few bills on the bar, she headed for the street, making sure to walk so as not to allow her thighs to rub together. She couldn't face the crowd at the office looking like this. Even if she cleaned herself up, there were still the bruises and the rope burns. No, she couldn't face them; she had to go home. Once there, she planned on taking a nice hot bath and having a nice cold drink. Then perhaps she'd be ready to examine the tattoo again, the one he'd engraved into her tender flesh . . . Maybe this was his idea of a replacement for the charm he never gave her.

When she'd first seen it, it seemed to be a hideous reproduction of a death head of some kind. It sort of resembled a skull. Then she decided she maybe hadn't been looking at the damned thing at the proper angle. But it was hard to get a good close up view of a tattoo on your inner thigh.

He'd licked it with his tongue to help reduce the pain after it was over and she moaned; it came to her now and magnified her shame.

What the hell have I come down to, she wondered, that a man such as this could satisfy my lust? That he could've done those humiliating things to my body, all in the name of good clean sex, and in the end, I'd still be satisfied enough to want more? She stood on a corner near the bar and tried to hail a passing cab and hide her outward shabbiness at the same time.

But then she realized that nobody was looking at her, this was New York City. Hell, these people were used to the strange, the bizarre. Who cared? That's right, June girl, she told herself, who cares? Nobody! Here you are, accepting crumbs from a bastard you would've spit on ten years ago, getting yourself so beat up that you're ashamed to walk the streets, and now you're wondering if he'll ever walk into your life again.

For what? More humiliation? Another tattoo?

Getting a cab was impossible, not one would stop. She sighed, figuring she probably could use the exercise and started to walk uptown in the direction of her apartment. She lived pretty close to Samantha. Samantha! If luck was with her,

Samantha was home. She'd told June over dinner last night that she had a pretty special appointment in the early afternoon, then she intended to go home. June glanced at her watch. It was after three; Samantha might be home. It didn't hurt to stop by and see.

If anybody could help her straighten out her life before things got worse, Samantha could. Samantha was different from most of the people June knew; she was compassionate, and full of empathy for her fellow man. She would understand June's predicament, and how her social life was on a downslope. She'd tell June what to do. Samantha didn't let men boss her around or control her emotions. Samantha was one smart cookie.

A cab stopped up ahead and two elderly men got out. June almost knocked them down claiming the cab as her own. Then she gave the driver the address while he gave her a suspicious once over. "I've got the money for the fare!" she said, then reflected on her past again. Ten years ago this cabbie wouldn't have worried about money. Hell no. She looked so good then he would've been more than willing to take it out in trade!

Ramona Blattfield stood in front of Bridge Gate Court and wondered if it was safe to go inside alone. Although the killer usually confined his killings to the evenings, he could've changed his routine, like most people do at times, just to break the monotony.

If murder and mutilation could ever be boring to a maniac!

She glanced in through the glass on the front door and saw a tall good-looking gentleman in a suit ducking into the corridor where most of the murders had taken place, and decided to go in. He obviously wasn't the killer, and with him around the killer would think twice before trying to kill a helpless woman. In fact he had the look of a cop, a plain clothes cop, so this made her feel safer than ever.

There were two small packages in the shopping bag she was carrying, the one with the wooden handle, and Ramona realized now that she'd risked her life by going out to shop. The killer could've gotten her either on the way out or on the way in. But these packages were purchased for Jeffrey's sake, so it didn't matter what happened to her, not really.

She'd called the boy forth, into this horrid world, but only to speak with him, to hear his voice again, to feast her eyes on his gorgeous face. And now she couldn't send him back. So the guilt was hers. But she'd found a way to rectify things, to lessen that guilt. So going out was worth the risk.

Last night, after Jeffrey had told her about a horrible experience in his past, her heart nearly broke out of pity for him. Then, when he insisted she go to bed, and that he'd stand guard, she pretended she was all right and went to bed. She even acted cheerful when she said good-night. But she wasn't. She was dying inside with grief over what had been done to him when he was alive.

And as she lay in bed, a wonderful idea suddenly came to her; something to make amends for what she'd done to Jeffrey and to help him forget his past. She remembered him saying he'd spent many hours talking to Uncle Max, her brother, her late brother. She shuddered and pushed the elevator button. Max had been her brother, and God rest his soul, everyone had admired the man. But a bigger bastard never walked the face of the Earth! However, only Ramona and a few others had ever seen the real Max.

But Max was obviously good to the boy, so she could forget her hatred for him and call him forth to keep Jeffrey company. She clutched the shopping bag close to her side and wondered if she'd forgotten anything. There were rosemary and sage, and a bit of an oak branch to stir the mixture with. If memory served her right, she was all set.

When the elevator stopped on the seventh floor, she got off and stood searching for her door key when a hand came out of nowhere and grabbed her. Ramona was too shocked to scream. Instead she turned on her attacker, thinking that surprise was on her side since he'd never expect this. But to her amazement, she saw old Mrs. Anderson from 7C standing in front of her, looking as weather-beaten and bent as ever.

"Ramona, I can't get my door unlocked. I've been standing here for the last ten minutes fooling with the damn thing." The old woman seemed almost in tears. "And you've got a gas leak in your apartment. I saw white fumes coming from under your door."

Ramona glanced sharply at the door to her apartment to make sure Jeffrey was back inside before responding. "I'll help you, Mrs. Anderson, no problem." She also intended to help herself by bringing forth Uncle Max. It was more important now than ever. Jeffrey had to be made to stay inside.

* * *

"In the name of Jesus Christ, our Lord—" J.J. Holiman had been praying for strength, both in his upcoming battle with this new demon and in his meeting with Garrett Lang. He hadn't seen Garrett in years; people change, friends become like strangers. They act as though you were the one who imagined the relationship, when really there was none.

He was sitting in his hotel room when a knock at the door interrupted his prayers. He rose and approached the door with uncertainty: would this be the old Garrett or someone the old man would regret having called, a stranger perhaps. "Come in, son." He studied the man walking in the flesh of the boy he once knew and wondered if he'd changed all that much inside. "Sit down."

Garrett had certainly changed in outward appearance. Somehow he was taller than the old man remembered, and his hair was gray near the temples. They stood and stared at each other and said nothing at first. It was very awkward, making J.J. feel for a moment that perhaps he'd made a mistake in wanting to see Garrett. But there was an emotion in Garrett's eyes that the old man knew he'd seen before, and he knew he'd done right.

"Oh hell . . . J.J." Garrett extended his arms and embraced the old man, bringing back memories of the nights they'd spent studying together in J.J.'s library. "God, I missed you," was the only thing Garrett could say, but it was enough.

"So you made it, huh? Mr. Big Time Executive. Thought for a moment there you forgot your old professor."

"What're you doing in a hotel? You have my

address. You know where I live." Garrett released
him and sat on the edge of the bed, leaving the
easy chair for J.J.

"I got in around midnight—"

"I was up. You could've called."

"Well, it's okay. This isn't too bad a place." As
J.J. watched, Garrett scanned the room, making
the old man even more aware of its failings. The
wallpaper was dry and faded, peeling in spots,
the carpet was filthy and stained, the bathroom
reeked with the odor of urine and vomit.

"When I leave I'm taking you with me."

J.J. started to protest, but Garrett was having
none of it. "I have more space than I know what
to do with. Besides, I can't have you staying in a
place as impersonal as a hotel. Not you, J.J."

The old man said nothing, and tried to hide his
gratitude, but he knew that Garrett could see it.
He took a bottle and two glasses from a table near
his bed and poured them each a drink. "Let's
drink to us. To an everlasting friendship." They
quickly downed their drinks and J.J. poured two
more. Once he was seated in the easy chair next
to Garrett, he tried to avoid his gaze because
Garrett had that same old look that said he was
troubled by something J.J. had in mind. He sighed
heavily and waited for Garrett to speak, knowing
he was in for it this time.

"What's this nonsense about wanting to help
solve those murders? When're you gonna stop
and enjoy your retirement?" Garrett sounded
annoyed but there was a sparkle of amusement in
his expression.

"They need me."

"They? Who's they?" Garrett wanted to know.
But then, the answer was obvious: the police

needed him. "There've been seven or eight murders so far and no one's even come close to solving them. At this point the slaughter could go on indefinitely—"

"So the police need you—an old warhorse of a demonologist, to help stop this lunacy."

"Yes. And if I don't do something quick, it'll get to the point where no one can stop it." J.J. sat back and studied Garrett to see if he could read fear in his face, and he did. He was right about Garrett: the boy turned man hadn't changed all that much. "The Lord's on my side, but I still need you to help with the physical work." Garrett said nothing. He turned his head away and stared out the window. "If I wasn't so damned old, I wouldn't ask you, son."

"What're you up against this time?"

J.J. rose and got a book from his briefcase. "I don't know. This one has me puzzled. Generally, from the description of the murders and what's been done to the bodies, I can at least get some idea of the demon involved and it's name."

"What makes you so sure it's a demon?"

Garrett was facing him directly now. J.J. saw a coldness that hadn't been there before. He was more scared than the old man imagined. "Well, actually it's a bit more than a demon. I'll explain as I go on. But for now, it's the taking of those body parts that makes me believe a demon's invol—"

"Satanists do that all the time. They use the parts for their so-called religious ceremonies . . . They burn them. They even consume them. Isn't that what you said in the past?"

"Yes, I did say that. But somehow it's different this time. Satanists stick to fingers and heads."

He noticed a repulsion in Garrett, but continued anyway. "This creature takes different parts as the murders progress. He's specializing."

"Meaning?"

J.J. sighed and wished he didn't know the truth, wished he'd been clutching at straws, wished he was just a plain old teacher and nothing more. "There's a ceremony in here. In this book." He sat down and tried to choose his words so as not to frighten Garrett more than he already was. But it had to be said, he needed Garrett's help. "There's a ceremony in here that utilizes various parts of the body. As in phases of desperation. In other words, first you use fingers, and if that doesn't work, you use a hand, then an arm."

"Phases of desperation," Garrett repeated. "What you're saying is this, if the first ceremony doesn't work, you advance to the next higher level."

"Exactly." He'd taught the boy well. Garrett was following.

Garrett leaned forward and ran a hand through his hair; a nervous gesture from the past. Then he cupped his hands together and looked at J.J. again. "What's this ceremony for?"

"To straighten out a mistake." The old man waited for a response, but hearing nothing, he continued. "Obviously someone was fooling around with these spells and didn't altogether know what they were doing. They were asking my old enemy, Mephisto, for a favor. Now, whether or not the favor was granted, I don't know. I do know, however, that something went wrong. It backfired. What I think we have here is a man/beast. And he's trying to be all man again."

Garrett looked at him oddly then, and J.J. took it to mean that he didn't completely understand. He decided to drop the subject for the time being. They'd only just met after years of separation, and they had a lot of catching up to do. "Is that offer still open?" Garrett looked puzzled. "For me to stay at your place?"

"Sure is!" Garrett sounded relieved that the old man had dropped the matter. He rose and approached the closet with a smile on his face. "Your luggage in here? Come on, I'll help you pack." Then he stopped in the middle of the floor as though something he'd only just recalled disturbed him.

"What is it, Garrett?"

"I just remembered I have a date tonight. Maybe I'd better cancel. You don't come to visit every day—"

"You'll do no such thing. You're not changing your plans just because I'm here. I'm staying a few weeks, or at least until the murders are solved. We'll have plenty of time to catch up. Besides, I was up late last night, until about three. I'll go to bed early, that's all."

"I was up till about three myself. Funny, we were both awake. You should've called."

At that point, J.J. ignored the obvious, made no statement concerning the fact that he hadn't called, and instead responded in a fatherly way. "It's no wonder you're so edgy. You barely slept last night. I think you should take a nap before you go out on that date. If she's pretty, you'll need your strength."

Garrett smiled and said nothing at first. But J.J. knew he wouldn't let it pass. "Actually she's more than pretty. She's outright beautiful. And yes, *father*. I'll take a nap before I go out."

7

June DeSoto got out of the cab, careful not to disturb her painful tattoo and decided she needed another drink before speaking to Samantha. She was normally a gutsy broad, but this was beyond her: explaining how she'd gone out with a man she'd previously considered a joke. Then explaining how she'd gone with the knowledge that he intended to tie her to a bedpost and make love to her. But in her own defense, she intended to tell Samantha she had no way of knowing he would torture her first, then sock it to her.

And in such a way as to make her crave for more.

This was the point she would have trouble bringing across. Samantha was kind of old-fashioned in her thinking. And now June wanted to lay a horror story on her, one that told of a demonstration of depravity and lust in its lowest form. Oh yes, she needed a drink all right.

There was a bar down the street, off the main avenue. But before going inside, she looked through the front window to see if it was safe to go in. Not that she was in any danger, but because she was so messy looking. Someone might object to her being in there, drinking at the same bar as them. There was no one around but the bartender. She went inside and spent a couple of hours consuming more scotch than she normally drank.

Then she staggered back to Bridge Gate Court and strolled through the front door, using the liquor in her veins for courage. The foyer was engulfed in near darkness, but that didn't bother an old gutsy broad like June. In fact, at the moment she preferred the darkness: it hid her shabbiness. If she ran into one of those stuck-up tenants, they would be looking at her, at the filth of her clothes and wondering just what the hell she was doing in stately old Bridge Gate Court.

Her heels, she noticed, seemed to echo forever in the stillness around her. The racket was so bad it made her head throb even harder. She tried walking on her toes to reduce the noise, but she was so drunk—

Something moved in the shadows ahead. There was a corridor off to one side of the elevator. She could've sworn someone stuck their head out and ducked back in again when June looked their way. Ridiculous, she told herself. Nothing moved. It's called the drunken d.t.'s. The booze is making you hallucinate.

She stood still for a moment longer, only to make sure it was the effect of the liquor and nothing more, then she started towards the elevator again. Step after drunken step, one foot clacking loudly behind the other, she walked ahead using determination as her driving force.

And heard another sound . . . Like someone giggling . . .

Bitch, she cursed herself. You're so drunk that now you're giggling without even knowing it. Stop this! You want Samantha to be thrown out for the company she keeps? Her mouth was dry and she could've used another drink, but one more would've put her under and she knew it. No. She had to keep going before her courage ran out. She had to go right up to Samantha's apartment and knock on the door and tell Samantha how sick she was—sick in the head, rather than physically ill from the booze.

She started walking towards the elevator again, but something in the shadows of that corridor made her stop dead: a piece of cloth was sticking out near the bottom of the wall. It appeared to be the kind of material used in a man's coat. The heavier kind, nothing resembling the thin, flimsy, shit they used in women's coats. What the hell? Was someone standing there? And if so, it had to be a man.

June felt a stirring in her lower torso, the kind she usually felt when she was drunk and needed affection and there was a man in the immediate area. Without thinking twice, she dug into her handbag for her pocket mirror. Shit! What a mess. He'd never want her this way. Then again, she suddenly had second thoughts about wanting him. She was here to see Samantha, and nothing more.

But she was horny and needed some loving. Samantha could wait!

As she gazed into the mirror again, she realized there wasn't enough light to really do herself justice. Her make-up was a mess and needed quite a bit of patching up before she'd even look halfway presentable—

"You look fine."

She heard the sound of his voice and felt even more desire, if possible, stirring up her insides. What a wonderful sound that was: smooth, gentle, understanding—almost the same tone of voice as the creep who'd humiliated her the night before. Sadist or no sadist, old Mister Tattoo Artist had a knack for whispering in her ear and heating up her flesh at the same time.

But she felt a twinge of conscience gnawing at her along with the desire: she was not as young as she tried to look. It was dark in here, which was to her advantage. But what if he took her to a place where it was brighter than this? Then he'd be able to see her as she was, and he might feel taken.

"I'm not as young as I look." She put the compact back into her purse and waited.

"Age has no boundaries for me, Sister. . . . Uh . . . What is your name?"

"*Sister?*" She repeated the word and smiled. Either the guy was very friendly in using that expression, trying to establish familiarity right away, or he was downright kinky. Nuts was actually a better word. Or maybe he wanted to pretend she was a nun so he'd enjoy the sensation of laying one. Oh well, she'd slept with kinky guys before. One even wanted her to diaper him and play nursemaid. "Do you want to play pretend?" she asked, feeling a smile come to her face.

"I don't understand. I just want your name."

"June. June DeSoto."

"Sister June DeSoto," he said and giggled. June

wasn't upset by this, although she did feel somewhere deep inside that an experience with a weirdo every twenty-four hours was hardly called for. "Come here, Sister June."

As he stepped out of the shadows, the light from behind cast an eerie glow around his body; she couldn't see his face. Then she spotted his cape and was appalled because he didn't recognize her. This was obviously the man she'd just slept with. She also felt something more, she felt the heat from her body rise in invisible streams. She wanted him, could feel herself going limp with passion. "Hello again. How come you don't recognize me? Or remember my name? And what the hell are you doing here?"

"What?"

"Never mind. Let's just do it again."

"What do you have in mind?"

His voice was as soothing as ever. She wanted to brush his lips with her own, to feel his tongue, hot and wet, running the length of her body. "Let's go to your place. You know, like last night when you tied me up?" She wasn't sure because she couldn't see his face, but she could almost swear he was smiling.

"Why wait?" he wanted to know. "There's an apartment back here. It belongs to the superintendent and he's out for the night. We could go there and do it."

June felt her legs weaken with want. She didn't know if she could make it that far, but she had to try, she had to have him. She walked closer to him and further into the shadows before something struck her as being odd: he was wearing a cape with a hood. The man from the night before had been wearing a cape-like coat, true, but he was also wearing a regular man's hat, no hood. Suddenly the passions she wanted to quench were replaced by fear.

Soft voice or no soft voice, this wasn't the same man!

"Why do you hesitate?" he asked and giggled again.

June heard something awful this time in the sound of his laughter, something insane and mocking. This wasn't a man looking for a good time, be it kinky or not, this was a nut! She was halfway between the front door and the elevator and now the choice was hers. If she made it to the street would anyone respond to her screams for help? After all, this was New York! People heard screaming all the time and managed to ignore it. Then too, if she made it to the elevator, would the doors close before he got inside with her.

"Look," she stammered. "I don't know what you want, but if it's money . . ." She dug into her purse again, hoping she hadn't spent everything in the bars, wishing she'd kept a count.

"I thought we were going to do it. Isn't that what you had in mind? You want me to tie you up and stick it to you."

Something in his attitude had changed and that made her mad. He was now speaking to her as though she were a common whore. And that just wasn't so. Didn't she have a charm bracelet full of refused marriage proposals to prove her worth? "Listen, you—"

She looked up in time to see the glint of a knife in his hand, the light behind him reflecting off the metal of the blade. She couldn't think, couldn't scream, couldn't even swallow.

She backed up and tried to get away, but it was

no use. She wasn't quick enough to escape the first slash, nor ready for the sharpness of the blade against her flesh. She barely felt anything when the blade sliced her skin: it must've been really sharp. But she did experience the sensation of a liquid, hot and thick, running down the side of her neck and her eyes widened with horror and shock. She knew it was blood—her blood!

Time after time, again and again, he brought the blade down and found a new spot, one that hadn't been slashed before, to slice through. June fell forward with arms outstretched, her hands coming to rest on his shoulders. Weak as she was, she wanted to see him, to look into the face of the man who was killing her, to take the image of his countenance to her grave. It was too dark though, she couldn't make out his features.

And then the most amazing thing happened. He stopped his maniacal slashing and dragged her back into the shadows of the corridor where he threw her roughly to the ground. As she laid there and wondered what was next, the sound of a zipper coming down answered her question. He wanted to do it, to screw her while she was bleeding to death. Well she wouldn't let him. The bastard! What a nerve!

She clenched her thighs tightly together but couldn't keep the hold. The tattoo was burning from the pressure. She tried punching him in the head when he bent down to slice off her panties, but even that was more than she could manage. When penetration was finally complete, she told herself she couldn't respond. But it was so good . . . he was so gentle . . . She looked up into his face and wished that she were already dead. It seemed as though there was no skin—

Samantha was inside her walk-in closet when something dawned on her: she wasn't afraid of being in there alone. She stopped trying to select a dress for her date with Garrett Lang and thought about how she'd taken a shower with no fear, and now she was in here doing this, also with no fear. It must've been her infatuation with Garrett that was causing this.

He was her dream man, her dream come true, a walking, breathing, replica in the flesh of the man she'd spent the last five years with. At this point, she didn't even remember coming home or walking through the semi-darkened hallway downstairs. And that was dangerous. Of course, it had still been daylight when she walked to the elevator, so it wasn't that dark. But still, there was a murderer roaming the halls of Bridge Gate Court . . .

She'd been careless, but only because of meeting Garrett, only because he made her feel she was invincible and nothing hurtful or hateful could touch her or harm her now. She selected a beige dress that came down to mid-calf and walked from the closet. Once outside though, she hesitated and wondered if she should wear the black and white one. It was pretty too.

Then she quickly decided to stay with the one she had. Morgan said that beige went so well with her dark auburn hair and brought out the tone of her honey brown eyes. She slipped the dress over her head and allowed her thoughts to wander back to her meeting earlier in the day with Garrett Lang, and she had to smile in spite of herself. First dropping her projections, then stammering like a fool! It's a wonder he even wanted to make a dinner date with her after all of that.

What a beautiful man.

Even more so than she imagined in her dreams.

What were the odds, she wondered, of dreaming about the same man for so many years only to meet him in the flesh? A million to one? Or a billion perhaps? It was a bit spooky when she stopped to analyze it. But then, who cared! He was there, he was alive, and he was hers—for the night at least. It was perfect, like something out of a novel.

Then again, there was such a thing as being too perfect . . .

Garrett Lang was almost too perfect and matched her dream man so well she was frightened for an instant. Maybe she'd wake up and find she was still dreaming. Maybe he'd turn her dreams into a nightmare. After all, nobody could match the image others have of them. Maybe he was awful in bed, a beast! Or worse yet, maybe he was one of those slam-bam-thank-you-ma'am kind of guys with no consideration for the women they were sleeping with.

What? Did I think that, she wondered in amazement.

Samantha was putting on her shoes, the beige ones she'd bought to match her dress, when the front doorbell rang. That puzzled her. If it was Garrett, he was about an hour ahead of time. When it rang again, she rushed to the door, thinking it might've been Ramona Blattfield come to borrow a cup of sugar or some tea. She glanced through the peephole and was amazed to see Ron Wheatley standing outside.

She released the bolt on the police lock and let him in, but not before noticing a look of admiration in his eyes. "Hi," she said and tried to act casual. Ron was interested in her, he wasn't a phony. Otherwise he wouldn't be here now. But, instead of feeling elated, she felt a bit depressed. She'd promised to go out with him first. Now here she was dating Garrett.

"Hi, yourself," he said and smiled, soaking her up with his eyes. "You look beautiful tonight. But then you are beautiful, Samantha." She started to say something but he stopped her and turned his attention on the shadow of the winged gargoyle on her window. "I came here to make a confession. When I stopped by last night and told you it was part of a police investigation, I was lying."

"What! But why?" The man was a liar, hardly in character with someone to replace her dream man.

"I used a flimsy excuse beccause I had to see you, to see what you looked like," he said and turned to face her, "I knew you weren't connected with the murders. But Jose Torres wrote your name down and said you were as beautiful as his Louisa. While I never met Louisa, I still had to come up here. I'm sorry."

"And now, why the confession?"

"Because I've been thinking. If we're gonna have any kind of a relationship, it has to be based on honesty."

Samantha smiled and felt a fluttering in her stomach. He'd lied to her, but it was for such a wonderful reason. He must've been a very lonely man despite his good looks. "Would you like some coffee, or a drink?"

136

He smiled back. Probably because he realized her offer meant forgiveness. "Only if it's no trouble. I see you're all dressed up. Going out?"

"I have an hour before Garrett picks me up." She was halfway into the kitchen before she realized what she'd said. She turned in time to see a tinge of hurt in Ron's eyes. Samantha felt she'd blown it with Ron, as she almost had with Garrett earlier. Saying and doing the wrong thing seemed to come naturally to her lately. "It's just a business kind of thing," she said quickly. "We're having dinner to go over the proposals I gave him today."

Ron leaned against the frame of the door, his tall, muscular body as appealing as ever. "Oh, I see. This's the guy you had that meeting with today." He smiled, but it wasn't warm. "Have to give him credit. He works faster than I do."

"Oh, come on," she said and walked back toward him, wondering if he'd noticed the glow on her face when she opened the door, the glow that was there because of Garrett Lang. "Don't be like that. It's just business." She touched his arm, her hand coming in contact with raw muscle. Her stomach began to flutter again. She looked up into his eyes and suddenly realized she was in the middle, between two men who'd just walked into her life, a position she couldn't have imagined a week ago.

His rough features cracked into a smile again, and this time she could tell he meant it. "I'm sorry," he said. "I really have no right to be offended. I don't own you. Not yet!" He clutched her shoulders with both hands and she felt he was about to kiss her, really kiss her, and not on the cheek as he'd done the night before. But he didn't. "Coffee sounds—"

He stopped in mid-sentence and grabbed his head with both hands, the smile on his face changing to a grimace of pain. He started to crumple and Samantha panicked. "What's wrong? What is it?"

He pulled away from her and staggered towards the door, leaving Samantha alone and in shock. As he left, she heard him say something that sounded like, "The beast . . . He's done it again!"

She walked slowly toward the door and closed and locked it behind him, her mind a complete, forced, blank. She wasn't about to let his words roll around in her head and drive her crazy. She didn't care what the phrase meant. She already had a pretty good idea, except she didn't know how Ron knew what was happening.

She sat down on the sofa in the living room and snapped on the television to watch the evening news, or whatever else was on, until Garrett came to get her. But it was difficult to watch the news while glancing over her shoulder at the gargoyles, wondering when they'd come alive.

Charlie was listening to the waves below slapping at the side of the boat. It was a warm, clear night, the moon high and full in the sky. He thought about Morgan and how he should've been grateful to have a beauty such as this beside him on the deck of his yacht. But he wasn't happy. He was angry because she'd either lied to him or she'd hidden most of the truth. There was more to the story about her childhood and her father than she cared to admit to anyone.

She'd told Charlie earlier that her father was greedy and stingy, so he was keeping his money to himself. But he knew there was more to it than that. His problems with Morgan had been of a sexual nature almost from the beginning of their relationship. Sometimes he'd be deep in the throes of passion, holding onto her for all he was worth, and he'd get the feeling that he was the only one involved in the act, that she could've just as well been reading a newspaper or studying the cracks in the ceiling.

And yet, there were other times when making love to her was incredible: she was responsive and hungry, almost animal. It had him puzzled.

She must've sensed his uneasiness, because she kept running her hand down over the small of his back to calm him. But it wasn't any good, not for him. He wanted her, really wanted her, as in 'wife,' to love, to cherish, to bear his children, and he couldn't do this with a liar or a deceiver.

"Let's have it," she finally said, her voice filled with resignation. "What'd I do now?"

"Nothing!" He wasn't about to make it any easier on her than she'd made it on him.

"Charlie!" She glared at him and started to walk away, but he knew she'd be back. She loved him as much as he loved her. He was sure of it. "Talk to me! Damn you!"

He turned and faced her head on. "When you're ready to tell me the truth about what happened with your father—"

"I've already told you everything. What more do you want?"

She was as angry now as he, her face twisted into a scowl, but still looking cute to him. "Morgan. We can't go on like this. I want you to be mine—"

"Oh, balls!"

"Completely mine. In here," he pointed to his heart. "Now either you talk so it'll be out in the open and we can both live with it . . . Or you can continue to hide it to yourself and make both our lives a living hell." He'd spoken softly and articulately, but he was raging inside.

"Okay, okay."

The tone of her voice had traveled several degrees of emotion in an instant: from a harsh growl to a soft, subdued whisper. That meant she was ready to tell the truth, really ready.

"You ever had problems, Charlie?"

"Everyone has, but right now I'm more concerned with what's tying you into knots and coming between us."

"It's very simple, there's a love-hate relationship between my father and me. He loves me, I hate him." She went over to the rail of the ship, leaning back against it, she turned to face Charlie. "You see how skinny I am? Wanna know why?" He remained silent, hoping to give her the courage to go on. "To begin with, I killed my mother. Well, not outright. But I killed her in childbirth. Moments after she had me something went wrong and she began to hemorrhage. The doctors couldn't stop it, so she bled to death."

He saw tears lining her face and wanted to go to her, to wrap her in his arms and comfort her. But she had to do this by herself, otherwise she'd never get rid of the pain.

"Anyway, from the time I was able to walk and talk, that's what my father kept reminding me about: that I killed my mother. And it was up to me to take her place." The last part was spoken so softly that at first he thought he'd heard wrong. But then she repeated it, her voice choking with emotion. "He wanted me as a woman, but not until I reached womanhood. So I was able to grow up halfway normal, if you could call it that. He kept telling me I'd be his when I came of age.

"Then I noticed something. From the pictures he kept of my mother, she was, well, not fat, but heavy-set. She had large breasts and wide hips. Then I figured it out. If I stopped eating and stayed skinny, my father might want me as a daughter and not as a woman."

"Jesus!" Charlie rose and went to her, holding her as close as he could, wondering if she could finally sense the love he felt inside. "Then he never touched you."

"No," she said, her body shuddering against his. "But what he did was just as bad. The mental cruelty, talking about how we were gonna live as man and wife when I came of age. So, when I came of age, I left."

"He's mentally ill, you know. He has his emotions mixed up. You see, Morgan, something I learned over the years. There're various degrees of love. There's the love you have for your parents, that's one degree. Then there's the love you have for your friends, still another degree. The love you have for your spouse is another. Sometimes people get their degrees of love mixed up and imagine themselves in love with their children. They mistake affection for sexual love."

"Now you make my father sound normal."

He looked down at her and realized she was being sincere. "Not normal, but not so different from hundreds of others.'"

"But, Charlie, he was raising me to be his wife. He insisted I learn how to be the lady of the house, to handle the servants and take on the responsibilities of making his life at home a pleasurable experience—"

"At least he never assaulted you sexually. Thank God for that much. There're a lot of women walking around today who have terrible secrets buried in their hearts. Whose heads are screwed around backwards because they were assaulted either by their fathers, or by an uncle or a family friend." He looked down at her then and realized there was something wrong. She didn't seem to be listening. Her mind was a thousand miles away and there was an awful expression on her face. "Morgan?"

She was close to being hysterical and began to talk rapidly as though what she had to say had to be said before she changed her mind. "He used to make me undress. And lay in his bed and then he'd undress and play with himself while he looked at my body—"

"You said he never touched you!" Charlie was in a rage by now. But she hadn't lied this time, rather she'd omitted part of the truth.

"I didn't know how to tell you. It was so sick. No, it's true he never touched me. But he made me feel ashamed. He made me wish I was dead." She looked up into his eyes then and he wanted to smother her with his love, to tell her it was all right. But she didn't give him a chance to speak. "I ran away from home and began to have affairs with all kinds of men to get back at my father. He wanted me pure and untouched until I came of age. Well, this was my way of evening the score between us.

"But, Charlie, when I met you it was different. You wanted me as a person, not a bed toy. And I've tried to love you, I've tried to show you the affection I never could show anyone else, any of those other men. And I'm still trying. Please, Charlie, don't hate me for the things I've told you. Please love me.''

''I do, honey. I do.'' He brushed her face with his lips and whispered to her, his voice as gentle as he could manage. ''Now that the truth is out, we can both help each other. I realize you're not using me as a fool because I have money and can give you things.'' She started to protest, but he stopped her. ''It isn't easy being a tub, you know, a fat man. You're never really sure that someone loves you for yourself and not your money. I understand about what you've told me and why you're sometimes cold and withdrawn. And we can both deal with it. Anyway, it could've been worse. What if you were secretly in love with another man? That's something I couldn't handle.''

Morgan smiled, her eyes aglow with love. Charlie felt warm inside. Suddenly she looked different, as though by telling him the truth, she'd released the plug that was holding her true emotions in check. He knew they'd make it this time. He'd help her forget the sexual abuse she suffered at the hands of her father. He also knew he'd kill the son-of-a-bitch for what he'd done to her if and when they ever met.

8

Her head was wrapped in an old newspaper he'd
found out back near the garbage cans. While
wrapping it, he'd gazed at it once or twice and
thought about how she'd died in the throes of
sexual ecstasy. Shame, he thought, she couldn't
stick around and enjoy it to the end. Then again,
her pleasure ceased when she saw his face. . . .

But she was no beauty either: she was wearing
too much make-up, and it didn't help. Most of it
was smeared. Her body was getting there as far
as age went, and it was heavily bruised. Whoever
the hell she'd slept with recently had done a
number on her. Beat her up, carved her body with
a knife.

And to think *he* was the beast, the one who
scared people half to death with his appearance. He
smiled at that because there was a fair share of
human beasts roaming the streets these days:
ones who had him beat when it came to physical
mutilation. The only difference was, they could
mingle in a crowd. Nobody was afraid of them.
And they kept right on swinging because they

looked normal; kept picking up broads and carving marks into their flesh.

Of course, this broad, the one he'd just killed and mutilated, wasn't an average woman. She was a nun! And because he killed her, some old bastard priest was bound to suffer with the worst erection yet.

Again he laughed but stopped to wonder if he'd done the sensible thing in leaving her arm behind, stuffed into a garbage can. The arm could've been used in the third phase. However, if he was following this right, both an arm and a head had already been employed, with no success. He was becoming more confused with each murder. But then, he was sharing his mind and his body with another. That's where the confusion came in. If he was in complete control and never yielded to his human counterpart, things would be different. There would be fewer mistakes, and no need for the body parts.

He was in an alleyway a few blocks from Bridge Gate Court, trying to make his way home, and trying at the same time not to think about J.J. Holiman and how his old friend was in town, when someone grabbed him from behind. He dropped the head and wheeled to face his attacker, his veiny, skinless lips drawn into a smile, revealing sharp dagger-like teeth. "Yes. Can I help you?"

An old man was standing before him, his body as dirty and crumpled as the clothing he wore. "Oh, Jesus!" The old man's face grew slack with shock when he gazed at the countenance of the beast.

"Can I help you?"

"I . . . I was gonna ask ya if ya had a drink . . .

But I think I had too much already . . .'' The old man looked down at the package lying at his feet, and saw a jagged piece of crimson flesh sticking out between the folds of the newspaper. "Oh, yeah. I think I had too much already,'' he repeated and turned to run. But the beast was faster.

The old man screamed, his voice a horrible wail of pain in the night, when the talons of the beast raked his neck, shredding the fabric of his coat, shredding his sweater, shredding his flesh. "Oh, Lord, oh, Lord,'' he wailed and sank to his knees.

"This is what I'll do to you, Holiman! You got away from me once!'' Again the hand with the clawed talons shot out and slashed at the quivering form on the ground, raking across the old man's head. Deep wounds, painful gulleys, appeared where moments before there had been hair and tender flesh. "I hate you!'' the beast raged, ignoring the pitiful wailing of his victim, using his razor-sharp nails as weapons.

When it was over, the body was shredded beyond recognition. The beast picked up June's head and continued on his way. He was satisfied at this point because, to a certain extent, he'd had his revenge on J.J. Holiman—on his memory at least, if not his body in the flesh.

His body in the flesh . . .

They would meet again, face to face, the beast was sure of it. The truth was revealed to him through the powers of his subconscious mind, the same way that J.J.'s presence in town was revealed to him. And this time, old J.J. would wind up like that hobo lying on the ground!

"Oh, yes, J.J.,'' he hissed through clenched teeth. "Asgar is back and he wants you!''

Garrett Lang walked into the lobby of Bridge Gate Court and glanced at his watch. Eight sharp. It was difficult to see anything as small as a watch because it was so damned dark in there, but he managed. He looked around and spotted the elevator back near an even darker corridor and shuddered. His dreams, or rather nightmares, had been more than accurate. He'd never been here in the flesh, and yet he was familiar with the layout of the place: the foyer, the elevator, the corridor where death stalked its victims. He'd been here many times at night, had walked these halls in his sleep . . .

Gail Lindman, his attractive, young secretary, had been one of the victims . . .

He felt bad about her death, mainly because there were times when he'd been tempted to ask her for a date. She looked good, she was classy. But then, what if he'd been deeply involved with Gail when Samantha came into his life. Samantha. Now there was a beauty! He pushed the button for the elevator and tried not to think about that darkened corridor, while allowing his mind to drift back to the first time he'd laid eyes on Samantha.

She'd sounded so professional over the phone. Then, when they'd met in his office earlier today, her confidence eroded in seconds. She was jittery and nervous and downright appealing. She wasn't the career woman he'd imagined. And that fact turned him on; she turned him on.

And you, you damned fool, he cursed inwardly, you almost let her get away with your business-like attitude. But it was only because he didn't want her involved in the mess he'd created.

Samantha deserved more . . .

But then, he'd already paid a heavy price in terms of loneliness. And so he too deserved more . . .

He had everything in life a man could want or need except for the most important thing of all: companionship—a good woman to come home to at night. Samantha was the fulfillment of a lifetime of searching; she was a dream come true.

The elevator was on the main floor by this time, and as the doors opened Garrett started to step inside. But he heard a noise behind him that was enough to freeze him to the spot. It seemed to be coming from that corridor, and made him wonder for one horrible second if the killer was hiding in the darkness. And if so, had he marked Garrett for death?

Garrett turned to face his attacker head on; let the bastard tangle with a man this time, he thought. He'd damn well lose. Then he remembered what J.J. Holiman had told him earlier and he suddenly became frightened. This wasn't anything human . . . Oh, it may've been human at times, but the human was mostly controlled by a demon. He backed into the elevator, his eyes scanning the darkness for movement.

As the doors closed, he breathed a sigh of relief. But the feeling didn't last for long because he wondered what would be waiting for him when he came back down with Samantha.

Standing in the darkened corridor, Ron Wheatley watched the elevator doors close with a certain finality, feeling they'd completely severed the bond between him and his old drinking buddy, Garrett Lang.

When Samantha mentioned having a date with 'Garrett,' a mental image of a man with the same first name came to him; someone from his past, someone close—a blood brother. Someone he now despised with everything in him. Garrett made it, while he, Ron, barely managed to keep one step ahead of poverty. But then Garrett had been bound and determined to make it, at any price. And Ron wasn't. Ron backed down, and ran like a fool.

And now, Garrett had it all. Garrett had Samantha.

Ron sank deeper into the shadows and knew he was wrong to stand there spying on Samantha's new boyfriend and dreaming of the past. There was a body beyond him, toward the rear of the corridor. A body with no head and one arm missing. He should've called it in hours ago, should've had the coroner here, and a police photographer . . .

He should've been looking for the other body, the old hobo. After he'd found the gruesome corpse behind him, the visions of the beast should've stopped. But they didn't. A tiny vignette of horror danced before his eyes while he stood there and watched in helpless anticipation. He saw the beast killing an old man, tearing his flesh to shreds as the man knelt at his feet. He should've been searching for that body right now instead of standing in the shadows of darkness, spying like a fool.

But Samantha mentioned having a date with 'Garrett!'

For him, there was no other choice but to make sure; he had to know if it was the same one. And it was. He was in a dreamlike state, his thoughts wandering back to the past, the YMCA where he'd roomed when he first left college and was trying to make a life for himself. He had dreams then, plans for the future. Then he met Garrett and discovered they had something in common: they both wanted wealth and power . . .

Only Garrett made it, where Ron failed . . .

He shook himself free and went outside to his car to call in the two latest murders, the ones he'd again witnessed in his sub-conscious as the beast was performing them. But somehow his mind stayed with the past. He recalled the last night he'd spent with Garrett; drinking, making plans, doing awful things. Garrett said it was all right to do those things, but Ron was scared, more scared than he'd ever imagined possible. And he ran. But something ran with him . . .

Now, try as he may, he couldn't shake the horror. And, try as he may, he couldn't shake the feeling that he'd done wrong by running.

He'd reached the car and was about to grip the handle on the door when he realized he was in one helluva fix. He'd have to send one of his men out to search the neighboring alleys for the hobo's body, without explaining how he knew there'd been another murder.

J.J. Holiman waited. Garrett had been gone for over an hour. That gave the boy plenty of time to pick up his date and leave the building. J.J. wanted to visit Bridge Gate Court to view the scene of the crimes, and he didn't want to chance running into Garrett. This Samantha, or whatever her name was, lived there. It was odd how everything seemed to be tied together somehow, and yet there were so many loose ends that the old man had trouble gathering them and putting the pieces of the puzzle into perspective.

Did the fact that Samantha had an apartment at Bridge Gate Court have any bearing on the case?

Gail Lindman, Garrett's ex-secretary, was killed there, along with several others. Was all that connected?

Then, according to the newspaper reports he'd read, the one Garrett obviously hadn't, Ron Wheatley was the detective investigating the case. If J.J.'s mind wasn't failing him, Ron Wheatley was an old friend of Garrett's, mentioned many times in those brief but all too few letters he received after Garrett moved to New York City. Was that significant?

Everything was tied together—somehow!

J.J. found himself wandering aimlessly through the huge penthouse that belonged to his former protege. He was searching for the door, the way out of this expensive tomb Garrett had bought himself. Then he remembered his books and he searched until he found his bedroom. One in particular had to be taken along in case there'd been another murder and the police were present.

He didn't want them thinking he was a senile old fool, and that book was his proof that a demon was involved. Of course, he was at a loss when it came to the demon's name—

No you're not, he screamed inwardly. You know its name, have known it all along. You were just too frightened to admit it to yourself. He's the one you came in contact with several years ago, the most dangerous you've ever faced, and you almost bought it, almost died but for your faith in the Lord.

J.J. had been aiding the police in the investigation of several murders, all with the signature of one killer, as he now recalled, and all had taken place in the same location, a boarding house for women. He'd gone to that house . . .

It resembled Bridge Gate Court! And yes, the victims were the same as now: young women who'd had their bodies mutilated in death by some demon maniac. J.J. had researched the method used by the killer beforehand, had gone through his books so thoroughly, that he swore his eyes would fall out from the strain. But it paid off!

He'd gotten rid of the demon—temporarily, though, it now seemed.

But that same method wouldn't work now. The demon was stronger and had control of a human. So it was different this time. J.J. had to get rid of the demon without destroying them both.

He tried to recall what he'd done the last time, and how the same method could be partly utilized to fit this very delicate case. He'd gone to the house carrying his Bible, his book on 'Exorcist Ceremonies,' and a bottle of holy water.

The house, as he remembered it, stood alone against a blackened sky, its chimneys reaching into the darkened clouds overhead like the fingers of a witch searching for its victims. Wind howled around him, whipped at his face and intensified his fears. The whole scene scared him.

But he prayed. He asked the Lord to aide him in his efforts, to give him the physical strength he'd surely need to defeat the evil because those demons can wear you down with their resistance, their lies and their blasphemies. He asked the Lord to give him the ability to listen to those

blasphemies and not lose his head. If J.J. grew
angry and responded in anger, the proper
ceremony would be either forgotten or performed
wrong and the demon would win.

He entered the house alone, a condition he'd
specified to the police ahead of time. It was just
too dangerous to allow anyone to accompany
him. The house was frightening inside; damp,
dark, and heavily shadowed. Things were hiding
in those shadows. Small, insignificant demon
creatures, pets of the beast were hiding, and
waiting for J.J. to make a wrong move so they
could pounce on him and devour his flesh.

But J.J. was smart; he ignored them. And using
the powers of his faith in the Lord, he ascended a
carpeted staircase to the second floor, where
most of the murders had taken place. And yet, his
mind was temporarily diverted by a she-bitch, a
siren of Hades. She was standing back near an
open doorway on the first level. He became
aware of her when he was halfway up the stairs.

He made the mistake of turning to look at her
and saw that she was naked and alluring, her long
brown tresses barely concealing the flesh of her
breasts. She sang songs of sexual splendor and
J.J., despite himself, began to respond. It had
been so long since he'd had a woman. But somewhere, somehow, he gathered the strength to
resist her, because eternal death and damnation
were part of the promise of her caress, and he
continued on.

The upstairs portion of the house was worse. It
was crowded with minor beasts, hideous half-
human, half-animal creatures, their voices rising
in a cacophony of anger. They were there to
protect the demon, and they were prepared to kill

to assure that protection. J.J. raised his Bible in the air for all to see and quoted first the 23rd Psalm and then the 91st, the Psalm of Protection.

He was scared that he might have to use the holy water, to waste it on these minor lumps of refuse. He was saving it for the demon beast. But they were driven apart by an unseen force, and a path was left for him to continue.

The room where most of the murders had taken place stood out in the sense that it was well-lit and warmer than the rest of the house. This was a trick, J.J. knew, employed by the beast to give him a sense of well being. But it didn't work. J.J. kept his guard up, entered, and began to pray in the name of the Lord, while watching for some sign of the beast.

There was a frilly, canopy bed in the middle of the room, and ruffled curtains hanging at the window. While he was praying, the curtains seemed to take on life of their own, rising and falling and emitting wailing sounds. Another trick meant to frighten him. And again, it didn't work. The Lord was on his side.

He was into his second prayer, as part of the ceremony of exorcism, when the beast put in an appearance. A roar—the voices of a thousand angry demons—shattered the air around him, and the beast rose from the ground. It was huge, more so than he'd imagined, and gruesome with its skinless body and dagger-sharp teeth. It was Asgar, demon lord of the fourth level in Acheron. J.J. was facing a most formidable foe and was tempted to yield his ground and run. But the Lord was with him and he stood like a man and chanted prayers of deliverance for himself and prayers of destruction for the demon.

But the demon moved close to his face as he prayed, and J.J. looked into those sadistic, manaical eyes and saw hell. For one instant, he'd allowed himself to be mesmerized by the beast—a mistake, because he dropped his Bible, his holy water, and his book on exorcism, and the beast laughed. J.J. would die. He'd let down his guard, had allowed himself to become enticed by the creature, and his defenses were gone. The beast grabbed his throat, encircled his neck with both hands and began to choke his life away.

"Lord," he prayed inwardly, "Lord Jesus, help me."

"Pray to your Lord. It'll do no good," the beast hissed as he read into J.J.'s thoughts and laughed again.

J.J. felt his eyes bulging from his head, his lungs burned from lack of air, the area around his throat was a raw wound. But above it all, above the pain and the suffering he endured, he became conscious of the wind outside. It was howling louder now, whipping heavily against the age-pocked, brickwork of the house, making the windows rattle and the eaves groan in protest. When the house began to rock on its very foundation, the beast became alarmed and released his grip on J.J.'s throat. Then he turned and faced the lone window in the room.

The old man seized the opportunity to suck in a long swallow of air and crumpled to the floor, but not before getting a stronghold on the genitals of the naked beast, Asgar's skinless flesh yielding to pain. The beast howled and came down with a deadly claw as J.J. rolled to one side, still holding on, driving the beast to his knees in agony. J.J. held him fast with one hand and reached for the

156

holy water, his fingers barely able to stretch over to the spot near the door where he'd dropped it.

"In the name of the Lord, Jesus Christ, I command you to be gone," J.J. shouted three times in rapid succession to nullify the powers of the beast while sprinkling his body with holy water. Asgar cringed and screamed in agony, the thunder of his voice causing a minor earthquake as the holy water seared his skinless flesh, leaving deep, steaming valleys of burning agony wherever it touched his body. "In the name of the Lord, Jesus Christ, I command you to be gone," J.J. shouted three times more because Asgar was a powerful demon. It would take the power of *six* to destroy a foe such as this.

And then he was gone.

J.J. had his book in his hands and had found the door to Garrett's apartment by the time the memory came to an end. He reached for the knob to let himself out, realizing he was troubled, and deeply so. The holy water and the chants had worked the first time, but he knew they wouldn't work again. Mainly because Asgar knew he was here, and Asgar was ready for him. J.J. would have to come up with something totally new to send the demon beast back to Acheron where he belonged.

Samantha rode next to Garrett Lang in the back seat of his limousine, her body close to his, and made up her mind to think before she acted and to think before she spoke. Earlier in the day she'd nearly blown the relationship with her nervousness, and now that she'd found Garrett in the flesh, she didn't want to do or say anything that would upset him.

Garrett, she noticed, kept eyeing her up and down every now and then as if he couldn't get his fill of looking at her. It started when he picked her up at eight, when she opened the door to her apartment and he stood there and couldn't say a word. However, there was something in his expression that told her he was silent because he was overwhelmed at the sight of her. And then, when they'd rode down on the elevator and crossed the semi-darkened lobby to the street, it was all he could do to keep his attention focused on what they were doing and not her.

The limousine halted at a red light. Samantha stared out at the people on the street and knew they couldn't be as happy as she was at the moment. This night was magic and she was Cinderella, on her way to a candlelight dinner with the prince.

"We'll be dining at The Captain's Table," Garrett said, breaking the silence between them. But instead of being pleased, Samantha was shocked, and disturbed. The Captain's Table was the restaurant he always took her to in her dreams: she thought she'd made it up, that it was a fictitious name. And now to find it was real. "I've taken the liberty of ordering lobster and filet mignon."

She wanted to scream because it was all too pat, all too much like her dreams, causing her to wonder if this was real. Was it happening or was she still asleep? She forced a smile. He was here, next to her, a breathing, sensual image born of her lonely imagination. And he was acting exactly as she had pictured he would. But things like this didn't generally carry over into real life.

"You look lovely tonight, Samantha." He reached over and touched her hand, caressing it with the same warmth and determination as he had these past five years in her sleep. "I have a confession to make, though."

Oh, you too, she wanted to say. Ron Wheatley also had a confession to make earlier. This must've been the day for revealing the truth. "Really? About what?" was all she could say, and even at that the words sounded choked. She didn't know what to expect from Garrett.

"I purposely left those proposals at home—the ones we were supposed to discuss over dinner." He held her hand even tighter, but not tight enough to hurt. "I wanted to use this opportunity to get to know you better. You aren't angry, are you?"

The warmth from his hand spread to her insides. She felt a rush of emotion and decided to enjoy this night to the fullest. It might never happen again. "No. In fact, I'm kind of glad you did. Those proposals are the last thing on my mind right now." She turned to face him and was quite unprepared for the touch of his lips on hers. Garrett reached across and cupped her chin, then bent forward and kissed her, gently at first, then with determination, as if he knew exactly where this kiss was going.

Samantha responded with everything in her. He was kissing her with the same skill, the same earthy knowledge of making love as her dream man. He released her chin and allowed his hand to wander through her hair, his extended fingers finally settling across the back of her head in such a way as to keep her lips pressed against his.

When it was over, he looked down into her eyes and started to say something, but stopped. Then he smiled and again brushed his lips against hers.

"I was about to apologize for what I've done," he said, using the same tone as Dirk or Lance would've in her sleep. "But I can't. I'm not sorry it happened. Samantha, I've spent a lifetime searching for someone like you. And while we don't know each other very well yet, I feel that you possess the qualities I've been looking for in a woman. And now there's no time to waste."

He'd said it in such a way as to shatter the romantic allure of the moment: it sounded desperate, as though he had only months to live. But he looked healthy enough.

There was another reason for his wanting to move things along, to develop their relationship quickly. She started to ask him why, but then the limousine stopped and she glanced through the darkened plate glass window nearest her and saw that they were in front of The Captain's Table, and she decided to wait.

The restaurant was a shimmer of rich carpeting, expensive linen, and elegant crystal. Samantha had never seen anything like it in her life. It was a far cry from the diners back home in the small town where she'd grown up.

A maitre d' greeted them at the door, a small, thin man who wore his black tie uniform with grace and style. "Monsieur Lang and Mademoiselle . . ."

"Croft," Garrett volunteered. "A table for two."

"Yes. You made a reservation. The usual, Monsieur?"

Garrett nodded with authority and the maitre d' led them to a table on the terrace overlooking the water. At that point Samantha recalled part of her dream: when they were out on his yacht, he'd said that The Captain's Table had docking space for boats. Then she dismissed it from her mind because it was something more to make her wonder if she were still asleep.

"Menu, please," Garrett said to the maître d' then turned to Samantha. "I've already ordered the house special, but I'd like you to take a look and see if there's something else that strikes your fancy. The food hasn't been prepared yet, so we can always change our minds."

He was so polite and aware of her, wanting to please her at every turn. She felt she'd either died and gone to heaven, or she had to be dreaming.

The menu, when it came, was written in French. She stared at the damned thing with annoyance while Garrett scanned it as though he could read and understand every line. And he probably could, she thought, reminding her of another point in this relationship: she was slightly out of her league. This wasn't the same as dating a guy on her own social level and winding up in a pizza joint or a steak house or even a Greek restaurant in the Silk Stocking District.

This was the big time.

What the hell did he see in her?

People like Garrett Lang mingled with aristocrats and upper crust sophisticates because they spoke a common language, lived similar lifestyles. Samantha was a small town bumpkin, hardly the type to qualify.

Therefore, she concluded, she had to be asleep, had to be dreaming this. And if so, it was the best dream ever because it was so real, so lifelike—

"Monsieur Lang? May I take your order please?"

Garrett smiled and turned to Samantha. She wanted to die. He was about to ask if she'd made a selection from the menu. If she admitted the truth, told him she couldn't read French, it might remind him of the gulf in social levels between them. And after all, this was her dream, so it had to remain perfect.

"I'll stay with the house special, Garrett. I trust your judgment." He smiled and spoke a few phrases to the waiter in French. He seemed pleased that she'd allowed him to take control. But that's how it was in her other dreams. Dirk or Lance was always in control, making her feel feminine and vulnerable in a wonderful sort of way. Yes, everything was the same.

Except for one thing: she'd never been to The Captain's Table in her dreams, never. Although he'd asked her, she usually deleted the lunch part and advanced to the bedroom scene; probably because she was forever in such a rush to be in his arms, to feel the weight of his body on hers, the warmth of his flesh inside her. Then again, maybe she hadn't been to The Captain's Table because she wasn't able to picture this much luxury, not even in her sleep. But she was doing it now.

Garrett touched her hand, bringing her back to the present and her wonderful ongoing dream. "Will you excuse me for a moment? I have to make a quick phone call. An old friend is visiting for a few weeks—I'd like to make sure he's comfortable."

"Take your time," she said and smiled. Then she watched him rise from the table and enter a private office near the back of the restaurant, his body moving with the same self-assurance and confidence as it had these past five years. He was like poetry in motion. You're lucky, she told herself, this is the best dream yet.

While she waited, Samantha scanned the restaurant. It was large and well laid out; the tables spaced far apart so that nobody was crowded. And the chairs were cushioned, with arm rests—nothing like the fast food places she was used to. And the people were different as well. They were well-dressed and spoke in soft, subdued tones. Was this how the other half lived, the ultra rich? From what she remembered of the menu, prices started at seventy-five dollars for one dinner alone, topping her lunch budget for two weeks.

A waiter emerged from the kitchen with a flaming dish on a tray, held high overhead. She listened to the ooh's and aah's around her and tried to remain calm. But the fire, along with the odor of burning animal flesh, brought back memories of the rapist back home . . .

The flaming bodies . . .

She was suddenly transported back in time to the woods near her home, that place where oak and maple grew wild, their branches long and heavy with leaves. That place where birds nested in those trees and had babies. Someone came there and hid until a young girl went by, and that someone caused a crack in the sanctuary of her mind, for it was like being in church when Samantha went to her woods.

There were rapes, murders, flaming bodies . . .

Her best girlfriend had been one of those victims. Samantha herself had found the body . . . Jeannie had been missing for several days, and although Samantha knew better, she'd gone to the woods to search for her friend. Maybe she just ran away, Samantha had reasoned at the time, not wanting to admit she might be dead. Maybe she'd had a fight with her parents and was hiding in the woods until things cooled down.

But something so simple wasn't meant to be. She was dead all right. First Samantha found her panties, the monogrammed ones; they'd each purchased a set at Genung's in Peekskill. At the time, both she and Jeannie felt there was something daring about walking around with your initials on your underwear. Samantha looked at those panties dangling on the branch of a bush and fought the instinct to run for home and safety, to call for help.

Her flesh crawled with fear but she stayed and kept searching, numbly telling herself that just because she'd found the panties where she had, it didn't necessarily mean another murder.

Then she found the body. Or what was left of it after the fire went out. Jeannie's face was unrecognizable; it was black and shriveled, and one eye was gone . . . Samantha knew it was Jeannie only because of the tiny gold locket lying next to the corpse. Jeannie had gotten the locket from her parents for Christmas. It was the first really expensive piece of jewelry the girl had ever owned. And the last.

She stared down at the body and felt her stomach heaving with fear and grief. The overwhelming odor of cooked flesh stung at her nostrils and she screamed and screamed and screamed.

Samantha was forbidden from ever going back to her quiet place, from ever going back to the spot in the center of the woods where she went to air her gripes, to think things out. "It's just too dangerous,'' her mother had said. But Samantha did go back. Not because she was an unruly teenager. She went back because of her stubbornness: she just couldn't accept the fact that someone mentally deranged had turned her place of beauty into a horror haven.

She remembered the last time she'd gone there. God, what a glorious day. Late fall and Mother Nature was dong her thing, making preparations for the coming winter months. The leaves had shed their greenish pallor and were now done up in various hues of brown and yellow and gold, all blended together in a soundless cacophony bursting with the miracle of life. It was wonderful to be able to walk through the woods and view the wonders God had wrought when He created the Heavens and the Earth.

And the birds, those who'd nested in the trees, their babies now grown and circling the nests. She stopped walking at one point to wonder when the birds would leave: some of them flew south when winter was near

She heard a twig snap under foot . . . but it wasn't under *her* foot.

Someone was walking through the woods . . .

Someone close.

Samantha's mind began to wander as it usually did when she was alone and afraid. She saw her girlfriend, her late girlfriend, the one she grew up with, the one whose face she couldn't recognize the last time she'd seen her. Some demon fiend had taken a teenager who'd been so full of mischief, so full of love, and had turned her into a hideous thing, had turned her shapely body into a small, shriveled, blackened hull. But not before raping her first.

She heard another twig snap. It was closer this time, and she knew she'd better run.

But she didn't run fast enough. He was faster.

He was a big man, and he wore a ski mask. She could recall lying on the ground with him on top of her, his body doing awful things to hers, and as she lay there and felt a gut-wretching pain burning the area between her legs, all she could manage to do was to look at his eyes through the small holes in that mask. He was crazy—

"Samantha?"

She heard a voice calling to her and didn't want to answer. It was a man's voice. The bastard! What did he want? She was being raped, wasn't that enough? But the son-of-a-bitch was persistent and so she responded despite her annoyance and found herself still seated in The Captain's Table with Garrett Lang staring down at her as though she was the one who was crazy and not the rapist.

J.J. Holiman wasn't home when Garrett called. He was on his way to Bridge Gate Court to check out the murder site and to try and stop his old enemy, Asgar, from going any further. But when he got there, he wasn't prepared for the sight that greeted him, the sight of June DeSoto—a headless torso with one arm missing.

"Hey, pops. You gotta move on. We don't want no rubber neckers hangin' around." There was a uniformed officer guarding the body. He was looking down at J.J. with cold steel-gray eyes and the most threatening glare the old man had ever seen.

"But you don't understand," J.J. said as politely as he could, "I'm here to help."

166

"Move it, man!"

"What's going on?" Ron Wheatley had finally gotten himself together enough so that he was able to perform the same tasks he usually did whenever a body was discovered. He made sure the coroner was on the way; that the lab men had taken their photos and searched for evidence; and that the body here as well as the one in the alley blocks away wasn't disturbed. It was the same old routine, but it was never boring. He looked down at the old man. "Who are you?" he asked, his tone full of annoyance.

"J.J. Holiman. I'm here—"

"Come with me." Ron said and led the old man to his car out front.

J.J. was puzzled. Not by his words, but by the way he'd spoken, as if he recognized the old professor's name and knew why he was there. "We can talk in here," Ron said and held the door on the passenger side. J.J. climbed in and waited until Ron was seated next to him before he spoke again.

"Do I know you? My mind's been playing tricks on me lately. Old age, you see."

"I'm Ron Wheatley—"

"Oh, yes! I read that you were investigating the case." The old man was excited now. Garrett must've told Ron about him, about how he'd aided the police so many times in the past. J.J. wouldn't have to prove his worth this time, not to Ron Wheatley.

"You're Garrett's former professor. He's told me a lot about you." Ron was studying J.J. with the oddest expression on his face.

"And he mentioned you, Ron, quite a few times in the letters he wrote after he left college."

There was silence between them for a moment. Ron had something on his mind but had trouble saying it. J.J. noticed the workings of his jaw, the worried look in his eyes. "Does this mean . . . You coming here, does it mean there's . . . Oh, Christ." Ron turned his gaze away. He couldn't finish the sentence. J.J. helped him.

"I think a demon's responsible for the murders, if that's what you're trying to ask me."

Ron said nothing, but continued to stare straight ahead. It wasn't that he didn't believe the old man. His silence betrayed his fears: he was terrified by the thought of taking on an unnatural force, something J.J. had come across many times before in his work with the police.

"Can you prove it?" he finally asked, turning to face the old man. J.J. nodded silently. Ron closed his eyes and sighed heavily before speaking again. He was obviously overwhelmed by the truth. "Can you give me something to present to my captain? Something concrete that he can look at and know you're not a fraud or a nut?" Again J.J. nodded silently. "That's what I was afraid of. You know what you're talking about and it scares me."

"Don't let it. I'll be here when I'm needed."

Ron smiled then, but it was a weak attempt. "So," he began in an effort to change the subject, "how's Garrett doing?"

It was J.J.'s turn to be dumbfounded. Ron lived right here in the city; Garrett's office was in his precinct. "How long has it been since you've seen Garrett?"

"Years. We lost touch."

"We can't have that. Listen, I'm staying at Garrett's until this case is solved. Why don't I

invite you up for a drink and to say hello? I'm sure
Garrett won't mind. In fact, he'll be happy to see
you." J.J. wondered what caused the absence in
years. These two had been best buddies.

"I'd rather not, if you don't mind." Ron wasn't
smiling now. "Garrett and I aren't on the same
wavelength. We haven't been for a long time
now. He's wealthy, he made it. And I'm—"

"You're just a cop, in other words? Hell, son,
Garrett isn't like that. He's not so stuck-up that
he'd forget his old friends." Ron turned his face
away for the second time, making J.J. think there
was more to the split-up of this friendship than
Ron was willing to admit. He decided to drop the
matter for the moment.

"Getting back to the murders," J.J. said, "Can I
see the body inside?" Ron turned to face him but
didn't answer. There was torment in his
expression. "What's wrong, son? You do want
my help?"

"Yes," he answered quietly, then he seemed to
lose control. He started to talk again, but it was
fast, too fast. He acted as though he'd been
holding this in for a while. "Look, there's something I have to tell you. If I don't tell someone, I'll
go crazy."

"Shoot."

"All right. But you have to promise to keep this
between us."

"If I can."

"What the hell does that mean?" Ron asked,
his mouth tight with indignation.

"Just what it's supposed to. If this has anything
to do with the murders, I might not be able to
keep my promise. I mean, I'm here to help stop
the bloodshed. If you're withholding some

169

important facts, how can I promise to keep it to myself?"

"I see. I guess you're right. The only problem is, I don't really know if this has a direct bearing on the case or not." He laid his hands across the top of the steering wheel. J.J. noticed they were trembling. "To begin with, according to what Garrett's told me, you've done a lot of research on the occult. While I don't know if my problem comes under that heading, I do know you're capable of finding the answer.

"Everytime a murder's been committed, I was there . . . in my mind. I've seen the victim's face, I've heard the pleas for mercy. It happens in my sleep, and it's happened once or twice when I was awake."

"Have you ever seen the killer's face?"

"No. I've only seen him from behind."

"Give me a description."

"I can't. He wears a long cape that covers his whole body. Do you think it's really happening at the time I get these mental images?" His hands were still trembling, but no longer resting casually on top of the wheel. He had a tight grip on it now.

"The only way I can tell if what you're seeing borders on the truth is if you can give me a description of the killer. I know what he looks like. Your description would not only confirm it, but it would prove to both of us that you're having psychic exper—"

"Psychic? You mean like in mind reader?" He sounded angry.

"Have you ever experienced anything like this before?" J.J. asked.

"Hell, no!"

The old man was silent for a moment, obviously

absorbed in thought. ''Has anything happened in your life recently to cause you to go into shock?''

Ron's head fell forward on the wheel. J.J. thought at first he'd fainted. Then he realized it was a reaction to his question. J.J. had hit on the truth, and a painful memory had emerged in Ron's mind. But he didn't feel it was his place to ask what happened. Ron would tell him if he wanted J.J. to know, so J.J. continued. ''Many psychics have developed their powers to foresee the future, or, as in your case, to foresee the present through the eyes of another, after a violent shock in their lives.''

''It happened about two years ago. So why am I seeing these visions now? Why not before this?'' Ron's voice was low, barely audible.

''A delayed reaction is not uncommon, son. Then again, perhaps you've been having experiences all along, small ones that you've been ignoring. For now, I think we should drop this. Give yourself time to think on it, and we'll discuss it again. Meanwhile, is it all right if I examine the body?''

Ron was anxious to comply with his request this time, as if he'd do anything to get off the subject of what happened two years before—the traumatic shock that might have left him psychic.

9

Garrett's chauffeur went downtown along Second Avenue to East 34th Street, crossed over to the west side near Madison Square Garden and headed north, up past Times Square to Central Park West. Samantha knew he was taking the long way home. It would've been easier to take one of the transverse roads across Central Park to Dridge Gate Court. But Carrott must've had something in mind when he told his chauffeur to take his time.

Garrett's silence had her puzzled, though. He hadn't said much since he'd interrupted her living nightmare about the rapist. And now she wanted to die: she'd blown it this time for sure, with no hope of sealing the crack in their relationship. Oh Garrett, she sighed inwardly, please forgive me for being such a fool that I was thunder-struck by the past. Please!

And to think it started with a tray of flaming meat.

"What happened back there, Sam?" he asked.

Sam? to her knowledge, no one had ever called

her that except for her dream man. But she wasn't angry. Garrett was, in his own way, giving her a second chance. "I don't . . . the tray the waiter brought out after you left. It was in flames. It brought back mem—" She couldn't go on. Her throat was a lump of grief. Tears stung her eyes. She bowed her head away from his stare.

"Oh, God, Sam, I'm sorry. Whatever it reminded you of, the memory must've been a painful one."

He reached across and drew her closer to him. She felt comfort in the warmth and strength of his arms; felt her body go limp from the heavenly scent of his cologne. He cupped her chin and ran his lips across her face until they reached her mouth. His kiss was hot and sweet, filled with a desire for more.

She moaned involuntarily and felt her body, her soul, and the hesitant part of her that recalled the rape, all surrender at once. She wanted him with the same yearning she felt in her dreams. And if he persisted, she would allow him to make love to her there, in the back seat of his limousine.

One of his hands had dropped to fondle a breast. She leaned into it, almost able to feel his flesh against hers, naked and alluring. Oh, Lord, thank you, she prayed silently. Thank you for making me whole again. The rape was unimportant at this point.

The rocking motions of the limousine came to a sudden halt. Garrett stopped kissing her and turned to stare, his gaze focused on the large stone lettering in front of her building: Bridge Gate Court. His face became a mask of torment, the hand on her breast became stiff and awkward. He was frozen, his mind locked in on some horrible event.

"Garrett? What's wrong?" He couldn't stop now. She wouldn't allow it. She was all worked up, ready for love.

"Nothing." He turned back to her, to silently ask for her forgiveness because the mood was gone, broken beyond repair. "Gail Lindman, my secretary . . . She was killed here."

"You poor thing. She must've been special to you." Samantha was saying and doing the proper thing. But deep inside she was burning with disappointment. "I feel bad, making you come here—"

"Don't be silly. This's where you live." He smoothed her hair back from her face. "I'll get used to it. I have to. You're the one I've picked to spend a lifetime with. Or am I moving too fast?"

She wanted to scream 'No!' but didn't. Instead she turned coy. "Keep kissing me like you did a few minutes ago and you've got a deal."

"Darling," he said and bent to kiss her. But the kiss was different from before. There was no promise of love and fulfillment. Rather it was a half-hearted effort at saying good-night.

He pressed a buzzer on the back of the seat and the chauffeur appeared out of nowhere to help them from the limousine. As they walked arm and arm through the front door, she felt his body stiffen next to hers. He isn't handling his secretary's death very well, she thought, and wondered just how close they'd been.

"The owners are supposed to improve the lighting sometime this week," she said, making light conversation to get his mind off Gail

Lindman.

Garrett glanced at the lights as though he were noticing for the first time how dim they were. Then he turned and grabbed her roughly by the shoulders. "Sam, I want you to come and live with me, now, tonight before you get killed too!" He sounded hysterical and it scared her. This was so unlike the image of her dream man.

"Garrett, I—"

"Don't argue!"

"Look, we've only just met."

"I don't care. I can't lose you, Sam." She felt his grip loosen, saw his face soften. "It doesn't matter if we've known each other for only a few hours or a few years. There's a maniac on the prowl."

That was true. She had to agree with what he'd said. And yet she'd dealt with a maniac before. Besides, he was moving too fast now; she felt funny inside. "He only strikes at night. Down here." She pointed to the darkened corridor near the elevator and watched him turn pale. "I've been staying in my apartment at night."

"And what if he changes his modus operandi?" Garrett fumed. "What if he starts breaking into apartments? Sam, he's crazy."

So was the rapist, she thought, and she got away from him. "Give me a day or so to think about it, Garrett. I just can't move in with you as if it were something I did all the time."

He sighed, the sound coming from deep within. "Okay, you win. But only for a day or so." He led her to the elevator and punched the button. "You can have your own room, you know. I didn't ask simply to acquire a bed partner."

She leaned against his shoulder, her body

caving in under the spell of him. "I know you mean well. And it makes me feel good inside to realize that you're so concerned about my safety. I've never loved a man in a sexual way. . . . never really been with one, please be patient?"

"I promise."

Once they were upstairs, Garrett used her key to unlock the door. Then he checked the entire apartment for intruders. When he was satisfied that she'd be safe, at least for the time being, he drew her into his arms for one more good-night kiss, his hazel eyes sparkling with desire. Samantha's arms climbed up and around his neck; her body responding to the tender force of his hand at the small of her back pressing her forward. She felt the rise of his manhood and wanted this night never to end. But it did, as he suddenly withdrew himself from her embrace and whispered goodnight along with a promise to call her in the morning.

She was disappointed because it ended just when she was ready for so much more. And Garrett seemed to be in the same frame of mind. But then she remembered what he'd said downstairs about Gail Lindman and realized she'd have to wait until they found a better place. His apartment perhaps.

She was on his yacht, below deck, his naked body steaming hers to new heights of desire. He was lying beside her, his tongue tracing a maddening path from her breasts to that forbidden area where her legs parted. "Oh, God, Garrett, please," she moaned, anxiously awaiting penetration, wanting with all her heart to feel him inside of her, strong and hard, yet gentle.

Garrett heard her and smiled, his eyes literally flaming with a similar desire, his body consumating the act as a moan came from deep within him. She looked up into his face and felt herself rising and falling in the same rhythmic pattern as he.

"Samantha!"

"Samantha!"

She heard a voice calling her name and at first thought it was Garrett, whispering in the throes of passion. But there was something angry in the tone of the voice. She heard outrage, shock, a hint of desperation.

"Samantha!"

She looked beyond the mound of Garrett's shoulder and saw Ron Wheatley standing in the frame of the door watching them, his body slack with defeat, his gaze dull. "How could you?" he asked, "And with him, of all people!"

Samantha shot bolt upright in bed, her nightgown sticky with sweat. What had started out to be the best dream ever, had suddenly been reduced to the level of a nightmare. Ron Wheatley caught her in bed with Garrett! And yet, it was just a dream and nothing more, she told herself. But it was so real, so true to life . . .

There were two men now, two who'd suddenly entered the picture. Two very sexy and desirable men who wanted to dominate her and who would, before long, force her to choose between them. And it promised to be no easy task since both were handsome and charming and appealing.

Then again, Garrett was wealthy and Ron wasn't. But that didn't make the choosing any easier. Money wasn't everything in life, and money certainly couldn't take the place of happiness even though Garrett was her dream man in the flesh . . .

Something about Garrett disturbed her. He was perfection personified, but he was also nearly too perfect, as were his actions. Like taking her to The Captain's Table for instance, the place he always took her in her dreams. Where did the dreams end, she wondered, and reality begin?

Then, for one fleeting instant she relaxed and a dark corner of her brain was stimulated into action. A secret, one she'd buried in the deepest recesses of her psyche years before, emerged to torment her. What made her so bold as to imagine that the choice of having either man was hers? What would either of them think when they discovered the truth about a horrible event in Samantha's past?

Samantha had killed a man, years ago.

She torched the rapist. Struck him on the head with a rock while he was in the throes of orgasm. Then she rolled him off of her and grabbed the can of gasoline strapped to a band on his waist. Some of it spilled on her and she was burned too. But not as badly as he.

She burned his balls.

Torched the bastard!

Took a match from his shirt pocket, lit it, and watched him turn into the same blackened hull that Jeannie had. She watched him burn and blister, his body a crackling, smoldering, mass of agony. She watched his eyes through the holes in the mask melt and fuse into one.

She smiled then and discounted the rest: the police investigation, the subsequent dismissal of the charges against her. Oh yes, she fixed that bastard and got away with it. In fact some folks even considered her a heroine.

The newspapers played it down, refusing to print her name because of her age.

But she lived in such a tiny town that everyone knew it was Samantha.

Odd that she was able to forget about it except for those occasional times when her spirit caved in under pressure and she could recall, with great accuracy, just how the rape had ended. And all this time she'd been wrong about going home: it certainly was safe. Samantha had made sure of that. She smiled again, then laid her head back down on the pillow to dream once more of her dream man.

Detective Nick Candeles sometimes worked partners with Ron Wheatley, but Ron was alone on this one. And that was good enough for Candeles. Viewing a corpse who'd been shot or stabbed didn't phase him in the least: he'd been working homicide for fifteen years. But take a corpse who'd been mutilated, he couldn't handle it. This latest one even had a tattoo!

He passed the coroner's report across to Ron Wheatley—their desks were face to face—then removed his jacket from the back of his chair and left on his own assignment. There'd been a murder in the park: a mugger shot a victim once through the head, splattering his brains in all directions. Well, he thought wearily, at least the body hasn't been mutilated.

Ron Wheatley read the coroner's report and something in it struck a nerve. The victim had recently been tattooed. There was a small death head on her inner thigh. The killer's signature!

He rose from behind his desk and strode toward the back stairs, the ones leading to the basement where the computers were. During the course of his investigation of the Bridge Gate killer, several weirdos popped up who liked to do strange and unusual things to womens' bodies. One of them was a tattoo artist and this was his signature. He also got his jollies from tying his ladies to bedposts. That would explain the rope burns on June's arm, the one he'd left behind, still attached to her body.

Then too, the guy wore a cape-like coat. Ron remembered that coat from their first meeting in the station house. He wanted to book the bastard then because of the coat. But Ron was the only one who knew the killer wore a cape, because he'd seen it in his dreams. There wasn't enough evidence to hold him, so he was released.

But now things had changed. The killer had gotten sloppy; had left his signature all over the body. Ron's head swam with excitement. This was the first real lead since the murders began, ten mutilated bodies ago. He sat down in front of a vacant computer and had to steady himself because the room was swimming along with his head. He'd been working much too hard and getting little or no sleep.

Well now, maybe things would be different, he thought. If this bastard—the tattoo artist, the one recorded on a long rap sheet in the computer—if he was the one, then Ron could relax and take a few days off. He and Debbie could—

Could what?

Go someplace?

Him and his legs and her on her dead stumps?

He punched a few keys, his guilt coming

through in the form of angry fingers abusing a computer, and waited until the right name and an address to go along with it flashed on the screen. Then he hurriedly keyed the print-out button and waited. His body was a mass of anxiety. This was the one, the killer/mutilator. He was sure of it.

And if all went well, he'd have the bastard in custody in a few hours, at least by one or two in the morning. His mouth worked its way into a smile, the hardness of his jaw yielding to relief. J.J. Holiman was wrong; no demons here, just a maniac who'd mimicked the actions of one by chance. He couldn't wait to call J.J., to tell him thanks but no thanks, your help is no longer needed. Because then he wouldn't have to tell J.J. about the shock he'd suffered two years before, the shock that supposedly rendered him psychic, as J.J. had suggested. He wouldn't have to mention the melodrama that haunted his waking moments, and only stopped when this killer/mutilator thing began. One nightmare had risen to replace another. . . .

He saw himself with Debbie at his side, high-powered rifle in the crook of his arm, strolling through a section of the Adirondacks. Debbie's legs were strong then, strong and healthy and firm. Good for everything from walking beside him to wrapping them around his body at night. Yeah, she had some good legs, he thought.

But on this particular day her legs weren't that good: they pained her. She was 'tired of walking aimlessly in circles looking for game to blow holes through.' And she was 'cold besides,' and wished she hadn't been 'stupid enough to let you talk me into going hunting up here—in snow country—in the dead of winter!'

Debbie was wearing a brown jacket; the memory jabbed at his gut. Why hadn't she worn the bright orange one he'd bought especially for her? Hunters had accidents all the time and shot each other by mistake. How often had he read about it: a hunter shooting at moving bushes thinking it was game only to wind up nailing someone through the head or the back? The orange jackets were used as a safety measure, to let another hunter know you were human and not an animal in hiding. Debbie, *why?* he moaned to himself.

But then the answer was simple: she hated orange, it wasn't 'her color.' Oh, God! Debbie had to pee; had gone into the woods to his right. But that spot didn't suit her, she was fussy. She doubled around behind and somehow wound up across the road in the opposite direction. Ron heard movement, saw something brown!

And God help him, he remembered Debbie's jacket. But she was on the right side of him! The thing he spotted was to his left! And brown meant a deer. He raised his rifle to his shoulder and fired.

Her voice, the maddening sound of her screams still came to him in the night. The sight of his finger on the trigger still came to him at night. He'd pulled back so fast, wished there was some way he could do it over, some way to make himself wait a few seconds longer. As soon as he released the shell, that tiny piece of bone-crushing, spine-shattering metal, he wanted to die. It was only then that he realized he was shooting at Debbie. She'd stepped into a clearing in the woods and he saw her, saw that shell tear a gaping hole in her back.

Tears, hot and angry, stained his face. He grabbed the print-out and ran for the stairs, taking them two at a time. The squad room was nearly empty. He looked at his watch—11:00—and figured she might still be up. He lifted the receiver and dialed, then waited until her voice whispered into the other end of the line. And oddly enough, she was in a good mood, considering the time of night he'd picked to call. "Hello, Samantha. This's Ron. I called to ask if you'd like to have lunch with me tomorrow."

He held on, hoping against hope that she'd say yes. Samantha was important to him now. She was more than just another broad he'd talk into bed. Samantha was intelligent and understanding. If anyone could make him forget about Debbie and how badly he'd hurt her that day in the woods, it would have to be Samantha.

"Glorie, oh, Satanus," he said, the words torching an angry spot in his brain. The beast was out, in control; his human counterpart asleep after wearing himself into exhaustion with his senseless emotions. "Satanus, lord of the highest level in Acheron, answer me! Why do you punish me so?"

But there was no answer, not for him. His lord and master had taken offense to a minor sin committed by the beast. And in his wisdom, old Mephisto doomed Asgar to a lifetime of misery: a lifetime to be spent trapped in the body of a human until the human expired or Mephisto forgave him, whichever came first. And to make matters worse, Asgar was compelled to serve the human, to be no more than a slave to his whimsical fantasies, even if it meant gathering body parts for ceremonies to make the human whole again. For the human suspected that the beast was part of him and controlled his sleeping brain.

"But dear Mephisto, the infraction was minor! It hardly warrants this sort of punishment." Still, the beast had sinned, had released a child of God from the pinnacles of hell!

The beast was, or at least had been, in charge of the fourth level in Acheron; a plateau surrounded by a mountainous range of steaming rocks flowing with lava where victims were tortured. Small demonic creatures, pets of the beast, enforced continuous torment according to the grade of sins charged against each prisoner. Although Mephisto's creed was based on the seven commandments of evil, better known as the seven deadly sins—greed, pride, envy, anger, gluttony, lust and sloth—Mephisto tolerated nothing from those beings who weren't one with his legions of demons. A form of entrapment, he thought, and smiled.

Asgar remembered the human victims and how each fared under the whip of his pets. He fondly recalled their moans of agony; their vociferous screaming; their shredded flesh peeling from the leather straps coated with razors. And there were the steaming mountains surrounding his level— hot, blistering, rocks coated with flesh.

Many of the prisoners, weary of torture and looking for escape, took to the rocks, seeking to climb to the next highest level where perhaps the method of torture was less painful. But the rocks were too steep, the heat too intense. They either fell back into their chasm of agony or they melted, their skins fusing onto the rocks. Some even attempted to escape by using the fused bodies of others as stepping stones to freedom. None made it.

If you didn't count the one he helped to escape, the child of God. . . .

Mephisto, though wise as the ages, was known to blunder now and then. Sometimes he trapped the wrong soul, a Christian one, and brought it down to Acheron with the rest for an eternity of damnation and suffering. Asgar was mostly amused by this because the cries of the pious and the meek were often filled with indignations as well as sorrow, making their torture a joyful experience. And yet, there was one who got through to Asgar; one who cut a wedge into the very blackness of his heart.

There was a child of perhaps five or six—a girl, with long, black, tresses and bright, blue eyes. Bringing her there had been a mistake. No evil in her; even the hags who controlled his pets were reluctant to order any form of torture for this child, for she was love in the flesh. Her soul, her thoughts, her very being were nearly as spotless as the Christ Child's. Everyone was afraid to touch her, afraid of retaliation from the God of the humans.

Asgar knew it was wrong to have helped her escape, knew he'd be punished by Mephisto for releasing her soul from the depths of hell, but she was useless; she could not be tortured. Besides, helping her escape was such a minor sin. He was certain that any form of forced recompense on his part would be just as minor. But it wasn't. Mephisto was enraged; his voice and the words he'd spoken nearly shattered the bulwarks of Acheron.

"SINCE YOU LOVE THESE HUMANS WITH SUCH FIERY PASSION," he raged, "YOU MAY NOW SPEND A LIFETIME LOCKED WITHIN THE SOUL OF ONE."

Asgar sighed. A lifetime was the worst part of it. The human was young, a lifetime meant fifty years or more of being only partially in control, of being a slave to the lowest form of life in the universe. Again he felt that his sentence had been too severe, for the punishment barely fit the crime. To think he wasn't the only one willing to release the child, and yet, he was the only one who was punished! If he had it to do over again, he'd burn the little bitch's ass along with the rest. Christian or no Christian, loving soul or no loving soul.

Asgar flinched from the glare of the sun streaming in through the bedroom window. It was morning, hardly his favorite time of day. He yawned, his teeth gleaming like daggers of steel and closed his eyes to yield control to the human once again.

Samantha had lunch at Clancy's, a steak house in the Fourties near Eighth Avenue. Ron Wheatley was beside her, encouraging her to choose whatever she wanted from the menu. Thank God it was printed in English. How different this was from last night's dinner date with Garrett. There was no plush carpeting, no heavy linen table cloths, no crystal stemware. The atmosphere of the place suited her just fine: she could relax and be herself.

Ron looked tired. His eyes were underlined with rings of exhaustion. Still, he smiled and kept his attention alert and focused on her. "Ready to order?" he wanted to know after she'd been through the menu twice. She wasn't normally this fussy, but the prices were a bit steep. How much did cops earn these days, she wondered?

"You order for me," she said, deciding this was best. Only Ron knew what he had in his wallet. Ron beamed, training his pale blue eyes first on hers, then on her full sensual mouth. She felt warm inside and not as nervous as she had with Garrett the night before.

Ron picked prime ribs and salad for both of them and an obscure red wine. After the waiter left she studied his face, the workings of his jaw. He wasn't as tense and strung out as the night they'd had coffee together in her apartment. Or as tense as last night when he'd grabbed his head and shouted. 'The beast. He's done it again.' She was still puzzled and wondered how he knew so much about the beast, yet she preferred to let it go and not ask questions.

"How was everything last night?" Ron asked, breaking the barrier of silence between them.

"You're referring to my date?" she wanted to know. He nodded. "It was all right," she said, wondering if he was asking out of curiosity or politeness.

"Just all right?"

"Yes." She had to downplay her affection for Garrett. After all, Ron had showed up in her dreams and just about wanted her to choose between them: him and Garrett. No use turning a dream into a waking drama. "He's very nice," she added.

"And how about me, Samantha? Am I just as nice?" There was an edge to his voice resembling jealousy.

She smiled, hoping he'd take it as an answer.

But Ron was persistent: he wanted to hear her say it, to tell him she'd grown attached to him in just the few days they'd known each other. "I wouldn't be here now if I didn't like you," she said finally.

"Good! Because I have a surprise for you. I'm taking a few days off and I want us to go away somewhere."

He'd said it matter of factly, as if this was something he did everyday; asked a woman he barely knew to go on vacation with him. She was astonished at how fast he was moving. Garrett had done the same thing the night before, only Garrett wanted her to move in with him. Ron was still a step behind. "Well," she began, not really knowing how to put her refusal into words that wouldn't hurt his feelings. "I can't take time off. There's a lot of work to be done on my accounts."

"Okay," he said using the same tone of voice he'd used when he asked her. "I understand."

But he didn't. He looked hurt. She wanted to tell him the truth, why she couldn't say yes to his offer: she'd never really been with a man. Going away with him would've been a signal that it was okay for them to sleep together. Why couldn't she tell him, she wondered? She told Garrett.

When the food came they ate in silence, then left the restaurant. Samantha knew he was troubled by her refusal to go away with him and wished the subject would come up again. Maybe next time she'd be honest about it. Ron drove her back to Bridge Gate Court and insisted on taking her straight to her door. Once there she invited him in for coffee. He said yes.

"I have to tell you something," he said when they were seated in the kitchen. He was so full of confidence she didn't know what to expect. Maybe he would ask her to go away again. "It'll be on the evening news. I caught the killer!" He stopped and waited for her to react. But she didn't. This wasn't what she expected him to say. "Did you hear me, Samantha? I caught the killer!"

She closed her eyes and tried to focus on the importance of his words: he caught the killer. She needn't be afraid anymore, nor stay confined to her apartment at night like a criminal. And she needn't fear the gargoyles! "Oh, God," she said, "Then it's over."

"Yes."

"But how?" Her eyes were open now and she imagined they must've been glowing with curiosity. "Who was he? Does he live here, in this building?"

"He's a slime who lived in the Bronx." He got up then and paced the floor, hands in his pockets. She watched him, the muscles of his jaw quivering with excitement. "I knew he'd slip up someday. They all do. You see, this guy loved to tie his victims to bedposts—"

"What!"

"He tied women like animals before making love to them. Why? Have you heard of him?" He stopped pacing, his gaze focused intently on Samantha, measuring her reaction. She didn't know what to say. June DeSoto had laughingly mentioned someone with a similar fetish. She wondered if it could be the same man.

"No," she lied. "I was just shocked, that's all."

"Anyway, we found a body with rope burns on one arm and around the ankles. She'd been tattooed on her inner thigh."

"Oh, God! He tattooed her? But why?"

"Because he was sick, that's why."

"But I don't remember the others being marked this way. Just mutilated." She had trouble saying it. How could one human do this to another, she wondered?

"This was the one he slipped up on. When he left his signature on her inner thigh, we had him!"

"And this body was found downstairs?" It couldn't be June. Besides, June laughed at her psycho, thought he was a joke. No, she told herself, there's no need to worry. It's not June! "Was she in the corridor near the back alleys?"

"Yes, where most of the other bodies were found. And don't ask me why he picked Bridge Gate Court to do his killing. That's still a mystery. But he's in custody. He'll talk."

"Thank God it's over," she said, her entire being flooded with relief. "Is this why you're taking a few days off?" She wanted to change the subject, to return to his original train of thought, to tell him she'd never really been with a man

"Yes, this is why I'm taking a few days off." He sat down opposite her, his eyes glaring with excitement. The coffee was ready, she noticed. But she stayed where she was, waiting for him to ask again so she could explain her refusal. It was important to her; he was important to her.

"I'll probably get a promotion," he said, reaching across to touch Samantha's hands. "And I have this poor woman to thank. I mean, it's awful. She's dead and she died in agony. But I have June DeSoto to thank."

Samantha heard the name and felt herself go limp, felt anger welling up inside. Another friend had gone and gotten herself murdered. Why did life forever repeat itself? "June DeSoto?" Her voice was weak, the words strained.

"Yes. She had identification in her purse." He looked at her, at her shocked expression and his jaw went slack. Then he spoke very slow, his words strained as well. "You didn't know her, did you?" But she didn't have to say anything. Her tears were the answer he was looking for. She felt pressure on her hands. He was squeezing them tightly now. "Oh, Samantha, I'm so sorry. Christ! I feel like an idiot."

"Don't. You had no way of knowing."

"Yeah. But I keep telling you things I shouldn't." He suddenly rose, only to drop to his knees beside her, to hold her, to comfort her. She cried with her head resting on his shoulder, one of his hands gently massaging the back of her head. "I'm sorry," he repeated bending forward to brush his lips against her neck. "Don't be mad at me."

She wasn't. He didn't realize she'd known June. He only mentioned her name in excitement. How could she be angry? The truth was, her emotions were racing in another direction. The feel of his lips on her neck, his hand fondling her head. . . . Samantha was experiencing something, but it was more in line with the way she felt when Garrett touched her last night . . .

But this wasn't Garrett.

"You're sweet, Samantha," he said softly, in her ear, "And so beautiful." He lifted her chin and pressed his lips against hers, a moan of desire coming from deep within him. She responded, her body going limp, her lips yielding to his intentions. But then he tried to force his tongue into her mouth and she froze.

"Please let me," he pleaded and she did, parting her lips, moaning herself from the thrust of him, the sweet taste of his tongue, the feel of his hand, first manipulating the nipple of one breast through her closed blouse, then hurrying with the buttons, pulling her bra up to lay his bare flesh against hers.

His mouth suddenly deserted hers and roamed down to her breast, his tongue drawing crazy circles before sliding his lips over it, engulfing it with passion. She leaned into him, wanting to experience this, wanting to know what it was like to love a man when she was awake. He stopped caressing her bare breast and rose, lifting her into his arms.

"It's this way," she said, guiding him to her bedroom. He laid Samantha across the bed and began to undress her, his hands gentle and knowledgeable, not rough like the rapist's. This wasn't anything at all like the rape, she thought, and watched while he quickly undressed to get on with the business of making love.

When it was over, she laid in his arms and cried, but not out of sadness. Rather she cried because Ron's gentleness had freed her mind from the bonds of fear. No longer would she be content to dream about love, not now, not when he'd opened the door to reality. Sex didn't have to be painful or hurtful. It also meant the tender sharing of mutual emotions between lovers.

He kissed her, his eyes full of concern. "Did I hurt you?" he stopped to ask. "Is that why you're crying?"

"No," she said and forced a smile. "This was my first time. And it was so wonderful!"

"I'm glad," he said, and again brushed his lips

lightly against hers. According to the clock on her
end table, it was after four. Ron glanced at it and
shook his head. "Damn it! I didn't think it was
this late. I have to get going. There's a mountain
of paperwork on my desk."

Samantha understood. She had an equally large
pile on hers. "Could you drop me at the office?"

"Now? At this time of day? I really wish you'd
stay home."

"You caught the killer, remember?"

He bowed his head and sighed. "There's more
than one pervert in this world. But if you must go
to the office this late, I'll not only drive you, I'll
pick you up when you're through."

"Oh, Ron, you're such a doll," she said, rising
unashamedly, her nakedness not as important as
it would've been a week ago. "I'm taking a
shower. Care to join me?"

"Why not, you little hussy?" he said, his face
working into a smile. "I introduce you to sex and
now it's 'let's take a shower together.'" She
laughed when he got up to follow her into the
bathroom, his heavily muscled frame so trim and
appealing. "By the way," he said, growing
serious for a moment, "Are you on the pill?"

The pill! Morgan had warned her to get some if
she was about to become sexually active. But
she'd forgotten because she never dreamed this
could happen. "No," she answered, wondering
about pregnancy.

"Well, don't worry," he said, patting her bare
behind. "I'm sterile. Always have been and
always will be."

His smile threw her off. "How terrible!"

"Not really. Some people are meant to have
children and some aren't. I've accepted it."

She turned on the faucets and stepped under a torrent of warm relaxing water with Ron following behind. The pill; he'd mentioned it and by doing so jarred her memory. She'd have to call a doctor and make an appointment to get some pills. After all, even though Ron was sterile who was to say he was the last. There was Garrett to consider as well.

10

The office was deserted by the time she returned, after five. The secretaries had left for the day and the other agents normally didn't return until seven or seven-thirty to make phone calls. Samantha had the whole place to herself. Yet, somehow she was uncomfortable about being there alone and a bit scared even knowing that the Bridge Gate Killer was in jail. As Ron had said, he wasn't the only kook around.

Sitting at her desk, she tried to keep her attention focused on a pile of paperwork and not on those awful background noises. A clock was ticking on the wall behind her, making her aware of its constant rhythmic sound. A faucet was leaking in one of the bathrooms, and the plopping noises were maddening. Someone must've left a door open—

Then there was the sound of footsteps, deliberate ones, coming down the hall toward her.

Someone was here and didn't care if she knew it or not.

The door to the office was locked, wasn't it?

She couldn't remember, and yet it didn't matter when the person in the hall probably had just as much right being there as she did. It was either a security guard or a cleaning woman. She sat still and stared anxiously when the outline of a figure distorted by thick green puckered glass stopped on the other side of the door.

From somewhere outside, probably in the alleys below, the sound of a cat engaged in battle rose to startle her. The knob was turning but the door didn't open: it was locked. She heard the knob rattle, watched it being twisted with violent jerking motions, heard the glass slam in its frame as someone tried to force his way in!

Every agent had a key, as did the secretaries, the cleaning women, and the security guards. She didn't know why this was coming to her now except that she was frightened and trying to be rational. But even rationality has a way of reversing itself, causing more panic. If the person outside had no key, he didn't belong there. She got up and silently crept towards the door—

"Samantha! Samantha Croft! Are you in there?"

She heard a deep voice, one laced with impatience and hatred, saw the outline of an overcoat or a cape and had to fight to keep from fainting. It was still springtime, but so close to summer that most people didn't wear coats. The Bridge Gate Killer wore a coat! No, a Cape! But Ron had him in custody!

"Open the door, bitch! I know you're in there!"

Bitch! He called her a bitch! At first she wanted to open the door and slap the bastard. But she didn't: that would've been a foolish move. Probably just what he expected. Her heart was pounding heavily. Ron was supposed to come back and pick her up. What time did he mention, she wondered, before it came to her: she had to call him. Otherwise he'd stay at the station house.

"Who's in there? I know someone's there. I see a light on!"

Oh, God, that voice, that awful, horrible, raspy voice. It reminded her of the rapist; it had the same hateful tone. As she watched, the shadow on the door disappeared from sight. She held her breath and wondered if it was safe to leave. She couldn't stay there, not now, not when she was alone, not when there was a psycho loose. And he knew her name.

The sound of breaking glass iced her spine and traveled to the base of her neck. She turned toward the window across the room and saw a man wearing a coat or a cape. He must've climbed through a hall window and walked the outer ledge of the building. He wanted her awfully bad and now he was coming for her.

"Are you Samantha?" he wanted to know as he approached her desk and stared hard into the shadows where she was hiding. "Answer me!" he commanded, but she couldn't. She was speechless; her vocal cords were constricted with fear. "I'm Phil Housner," he said, "Morgan's father. Are you Samantha Croft?"

When he bellowed the last part, Samantha came alive; she felt rage building. Who the hell did he think he was yelling at? "No wonder Morgan can't stand you. You nervy, belligerent, bastard!"

He smiled in response, but it wasn't friendly, making her feel colder inside. "Is that what she said? That she can't stand me?"

"What're you doing here?" she asked, ignoring his question. "How did you find me?"

"I questioned your neighbors."

"You did what!" He had more nerve than she imagined possible. "You knocked on doors? Asked my—"

"Well, neither of you were home." The smile on his lips had been replaced by a thin line of defense. "I gathered that Morgan was still in Bermuda with her pig boyfriend. I wanted to leave another message."

"Make it quick. Then get out!" She unlocked the door and held it open for him.

"Tell her I'm waiting. Tell her I haven't forgotten our agreement. And tell her I'm running out of patience!"

Then he was gone, leaving Samantha alone and shaken. She closed the door behind him and was about to lock it when a fist came up against it. Someone was knocking, but the sound was gentle and polite. "Yes?" she said without opening the door.

"Samantha Croft?" came the muffled reply.

She sure was in demand tonight, she thought, wondering who this was. "Can I help you?"

"I'm Nick Candeles, Ron Wheatley's partner. I came to drive you home."

She opened the door and was face to face with a tall, stocky man, apparently of Italian heritage. "I was just about to call him. Why didn't Ron come himself?"

Nick Candeles glanced down at his feet. "Ron left real sudden like. Asked me to pick you up." He extracted a piece of paper from his pocket. "He wrote down the address and your office number."

This wasn't like Ron: sending someone else and not calling. "What happened? Did he become ill?"

"Well, yeah. I guess you could say that." He looked at her, but didn't say any more. He hesitated a moment, then added, "Is he a real good friend of yours?" Samantha nodded. "Then I guess I can tell you. We were talkin' about different cases we worked on . . . and I was tellin' him about a case I handled when I was stationed upstate, before I came here. Something about a guy hunting out in the woods with his business partner. He shot and killed his partner, supposedly by accident. Only I think he did it deliberately. And he got away with it. And believe me, lady, I wouldn't have said anything if I didn't feel that way."

"And?" This was puzzling.

"Then he asked me what I meant. So I told him. Anyone can get away with anything they want if they do it right. This guy I was talkin' about, he went up there to hunt, but instead of game he was huntin' his partner." He again eyed the floor as though he couldn't go on, but he did. He kept talking. "Ron and I didn't always work together. I didn't know . . ." He scratched the back of his head. "At this point my tongue should've fallen out. Ron got real pale and mumbled something about you, wrote down the address and left."

Samantha stood and looked at him a moment longer before going back to her desk to retrieve her purse. This was all so confusing. First that bastard Phil Housner broke in, scaring her half to death, giving her a message to pass on that she didn't understand. Now this. Ron was harboring a secret, something out of his past, something terrible. At that point, she'd had enough. She grabbed her purse and followed Nick Candeles to his car, vowing to go right to bed when she got home. At least when she dreamt of her dream man there were no unwanted mysteries to solve.

"Tell me," she said, turning to Candeles before getting into the car. Curiosity was getting the better of her. Besides, how could she help Ron live with his secret if it remained one. "Did you find out why Ron acted that way? Did anyone tell you why?"

"Yeah. Ron shot someone during a hunting trip. But it was an accident. Geez, lady, I feel bad. I really didn't know anything about it or I wouldn't have opened my mouth like I did."

"Who was it?" She just had to know.

"His wife," Candeles answered. Then he helped her into the car and drove away.

Ramona Blattfield heard it on the evening news and was able to relax for the first time in weeks. Her whole body went slack with the joy of it; the Bridge Gate Killer was in jail. Now she could go on with her life: she could bring Uncle Max here to walk beside Jeffrey, to help keep Jeffrey in her apartment where he belonged.

Although she'd gotten the basic ingredients for her ceremony days ago—rosemary, sage, and a sliver from the branch of an oak tree to stir the mixture with—she'd let it go, let Uncle Max stay where he was for a while longer. After all, the ceremony had to be performed with a clear head, otherwise things could go wrong, bad things could happen. She might've conjured up a stranger instead of Uncle Max.

And so she waited. But for what? A good night's

sleep perhaps? One that wasn't so full of dreams of horror and mutilation? One that wouldn't cause her to rise in the night and sit by the window waiting for the sun to come up? Now things had changed. The killer/mutilator was in jail where he damned well belonged and she could go on with her plans.

Jeffrey floated in as the announcement was made and drifted down beside her. He was dead, she knew, and had been for a long time, but that didn't stop a look of relief from crossing his face. Jeffrey still had feelings. She squeezed his hand and laughed when hers closed on a puff of air. He was vaporous, he was gaseous, he wasn't solid. How often had she forgotten this up until now? Fifty times? A hundred? The truth was she'd forgotten every day but only because she still had trouble accepting his death.

"Okay! Aunt Mona!" he said, his voice full of exuberance. "They caught the bastard!"

"Jeffrey! You curse like that again and it's soap in your mouth for sure," she said scowling, her face drawn tight with displeasure. But then she thought about what she'd said and burst out laughing. Jeffrey did the same. "Put soap in your mouth," was all she could manage in between spurts of laughter. Jeffrey's face had small vaporous dots running down the cheeks: tears, she assumed, from laughing so hard.

But it was good for them to let go, to really release the inner tension they'd both harbored for weeks. She snapped off the news and went into the kitchen for some tea and cake. Sweets were a form of tranquilizer for her and not really necessary tonight, since she wasn't depressed or angry. She was celebrating.

"May I have some too?" Jeffrey asked.

She studied his face and saw that he was serious, and she stopped smiling. Jeffrey didn't eat, couldn't eat, not since he'd died. But she cut a healthy wedge for him anyway, put it on a plate and slid it across the table. As she watched, he bent over and started to bite at the cake with his vaporous teeth. "Jeffrey! For God's sake use a fork. You're not a dog."

"I can't. My hands won't hold one."

That was true, she thought, and watched him gobble his cake like an animal. Only instead of being more depressed because of his plight, she laughed when the cake he'd bitten into floated down the front of him and landed in a heap on the table. "I guess you still can't eat."

"Thought I'd give it a try anyway." He beamed at her but suddenly grew serious. "That stuff in your bag. What's it for?"

"What bag? What're you talking about?"

"The shopping bag in your bedroom."

"You looked in my bag?" She was horrified. "You snooped into my personal things?" This was so unlike Jeffrey.

"Aunt Mona," he began, his voice patient yet tense. "The bag was open. I saw what I saw when I floated over it. There's a whole lot of strange stuff in there."

"Herbs and spices," she lied, hoping he'd believe her. Bringing Uncle Max here was to be a surprise. But Jeffrey didn't fall for it. He always was a wise little bugger, she thought.

"It's the same stuff you had when you brought me back. What's it for?" he wanted to know.

She could see that she was losing: he was onto her. "I . . . I wanted to bring Uncle Max back to keep you company."

"But you can't! Because then we'll both be stuck here."

"I have to, Jeffrey. You're so lonely. Uncle Max will help."

"Let me think about it," he said then as if the final decision were his. Ramona, however, knew better. She'd go ahead and do it whether Jeffrey wanted her to or not. "It might turn out bad," he continued, "Uncle Max might not accept being confined to your apartment."

"Well, he'll just have to! You're a young boy, you shouldn't be alone so much. And I'm no company, not really . . ." She stopped suddenly. Another idea had just crossed her mind, and it was the best ever. She looked over at Jeffrey and smiled. "Were there any girls your age? You know, ones who died before you did?"

"Oh, Lord," he moaned. "Tell me she's not gonna fill this apartment with dead people. Please, Lord, say it isn't so."

"You know, Jeffrey," she began, completely ignoring him. "If I bring back Uncle Max, I have to bring Aunt Sadie too."

J.J. Holiman watched the news and shuddered: the Bridge Gate Killer was in jail. They showed a fast shot of him, hands manacled behind his back, being led to a waiting police car, his head slightly bent to one side to avoid the glare of the cameras. J.J. watched for a moment longer, then snapped off the set and went to his room to give it more thought. Garrett was away; he'd left early after saying something about going to the Hamptons on Long Island 'to forget.'

Although he had no idea what the boy intended

to forget, J.J. figured it was good for Garrett to get away now and then and just let go. Besids, J.J. had important work to do and Garrett was afraid of the explanation J.J. had given concerning the Bridge Gate Killer: that he was only partially human, that he was more demon-beast than anything. So Garrett's presence would've been a hindrance to what he had in mind.

Once J.J. was safely locked in his room to avoid contact with Garrett's servants, he thought about the man he'd just seen on the news. A mental image of the alleged killer rose up before him and he shuddered again. The man was tall and lanky, was dressed in a cape-like coat and was as spooky as spooky could be, but he was no killer! The demon in him, that was the killer! The mutilator! And bars wouldn't hold a demon, no way in hell! So if the police thought it would stop now, they were mistaken.

He considered calling Ron, but didn't. Something inside him kept telling him to wait. But wait for what, he wondered? And yet, the answer was simple: the man they'd caught and jailed wasn't the one harboring the beast! Asgar was too smart for that. Hell, any fool would've been suspicious of the creep he'd seen on television. Most people would've been afraid of someone who dressed like the Phantom of the Opera and whose complexion was laced with the pallor of an under-taker.

Oh no, he wasn't the one. Asgar wouldn't draw attention to himself. Therefore he'd hide in the body of a so-called normal man: one whose outward appearance conformed with the rest of society. At this point J.J. realized why he'd shuddered at the news that the killer had been caught, why he felt anxious inside and not relieved. The person harboring the killer was still loose, but the police felt differently. And so the entire burden had been passed over to J.J. He had to keep looking, had to keep searching, had to keep hoping he could find the right person and exorcise the beast from his body before he killed again.

J.J. rose and picked up the telephone from his bedside table. Garrett had left a car at his disposal. He dialed a few numbers and gave the chauffeur instructions. He was on his way to Bridge Gate Court. He wanted to look for clues, make his deductions, and perhaps learn the identity of the real killer; an easy feat to accomplish, now that he wouldn't be tripping over the police.

He strolled the woods with the head under his arm and searched for a proper place to perform his ceremony, a place that wouldn't be crawling with campers or tourists. He'd been here before, had walked beneath the trees and the sky, had prayed to his god, Mephisto, in these woods asking for forgiveness; so he was familiar with his surroundings. He lifted his robes and stepped over a half-rotted log, conscious of the clacking noises of the candles in his inner pockets.

There was a small clearing in the path ahead where the moon and stars shown down as though it were daylight. If he stood in that clearing, under the full moon, his god would surely be pleased that he'd picked such a favorable position in relation to the universe. He would be at the apex, the highest point in the pentagram of his lord; for Satan worshiped the moon as the key to all. And,

instead of its being the climax to the secret of life,
the moon was the beginning . . .

He stumbled over a long branch and bent to pick
it up. The branch would make an excellent stake
for the head. The third phase of his ceremony to
rid his soul of an evil creature was to begin
tonight. Again he intended to beseech his lord and
master to free him from the bonds of the beast he
felt was part of him. Of course, nothing had
worked up to this point, and that caused some
doubt: did the demon in his dreams exist only in
his sub-conscious mind or was it real?

If it was real, surely his lord would've
responded and freed him by now. So he could've
been wrong. But then the dreams continued, as
did the murders. And as always he awoke to find
body parts lying at the foot of his bed . . .

He tried to recall the first time it happened, the
first time he found some fingers, their blood
swelling the carpet into a crimson stain. He
wanted to scream, but dared not for fear that
someone might hear. Besides, there was a
woman in his bed. He kicked the fingers under the
footboard and hoped they'd disappear. He
couldn't face it, couldn't make himself admit that
the dream he'd just had, and the beast in that
dream, were somehow connected with those
fingers.

But he'd seen the beast chewing them off that
woman's hand!

And there had been a terrible burning sensation
in his groin. He jumped into a shower and swore
he wouldn't look, but the beast had urinated in an
alleyway, had used those terrible claws on his
penis. And when he finally looked, he was raw,
the skin puffy and sore. The beast controlled his

sleeping brain! He was sure of it. He strolled further into the woods using the branch as a walking cane and decided to use the full moon as his guide. The point where the moon beamed down ahead had to be the clearing he was searching for. And it was.

He stopped to examine the clearing. It was perfect, surrounded by wild shrubs and trees. He walked to the center and drove his branch deep into the ground, for such was his physical strength since he'd become united with the beast that no task was too difficult or tiring. Once the stake was secured, he placed the neck of the head over the spiked top and pulled down hard, ignoring the squishing noises the head made when it slipped down over the wood. He had to ignore it; there was much to be done and he had no time for human emotions. She was dead, had died at the hands of the beast, and he was determined that she should not have died in vain.

He went to the edge of the clearing and began to dig a line into the soft earth with the tip of his shoe, a line that would encircle the stake. This was to be the outer rim of his pentagram. "Satan, lord of the elements, lord of the kingdom of the earth, hear me, your servant, as I beseech you to grant one last request. Hail, Satan!" His voice echoed in the night and it scared him. What if someone were to hear and come running out of curiosity? Would the beast in him emerge to kill again?

"Satan," he began once more, only softer this time, "I call you forth as my lord and master to ask your forgiveness. Hail, Satan!"

With great care he completed the outer rim, then fell to his knees to hand carve the elements of the pentagram into the soft earth beneath him. He again listened to the clacking noises of the candles and grew impatient to continue, to get this over with. How many times had he performed this same ceremony, he wondered? Too many, was the answer. Too many times he'd taken human body parts and offered them as sacrifices to his god only to hear nothing in return.

Then again, perhaps those parts were an insult to Mephisto. What were a few fingers and an arm compared to this, a head, the holder of the subconscious mind, the holder of the third eye, the holder of the focal point of the entire body? Mephisto would listen now; he just had to. The man approached the center of the pentagram and, standing near the staked head, began to pray while pulling the hood of his robe up to hide his face.

"Satan, lord of the winds from the four corners of the earth and the princes of hell—Satan from the south, Lucifer from the east, Belial from the north, and Leviathan from the west. Take this, my sacrifice, as yours. Take this humble offering in thy name . . . Satan, lord of the Earth and surrounding planets, lord of the creatures that dwell therein, lord of the creatures of the night. Hear me, I beseech thee—"

"What the fuck's going on, man? You must be on some good shit!"

He turned and found himself face to face with a young man, the strangest looking creature he'd seen in a long time. One of those so-called punk rockers, the sides of his head were shaved, but not the top. On top he sported a brilliant blue mohawk tipped with red. But it wasn't his hair that caught the man's attention the most; it was his clothing. He was wearing black leather, which was pleasing because black was the color of the creatures of darkness. And it blended well except that he was also wearing chains and razors for ornaments. "Hey, man, you wanna split some of that shit? What'cha got? Crack?"

As the young punk rocker approached him, he felt his body going through a strange metamorphosis, felt the beast he suspected was a part of him coming to life. His teeth were changing, growing, becoming pointed at the ends and so dagger sharp they cut the inside of his mouth. His fingers ached near the tips; his nails were turning into talon-like blades of steel.

"All I got is some cocaine. But ya get a better high with crack—Oh my God, you musta been out of it but good. That looks like a head . . . It is a head! What the fuck? Oh, shit, no—"

Asgar grabbed him by the throat and started to dig his teeth into the soft layers of skin and outer membranes surrounding his jugular vein. Then Asgar began chewing through the tough, sinewy muscles protecting the vein and stopped to smile when the hot and salty blood touched his lips. He heard his victim gurgling and released him, watched him fall to the ground and rock back and forth, his hands at his throat to stop the flow of blood. But it was too late. Asgar held a piece of the vein between his teeth. Nothing could stop his death now.

"Gloria, oh, Satanus," Asgar bellowed, undaunted by the fact that this creature might've had companions. If he did, Asgar would kill them too, for this was the greatest sacrifice of all, the giving of a human life to his lord and master. "Hear me, Satanus," he shouted, his voice quaking the very earth beneath his feet. "Hail, Satan," he bellowed and Satan heard and made his presence known. As Asgar watched, the young man's body turned into a quivering ball of fire, the flames reaching high enough to dance among the treetops overhead.

Oh, yes, Satan heard, and Satan was pleased; he'd accepted the offering. And perhaps this was a good sign. Perhaps the beast would be freed now, freed from the encumbrance of his human counterpart before the next moon.

Garrett Lang woke up as if from a trance and found himself on the balcony of his mansion in the Hamptons. He wondered how long he'd been standing there, in that very same spot, reminiscing about Bridge Gate Court and the beast who haunted his dreams. But then he realized it had been different this time: the beast wasn't roaming some apartment building in New York City. No. The Beast had been out in the woods. . . .

He gazed at the woods behind his house and felt he was losing his mind. This was ridiculous. How could the beast be standing in a moon-filled clearing in the woods when so far his crimes had been confined to one area? Each and every murder to date had taken place where Samantha lived. Samantha!

Oh, but she was beautiful. And he'd had his chance, could've held her in his arms and made love to her. And did he? No! He'd been so taken with grief over Gail Lindman's murder he was unable to perform. Then again, was it really due to his secretary's murder, or was it because he nearly went into shock when he went to get

Samantha? Was it because he knew he'd been to Bridge Gate Court in his sleep, had wandered those halls with the beast?

That was even more ridiculous, he thought to himself. Of course he was overtaken with Gail's death. It couldn't have been the latter. Then why did he feel he was experiencing *deja vu* when he entered Bridge Gate Court? Why? The answer was simple enough: because most of those old, luxury buildings in that area resembled one another. If you've seen one, you've seen them all. While he might not have been in that particular building before, he'd been in others and the memory had stayed with him. Hence, *deja vu*.

He straightened himself to full height and breathed deeply of the warm night air. It was wonderful being here in the Hamptons where everything was clean and green and alive. It was too bad he didn't feel as alive inside, but that was only because he was alone. At least at this point he was. But what about before, when he'd been in a trance and had been walking those woods with a head under his arm? He wasn't alone then. And later when that punk rocker showed up, he watched the beast destroy another human life.

Garrett had pains in his head and knew he couldn't go on. It was just too awful to keep remembering the same thing over and over until he felt he was going mad. He wanted to forget; had to forget. He walked back inside and picked up the telephone, hoping she was home and would say yes. "Hello, Samantha? It's Garrett. Listen, I'm out here on Long Island. Would you like it if I sent my limo in to pick you up? . . . Yes, dear. Yes, for the weekend . . . You will? Great . . . Oh, I see . . . No, that's fine, don't worry about it

. . . I'll see you in the morning then.''

Ron Wheatley stopped running from his past when he wound up in those very same woods in the Adirondacks where he had aimed a rifle and shot Debbie in the back. He parked his car and walked until the clearing came into view—the one she'd stepped into when he pulled the trigger. He was here because he wanted to see that clearing again, to work it out in his mind.

Could the situation have been as Nick Candeles described it, even though Candeles was discussing someone else? Did he shoot her on purpose then lie and tell himself it was an accident? What had been going through his head when he pulled the trigger? And why was he now experiencing a sensation that didn't belong?

It seemed he was in the body of a man, a man-beast, and the man was carrying a head through the woods to a clearing. The head was then staked on top of a long tree branch. This was a ceremony of some sort. A pentagram was drawn. Words were chanted. Oh, God! No, go back! Don't take another step! There was a strange-looking young man, and he was flirting with death only he didn't know it. No! Don't! Get away from that stake—Ron buried his face in his hands and tired to stop the visions. But it was no good. He was watching the beast kill that strange young man, the one with the red-tipped mohawk.

Ron stood in the midst of some large trees and held his head to quiet the throbbing pains inside of his skull. Then he forced his mind to go blank. He wouldn't go on, wouldn't watch another murder. This was more than one person could take; more than he could stand. Why was this

214

happening? Then he remembered what J.J. had said, about how he could've developed a sixth sense due to a traumatic shock. This thing with Debbie had been extremely traumatic, enough to shock him to hell and back.

But the visions only began when the beast started his murderous rampage. This thing with Debbie happened two years ago. It couldn't be connected. Then again, J.J. said he might've been having brief unimportant psychic experiences all along and had ignored them because he didn't recognize them as such. Whatever it was, whatever was causing those visions, he knew he couldn't stay in those woods, not when the beast was there also.

He turned and ran for his car and the long trip back to the city. He'd give more thought to what took place with Debbie at a later date, when his mind was free and his heart open to the truth.

But the strangest thing happened when he got back to his car. He was able to look through the window on the driver's side and see himself behind the wheel, fast asleep: the drive up had been too much. And the truth became self-evident: this had been *another dream*, not a *waking experience.* He hadn't been walking through those woods side by side with the beast with a clear head and open eyes. Hell no. He was doing it in his sleep as usual, and as usual, he and the beast were one!

Samantha had been in a state of shock when Garrett called inviting her to the Hamptons for the weekend. And she'd said yes so quickly she later wondered if she did it to get even with Ron. Ron was married? But he went to bed with her! And after asking her to go away for a few days! Why didn't he take his wife on a trip instead?

But no, he asked her, Samantha. And after she turned him down he never asked again. And she wanted him to ask again. Especially after they went to bed and made love. If he'd asked her then she would've said yes. But he didn't.

Therefore, she concluded, he asked only to lure her into bed: it was part of his line. He had no intentions of taking her anywhere. He used the idea of a trip as an incentive. Once he got his way, that was it. He didn't even come back to the office to pick her up. He sent his partner, Nick Candeles.

She wondered if the story Candeles had told her was true: about how Ron shot his wife. Did they make it up between them as an excuse for Ron not to come back and drive her home? Was that Ron's way out? He'd lied to her, laid her, and now he'd left her. The bastard!

But what if Ron shot his wife dead? This would explain why he couldn't take his wife on a vacation. Then again, Candeles never mentioned that part of it, and if she were dead, he would've told her. She glanced at her watch and decided it was time to start packing. Although she wasn't leaving until morning, she wanted to be ready when Garrett's chauffeur arrived.

Samantha approached her bedroom and was grateful because she'd left the lights on in there; now she wouldn't be walking into a darkened room. In fact, most of the lights in the entire apartment were on. But only because it was late at night and she felt safer this way. She'd done this even knowing that the killer was in jail because he wasn't the only nut-job around. Look at what happened with Morgan's father, she thought. The man was violent and unreasonable; he reminded her of the rapist. But she'd torched that bastard, so there was no earthly connection.

Still, Phil Housner was a horror on his own, a wealthy horror. And it must've been nice, she thought, to have so much money that you usually got your own way. He cut Morgan off without a penny, and yet continuously hunted her like an animal. When would it stop? Samantha walked into her closet and pulled a suitcase from a top shelf. This wasn't going to be easy: choosing a wardrobe to spend the weekend in. If only she knew what Garrett had in mind, such as where he would take her and what the fashion scene was like out there in the Hamptons.

But all he would say over the phone was that he had a mansion and she'd have her own room. She selected a few dresses and then some tailored slacks with matching blouses before she'd allow any further thoughts to enter her head. Then she found herself wondering where Ron would've taken her had he been on the level. He had no mansion, no limo. All he had was himself, and that had been enough until she discovered he was married.

She carried the clothing to her bed where the open suitcase was waiting and sat for a moment to think things over. Before discovering Ron's secret she would've had to choose between two men. Now the choice was easy: *Garrett* wasn't married. Oh, God, he just couldn't be! What Ron had done to her was enough . . .

"Ron, why?" she said aloud. "Why did you deceive me?" She'd been honest with him. Had given herself to him. And he'd been the first to have his way with her—not counting the rapist or the man in her dreams. And it was a beautiful experience. Only now that same experience made her feel cheap and used, because he was married!

She rose and folded her clothing neatly, then went into the bathroom for her toiletries, her mind growing hard with hatred for Ron Wheatley. She'd heard about men like him before. Even Morgan, as smart as she was, had run into a few: the liars, the users, anything for a lay. Well now, *fuck him*, she thought.

Once her packing was finished, she went back into the living room and lay down. Although she'd told Garrett not to send his chauffeur until morning because she was exhausted and couldn't make the trip to Long Island before then, that wasn't the whole story. The truth was, she'd feel much better if she waited and rested and had a chance to forget the hurt that Ron Wheatley had caused.

She was on his yacht in the middle of the Atlantic. She was at the wheel and watched him as he stood up front by the bow of the ship. He was naked, and when he turned to face her she wanted to die: he was perfection personified, his long, muscular, body heating her flesh even from a distance away.

"Ron," she called and watched him walk towards her, his hips swaying with confidence, his body poetry in motion. He was smiling, his pale blue eyes sparkling with lust. Oh yes, he was ready. He was moving faster this time, had even removed his clothing before the dream began. And that was different, something he never did before.

"Would you like me to take the wheel?"

someone asked . . . Curiously enough it was a woman's voice, and it came from behind her. Samantha turned and saw an attractive young woman with a rifle strapped to her back. "I'll take the wheel while you go to bed with my husband," she said and smiled.

Samantha felt angered by her words. The son-of-a-bitch was married! What nerve! She turned to face him, to confront him with the truth—but he was holding the rifle in his hands now and aiming it at her. Or was it because she was standing between him and his wife, and he wanted a chance to shoot his wife again? She saw flames bursting forth from the barrel, but heard no sound. He must've been using a silencer, she thought, and closed her eyes to wait for the shell to tear at her flesh.

But it didn't happen. The shell passed through her without causing any damage, only to lodge itself in the body of the woman behind her. And yet, the woman felt no pain. Rather she smiled and said, "Thank you, Ron." Then she took the wheel from Samantha's hand and began to maneuver the yacht further out into the open water. Samantha stared at her dazedly, watched the hole in her body grow larger, watched blood pump through that hole, felt Ron taking her own hand to run it over his naked body while he leered in her face—

She sat bolt upright and found herself on the couch in the living room. The television was still on, but the station had gone off the air. The lights overhead were glaring in her face. Her mouth was dry. She swung her legs over the side of the couch and held her head for a moment, deciding not to think about that dream or what had turned it into a nightmare. She wanted a hot cup of tea and a hot bath and nothing more; no thoughts, no memories.

She got to her feet and started for the kitchen, but something made her stop and turn, stop and look back over her shoulder. Someone was watching her, she could feel eyes burning into the back of her head. Then she saw him: a man wearing a cape with a hood. No, a shroud, a death shroud . . . He was standing near the window where the gargoyles were and the window was open. He'd gotten into her apartment. Garrett had said this would happen. That he might change his, 'modus operandi,' and forget about killing in that corridor downstairs.

She stared at him for a long time, wanting to see his face, waiting for him to make his move. And when he did, she screamed and screamed and screamed.

11

J.J. Holiman had spent seven hours going through the building at Bridge Gate Court searching for evidence of the real killer's identity. But he was stumped. There were no clues! The bastard had been careful not to drop a shred of clothing or anything similar that would've led back to his door. J.J. was about to give up when he bumped into a garbage can in the alley, knocking it over. The can fell over with a clacking noise and the lid landed beside it, spinning loudly on its rim.

He looked up to see if the noise attracted any attention, but there wasn't a soul in sight. The tenants were probably used to such noises. He sucked in a heavy breath of air, relieved because he hadn't been caught where he didn't belong, and bent to pick up the can and found himself staring at an arm.

An arm with a bloody severed end was lying among the trash on the ground; an arm with a charm bracelet attached; a body part, he knew, from one of the latest victims. He figured it belonged to the woman whose head was also

missing, the body found murdered and mutilated
in the corridor behind him.

Strange, he thought, that the mutilator had left
her arm behind. But from the reports Ron
Wheatley had shown him earlier, the fool had
already stolen and used an arm in one of his
ceremonies. Of course the report didn't say that
the arm had been used in a ceremony. But it did
mention that an arm had been taken from one of
the first five victims. And it hadn't worked then,
hadn't been accepted by Mephisto as a gift to
exorcise the beast from the human. Knowing this,
the killer had left June DeSoto's arm behind.

Then why did he take and keep her head when
he'd already used a head too?

The stupid bastard! Why was he confused? Had
he killed so many women and had taken so many
body parts he couldn't think straight? He'd taken
a head from victim number six: Gail Lindman. J.J.
rose and was searching for something suitable to
wrap the arm in when someone screamed in one
of the apartments above. And from the sound of
it, the woman doing the screaming was scared to
death, as though she were facing the unbearable.

The killer? And if so, this was all he needed to
prove his theory: they had the wrong man in jail.

Ramona Blattfield was awakened by the
screams; the same exact screams she'd heard
when the Bridge Gate Killer was doing his thing in
the hallway downstairs.

But he was in jail. Besides, these screams were
coming from up here, on the seventh floor. So
someone was hollering for a reason other than
being killed. And since it was the voice of a young

woman, she assumed a man was beating his wife.

She started to go back to sleep, but the idea of a woman taking a beating enraged her. She wasn't sitting back and letting the bastard get away with it. First she called the police, and what a load of bullshit that was. As soon as she gave the location —Bridge Gate Court—on comes a detective.

"Tell me what happened," he said. "Someone's being beaten to death," she answered. "Instead of discussing this over the phone, come over here and do something about it!" Then she hung up and ran for the front door.

Jeffrey was just floating through it by the time she got there, and that enraged her even more. But she couldn't do anything about it then. She'd nail Jeffrey's ass later on, when this was over. She released the bolt on her police lock and threw open the door to find Samantha Croft standing in the hall screaming, and not a mark on her.

"He's in there," Samantha yelled, pointing to the open door of her apartment. "I saw him, The Bridge Gate Killer. He was wearing a shroud!"

Ramona wrapped Samantha in her arms and patted her on the back. Although she knew that the younger woman had obviously been having a nightmare, she didn't argue the point. The Bridge Gate Killer was in jail. Besides, even if he wasn't, what was he doing in someone's apartment when all along he'd mainly confined his killings to a corridor downstairs? He never came up here, and certainly never entered anyone's apartment.

Then again, if Samantha was right and hadn't been dreaming . . . No, it was too awful to think they had the wrong man in jail and that now they weren't even safe inside their apartments. She glared at Jeffrey over Samantha's shoulder and he went back into her apartment. "Now, now, dear," she told Samantha in as soothing a voice as she could manage under the circumstances, "You just calm down. The police are on their way."

Like Ramona Blattfield, Detective Nick Candeles thought this was bullshit too. Ron Wheatley hadn't come back yet, and as Ron's partner this was his call. He shuddered, his body quaking all the way over to Bridge Gate Court. He was aware they had the killer in jail, but something crossed his mind after that nasty bitch hung up on him: what if they had the wrong man? It wasn't as if it couldn't happen and hadn't happened before. And if that were so, then he was on his way to view a mutilated body.

At Bridge Gate Court, a crowd had gathered. "What's up?" he asked a patrolman in front of the building. "What happened?"

"Upstairs, on the seventh floor. We have a young, white, fe—"

"Never mind the bullshit!" Candeles bellowed, "Just give it to me straight!"

"Some woman claims the Bridge Gate Killer was in her apartment."

"Is she dead?"

The patrolman stifled an obvious guffaw before answering with, "No. I was just talking to her."

Candeles started through the front door and heard laughter behind him followed by, "How the fuck could she tell me she'd seen the killer if she was dead? What an asshole!" But he ignored it and kept going. He had better things to do other than to spend his time arguing with a smart ass patrolman.

Samantha was in Ramona Blattfield's apartment by the time he got up to the seventh floor. He followed Ramona to where she was and again fought the urge to tell someone off. He'd recognized Ramona's voice. She was the nasty bitch who'd hung up on him.

Samantha was still shuddering when he reached the kitchen; her whole body quivered with fear and he wanted to die. This was Ron Wheatley's girl, the one he'd driven home earlier. And hell, Ron should be here now. But he hadn't come back from wherever he ran to when Candeles' remark brought back the past.

"Tell me what happened," he said as gently as he could. But it didn't come off the way he'd meant it. He had a rough voice, made even more so by the years he'd spent on the force. Then he had to consider the fact that he was a big man, too big and hefty to appear gentle. "Did you see his face? Can you tell me what he looked like?"

Samantha recognized Candeles, but was so distraught she couldn't do anything but answer his question. "No," she sobbed, "I didn't see what he looked like. He was wearing a cape. Or a shroud. You know, like they used to bury people in. There was a hood covering his face. Besides, I was too busy trying to get out of there to really look at him. I'm sorry if that sounds sarcastic. I didn't mean it to."

"I understand." And yet he didn't: at least not the part about the cape. The Bridge Gate Killer wore a cape, but he was in jail, and unless they had the wrong man, this was an imitator, which made things worse. Every time a string of murders was committed by a psycho, another one came out of the woodwork to imitate him. Christ! This was awful! Imitators were sometimes worse than the nut they were imitating. Then again, she was alive; he didn't kill her.

"For whatever it's worth," he said, still trying to sound gentle but not succeeding, "There are patrolmen all over the area. If he's around, we'll find him. Is there someone you know you can spend the night with? We'd like to check your apartment thoroughly, in case he left fingerprints or any other clues."

"She can stay with me," Ramona Blattfield said, putting her arms around Samantha with an air of protectiveness.

"That's all right, Ramona. I appreciate the offer, but I have a friend out on Long Island. He'll send a car for me if I call. I want to get as far away from here as I can."

Ramona smiled and smoothed Samantha's hair away from her face. "I don't blame you. And you can use my phone to call."

"I'll do it," Candeles said, "What's the number?" While he dialed, he wondered how many 'friends' the lady had. Up until this moment, there'd just been Ron. Now she had a 'Garrett Lang' as well. "Hello," he said, speaking into the receiver, "Is Garrett Lang at home? . . . Oh, I see. Do you know where he's at or what time he'll be back? . . . No, no message. I'll call him again in the morning."

This was a bitch, he thought to himself. The lady had struck out all around. First Ron was nowhere to be found, and now Garrett Lang wasn't home. "You'll have to stay here for the night," he told Samantha. "But don't worry. I'll be in your apartment right next door if you need me."

J.J. Holiman hid the packaged arm in the darkened corridor downstairs. Then he rode the elevator from floor to floor, stopping on each level, trying to determine just where the screams were coming from. When he got to the seventh, he heard Samantha and Ramona discussing the killer and the police and rode on up to wait until things cooled down a bit. He had to talk to Samantha and it had to be alone. Even if Ron Wheatley was in charge of any investigation when it came to Bridge Gate Court, Ron might not give him a free hand to question the woman who'd just sworn she saw the killer. And J.J. had to have the facts; what he looked like and what he'd done.

After an hour or so, J.J. figured it was safe to make his move. He took the stairs down to the seventh floor and was about to knock when a tall, burly man opened the door to Ramona's apartment They were both startled, but J.J. recovered faster, especially when the man displayed a badge and began to ask questions. "I'm J.J. Holiman—"

"Really!" he said and J.J. knew it wouldn't be easy getting past him. From the looks of him, he was a real hard-nosed cop.

J.J. thought about the badge he'd seen. This was a detective too. Then where the hell was Ron Wheatley, he wondered? "I'm a close, personal friend of Detective Wheatley—"

"And?"

"Well I heard a woman screaming—"

"Listen you little fraud. You ain't no friend of Wheatley's. I know them all, and you ain't one of them! You're just a shit-headed snoop. And if you ain't gone by the time I count to three, you're dead!"

"But I'm a demonologist. Ron knows me! I came here to help."

"One—"

"Call Ron. He'll verify this."

"Two—"

"Call Garrett Lang. He knows me too." This was awful. He just had to get inside and speak to that woman. Yet there was no way to get around this gorilla blocking the doorway. However, at the mention of Garrett Lang's name, the detective stopped counting. And the expression on his face turned from anger to confusion.

"I just called Garrett Lang. He's not home. Do they know each other? Ron and Garret Lang?"

"Yes. They're old friends. Why?"

"How long's it been since they seen each other?"

"At least ten years. Why?" This was ridiculous. So much time wasted answering questions when J.J. had to see that woman, and fast. The killer was probably miles away by now; it had been over an hour since she screamed.

The detective lowered his voice and sneered. "Their mutual girl friend's inside. Wait'll they find out they're both screwing the same broad."

J.J. had to think fast. Mutual girl friend? Garrett came here to see Samantha Croft. Was it possible that she knew Ron as well? And if so, were they both aware of this? "Samantha Croft? Is she the one who screamed?"

"Yeah. Said she saw the Bridge Gate Killer in her apartment—"

"May I see her? I really am working on the case

with Ron."

"Well, I don't know. She's pretty beat—"

"Why don't you ask her? Tell her what I've told you. That I know both men."

"Kind of like blackmail, huh?" Candeles leered. J.J. felt his stomach turn but he smiled anyway. If this was the only way to get to see Samantha, making it appear lurid, he had to go along with it. "And you say you're a demon—What was the rest?"

"A demonologist. I investigate murders and have helped the police in the past."

"Is that the same as being a criminologist?" J.J. nodded in agreement. He'd go along with whatever it took to see Samantha. Candeles motioned for him to wait while he went to speak to Samantha. Then he came back and showed J.J. inside. "She'll see you. But only for a minute or two. Says she's tired."

J.J. found a distraught and exhausted Samantha sitting in the kitchen drinking tea with Ramona Blattfield. He smiled and had to admire Garrett's taste in women, and Ron's as well. "You wanted to see me about what happened a while ago?" she asked, her eyes trained on his face. J.J. felt his stomach flutter like a schoolboy's and had trouble answering because of the lump in his throat. "You're Garrett's house guest. Am I right?" He nodded. "I'm Samantha Croft."

J.J. was disappointed. He hadn't gotten much information from Samantha, other than the fact that she'd seen, "someone doing a great imitation of the killer." Detective Candeles had her convinced that the killer was in jail and the guy in her apartment was a "nut-job imitator." If only she'd seen his face, J.J. would've known the truth. No one could gaze upon Asgar's skinless countenance and mistake him for anything other than the murderous bastard he was.

He walked through the front door of Bridge Gate Court and out into the raw night air. The streets were nearly deserted, making him wish he hadn't sent Garrett's chauffeur home. But then the chauffeur had mentioned something about taking a friend of Garrett's to the Hamptons in the morning. J.J. knew he'd probably spend hours going through the building looking for clues, so he sent the chauffeur home. What a mistake that was. Now he'd have to walk home, unless he was lucky enough to find a cab along the way.

He had to go from West 72nd Street and Central Park West to First Avenue and East 59th Street to get to Garrett's. A lot of walking for a man his age, but he had little choice. The chauffeur was gone and that was that.

Of course, J.J. didn't relish the idea of going through Central Park this late at night: he'd read so much in the papers about muggings and murders, and considered taking an alternate route. Then again, the media had a knack for making things seem worse than they actually were.

He entered the park and walked without incident until he was a little beyond Strawberry Fields, the section named in honor of John Lennon, when he realized he wasn't alone. Something or someone was taking a route parallel to his, only they were walking back in the bushes while he was on the main road. He stopped once or twice and tried to analyze the footsteps . . . It could've been a dog or a cat, but the noises they made were hardly similar to what he was hearing. Besides, the footfalls were heavy, too heavy to belong to a small animal. No, this was a large animal, a human animal. He began to sweat and felt his heart thumping in his chest. He was old and knew he'd damn well lose in hand-to-hand combat with a mugger. If it were a mugger. So he kept walking.

Footfall after footfall, step after step, the person in the bushes walked along beside J.J.

And then the unseen stranger began to giggle.

The Bridge Gate Killer liked to giggle!

A stupid thought at a time like this, but it came to him suddenly, before he could stop it from entering his head. Then something else came to him: his old buddy, Asgar—he liked to giggle. And Asgar was the real killer, not the pathetic spook they had in jail! Hell, the spook wasn't even the one harboring the beast. Oh God, the stranger giggled again.

J.J. began to run, forgetting his age, forgetting his heart, forgetting that if it were Asgar, the beast could outrun him any day. He stumbled once and almost went down, but regained his balance and listened to those footfalls keeping time with the rhythm of his own. Step after step his feet struck the pavement with fury, his heart pounding so hard it began to hurt.

Was this how it would end for him, he wondered? Was he about to die of a heart attack running away from a beast he'd defeated years ago? It wasn't fair. He'd spent his life fighting demons and always imagined going out in a more spectacular manner than this, perhaps locked in fatal combat with some master demon. But this, a heart attack, this was embarrassing.

He tripped over a curb and fell forward, his hands outstretched to muffle the blow to his face. Both knees hit hard, and his face hit the pavement, stunning him so that he was unable to get up right away. The parallel footfalls had stopped running. Now they were casually strolling in his direction as he lay there, on a cold sidewalk, helpless and bleeding. He rolled over onto his back, angered at the thumping of his heart. He tried to sit up when a form came into view, a man, a large one, wearing a hooded shroud. Asgar!

"J.J. Holiman. How nice that we meet after all these years."

His voice thundered heavily in the still night air, quaking the pavement beneath his body. "In the name of the Lord Jesus Christ, I command you to be gone," J.J. shouted three times in rapid succession.

"Are you starting that nonsense again?" Asgar wanted to know.

J.J. ignored his taunts and continued. The last thing he could afford to do at this point was to give in to the torments of the beast. His prayers and his demands would work: they always had in the past. Asgar wouldn't dare challenge a direct plea to the Lord God above. He was smart enough to be wary of the wrath of God.

"I leave you now, old man," Asgar said and turned as J.J. knew he would. "But as you know, I will be back and we'll see who wins next time."

J.J. struggled into a sitting position and watched Asgar disappear from sight, then surveyed the damage to his body. A few bad bruises, some sprains, possibly a broken nose. He slid his legs over the edge of the curve and cringed when his feet touched the ground. He was in no shape to be walking to First Avenue or any place else.

He looked around for a pay phone, but there was none in sight. Just then a limousine came flying around a curve a few feet away and headed straight for him. He flung himself back onto the sidewalk and prayed, the wheels of the limo bumping off the raised pavement near him as it came to a screeching halt. It was Garrett's car, complete with chauffeur.

"I couldn't sleep. I was worried about you roaming around in that building by yourself," the chauffeur said once he was at J.J.'s side. "I went through the whole place and you were nowhere to be found. I figured you walked. Jesus, lucky for me I thought to try the park. Mr. Garrett would kill me for sure if anything happened to you. Are you all right?"

"Yes. I just fell. Would you help me up?"

"Are you sure? Maybe I should call a doctor or an ambulance."

"Hell no, man! Just get me to my feet. We've got some traveling to do.

"Traveling?" the chauffeur asked while he helped J.J. into the back seat of the limo.

"Yes, traveling. Take me to St. Patrick's Cathedral. I have to do some serious praying."

"It's closed at this hour," the chauffeur said.

"Then I'll kneel on the front steps. Let's go."

The great cathedral loomed on Fifth Avenue like a leftover from another era, its ornate stone spires piercing the night sky in brilliant contrast to the surrounding walls of metal and glass. The main doors were tightly closed, as the chauffeur had warned, but J.J. was drawn by a shaft of light into a small side entry door that stood ajar. Gratefully he hobbled in and looked up at the high domed

ceiling, the crystal chandeliers, and the paintings.
He knew he'd never been inside of a church so
magnificent in his life.

J.J. walked to the long aisle in the center of the
church and genuflected as best he could. Then he
took his time getting down to the first pew in front
of the altar. He was here to talk to his God
through Jesus Christ, His son. He was here to ask
for strength of mind and spirit in his upcoming
battle with Asgar. He was here to ask the Lord to
spare what little was left of his life should He see
fit to do so. He genuflected again and entered the
aisle to pray.

His head was bent in prayer when he sensed
someone staring at him. Probably another
devoted follower of God who, like himself, had
come in late at night to pray, he surmised, and
kept his head down in solemn worship. But it was
no good: whoever was doing the staring hadn't
stopped, and J.J. sensed it. Eyes were glued to his
face! Oh yes, he felt them studying him from
somewhere near the front of the church, not the
rear. And yet, he was in the first pew.

He glanced up in time to see someone dressed
in black robes entering a confessional chamber off
to one side, near the altar, closing a curtain
behind them. It was a priest. J.J. had only seen
him from behind and the lighting wasn't that
good, but the man's head had been bowed in
prayer and his hands were folded across his
chest.

He wondered why a priest was here, giving confessional services at this time of night. For all he
was worth, he couldn't remember another priest
who'd done the same in the past. But this *was* St.
Patrick's Cathedral, and this *was* New York City,

the town that never slept. So maybe the priests here offered late night services.

And that was good too. J.J. hadn't been to confession in weeks and although his sins were few, he felt a sudden need to bare his soul. He rose with great effort, cringing at the pain of his bruises and entered the first chamber, drawing the curtain across for privacy.

"Yes my, son," the priest said in a soothing voice.

"Forgive me, father, for I have sinned," he said and leaned closer to the screened partition separating him from the priest. He wanted a closer look at the holy man, but the mesh of the screening had been woven in such a way as to insure complete privacy for both parties. "I have sinned," he repeated.

"Haven't we all?" the Priest mumbled dryly, in such a low voice that J.J. wasn't sure he'd heard it correctly.

"I'm sorry, what did you say?"

"Nothing, son. Nothing. Now, tell me how you've sinned."

"I coveted another man's woman." He'd wanted Samantha; had been beguiled by her beauty. "And I wished someone dead." He was speaking about Asgar at this point and felt it wasn't really a sin in the normal sense, but he had wished death to a living creature, if by any stretch of the imagination Asgar could be thought of as a living creature.

"What do you feel your punishment should be? What would equal your sins of the flesh?" the Priest wanted to know, asking in the same, soothing, disturbing tone of voice he'd used throughout.

"What?"

"We're very liberal minded around here, son. We try to work along with our sinners."

J.J. couldn't believe he was hearing this. At first he was too astonished to reply. But then he sucked in his breath and started to answer the priest with a suggestion of ten Hail Marys and ten Our Fathers when something stopped him, something that had been there in the booth with him all along. There was a terrible odor; he'd noticed it when he first came in. Then it had been subtle, but now the stench became overpowering. It was a mixture of feces and urine, reminding him of the smell of the public toilets in subway stations.

"I'm waiting," the priest said.

J.J. listened to the voice, heard it as though for the first time since entering the booth, sniffed the air and felt a sinking sensation burn at the base of his skull. He was trapped in a tiny confessional chamber with Asgar! He tried to steady his nerves. He had to escape, to get out and away, but the rear door of the church was very far away. His knees throbbed, his whole body ached from the fall. He'd never make it.

Asgar sensed his hesitation, felt J.J.'s mind working overtime, scanned his brain and saw the truth: J.J. was wise to him. He giggled then for the joy of his position. He had the old bastard right where he wanted him, trapped and helpless. He bowed his head and briefly thanked his god, Mephisto, for the taste of victory that was in his mouth. However, he didn't strike then because it would've been too quickly over and done with. And J.J. had to suffer, had to squirm, had to beg his God for help knowing it was useless. Asgar was the victor!

"I'm waiting, son," he said carrying on with the charade, dragging it out for all it was worth.

"In the name of the Lord, Jesus, Christ," J.J. began, hoping to finish the phrase at least once before Asgar struck. But it was no good. Two demon claws came through the screen in front of him and clutched him by the throat, squeezing the life from his body, making his eyes bulge in their sockets. "Oh, Lord, help me!" he screamed inwardly, knowing that Asgar was reading his thoughts with amusement because he giggled and squeezed even harder.

What a way to wind up, dead at the hands of a demon whose actions would now go unchecked. There would be no successors to his work: he'd had no children, had lost Garrett . . .

J.J. was nearly dead when a light shone in his face. He wondered if it was the magnificent fabled light of everlasting life: an entrance to the kingdom of the Lord. He was dead and at rest, he surmised, content to be free from the worries of existing on that hellhole of a planet called Earth. However, something so wonderful wasn't meant to be. The heavy clawed pressure of Asgar's hands had vanished from his neck and in its place he felt the soothing touch of a wet cloth. He opened his eyes and found himself face to face with a priest. A real one.

"Easy, my son," he said. "You've had a terrible ordeal. Tell me, what in the name of God was that creature? Was it a . . . demon? And what was it doing in my church?"

J.J. tried to speak, but the soreness in his throat

prevented it.

"I know, son. It's hard to talk with your throat half-crushed. But Lord, God, that was a fierce looking creature. And he nearly had you dead. I heard noises and I ran to the front of the church and I found him choking you. I cried to the Lord for help and the beast ran!"

Samantha wanted to sleep, needed it desperately, but the memories of the horror in her apartment lingered to haunt her. That awful man, she thought and shuddered, standing there watching her as though she were a specimen under a microscope. He wasn't there to murder her, it seemed, only to stare. Yet how was she supposed to know this? If she had, maybe she wouldn't have been so frightened.

Ramona Blattfield had graciously allowed Samantha to use the sofa in her apartment, which was puzzling in its own way. Ramona had a spare bedroom, but she kept the door closed and locked as though she had something to hide, or worse yet, as though someone was hiding in there. Samantha alternated between thinking about the experience in her apartment and watching the door to the spare bedroom.

She rose at one point and considered making another cup of tea. Ramona had told her to feel at home. And yet it was so late at night she was afraid the noise would wake Ramona. She lay down again and tried to force sleep, tried to force herself to enter the unconscious level of her dreams. Once there she intended to spend the rest of the night in the arms of her dream man—

A puff of smoke was coming from underneath the door to the locked bedroom!

She sat bolt upright and wondered if there was a fire. But she didn't smell smoke. Therefore it was dust . . . Had to be dust . .

Moving her way!

She dared not scream. Ramona was still trying to recover her nerves from the last time Samantha had screamed. Then what should she do, she wondered? But the answer was simple, she had to go to sleep. A funnel of dust couldn't hurt her and if she were locked in her dream man's arm she wouldn't be here awake watching it swirl above her head . . .

She was on his yacht in the middle of the Atlantic, headed for Bermuda. He was standing up front, at the bow of the ship, while she remained at the wheel. And his name wasn't Dirk or Lance or even Ron: it was Garrett; her original dream man. His long muscular tan frame caught her attention, as did his hazel eyes and the hint of gray flaring at his temples.

God, he was beautiful. He was everything she'd ever wanted in a man and more; he was perfection personified. She found herself wondering if he was ready, did he want her as badly as she wanted him? She wanted him so badly her insides were fluttering. But he'd said to wait because they weren't alone There were people below deck. What people? She hadn't seen them, hadn't noticed anyone coming aboard when she got on with Garrett.

Maybe they were already there; maybe they'd boarded earlier. She smiled, because that meant Garrett wasn't the loner he pretended to be.

Otherwise why would he have invited others to join them? And now that she'd accepted their presence on the yacht, when the hell was he going to ask them to leave?

"But, Samantha. I'm here to protect you," someone said, someone who was coming up the stairs in front of her. And when she looked she saw Detective Candeles followed by that funny little man, J.J. Holiman. "We're both here to help. Ron isn't around, and Garrett's gone."

She glanced at the bow of the ship and saw that it was so: Garrett had suddenly disappeared. Now where the hell did he go, she wondered? He couldn't be below. He would've had to pass her to get there. Maybe he fell overboard? But then she quickly dismissed the thought because he would've shouted for help and since he hadn't, he was still aboard. "What are you protecting me from?" she asked Candeles. "I'm not in any danger."

"Oh yes you are," said the little man known as J.J. "Just look behind you."

She didn't want to turn. She'd been through enough for one day. There was an awful creature in her apartment and then there was some floating, moving, breathing dust in Ramona's. Enough was enough. But someone was standing behind her. She felt breath, hot and stale and foul, on her neck. Something sharp came up against her back. A nail. Someone was poking her with their nails. But oh God, those nails were as sharp as razors. And someone behind her was giggling.

She turned despite her anxiety and was face to face with a hideous creature. She couldn't really see him because he was wearing a hood covering, but she knew he was hideous because of his hands. His nails resembled clawed talons. She stared at the hooded head while those clawed talons were raised up high and brought down with such sudden swiftness she barely had time to scream, had no time to move, couldn't stand the feel of her own blood running from a hole in her throat. . . .

Samantha woke up and held onto her head, letting her hands slide slowly down to examine her throat to see if the creature in her dreams had torn her throat open with his talons. But no, it didn't happen. Her throat was untouched. She sat up and swung her legs over the side of the sofa. She needed a cup of tea, something soothing to help her through the night. But she couldn't move. There was a huge ball of dust in front of her, blocking her path. And God help her, a face was staring at her from the center of that dust.

12

Samantha didn't scream. Either she was braver than she thought or the shock of seeing a face in the middle of a ball of dust was so unnerving she couldn't scream. That, coupled with the psycho who'd broken into her apartment, made her so upset she spent the rest of the night sitting in Ramona's kitchen drinking tea. The ball of dust didn't follow her there.

Ramona got up at half-past nine. Samantha heard her moving around in the bathroom and plugged in the coffee pot.

After a while, Ramona came and joined her in the kitchen, a perennial smile turning up the corners of her mouth. Samantha smiled back and said good morning, but didn't mention the dust or the face she'd seen in the midst of it. If Ramona was unaware of the strange creature living in her apartment, she might start to believe Samantha was crazy.

But then Ramona had to have seen it at least once. Otherwise why did she keep the door to her spare bedroom closed and locked? Didn't she know it would eventually float under the door and escape? Dust was hard to confine to one area, Samantha thought and smiled again.

"My, but you're in a good mood today, considering what you've been through. And you made coffee? How nice." Ramona poured herself a cup and stared off into space. "Strange how some tea drinkers start the day off with coffee," she said and automatically started to squeeze lemon juice into her cup.

"Don't!" Samantha said. Ramona was upset too; the smile on her face was a front. "It's bothering you too, isn't it?"

Ramona turned and stared at her and said nothing at first. She was biting her lower lip, and tears were misting her eyes. She carried her coffee back to the table and sat down, tracing an invisible design next to her cup with the finger of one hand. "Yes, it bothers me," she said quietly, then looked up into Samantha's face, her eyes dull with fear. "He got into your apartment! And even if that cop was right, and this is an imitator, he didn't do things quite the same. He isn't confining himself to that corridor downstairs. He's coming into our homes now."

Samantha felt awful, more for Ramona than herself. She'd already faced her ordeal and lived to tell about it. What if Ramona wasn't so lucky? The phone rang, shattering the stillness around them. Ramona looked at Samantha, rolled her eyes with impatience, and got up to answer it. "It's for you," she said, motioning for Samantha to take the receiver from her hand.

Who could this be, Samantha wondered? Nobody really knew she was here. "Hello?"

"Hello, dear." It was Garrett. "I understand

you went through a terrible ordeal last night. A Detective Candeles called a while ago. He gave me this number. I'm sorry I wasn't here when you needed me.

"It's all right, Garrett." Ron wasn't around either, she thought dully.

"Are you still planning to spend the weekend?" he asked, something anxious in his voice.

"Yes, I am. As a matter of fact, the reason Candeles called last night was because I was coming then—"

"Oh, God! I'm sorry."

"It's okay. You don't have to keep apologizing. You didn't know. I'm sure that if you knew I'd changed my mind, you would've been home."

"That's for sure. Anyway, I got lonely and went out for a ride alone, in my Excalibur. Drove around for hours. Normally my chauffeur's with me, but I left him in the city, at the disposal of my house guest."

"That would be J.J. Holiman?"

"How do you know his name?"

"He was here last night," she said and suddenly realized the tension had left her body. Speaking to Garrett was as good as taking a tranquilizer. "J.J. Holiman came to see me."

"I don't understand."

"He's helping Ron Wheatley with the murder investigations."

"Ron Wheatley! You know him too?"

Garrett was tense, his words strained. She didn't know how to answer: she certainly couldn't tell him she'd dated Ron. "He asked me a few questions about the murders."

"And?"

"That was it," she lied, not really wanting to,

but feeling it was better this way. Garrett sounded as though he didn't care for Ron Wheatley. "Was he a friend of yours once?"

"Yes. Over ten years ago. I don't bother with him now, though. But let's not discuss him anymore," he said, his mood picking up. "Let's talk about us. My chauffeur will be there shortly. J.J.'s coming along too. He had a nasty accident last night."

"Oh, I'm sorry to hear it. I hope he's all right?"

"You can't keep an old war horse like J.J. down for long. He's fine. Just banged up a bit as I understand it. Anyway, I'll say good-bye for now. And I'll see you in a few hours."

Samantha hung up and turned to Ramona. "He's the one I'm spending the weekend with," she said casually and was amazed by her own candidness. Ron Wheatley had opened the door to exploration and honesty. She was grateful for that much, even if he was a bastard!

"Good. I'm glad," Ramona said and smiled, really meaning it this time. "You're a young beautiful girl. You need the companionship of a good man."

Samantha had mixed emotions at this point. She hated the idea of leaving Ramona behind, alone and maybe at the mercy of the Bridge Gate Killer imitator. But then she remembered the face in the funnel of dust and knew Ramona would have plenty of company.

J.J. Holiman's heart was all aflutter; he was going to be spending the next few hours riding out to the Hamptons in the back seat of a limousine with the beautiful Samantha. While he was aware she'd never see anything in him due to the difference in their ages, he hoped they'd at least become friends. He'd never had a real close woman friend in his life.

Up until now the idea of remaining a bachelor had struck him as being a purely unselfish choice. But then he thought of Samantha again and was able to look back and see what a stupid mistake he'd made. He'd doomed himself to a lifetime of loneliness and probably would die the same way —alone.

J.J. had taken a shower and was gently toweling his body, avoiding the bruises he'd gotten in the park and then in the cathedral. He stepped in front of a mirror and noticed a mark on his shoulder that hadn't been there before last night. He leaned closer to the sink to get a better look at the damned thing. From far away it appeared to be a small, red welt with numbers on it. And that made him cringe.

"Dear. Lord," he prayed aloud, "Please let it be something else." But it was the same close up as it had been far away, and he wanted to die. Asgar did this to him, the foul son of a bitch, and probably when his guard had been down, when he'd been unconscious and unable to ask his Lord for His divine protection.

That was the only time Asgar could've succeeded, could've branded J.J. with the mark of the beast and gotten away with it. But then he realized that wasn't so. Even if he had been half dead, Asgar wouldn't have dared touch him if J.J. had a totally honest relationship with the Lord. The truth was, he doubted His existence at times. And that made J.J. the worst kind of fool possible. How many times did he have to witness a miracle; how many times did J.J. have to see a more than visible sign of the existence of a higher force to believe God was there?

Hadn't the Lord saved his life so often that he'd lost count? Hadn't the Lord stepped in when he'd been engaged in hand to hand battle with Asgar in that old boarding house for women that resembled Bridge Gate Court? He saved him then too. And so, his faith should've been unshakable. But it wasn't. It wasn't too solid during those good times when nothing bad happened and he was at peace with the world. Then he'd sit back and wonder if those miracles really happened or had they been nothing more than the figment of an over-active imagination?

He'd had the audacity to question the existence of the one Person who kept him sane and whole, and now he was paying for it. He saw a tiny circle dug into the red welt in his shoulder with three equally tiny sixes in the center of it and considered suicide.

Normally this mark meant you were one with Satan; a follower, a disciple and open to demon possession. But J.J. was a Christian. At the moment he felt the presence of the Lord inside of him despite the mark. So now what, he wondered? Would this make his lifelong struggle against the forces of darkness even worse than it was before? Would he have to fight against himself as well?

He wondered if he were the same person deep inside. Usually when he battled demonic forces, he filled his soul with love for his God and went into the battle knowing he was at peace with his Creator—at least he imagined he was. Now, however, since he'd been branded and cursed, how would he really feel in his heart, in his soul?

Would he tend to see things differently and find himself in sympathy with the demons? Oh, God, it was just too awful to think that way.

He examined his hands for the telltale signs of them changing into talons. Then he curled back his upper lip to see if his teeth had grown. The mark was more than just a sign of the brotherhood of Satan: it changed you in different ways. Provided of course you were evil to begin with. Perhaps being a Christian would help and the mark would remain as nothing more—just a mark, in line with a tattoo.

J.J. knew it was time to get dressed and ready to go pick up Samantha, beautiful Samantha . . . He suddenly realized he wanted to *fuck her brains out!* But would she have him? No! And just because he was old and she wanted her fill of young bucks. Well, he could still get it up when the mood struck him, so maybe he'd fuck her anyway and prove her wrong! Jump her bones and tease her until she begged him for it.

The chauffeur was downstairs when J.J. got there, and ran to hold the door and help him into the waiting limousine. J.J. thanked him courteously and watched through the rear window as the chauffeur put his suitcases into the trunk in back. J.J. had to admire the man because he was so conscientious about his work, always willing to go that extra yard; a quality not easily found in workers these days. At that point he figured he'd say something to Garrett, put in a good word; maybe earn the poor guy a raise.

Then he turned back to face the front of the limousine, snapping on Garrett's television to catch some of them quiz shows he never enjoyed before. But he couldn't concentrate on his program: his mind was still on the chauffeur and he kept thinking about what a sap-sucking, asshole the guy really was. Always shining up to this one and that one, brown nosing till it hurt. Well now, fuck him, he thought. J.J. had more important matters to think on, such as how he was grateful the mark of the beast hadn't changed him all that much.

Samantha had never been one to sit and wait for long. Even as a child, if she was alone and something had to be done, Samantha did it and to hell with everyone. Never mind that she was a female and needed somebody to lean on. Samantha had been born with one strike against her— *impatience*, which only naturally led to the second strike—*independence*.

She recalled the time when the urge to come to New York City had been a burning desire and her parents told her to wait, to sleep on it for a month or so. *Sleep on it, like hell,* she wanted to scream. *I can't wait, I've already made up my mind.* And so she packed her bags and left. She even walked the mile to the train station carrying a suitcase in each hand, because she couldn't wait for her father to drive her.

And now, as she was saying a temporary good-bye to Ramona and dragging her suitcase downstairs, she thought about that day and wondered how things would've gone if she'd waited for her father. He might've talked her into staying home. And perhaps she should've stayed. So far her life in New York was running parallel to her life at home. And so, all she did was run from one bad situation to another: from a rapist to a killer.

But he was dead, she reminded herself; the rapist was dead. There really had been no need to leave home. But there was a need to leave Ramona's apartment. That ball of dust, the one she didn't mention to Ramona, provided all of the *need* she'd ever need or want.

When the elevator reached the ground level, she glanced at her watch and realized how early she was: the chauffeur wouldn't be there for another half hour or so. A long time to wait. And what's the difference if she did her waiting upstairs or down? At least in Ramona's place she could sit and drink coffee and be comfortable.

And perhaps wait for the funnel of dust with the face in it to return? No way! She couldn't wait up there.

She stepped off the elevator, dragging her suitcase behind and wondered whether to wait in the hallway, or wait outside and stare at the park across the street? The park reminded her of her beloved woods back home, which in turn brought back unwanted memories of the rapist. Therefore it was best to wait inside.

Samantha was dragging her suitcase down to the front door when she made the mistake of peering into the corridor to her left, the one where most of the murders had taken place. But she was safe now; the killer was in jail. So there certainly was no harm in looking, since there was nothing to see. But there was.

A package was lying near the middle of the corridor, something wrapped in newspaper. Something neatly bundled and waiting for its owner to return. That should've been enough to make her continue on her way. But she walked into the corridor and kept her attention focused on the package, not wanting to think about the dimness ahead, or the murders, or anything unpleasant. She was really curious now and not about to turn back, so she kept her mind on a straight path and didn't let it wander. And yet it did, mainly because the package had such an odd shape to it.

It was long and narrow, but not too narrow. Could it have been a body part, one the murderer had dropped in his haste to leave? And yet, the whole idea was ridiculous. Why would the police leave it behind? But then the answer was simple: the police hadn't taken it because the murderer had wrapped this stolen body part in filthy newspaper. They probably assumed it was garbage left there by a lazy tenant for the super to dispose of, for Jose to carry out back where the cans were. But Jose was dead. The killer got him too.

Since she was more than satisfied with her 'lazy tenant' theory, and Jose was dead, she decided to carry the package out back to the cans herself. She bent to pick it up and tried not to think about how it felt—soft and stiff—about the same as a body part would feel after rigor mortis had set in. *Just carry the damn thing and keep your mind blank,* she reminded herself.

But something was jingling inside of the package . . .

Well, not jingling, actually more in line with *tinkling* . . .

June's charm bracelet had tinkled. And she was dead too, along with Jose.

The package suddenly became a hot potato in her hands and she dropped it. It fell to the ground with a sickening thud, and the package split, revealing its contents. Tiny white maggots were threading their way in and out of the flesh where the arm had been severed from the body. There was a charm bracelet down near the hand. The fingernails were long: had been painted red. It was June's arm!

Samantha stepped back and screamed and screamed and screamed.

Ron Wheatley was in the station house when the call came: a woman was screaming down in the corridor of Bridge Gate Court. He grabbed his jacket and ran to his car, turning on the sirens after placing a hand-held flasher on top. This was a code three, which called for sirens and flashing lights.

All the way over to Central Park West he tried to force himself to remember that the killer was in jail and nothing could've happened. But it wasn't easy, especially after what took place last night when he and the beast had been one again, when he and the beast had performed a ceremony in the woods, when he and the beast had killed a young punk rocker.

Then again, he wondered if it were true. Had it all taken place exactly as he saw it, or had he been dreaming? Because if it wasn't a dream, then he was going through one of those psychic experiences J.J. Holiman had mentioned, and that was a terrible thing to face. The very word 'psychic' lent an air of credence to his imaginings. In other words, it really happened as he saw it. Everything about last night was true and they had the wrong man in jail and now this woman was screaming!

* * *

Samantha was half-hysterical and still crying when Ron reached her side. The sight of her seemed to throw him off balance at first. But then, when he recovered he took her in his arms and thanked God she was still alive. What happened, he wanted to know? She told him about the arm and he held her even tighter.

But she was still angry with him. He had no right to be so affectionate, wanting her with the passions that he did. And yet, when his arms enfolded her body she caved in and had to fight to keep from remembering his tenderness—the way he made love to her, the way he awakened her own passions and made her whole again.

As he held her, he brushed her neck with his lips and she moaned involuntarily, forgetting her panic and nausea. But it was no good; Candeles had told her he was married. And so Ron had no right doing this, and she, Samantha, had no right being so responsive. Damn his wife, she cursed inwardly! And damn him too, for making her love him!

"What are you doing down here? This corridor is dangerous. It's so dark—"

"I saw something. A package. And it made me curious."

"You know what they say about curiosity," he said, pulling a mini transmitter from his back pocket. After pushing a button, he spoke into the mike while she listened. "Headquarters . . . This is Detective Ron Wheatley. I answered the call at Bridge Gate . . . Yeah . . . Nothing serious. I can handle it. No back-ups are needed." Then he pocketed the transmitter and started to embrace her again when something made him stop and look back over his shoulder. "That suitcase. Is it yours?'' he wanted to know.

He seemed so down in his attitude: Samantha felt sorry for him until she remembered his wife. Then the 'get even' side of her personality took over and she smiled. ''Yes. It's mine.''

He stepped back and concentrated on the tile floor beneath his feet. ''You're going away? Isn't this kind of sudden?''

''Yes it is,'' she said, amazed at the coldness in her voice.

''Do you wanna tell me why? I mean, yesterday when I asked you about going away for a few days you couldn't. You had too much work on your desk. And now . . .'' He looked at her, and she saw something depressing in his gaze.

''You asked me once and I said no. Had you asked again I would've said yes.''

''Oh God, Samantha! I wanted to give you time to get used to me before asking again. That's all. I was the first man in your life, and I wanted you to feel comfortable with me. You make it sound as though the only reason I asked was to get you to go to bed with me.''

''Well, didn't you?''

''No!'' he answered quickly, then he sighed and spoke again, only his voice was softer, almost pleading. ''Honey,'' he said, his hands touching her shoulders, ''Believe this: You mean a lot to me. You did when I made love to you, and you do now. I never used you. In fact, I think I'm falling in love with you.''

Samantha brushed his hands away, although deep inside she didn't really want to. And yet, she had no choice. She was decent, she was moralistic, and as such, she could never be the other woman in his life. ''You have no right to fall in love with me! Not when you're married!''

His face dropped; he looked like he'd been slapped. He didn't ask her how she knew. Rather he stepped aside and watched her walk toward the front of the corridor. ''May I ask who you're going away with? Or will you be alone?''

''I won't be alone,'' she shouted back over her shoulder. Then she turned and seized the opportunity to lash out at him once more. After all, Garrett Lang had recognized Ron's name this morning on the phone and he obviously disliked Ron. Therefore, Ron had to feel the same way about Garrett. ''I'm spending the weekend with Garrett Lang!'' Gauging from the expression on his face, her words had cut him to the bone. She felt satisfied.

''Miss Croft?''

She turned and saw a man dressed in a uniform, and assumed it was Garrett's chauffeur. ''Yes. I'm Miss Croft,'' she said, enjoying this because Ron was suffering now, the same way she'd suffered last night when she discovered he was married.

''Mr. Lang sent me. I heard you mention his name.'' Then he looked down at the suitcase next to his feet. ''Is this yours?''

''Samantha! Please don't!'' Ron yelled.

But she ignored him and nodded to the chauffeur. ''I'll take this to the car,'' he said, and picked up the suitcase. Samantha followed him.

After she was gone, Ron balled up a fist and struck the nearest wall. ''Damn you, Garrett! You won again, you bastard!'' He cringed from the pain, but somehow he couldn't stop cursing Garrett. ''You got the money and now you've got my girl . . . You fucker. And you don't need her, you can have anyone you want. Why Samantha?''

"Are you all right, mister?"

He turned and saw a group of tenants watching him, his insides flipping from the embarrassment. They'd heard every word. Then he got angry. Where the hell were they a while back when Samantha was screaming? Hadn't he found her alone and helpless? And now, now when it was all over, now they come down here! The cowardly bastards. "Yeah. I'm fine," he muttered and picked up the arm.

He was about to wrap it up, to hide the gruesome disgusting thing from the tenants, who weren't used to such things. But then he thought about getting some instant revenge for their cowardice, for what it might've cost Samantha had the killer been here himself and not this arm. And he turned and displayed it while they froze in silence. "She screamed because she found this! The killer left it behind." Then he walked down the hall towards them, forgetting the pain in his hand, smiling while they shouted protests and scattered. "You all have a good day now, you hear?"

After taking the arm to the police lab downtown he went home. He needed time to think, to lay out his plans; he wasn't about to let Samantha go without a fight. Garrett was rich and charming: not an easy man to take on. But he was willing to do it for Samantha. She was a prize worthy of a good battle.

Debbie wasn't in the bedroom when he got home. He went through the house calling her name and was amazed to find her out back on the patio in her wheelchair. She's finally decided to join the world of the living, he thought, and wondered why she'd gotten out of bed. But he didn't question her because she looked depressed. And if she was depressed, he didn't care to know why. Her constant whining and nagging were doing a number on him.

Ignoring the expression on her face, he brushed her cheek with his lips, smiled and said good morning. But she didn't smile back. And in a way he couldn't blame her. Debbie didn't have too much to be happy about these days; although he still hoped she'd keep her feelings to herself.

"I made some coffee," she said, "It should be done now."

"Where's the housekeeper?" She couldn't have done this alone, gotten into her chair, made coffee.

"I told her to take the day off."

"Why?"

"Because we have to talk. You and me. I let her go because I had a feeling you'd be home early."

Maybe the trauma they'd both experienced two years before had left her psychic as well, he thought, and went on into the kitchen where he found the coffee and some fresh danish. He made up a tray, filling it with two coffee cups, a pitcher of cream and enough pastry for the both of them. Then he went back outside and tried to smile at her, tried to lift her spirits because he did owe her in terms of emotional support for what he'd done, even if it was an accident.

But she wasn't having any of this, she was down and depressed and couldn't be brought out of it. "Your lawyer called today. We're getting a divorce!"

Ron nearly dropped the tray. His hands were still shaking when he laid it on the table beside her. "What?" he said.

"It's the only way to get additional aid from the government. . . ." She let her voice trail off, put her head into her hands and cried. Ron went to her, wrapping his arms around her shoulders, but his body was stiff and unresponsive and she must've felt it too. She broke away and faced him again. "I know you probably don't love me at this point," she said, "And I can't blame you."

"Debbie, listen." It was true: he didn't love her. But she was sick, too sick for him to allow her to accept the truth. He had to lie. "I—"

"No, Ron. I won't listen. I have the floor now. I want you to file for a divorce. I've read about this in the papers. And you probably have too. About how there's a married couple and one of them becomes handicapped and the government won't supply the necessary funding to help them. Do you remember that woman who had cancer? Remember the one with the six kids? Remember how her medical bills and such were taking her husband for broke? He had to divorce her so that she'd qualify for government aid."

He listened to her and felt dead inside. He wanted Samantha and he wanted his freedom. But now that both things were being handed to him—for surely Samantha would change her mind if he was no longer married—now that he was getting his way, it was like a knife through his heart. He couldn't do this to his wife, not after what he did to her two years ago. "Debbie, I know what you're saying is true. But there has to be another way."

"There isn't. And I want to tell you something.

About the shooting—"

"I don't wanna discuss it," he said and started to walk out, but she stopped him.

"It was my fault!"

He stood by the frame of the door and stared into the house for a long time before it sank in: she was taking the blame for being crippled. But why?

"Think about what happened that day."

"I can't." He was crying now. But she didn't give in, didn't soften her tone or her attitude.

"We were walking in the woods and I was full of complaints, as usual."

"You were cold and tired."

"Bullshit! Ron, listen. At this point I've had nothing but time on my hands. Time to think. Time to go over it in my mind. And I know the truth even if you can't see it. So let's go over it again. Just once more to clear you of the guilt you've been carrying for the past two years."

"Do we have to do this now?" he wanted to know. Either she was about to convince him he'd done nothing wrong, or else it would backfire and he'd feel more guilty than ever. He couldn't face it, couldn't take any more.

"Just listen. I was full of complaints as usual. Remember, Ron, I was forever complaining about something or other? It's called wanting your own way. I was determined to make you miserable for dragging me up there to the Adirondacks in the middle of winter. I mean, you were a bastard in my eyes for taking me someplace where I'd be cold and where I'd have to walk.

"I didn't want to go and I should've resisted and stayed home. But then I couldn't complain and that would've robbed me of the opportunity to manipulate you a bit more."

"Manipulate me?" He couldn't believe he was hearing this. But she nodded and he knew it was so. "You were trying to control me through manipulation?"

"Always," she said and continued. "Well, I was full of complaints and I wouldn't do a thing you asked me to without a fight. Such as wearing that orange jacket, even though I knew in my heart and soul that you were right about the jacket. It would've been safer to wear.

"Besides, it was probably a lot heavier than the brown one I was wearing. And you could've thrown that in my face. You could've told me to shut up about being cold. That if I were properly dressed I wouldn't feel cold. But you didn't. Instead, you acted as you normally did under those circumstances—you kept quiet and tolerated my abuse."

"I loved you very much."

"I know you did, Ron. And I took advantage of your love. But then it seems to follow a pattern with me. I did the same thing to my parents, used their love to control them. But, getting back to that day in the woods. If I'd been wearing the orange jacket, you would've known it was me when I crossed over behind you and entered the bushes from the other side. You would've known it was me if I'd said something about changing positions from one side of the road to the other."

He was beginning to get the point. She was right. Analyzing it from her point of view, it was her fault. And yet, she'd let him carry the guilt for two years or more. "Why didn't you say something when you crossed the road? You make it sound as though you kept quiet on purpose."

She sighed heavily and acted as though she wanted to stop now. But then he saw her body stiffen and she went on. "I did keep quiet on purpose."

"Debbie!"

"It was another way of controlling you. Never let him know what you're thinking. Make him ask. Make him beg. In other words, you were inferior to me and speaking to you voluntarily was lowering myself. You weren't worthy of my thoughts. And now, here we are. Me in a chair, an obvious cripple, and you—you don't sit in a chair, Ron, but I've made you a cripple too."

"Oh, God," he said and fell at her feet, burying his head in her lap, crying to release the tension he'd felt all along.

She brushed the back of his head and spoke again. "A few weeks ago I even enticed you into bed, knowing I wouldn't enjoy it. But I had to. You weren't getting it at home. And that was my way of keeping you from other women. But you're free now. I'm letting you go because what happened to me was my own fault. A case of manipulation that backfired."

He listened and said nothing, but continued to cry in her lap. It was her fault! That phrase went through his mind a dozen times before the guilt he'd harbored began to lift. And she was setting him free! But it was too late. He'd already lost Samantha to Garrett because he was married. And now that he was getting a divorce, Samantha wouldn't accept him, not really. She'd hate him even more. She'd never understand that Debbie wanted it this way. That Debbie was the one setting him free. At this point, the victory was a hollow one.

"Hey, sailor," Debbie said, to cheer him up. "How's about we go to bed just once more for old times sake? You know, as if nothing were wrong between us and we were still lovers?"

He looked up at her, wondering if this was another one of her attempts to manipulate him. And while he would've liked nothing more, he could't say yes. He didn't trust Debbie, not after she'd told him the truth about herself and about the accident. "No, I think I'll pass," he said. "You want some more coffee?"

13

Morgan Housner stood in front of Bridge Gate Court with her Charlie and made endless promises. Charlie hadn't wanted her to come back here ever because of the Bridge Gate Killer. But now the killer was in jail and Morgan wanted to come back this one last time to collect her things and to tell Samantha she was getting married.

"I promise, honey," she said, "I'll just pack and leave. If Samantha isn't home, I'll write her a note. Can I give her your phone number? I mean, it's unlisted and all—"

"Hey, skinny, it's soon to be *our* home phone number. Samantha's your best friend. Give it to her. Now what else?"

He sounded as though he were speaking to a child. But Morgan didn't mind. Charlie could baby her until the day she died and she still wouldn't mind. "Okay," she said, "I'm to make sure I have everything so I never have to come back here. I'm to call you in one hour to let you know that I'm okay. And when I'm finished I'm to call you to come and get me."

"Right so far. But you forgot something, didn't you?"

"I didn't forget. I'll never forget. I'm to remember always how much you love me." When he bent to kiss her, she let go and melted in his arms. Weeks ago Charlie had shown her how to give of herself—completely and with nothing held back. He helped her to shove her father's craziness to the back of her mind and be his, in her heart and in her soul.

When he stopped kissing her, Charlie glanced up at the facade of Bridge Gate Court and something in his face told her he was troubled. "I'd better take you up to the door. Maybe stay with you while you pack."

"Don't be silly," she said and smiled. "I'm safe —it's daytime. Even if the killer wasn't in jail, he only struck at night, remember?"

"Yeah. Well. . . ."

But he didn't sound convinced and he had to let her do this alone. Men had no patience when it came to packing. With Charlie there she'd forget half of everything. She spotted Ramona Blattfield coming down the street in their direction and figured this was a way out. "Hi, Ramona," she said and smiled. "Wait for me. I'll ride up with you." Then she turned back to Charlie, "She's my next door neighbor. I'll be safe with her."

"Yeah. Two women together."

She sighed in exasperation and gave in. "Okay! Take me upstairs if you must. But then you have to leave. I can't pack with you around. Deal?"

"Deal!"

"I'm so happy to see you back. And with such a nice young man at your side," Ramona said on the way up. Charlie smiled politely and waited for

Morgan to tell her the good news, that they were getting married. But Ramona didn't give her a chance to say a thing. "Samantha has a fellow, too. She left a while ago, with her suitcase. To spend the weekend with him."

"Samantha?" Morgan was astonished. While she knew Samantha had a boy-friend, she didn't know they'd reached the sleeping-together stage. "This is my roommate we're talking about? She's gone to spend the weekend with a man? Did she say who he was?"

"Oh, yes. His name is Garrett Lang—"

"Garrett Lang!" Charlie blurted. "You're kidding."

"You know him?" Morgan asked.

"Well, yeah. Not personally, but I know of him. He's rich, even more so than me. Hell, Morgan, we're talking a great deal of wealth here! And Samantha bagged him?"

Morgan couldn't believe she was hearing this. It had taken Samantha a long time to get started; she was a late bloomer and all that, but once she got her act together . . . "How old is he?" she asked, hoping he wasn't on his way out.

"He's in his mid-thirties. So he hasn't got one foot in the grave and the other on grease. Good for your girl friend. Maybe that'll relieve you of most of the guilt and anxiety you've felt over leaving her alone once we're married—"

"You're getting married!" Ramona shouted and grabbed Morgan, holding her in a gentle bear hug. "Oh, I'm so happy for you!" Then they parted and she studied Morgan's face with an air of seriousness. "Now we've got to start working on Samantha. She's got to get married too. Nobody should be alone. And if he's rich, that's good!"

* * *

Morgan waited until she was alone in the apartment before she'd allow her thoughts to wander to Samantha and her new beau. Oh God, but it was wonderful to know she wasn't deserting her roommate. And best of all, Samantha had gone and gotten herself a real catch, so that made it even better.

She went into her bedroom and into her walk-in closet to take a fast inventory. Most of her clothing was still usable. But there were a few items she could part with. Like those old blouses she'd mainly kept to wear around the apartment and go shopping in. She picked one off the rack and looked at it closely. This wouldn't do; Charlie was fussy about the way she dressed.

Hadn't he told her on the way over here to throw it all away and buy new at his expense? And yet, she wasn't about to take advantage of Charlie and his good nature by taking him for broke—

The doorbell rang then and she glanced at her watch. Barely half an hour had passed since Charlie dropped her off. Was he back so soon? Did he miss her this much? She ran and opened the door, all the while knowing she should've asked first, should've made sure it was Charlie. . . .

"Oh, I see you're finally back! You and your pig boyfriend must've gotten tired of one another—"

"Daddy! What the hell are you doing here?"

"Daddy?" He pushed his way into the apartment and slammed the door behind him. "Daddy?" he repeated, his mouth drawn into a thin cold smile. "I thought I told you to call me Phil!"

"I can't," she said and turned away from him. "You're my fa—" She couldn't finish. He grabbed her and spun her around so quickly she was left in shock. From the expression on his face she was afraid he was going to hit her. "What? Was it something I said?"

"I'm not your father anymore, little girl. You just remember that. You've come of age and you owe me—"

"But, Daddy—" She stopped when he raised his hand and struck her across the side of the face. "Oh, God," she moaned.

"Don't call on Him for help. Not now. It's too late for help, honey. Like I said, you owe me. You killed my wife—"

"But I didn't mean to. Mommy died giving birth to me, but it wasn't my fault. I didn't kill her on purpose." Her mind drifted back to her childhood: she was the lady of the house, groomed for an aristocratic marriage. Manners were important, and the way you carried yourself, that was important too. She was taught how to dress, how to speak, when to speak. Protocol was important: ambassadors were never seated next to movie stars. She wondered if the people who taught her knew they were grooming her for marriage with her own father!

"You killed my wife," he repeated, ignoring her objections, "And I'm here to collect!"

"I can't marry you. This is insane!" He raised his hand to strike her again, but didn't. Instead he grabbed her roughly by the shoulders and forced her to look directly into his eyes.

"I'm not speaking about marriage in the normal sense of the word," he said, his voice softer this time. "I found someone who'll perform a

269

ceremony—"

"What!"

"Yes, Morgan. A mock ceremony, but a marriage ceremony just the same. Of course, it won't be recognized by law, but we'll know it's just as real."

He was holding her shoulders gently now, looking at her the same way so many men had in the past. He wanted her. "And what if we were to live as man and wife . . . and had *children?*" She thought that might wake him up, if anything could at this point.

"So? That'll be great! I'd like to have kids. A son maybe."

Her stomach turned and she had to fight to keep from throwing up. "When, Da—Phil? When will we be married?"

"In a few days. Just as soon as I set things up. And to make sure that you don't run away again, I'm staying here until after the ceremony. I know Samantha won't mind."

Samantha! She suddenly remembered that Samantha had gone away and wasn't due back until Monday. This was awful: at least if Samantha were here she'd talk sense to Phil. Samantha was intelligent and had a way with words. When the phone rang behind her, she felt her heart jump with joy and hoped it was Samantha. But it wasn't, it was Charlie, poor Charlie. And Phil was crazy so Charlie couldn't come here. Phil would wind up killing him.

"The packing. It's taking longer than I expected it to," she lied.

"Well then throw it all away. I'll get you new stuff. No use agonizing over what to keep—"

"And besides," she continued, interrupting

him, wondering if he heard the dullness in her voice. "There's more to be taken care of than I thought."

"Such as?" He was losing his temper and she couldn't blame him.

"Well, Samantha just called. She's not coming back either. I have to break up the apartment."

"Oh, for—"

"Please. It's only for a few days. . . ." She let her words trail. Phil was listening and she couldn't go on.

"Is this what you want?" He asked, something anxious in his voice.

"Yes."

"You're not just putting me off because you've changed your mind and you don't want to marry me?"

"No. Don't be silly."

"Okay, skinny . . . Have it your way. Do what you have to if it makes you happy." His mood was on an upswing now. "And I'll tell you what. I'll even leave you alone so you can do your thing in peace and quiet. But only until Monday or so. Then I'm coming up to get you. Finished or not. Okay?"

"Okay." After he'd hung up she turned to face Phil and wanted to die. He'd taken his clothes off. Oh, God, she thought, he can't be serious.

"Now for a bit of prenuptial sex. You put on a few pounds, kid. You look great."

She'd done it for Charlie: had eaten herself ten pounds heavier because Charlie took the fear from her heart. He'd told her to relax; Phil wouldn't win this time. Morgan followed Phil's lead to her bedroom, grateful that he hadn't asked about the person on the phone. Because then she would've had to tell him about Charlie and about how they'd almost gotten married . . .

Samantha rode all the way out to the Hamptons next to J.J. Holiman, the peculiar little man who'd walked into her life the night before. And now, he was even acting more peculiar if possible. 'J.J. Holiman was his name. Demonology was his game.' And the way he kept leering at her. Well, she thought, at least he wasn't giving her time to dwell on finding June's arm, or time to dwell on that awful scene with Ron.

When at last the chauffeured limousine pulled into a hidden driveway in the woods, she was amazed to look ahead and see high wrought iron gates. Cold, steel-gray, and uninviting, they reminded her of a prison. There was a guard shack as well, complete with armed guards.

She looked beyond the gates, beyond the guard shack and saw the mansion that was Garrett's home, and it took her breath away. It was like a two-story hotel: white, brick-faced and elegant. Tall, marble, Georgian-style columns stood guard on the upper stairs of the house—she counted three levels of stairs in all leading to the main entrance—strategically placed lest anyone dare attempt to enter unseen.

After passing through the guard shack and staring at the uniformed guards with their holstered guns, she looked ahead again and saw a man waiting on the road to greet them. It had to be Garrett, she knew, and felt warm inside, her heart pounding heavily with anxiety. The limousine traveled along a white brick road, bordered on both sides by luxurious gardens.

Stone benches and statues were scattered here and there.

"Ain't this living?" J.J. Holiman wanted to know. "Garrett says he has a swimming pool out back and a tennis court."

She smiled despite herself and wondered why Garrett invited him along for the weekend. He was becoming a nuisance in every sense of the word.

"Sam," Garrett said, brushing her face with his lips once she was beside him, "I'm so glad you're here." Then he gently squeezed her body close to his for emphasis.

"Oh Garrett, I missed you," she said, hoping she wasn't being too forward. But she was glad to see him after what had happened to her these past few days. Unable to control herself, she trembled involuntarily.

"I guess you're still upset over last night, and I can't blame you. Please try to relax. I've got you now and nothing bad can hurt you. I won't let it."

She looked up at him and half smiled. "At least you didn't say 'I told you so.'"

He smiled as well and put his head down against her shoulder for a moment. "Right! About the killer changing his 'modus operandi' and breaking into apartments." Then he laughed and looked straight into her face, his hazel eyes flaring with passion. "It's impossible to bawl you out because you did what you thought was right. I'm just happy you're here to talk about—"

"Garrett, my boy."

They both turned at the same time to see J.J. Holiman struggling to get out of the limousine. Samantha felt Garrett's body stiffen next to hers;

273

she looked up at him and watched his face go pale with horror. Then he suddenly pulled away from her and hurried to help J.J.

My God, you're a mess," Garrett said. "Just look at you. What the hell did you have an accident with, a Mack truck?"

After lunch, Garrett invited Samantha to take a walk with him in the woods bordering the grounds of his mansion. She was unsettled by the idea because of what happened in those woods back home. But she said yes. J.J. had gone up to his room to take a nap, so she knew they'd be alone, she and Garrett; then she marveled at how much she'd changed in the past month. She wasn't frightened by the idea of being alone with Garrett.

And yet, she couldn't take credit for the change, not when it belonged to Ron Wheatley. Ron had shown her a different side of the coin by proving that a relationship between a man and a woman didn't necessarily have to be associated with force and violence. And so, she felt more than ready for whatever might happen with Garrett.

"You have a beautiful house," she said as they walked hand in hand down a path leading into the heart of the woods.

"I think it's nice."

Samantha laughed. "Just nice? Garrett! It's the most gorgeous, beautiful, wondrous thing I've ever seen."

He smiled and turned to look at her but kept walking. "And I think you're the most gorgeous, beautiful, wondrous thing I've ever seen."

She blushed and said thank you and felt warm inside. Garrett had such a way with words. But then this was no different from her dreams, when he was her dream man. "Do you own this property too?" she asked, referring to the woods they were walking in.

"Yes. I bought it to insure my privacy. But somehow privacy isn't important since I met you. There's no satisfaction in being alone anymore."

"I know what you mean," she said, glancing sideways at his face, at the gray flaring at his temples. "I used to enjoy being alone too, doing things my way. But now, it's awful. And now, when I'm alone, all I can think of is you." And Ron as well, she thought, if she were to be honest with herself.

"Oh, Sam," he said and stopped walking. "It's wonderful to hear you say those words. That you missed me as much as I missed you." He put his arms around her waist, pulling her closer. She raised her head to look into his face, his eyes, and spotted the trees above: it was the same view she'd had when the rapist was doing his thing. He felt her stiffen. "Please don't be afraid of me. I won't hurt you, Sam."

He bent down and kissed her, his lips soft and gentle, a whisper of passion in the wind. She moaned involuntarily when he increased the pressure, his kiss becoming more in line with a demand for satisfaction. Soft, spring breezes blew against their bodies as they were locked in the embrace of lovers.

She felt the breeze swirling down by her legs and stiffened again: she was wearing a dress—had been wearing one the day she was raped. Garrett felt her coldness and stopped kissing her. "Please Sam. I won't hurt you. I just want to make love to you here in these woods. Where everything is alive and beautiful. I thought it would be special for both of us.''

She tightened her grip on his neck and forced herself to be responsive. This was Garrett Lang, not a rapist with a ski mask covering his face. Garrett took her cue and kissed her again, gently forcing her lips apart to taste the savory nectar of her mouth, while gently forcing her lower torso close to his so that she could feel the swell of his manhood. Then he moaned and ran his tongue across hers, across her lips, across her neck, and began to carve maddening circles into her heated flesh.

When he started to lower her body to the ground, she didn't resist. There was a wonderfully warm sensation of grass against her back as Garrett lay down next to her and kissed her again, his hands working magic on her body. Starting with her breasts, he cupped one gently before enclosing it with his palms, massaging it through the fabric of her dress, driving her crazy, making her long for the feel of his hand against her naked flesh. Then he moved to her other breast and began again, heavy moaning sounds coming from deep within his throat as he did.

She wanted to die from sheer frustration when his hand deserted her breasts and wandered down across her stomach to her abdomen. He was taking so long, dragging it out when she knew what was coming next. She'd gone through this so many times in her dreams, and she was ready for fulfillment *now*. She felt him lifting her skirt, rubbing his hand along her inner thighs and she became more responsive than ever, her lower torso moving in rhythm with her passion. When at last he tugged gently at the leg of her briefs and touched the naked flesh beneath, she moaned and wanted this to go on forever, to never stop.

She helped him when he tried to remove her panties. And she helped him when he tugged at the zipper of his own pants. She was burning inside, as much as she'd been burning when he'd made love to her in her dreams. She touched him, felt his hardness and moaned again. Garrett moved on top of her, his manhood gently penetrating her body. Oh God, she thought, he was better than Ron. But it hurt too, because he was bigger than Ron, bigger than the rapist . . .

Rising and falling, the lovers forgot their inhibitions, forgot that they were out in the open woods, forgot everything but what was happening at present. At one point Garrett rolled, pulling her on top of him, holding onto her lower back, holding her body tightly against his. She moaned and felt she would explode before this was over. And when at last it was and they chuddered, caught in the throes of orgasm, she had to fight to keep from screaming.

"I love you, Sam," was all he could say afterwards as she lay on top of him, her head nestled gently against his chest. And although she wanted to respond, to say something equally as nice, she couldn't: not when her breath was coming in short spurts and she knew she must surely be dead. Nothing this wonderful could happen in real life. And it was about to happen again. Garrett wasn't finished; she could feel him growing inside of her, could feel his passion reawakening.

J.J. Holiman had an obstructed view of the lovers in the woods from the second floor window of the guest bedroom—obstructed by those damned trees, but he saw them nonetheless. He stood and watched for a while, aware that he had the same thing in mind when it came to Samantha, then went back to the bed and lay down, an erection swelling the lower part of his pants. When he realized it was there, he knew he had to face facts.

There was something wrong with him, something twisted in that area of his brain that controlled his emotions. Something had gone wrong. He wasn't using his head; nothing he said or did made sense. And he knew it as sure as he knew his name. Why just look at the way he'd made a horse's ass of himself in front of Samantha during their trip out here to the Hamptons. 'J.J. Holiman is my name. Demonology is my game.' Now he wished he'd died before he'd said it. What an idiot.

Besides, it wasn't like him to reveal his secrets to others, especially when he barely knew them. As a rule he aimed for anonymity, keeping his identity as well as his chosen vocation from the world. Of course he'd tell anyone who asked what he did for a living that he was a professor of economics at a small college upstate. But that was as far as it went. Because when it came to the other, the demonology, he kept it a secret.

Had to keep it a secret; you never knew who you were talking to.

What if he were to reveal his identity to a coven member by accident, or worse yet, to the high priest of a coven? He'd be dead meat, hunted down and killed by insane Satanists. Then too, the possibility of revealing himself to a demon disguised as a human beat everything else to hell and back. Why the son-of-a-bitch would have old

J.J. dead and buried before he was able to blink twice. So, like it or not, he had to live with his secrets. He had no choice.

And yet, he'd never had any qualms about his profession when speaking to the police. After all, he was there to help, and he couldn't if he wasn't completely honest. The officers he worked with had a right to know why he was getting himself involved in their murder investigations. Otherwise, how could he convince them that a demon was responsible? The only way possible was to tell them, 'I'm so and so and this is what I've devoted the better part of my life to.'

And after that, after he explained things as they were, they mostly welcomed him with open arms. But speaking to the police and speaking to an average person, one he knew nothing about, was two different things entirely.

And yet, only this morning, with Samantha in that limo, he ran his mouth off like he never had before. That alone showed him he wasn't thinking clearly. And there was more, it hadn't stopped there. Just a few moments ago when he'd caught Samantha and Garrett screwing—*No*, when he caught them *making love* out there in the woods— instead of being embarrassed about watching them, he became aroused instead and wanted to change places with Garrett! And too, the phrase he'd just used—*screwing*—well, it just wasn't part of his normal, everyday vocabulary when it came to lovers.

Degenerates screwed, not people in love.

What was happening to him? Was it the mark of the beast that was responsible for this change in him? He was confused and troubled. But only partly so because deep down inside of him the answer was fighting for a way out: he was one with the brotherhood of Satan. And as such, he had to fight even harder to keep himself on a straight path. He had to pray to his God for the needed strength to fight this thing in him, this demon within. He had to beg his God for forgiveness for doubting His existence and ask that the punishment be lifted.

And then he had to approach Samantha and apologize for acting like a fool this morning . . . No, he had to jump her bones and fuck her to death! When the thought entered his head, he tried to keep it away, tried to keep it from completing itself. But he couldn't; couldn't stop it. At that point his whole body began to shake, and the bed beneath him as well. He became frightened, more so than he'd ever been in his life, especially when he looked down and saw that his lower torso was vibrating in the violent rhythm of passion gone mad. "Dearest, Lord," he shouted, "Please help me. Please! Don't let this demon win the battle."

Ron Wheatley waited until Debbie was back in bed before he allowed anything to sink in. Then he sat in front of the television, picture on, sound off, and went back over it in his mind. Debbie said she was responsible for the accident. And while he didn't think so at the time, she proved it by telling him things about herself that he'd somehow managed to overlook up until now.

And yet, even now, even after she'd confessed everything, he still couldn't accept the truth: that Debbie had spent her whole life manipulating those she loved. And she manipulated him! She caused the accident herself, then waited two years to confess. The bitch! How could you do that to someone you professed to love with all your heart and all your soul and all your might? How could she?

And her lies cost him Samantha, because to him, hiding the truth was the same as lying. Whether you told an outright fabrication or kept everything hidden, it didn't matter. Lying was lying.

Ron picked up the phone on the coffee table and dialed headquarters, asking for Candeles' cousin when the desk sergeant answered on the other end. Candeles had a cousin on the force who was worth his weight in gold, and who readily accepted gold, in the form of cash or greenbacks, for various favors rendered. Ron wanted Garrett's phone number and Garrett's number was unlisted. Well hell, no problem. He'd get it from Candeles' cousin. Otherwise, how would he be able to speak to Samantha and tell her . . . what?

That Debbie had lied to him and he'd soon be a free man? Or maybe he'd tell Samantha he loved her and he wanted her to leave Garrett's side as soon as possible? Or perhaps he wouldn't tell her anything. Perhaps he'd just sort of act as though he needed someone to talk to. Then he'd speak to her with a sort of depressed inflection in his voice, sort of heap on the guilt.

At this point, Ron was willing to try anything, to do whatever it took to get her away from Garrett and back into his arms where she belonged.

Garrett was lying in bed reading the stock reports. It was late afternoon, too early to be in bed. But after making love to Samantha twice in rapid succession that day his legs were weak and shaky and he was a bit tired.

Samantha was standing in front of the window peering out at the woods, thinking about the ecstasy she'd experienced in Garrett's arms, the shower they'd taken together after coming back to the house, how they'd washed each other's bodies with pleasure. Something was bothering her, though. Something about those woods made her uneasy.

True, they reminded her of the woods back home and that led to memories of the rapist. But it was more than just the memory of her past that disturbed her at this point. She couldn't put her finger on the problem except that she was sure there was something unsettling about these particular woods.

"Penny for your thoughts, beautiful baby," Garrett said behind her, and she felt her skin crawl. Beautiful baby! he called her that once in her dreams!

"I was just staring at the woods and thinking about how wonderful it was a while back," she said, telling a downright lie. Telling the truth would've been awkward; about how something was bothering her and she didn't know what.

"It was wonderful, wasn't it? Come here and give me a kiss to show how much you appreciate me. It was hard getting it up twice in a row, if you'll excuse the pun."

She turned to look at him, anger welling up inside because he was talking dirty, but he was also smiling so she couldn't stay mad. Garrett was doing nothing more than speaking to her with familiarity, as lovers often did. Samantha had to learn to lose her thin-skinned attitude and enter the world of grown-ups. "If you weren't such an animal," she said, "it never would've happened."

"Oh! Now I'm an animal, am I? Hell, just a while ago I was 'Garrett dearest.' Now I'm an animal. So. Come here and kiss the animal and say thank you."

She burst out laughing. He really had a good sense of humor. She walked over to him, arms outstretched, mouth puckered in an exaggerated way, and was about to kiss him when the phone rang, startling them both. Garrett reached over and picked it up, his face dropping when he got to his feet and handed it to her. "It's for you," he said dryly. "It's a man."

Samantha couldn't imagine who it was. She started to say hello when Garrett interrupted with, "Who did you give my number to?"

She put her hand over the receiver. "No one. Except for the detective who called you."

"It doesn't sound like him. Find out who it is and tell him never to call here again."

She noticed an edge of jealousy in his voice, but ignored it. "Hello?" When Ron Wheatley answered she wanted to die. She'd already told Garrett that their relationship had remained on a professional level and had been connected with the murder investigation. Now what, she wondered? And Garrett was listening as well. How could she talk to Ron in a normal way with Garrett listening?

"Samantha, I didn't want to bother you while you were with him. I just called to say I love you."

That reminded her of the lyrics from a song, she thought. Then she noticed how depressed he sounded and felt a tinge of sympathy for him. "Really?" was all she could say under the circumstances.

"Is he listening to your conversation?" Ron asked indignantly.

"Well, yes."

"Okay, I get the picture. Don't say anything, just listen. I'm getting a divorce so I'll be free—"

"That's kind of sudden isn't it?" she asked, her anger building again. What was he doing this for? First he shot his wife and now he was divorcing her. Poor thing.

"Well, it's a long story, but partly it's being done for us."

"You know something, Ron? You really are a bastard! And a nervy one at that." She slammed down the phone and turned to face Garrett. When he narrowed his eyes and scowled, she wanted to run. He was obviously angry at her.

"Ron? Was that Ron Wheatley? What'd he call here for? Was this part of his job, part of the investigation he's conducting? Don't lie to me now, Samantha. I heard what you said and the way you spoke to him."

She was nervous; tears were welling up. "I lied to you about our relationship, Ron's and mine."

"I thought so! You were friendlier with him than you led me to believe. And now where does that leave us? Is this to become a *menage a trois?*"

"No. I met him before I met you. I liked him. But then I found out he was married—"

"Married?" he said, his gaze softening. "And he still wanted you." She nodded silently and Garrett half-smiled. "I really can't blame him for that. You are beautiful and intelligent and sensitive. Besides, Ron and I always did have the same taste in women, so I'm not surprised."

He walked closer to her, putting his arms around her body. Just the fact of him being so close heated her flesh. "I'm not surprised," he repeated, his eyes soft and passionate now. "And I know what's going on. You dumped him once you discovered he was married; am I right?" She nodded again, also silently this time. "Okay! Next time he calls I'll speak to him."

Samantha leaned her head against Garrett's shoulder, desiring the warmth and strength she received from his touch. "I'm sorry he called here. I didn't give him the number. Unless he got it from that other detective."

"Don't worry about it," he said, wrapping his arms tighter around her body. "But what happens when you go back to the city on Monday?"

"I don't understand," she said, and she didn't.

"He'll start calling you at home. But there is a way to stop him."

"How?"

"If you were living with me he'd stay away." Garrett drew her out at arm's length then, looking into her eyes so that she could see how serious he was. "I mean it, Sam. You could come and live with me. Besides getting rid of Wheatley, it would solve another problem between us."

"Such as?" She couldn't even begin to imagine what he was talking about. "I thought Ron was the only sore spot in our relationship."

"No, he's not. There's more. I want you to give up that job of yours. For now I'd rather you didn't call strangers on the phone and make appointments to go see them alone. It's just too dangerous. I'll support you. After all, money is no object with me. I have more than I can possibly spend in a lifetime, and I want someone to share it with. And that someone is you. What do you think? Will you do it?''

She didn't know what to say, she was speechless. Garrett was everything she ever wanted in a man and more; he was her dream man in the flesh. And under any other circumstances she would've screamed her answer. She would've said yes! But now she couldn't. Garrett only wanted her to live with him, to shack up, while Ron was willing to divorce his wife and marry her. She felt cheated by Garrett and couldn't answer right this minute. He sensed her hesitation and pulled her closer to him again, his movements marked by desperation.

''I know you're probably thinking of marriage. And believe me, Sam, I can't ask you now. Not until I solve some personal problems.'' He felt her stiffen. ''Those problems don't involve a marriage. I mean, I'm not married. It's not that. I only wish it were so easy. But I promise you this, once my problems are solved, we'll get married, have kids, the whole nine yards.''

''Oh, Garrett,'' she said and drew his face down towards hers. When they kissed she felt nothing but honesty between them, and not the deceit she felt with Ron. She also felt him becoming aroused again and playfully pulled away from his embrace. ''You really are an animal!'' she said and laughed.

''No! It's you!'' he said, putting on an act of innocence. ''You're doing this to me. Making me crazy. Twice in one day should be enough! Now you've got me shooting for three!'' He pulled her back into his arms and lifted her off her feet, carrying her toward the bed. ''If it's less thrilling than it was before, it's your fault, you little vixen. You've got me worn out but good!''

14

J.J. Holiman had dined with Samantha and Garrett, after which he retreated to the library to do some heavy thinking. He was no closer now to the killer's identity—the harborer of the beast—than he had been when he first entered the case. And time was growing short. But only in the sense that the mark of the beast on his shoulder had already caused a change in his personality; there were two forces in him now. There was J.J. Holiman and an unknown x factor.

And from what he knew on the subject—from his studies dealing with the mark of the beast—he would next be destroyed from the inside out. Soon he would begin to notice a severe malfunction of his vital organs, all of them.

Unless of course he choose to cooperate and be as one with Satan. Then life would go on indefinitely. But J.J. could never survive for long living the lifestyle of a Satanist, a servant to the powers of darkness; not after spending his entire life engaged in battle with the lord of lies. So his time was limited, and he had to make do with what little was left.

He sat down behind Garrett's desk and decided to make a list of what he'd come across so far. For one, he knew that the harborer of the beast was not the man they had in jail. He was someone more ordinary; less of an attention-getter; someone who could mingle in a crowd.

Then it dawned on him. The man he was looking for was someone who'd been seen in Bridge Gate Court many times, someone who'd gone in and out of the building without being noticed. How else could the demon within him gain access to Bridge Gate Court and commit his murders and not be caught? Only by being a visitor on a regular basis.

He made a note to question the neighbors. In doing so, one of two things might happen. Either he'd discover that the killer actually lived in the building or the tenants would give him a common name, the name of a man they'd all seen coming and going without becoming suspicious.

There was one he knew of already, one man who walked the halls of Bridge Gate Court day and night who was welcomed with open arms: Ron Wheatley! He started to jot his name down under the heading of 'known suspects' but stopped. To list his name was ridiculous.

Ron was a cop! He was there strictly on official business. He'd been ordered by his superiors to head the investigation, so that let him out. The man he was looking for went to Bridge Gate Court willingly, without being ordered to go there to protect the general public from a demon. And therein were the key words that would lead to the killer's identity—willing and protect.

The man he was looking for had to be there on

his own, without a desire to protect anyone. If he found a common denominator, if the same name popped up continuously when he questioned the tenants, J.J. would first have to determine if the man had come there willingly and, if so, in what capacity. Was he there to visit? What tenants had he come to see? Then he would question those tenants, those who played host to the suspect.

He'd ask if the suspect had come of his own free will. Was he someone who just dropped by whenever he felt like it? Or did the hosts, themselves, force the suspect to visit? Did they call the suspect on the phone and constantly hound him until he showed up? Free will was a very important factor here, because the killer went to Bridge Gate Court of his own free will. In fact, he was drawn there by the compulsions of the beast he was harboring.

Next J.J. had to determine how many times the suspect had actually visited. There had been a dozen or so murders to date, so the suspect had to have been in the building at least eight or nine times in the past month. Eight or nine times would've done it since the beast killed two victims in one night on two occasions that he knew of.

Now that he had this clear in his mind—the murderer's willingness to be there—the second part had to be considered: protection. If the suspect were there to protect, this would lend credence to his innocence. Unless! Unless the harborer of the beast wasn't sure that the beast was in him, that there was a demon within. The suspect might've gone to Bridge Gate Court actually believing he was there to protect someone, to make sure that his friends weren't harmed by the killer, only to have the beast in him emerge once he entered Bridge Gate Court.

That idea led back to Ron Wheatley. He was sent there to catch the killer in order to protect the tenants. And if the harborer of the beast wasn't sure the beast was in him, then Ron could be a prime suspect. And too, Ron was the only one he knew who fit the description of the man he was searching for. Ron was normal-looking in appearance; his body was the perfect hiding place for Asgar.

J.J. leaned his elbows on the desk and cupped his hands into a spider-like pose. He was thinking back, allowing his mind to dwell on his first meeting with Ron Wheatley. He thought about how Ron had mentioned being aware of the beast and the murders. Then he tried to remember his exact words. As far as he was able to recall, Ron had said something to the effect that every time a murder was committed, he was there . . . in his mind. He said he saw the victim's faces, heard their pleas for mercy. It happened in his sleep, and it happened once or twice when he was awake!

At the time, J.J., aware that he was dealing with a cop, had come up with the best possible answer he could under the circumstances. He told Ron that he might have been going through a psychic experience. What a fool. Ron told him a secret, something about himself that should've placed him on the list of prime suspects from the very beginning. And J.J. chose to ignore it simply because the man was a cop. But now, as he thought about it—really let go and allowed Ron's words to sink in—Ron could be considered a prime suspect. Except for one minor detail.

Ron was sent there by his superiors to investi-

gate the murders. Therefore, he would not have
had a reason to even enter the building if the
murders hadn't started in the first place. J.J.
realized he'd just now proven Ron Wheatley's
innocence with his own analysis of the facts.

And yet, the things Ron had told him, the fact of
being one with the beast, those things helped to
establish his guilt! And the only way to determine
the truth was to perform an experiment to
discover whether or not Ron Wheatley was
psychic as J.J. had said he was. Because if he
wasn't psychic, analysis or no analysis, Ron
Wheatley was the harborer of the beast.

Samantha had fallen asleep after dinner. Garrett
sat with her for a while, then went looking for J.J.
Holiman. J.J., his old friend, had lied to him, and
Garrett wanted to know why. It was impossible to
have as many lumps and bruises as he had from a
simple fall.

The old man had trouble walking, said his knees
were swollen, which could've happened in a fall.
Garrett conceded that much. And his nose looked
broken. That could've happened in a fall, too. But
there were marks around his neck, and no way in
hell did he get them by tripping over something.
Of course J.J. didn't know Garrett had seen the
choke marks because J.J. had done his best to
conceal them. Well, now J.J. could damn well
explain them, Garrett thought. Someone tried to
strangle him and Garrett wanted to know who.

J.J. was seated behind Garrett's desk, writing
something. When Garrett walked in J.J. glanced
up and smiled and called him 'son,' but Garrett
didn't smile back. Rather he stared at J.J. for a
long while before he spoke. ''When is it going to

end? When will you stop? When they kill you?"

"I don't understand," J.J. said, his eyes wide with innocence, but Garrett was having none of this.

"Look J.J., I know why you're hiding the truth, and believe me, it's embarrassing." The old man started to respond but Garrett stopped him. "Let me finish. You're keeping a lot from me because of my fears. Ever since we first met, I've been terrified of anything dealing with your world of demonology. So, keeping that in mind, you've decided to hide the truth to protect me, and I appreciate it. But those marks on your neck had nothing to do with falling."

J.J. sighed heavily and cupped his head with his hands. "No, they didn't. You're right." He looked up at Garrett, his face lined with torment. "I did fall, that much is true. But it happened when Asgar chased me through Central Park. He—"

"Asgar? You told me about him once. I mean, I remember the name." Garrett ran a hand back through his hair in frustration. "Then I can assume he's back, and he's the one involved in the Bridge Gate murders . . . the mutilations."

"Yes. He's the beast the human is harboring."

"What can I do to help?" Garrett asked, not really wanting to. But J.J. was old, he needed someone.

"At this point, nothing. It's just too dangerous."

"Oh, swell. Then I'll just sit back and wait for him to kill you next time."

"Garrett, sit down and let me explain what I've discovered so far. Then you be the judge, you tell me what I'm up against. You can also tell me if you still want to help. First of all, I went to Bridge Gate Court last night searching for clues," J.J.

began, telling the story from the beginning, leaving nothing out, studying Garrett's face while he talked.

Garrett tried to keep his face a blank, to show none of the fear he had in the past. J.J. was giving him every gruesome detail as a test. If Garrett failed, the old man would just go on and hunt Asgar alone. Garrett interrupted him at one point. "You said he'd already stolen and used an arm in one of his ceremonies, so he left the arm behind because it was useless. But he did take June DeSoto's head?"

"Yes. And why I don't know. He'd already taken a head from a previous victim. It may be that he's confused. Asgar isn't the smartest demon around. Or rather I should say he is smart, but he's just too damned lazy to think with his brain." J.J. then continued on, telling Garrett everything from the time Asgar attacked him in Central Park to the choking incident in St. Patrick's Cathedral.

When he was through, Garrett got up and opened a cabinet beside J.J., extracting a bottle of vintage brandy and two snifters. He poured them each a drink and said nothing for a long time. He was troubled. The battle with Asgar, the one J.J. had been waging for the past couple of decades was coming to a head. One of them would die soon. But demons didn't die, so J.J. would be the victim, the one to perish.

"Do you still want to help?" the old man wanted to know.

"Do I have a choice?"

"Garrett, I've told you time and again. Don't answer a question with another question, it's impolite."

"We're discussing the most terrifying subject imaginable, and you're worried about what's polite? The answer is yes, I will help." But he didn't want to, he wanted to run because now he knew the truth about Asgar: he was a foul, demonic beast from the pit of Acheron who would stop at nothing to achieve his goals. He was also cunning and deceitful, a true disciple of the lord of lies. When Asgar came for him, Garrett hoped he wouldn't be home.

"Well!" J.J. said, a hint of relief in his voice, "That's settled! Now, let me fill you in on what I've got so far in the way of suspects."

"Suspects?" Garrett didn't understand.

"The one who harbors the beast."

"Just to interrupt you for a moment. Does the so-called suspect know he's harboring the beast?"

"He may and he may not. Maybe he only suspects the beast is there. Thus the reason for gathering the body parts for ceremonies."

"But Asgar's doing the gathering for him. There-fore, the human must be aware of something!"

"Not necessarily, Garrett. His suspicions alone are cause enough to generate a need for the necessary tools to exorcise the beast—"

"But," Garrett cut in, "What must the human think when he comes out of his stupor? You know, the trance he's in when the beast is in control. What happens then? He must know something's wrong when he finds body parts in his home."

J.J. thought about this for a moment, then answered with, "I believe the shock of finding body parts is enough to send him—the human—back into a trance. I believe that when he performs his ceremonies, some part of his brain, the part responsible for his conscious actions, well, that part mercifully closes down. Therefore he sees his own performance of those ceremonies in the same trance-like state he's in when he's killing along with the beast.

"And, as I've said before, his suspicions of being one with Asgar are enough to generate a need within him for body parts to exorcise his unwanted counterpart. So the beast in him is doing the killing and mutilating to get body parts for ceremonies of exorcism. And before you ask me why Asgar is cooperating, I'll tell you. It's because Asgar is not entirely happy with the arrangement either. He doesn't like sharing his brain or his time with another. He wants out just as badly as the human wants him out.

"Now, if the killer is human most of the time, I may be able to exorcise the beast from his body. But it must be done before Asgar gets out. In other words, the human must be in control when the exorcism is done."

"What's the difference?" Garrett wanted to know. He was growing more confused by the minute. "If Asgar wants out as much as you say he does, then what does it matter who's in control, him or the human? Hell, you'd be doing the old boy a favor. He'd be very appreciative I would think."

J.J. smiled as though he'd just heard the stupidest question ever. "Asgar wants out, true, but on his own. With no outside interference from me or my kind. Exorcism is a very painful process to a demon. They really suffer physically, you know. Their flesh is literally burned to a crisp by the holy water. Their minds are branded with hot irons at the mention of the Bible verses I use and also by any mention of God's name. So I only hope and pray he's buried within the human when I go for him. Otherwise it's just too dangerous."

"But J.J., you've taken Asgar on in the past and defeated him. Why is it so dangerous now?"

"Because my old demon foe is wise to me. What's more, he's familiar with all of my tricks, all of the methods of exorcism I've used thus far. So he's ready for me this time, which means I'll have to come up with something totally new."

"Why can't you just get rid of him for good? Why must it be done time after time?"

"Because, Garrett, Asgar doesn't give up. Other beasts will face me once and then disappear for a century or so. You know, they're waiting until they're sure I'm dead to strike again. I mean, you never really get rid of them for good. The evil is always present, always looking for the opportunity to take over, to fill the world with images of themselves.

"But Asgar doesn't wait for anything. He continuously looks for trouble, for humans to dominate. Although this time I suspect he's in this human as a form of punishment."

"Punishment?" Garrett couldn't believe he was hearing right. "Who would punish a demon prince?" The whole idea was incredible.

"Satan—his lord and master! Satan is the only one capable of issuing punishment to so foul a beast as Asgar. And I know he's being punished for something, because otherwise why would he kill and mutilate bodies to gather parts for a ceremony to exorcise himself? Hell, those bastards, once they have a foothold they stay where they are—inside of the body. But Asgar's trying to get *out!*"

"I see. So by doing the opposite of what he normally does, he's telling you he's being harbored by force!"

"Exactly! And as I've already said, I only hope he's still inside when I go for him. If I face the human and not him, it'll be a lot easier and safer too."

Garrett rose to pour two more drinks. He was scared and trying not to show it. There was an important question he wanted to ask, and yet he couldn't voice it while he was face to face with J.J. He turned his back while he poured the refills and tried to act casual. '"Why do you imagine the human's being punished? I mean, he's linked up with Asgar, so he must've done something wrong as well."

"Whoever the harborer of the beast is, he always had a bit of the beast in him to begin with, so it was easy for Asgar to be placed where he was. Besides, as I told you back in that hotel room in the city, the human must've been fooling with Satanism, performing some sort of a ceremony, and he made Satan angry. Why, I can't explain at this point. So Satan is punishing him and Asgar both by linking them together."

"Who are the suspects so far?" Garrett's back was still turned and he was glad because when J.J. spoke again and uttered Ron Wheatley's name, Garrett wanted to die. He gave himself time to recover, then went back to where he was sitting, placing a drink in front of J.J., his hands slightly trembling.

J.J. stared at Garrett's hands, then acted as though he understood. "I know he was a good

friend of yours in the past. Did he ever do anything when you roomed with him to make you
feel he was involved in Satanism?''

''No,'' Garrett said, hoping J.J. hadn't noticed
the crack in his voice when he spoke. ''Ron acted
perfectly normal. In fact, I'm surprised that he's a
suspect.''

''Ron Wheatley walks with the beast in his
dreams.''

Garrett heard this and thought about it.
Although he'd never said anything to J.J., and
never would now, Garrett, himself, had walked
with the beast at times. He made no further
comment, but rather listened quietly while J.J.
explained in detail what Ron had told him. And as
he listened, Garrett tried to keep his nerves steady
and even. Ron's experiences were the same as
his. Oh God, it just couldn't be so. . . .

''Well, son,'' J.J. said, sipping the last of his
brandy and rising uneasily to his feet. He was still
in pain from the wounds the beast had dealt him.
''I think that's enough for tonight. Let's turn in.
We can continue this in the morning.'' Then he
quickly added, ''But not in front of Samantha.
She's frightened as it is, and I can't blame her
after what she's been through.''

Garrett had to agree with him about Samantha.
He wanted nothing more than to be able to
protect her further from the horrors she'd
suffered. He walked J.J. upstairs, making sure he
reached his room safely. Then he looked in on
Samantha: she was still asleep, her arms
wrapped around his pillow the same way they'd
been wrapped around his neck earlier.

And at first, he'd had the idea that maybe J.J.
was right, that he should go to bed. But he knew

he couldn't sleep, especially now since discovering the truth about Ron Wheatley. And to think he'd roomed with the guy and could've been killed at any time.

He shuddered and started back downstairs. Between what he'd learned about Ron and the horrors J.J. had just recounted, Garrett wanted a breath of air. A ride would do the trick: a ride would tire him out, calm him down. And since he wanted to be alone to think out his pact with J.J., he figured he'd take the Excalibur again and not bother his chauffeur.

He was almost out of the house when he heard giggling . . . maniacal giggling. And it seemed to be coming from one of the bedrooms upstairs. J.J. had told him earlier that Asgar liked to giggle and Asgar was a killing machine. Running as fast as he could, taking the stairs two at a time, Garrett searched his bedroom first to be sure Samantha was safe. Then he ran to J.J.'s room and found his old professor sitting up in bed reading a book. J.J. looked astonished when Garrett came bursting into his room.

"I heard giggling—"

"It was me, son."

"You!"

"Yes. I was thinking about Asgar, about how slick he imagined himself and it struck me funny. That's all."

Garrett said good-night again and closed the door. He knew J.J. was lying. Those noises never came from anything human, unless the old man was losing his grip, going crazy from the strain of trying to destroy a demon killer. So he let it go at that and headed out the door for his ride alone in the Excalibur.

* * *

Ron Wheatley was also alone that night and had opted for a ride to clear his head. Too much had happened during the day for him to be able to sleep.

He'd lost both of the women in his life and had never felt more alone except for the time his mother died, leaving him with no one to talk to, no one to share his dreams or his disappointments with. And that was the same feeling he was left with now.

Debbie had shattered the picture he'd set up in his mind concerning their marriage. And of course, while she felt she was doing it for him and not to him, it didn't matter now. And it didn't matter either that she'd freed him from two long years of mental bondage by confessing all because she'd done it too late. He'd already lost Samantha . . .

He pulled onto the Meadowbrook Parkway and drove until he came to the exit for the Long Island Expressway. He planned on taking the L.I.E. and heading west to the Midtown Tunnel and Manhattan. Manhattan was a lively town that almost never slept. And if you were in the same predicament—alive and couldn't sleep—there was always something happening in Manhattan.

He was sitting on the entrance ramp for the L.I.E. waiting for a break in traffic when he spotted a white Excalibur in the next lane. A real beauty it was, too. In fact, he couldn't take his eyes off it, or off the driver behind the wheel. Of course it was late at night and it was dark, so he couldn't be sure, but for the life of him it looked like Garrett Lang.

But then what would Garrett be doing heading

for Manhattan alone in an Excalibur when he had someone like Samantha spending the weekend in his mansion in the Hamptons? No, it was just too absurd to imagine him leaving Samantha behind to ride around in his car.

And thinking of Samantha just then brought out a bitterness in him he never knew existed. Samantha was another one like Debbie: they both had dangled their bodies in front of his eyes; both had given in to him when he was desperate enough to beg, then they both cut him off cold! Oh, yeah, Samantha was his wife all over again. A teasing bitch who made him fall in love with her only to turn right around and dump him!

That's what Debbie did, she just as much dumped him this afternoon. And yet, she was doing it for him; she was setting him free. But he alone knew the truth. Debbie was tired of manipulating his ass, so she was getting rid of him to make room for the next sucker. Never mind that she was in a wheelchair and had no feelings below the waist. She'd grab herself some poor fool who didn't know any better and she'd fuck him, work him over real good, while pretending she was enjoying it!

And Samantha would do the same thing to Garrett!

Ron's mind then skipped to the Bridge Gate Killer, and he wondered if some woman hadn't worked him over to the point where all he wanted to do was to murder and mutilate every bitch he could get his hands on! Coming on like they're something special. Acting so coy and innocent after making you hot and bothered: telling you they're virgins! Debbie did it and Samantha did too: acted like a couple of *nuns*.

Then, once they got their sex, well hell, they both dumped him. Only it took Debbie a bit longer than it took Samantha. Debbie fucked him over for two years before she had her fill. And now, in a way, Ron could understand and sympathize with the Bridge Gate Killer. Those bitches he killed, they picked on the wrong one when they picked on him!

And maybe he had the right idea, killing those women like he did. You didn't see him—the killer —sitting around, or driving around late at night, brooding and trying to forget what some bitches did to him! As a matter of fact, Ron was so angry inside he could kill some bitch right this moment and never regret it later: another nun like Debbie and Samantha perhaps?

The man walked through the door of Bridge Gate Court and couldn't imagine why he was there except for a strong compulsion deep inside, luring him, taunting him. And he wondered if the beast inside him was awake—if the beast existed, that was. He couldn't be sure, had never really been sure in the past. But if the beast was alive, and in him, and its foul, conniving brain was awake, then the beast was responsible for the compulsion.

He walked back toward the corridor where most of the murders had taken place and felt a deadness overtaking him: his brain was crawling with cold, sharp, spasms of shame. The beast had killed here; the beast had murdered and mutilated those beautiful women with the voluptuous bodies and it seemed it was being done for him! Because he wanted them dead, wanted their body parts.

Then he wondered about the woman at home, sleeping in his bed. How would she feel if the beast left body parts—gruesome, gory, stumps of once living flesh—how would she feel if the beast left them at the foot of the bed this time for her to discover? After all, she was an emotional cripple and couldn't really handle it. So, how would she feel?

His head ached: the beast was fighting for space. It was his turn to emerge, the man imagined. Otherwise why would he get these headaches followed by blackouts? Except that they weren't really blackouts in the normal sense of the word, because he was able to see what the beast was doing at all times, able to see the horror written on his victims' faces, and able to hear their terrified pleas for mercy.

But the beast showed no mercy. Instead, he went on and murdered his victims while enjoying his role in their deaths. He enjoyed being a physical participant in the destruction of human lives, enjoyed his part in the slaughter, the mutilation.

The man held onto the sides of his head and begged for mercy, begged for the power to keep the evil one subdued. And yet, no mention of the word 'God' came from his lips. He wasn't praying to a Higher Power, he was just begging for mercy, and that made him wonder too. When had he lost the ability to say God's name? Was it that night ten years ago when he and his roommate had been praying to another god? Is that when he lost his inner humanity?

Groping for the wall to steady himself because the pain was so intense, he let his head rest against that wall, felt the cold hardness of its surface dulling the throbbing in his skull—

Asgar pushed himself away from the wall and laughed. This damn wimp, the one he was sharing a body with, had had enough, couldn't take the sight of another murder. Well, that was too bad. Asgar was in the mood for killing. And since killing naturally led to the gathering of body parts, and because the man wanted his freedom as Asgar did, the man would awaken several hours from now and find whatever Asgar chose to leave him.

The beast stood back in the darkened foyer and waited for an hour or so. But no one came inside of the building. Those soft-breasted nuns were probably all in for the night. Therefore he had no choice other than to go looking for one. First, however, he planned on stopping at that Samantha's apartment as he had once before. Not to kill her, just to look at her; to feast his eyes on her beauty, her creamy flesh, her full sensuous lips, her well-rounded body.

The man in him had fucked her. And in Asgar's opinion, that was the only sensible thing he'd done since Asgar first became a 'tenant' inside of him. He pushed the button and waited for the elevator, got on when it came, and then pushed another button for the seventh floor.

It was quiet up there when he stepped off, except for an annoying voice, making incessant droning noises in the apartment next door to Samantha's. Probably some nun engaged in prayer, he thought, and put his skinless ear against the door to listen. And when he'd heard enough he knocked on the door so that she'd come and let him in.

Of course he could've dematerialized and gone

through the door without anyone letting him in. And too, he could've taken the door off the hinges. But it was more fun this way; making the bitch come and answer the door only to find Asgar waiting--waiting for her body parts.

"Cius, acarius, volanum," Ramona Blattfield said, and sprinkled rosemary into the wooden bowl in front of her. She was in the midst of conjuring up Uncle Max, and perhaps Aunt Sophie too, if she could manage it. Jeffrey didn't agree with what she was doing, so she gave him permission to leave the apartment until it was over.

She gave in to Jeffrey just this once, knowing she never would again. After all, the idea of bringing forth Uncle Max had been to provide company for Jeffrey. Therefore, if she did this right, if she managed to bring forth Uncle Max, Jeffrey would have no choice but to spend his time here, in the apartment, not floating around outside where he didn't belong. "Cius, acarius, volanum,"- she said, chanting with everything in her to insure success. "Rosemary and a bit of sage to bring forth Uncle Max."

She was in the middle of her next chant when suddenly a loud noise shattered her concentration. Someone was knocking on the door, the rapping sounds of their knuckles against wood chilling the base of her skull. She was frightened and couldn't understand why.

Was it because the noise had crept up on her with such ferocity when all had been quiet and still around her? Or was it because she was afraid the person on the other side of the door had heard everything she'd said? Would they think her a witch now? When the knocking persisted, she left her herbs and her wooden bowl to answer the door.

Whoever it was, she'd get rid of them in a hurry. She had to. Jeffrey was lonely, he needed Uncle Max. And the timing was perfect: she was working in conjunction with the new moon. "Who is it?" she wanted to know first before opening the door. Even with the killer in jail it just wasn't safe to let strangers in. "Who is it?" she repeated.

"Why don't you open the door and find out?"

Ramona felt a lump in her throat. What the hell kind of a way was that to answer someone? What was this, a wise ass? She considered calling the police, but didn't. She was still safely locked inside her apartment. He couldn't get her there.

"Well?" he wanted to know. "Are you opening the door or not?"

"Who are you?" she asked and marveled that a creep like this would have such a velvety-smooth voice. "I don't let just anyone in."

"I'm not just anyone. Think about it. Weren't you trying to conjure me up just minutes ago?"

Oh no, she thought, her heart skipping a beat. It was Max. She'd done it; she'd brought him here! And yet, why did he have to come this way, why through the door? Jeffrey sort of floated into her kitchen the night she brought him forth. But then Max always was a bastard; always had to do things *his* way. However, she had to be sure it was Max and not someone playing tricks to get in.

"'What's your name?" she asked because if he didn't give Uncle Max's name, then this was a trick.

"Uncle Max," Asgar answered.

Ramona tried to remember at that point whether or not she'd used his name when conjuring him up. After all, if this person outside had been listening at the door and had heard her chanting and was familiar with the occult, he'd know what she was trying to do—conjure up Uncle Max. But for the life of her, she couldn't remember using Max's name.

"Come on, bitch! Open the door!"

Those words were harsh, yet spoken with the same soothing tone of voice. It was Max! He sure hadn't changed much. Ramona released the bolt on the police lock and opened the door—and tried to scream, but he had her by the throat, had his nails inside of her throat—

Morgan Housner was in the shower when Ramona Blattfield was murdered. While Morgan normally enjoyed long, hot showers, this one was longer and hotter than ever. Phil's touch was on her body, her father's touch, and she had to wash it off. But then she somehow wondered if she could ever remove the feel of his touch, and if so, would she feel clean again?

Phil was lying in her bed outside watching television, waiting for her to come and lie down beside him for the night. They both needed their sleep, he'd said. After all, they were getting married in the morning. Oh, God, it was just too awful for words. She was marrying her own father; but by force, not by choice.

She stepped out of the shower and heard noises coming from the bedroom outside, then remembered that Phil had the television on. Those muffled, gurgling noises she heard had to be coming from the sound track of a murder mystery. She dried herself, splashed powder on, and wondered about the other noises she was hearing: scuffling noises, someone being slammed against the furniture.

Phil had left a sheer nightgown folded neatly over the top of the toilet tank. She picked it up and shuddered. This wasn't what she'd planned on wearing to bed, not with him anyway. But he enjoyed looking at her body so this is the way it had to be. If she went against his word, he'd beat her again.

She slipped the flimsy piece of nothing over her head, sucked in her breath for courage and decided to go out and face him. God knows, at this point she needed all the courage she could muster. He'd probably leer at her, because nothing was hidden, and then grab her once more before he rolled over for the night.

But she was ready for him. In fact she was more than ready, she was resigned to her fate. She had given up hope of ever finding happiness in this life.

Phil wasn't in bed when she opened the door, and the television had been turned off. Taking advantage of his absence, she hurried to climb into bed. If she was lucky enough to fall asleep before he came back, he'd leave her alone, at least for tonight anyway.

And one good night's sleep was better than nothing. She started to pull back the covers on the bed when something caught her attention: blood-stains. The bedspread was dotted with large drops of blood. But the spread had a red print so the blood had blended in and she didn't notice it until she was real close.

"Phil," she called, not really wanting to,

believing in the old adage about 'letting sleeping dogs lie,' but she had to. No matter what his sickness, the one that kept him climbing into bed with his own daughter, no matter what he was inside, he was still her father. "Phil," she called again, but Phil didn't answer.

Maybe he just didn't hear her, she thought. She hurried out to the kitchen because he was bleeding and needed her, but the kitchen was empty. Then she decided to look for him in Samantha's room, or Samantha's closet. She started to panic. Phil wouldn't just leave, just walk out without telling her.

She went back to the kitchen thinking maybe she'd missed him somewhere along the way, but the kitchen was still empty. Deep inside she was telling herself not to panic. Phil had gone out. But for what? A pizza? A container of milk? And why would he go anywhere without telling her? Why would he leave so abruptly when he'd been standing guard over her all weekend long, making sure she didn't get away before the wedding?

Right this moment, the idea that he'd left and she was free should've brought tears of joy to her eyes. But the tears welling up inside of her had nothing to do with joy; they were brought on by fear. Those noises she'd heard when she was in the bathroom, and the bloodstains . . . Something bad happened to him. Something bad could happen to her as well if she stayed there.

And yet, the only person she could think of who could be responsible for this, for the blood and for the body disappearing, was in jail. Besides, the Bridge Gate Kiler never took a whole body before, only body parts. So, whoever had done this had to be a totally different psycho; someone just starting out. And he started with Phil. He killed Phil and took his body. And maybe, just maybe he was coming back for her!

Morgan was close to hysteria when the doorbell rang, the sound of it searing the nerves at the base of her skull. She wanted to run and answer it, but maybe it was the psycho who'd stolen Phil's body. Worse yet, maybe it was Phil. Maybe he only cut himself somehow and had gone to the store for band-aids.

But she had band-aids, lots of them.

Then again, Phil didn't know.

And now he'd come back for the wedding tomorrow . . .

And yet Phil had an awful temper. He'd ring the bell and holler . . .

When someone knocked on the door this time instead of ringing the bell, her first impulse was to scream. The psycho, whoever he was, he wasn't giving up without a fight. Then he rang the bell again. But she still didn't answer. Instead, she went back to her room for a robe. She wasn't dressed for death—for rape maybe in this flimsy piece of shit Phil had bought her, but not for sudden death . . . or mutilation . . .

A lot of things were going through her mind at this point, and topping the list was the thought of calling the police. But they'd take too long. They'd never get there in time. The psycho was back, wanted more blood. Phil's hadn't been enough. When she returned to the living room to wait, something else hit her full force: maybe they had the wrong man in jail. So now the *real* Bridge Gate Killer was free to do his thing.

Then she smiled in spite of herself because she was giving the bastard a run for his money.

Getting to her and killing her wouldn't be all that easy. He had to work at it, he had to break down the door if he wanted her.

"Morgan? Are you in there?"

She heard a soothing voice and wondered how he knew her name. But then, maybe Phil gave it to him! Maybe Phil was trying to save his own skin and told the killer to go get Morgan!

"Honey, I know you're in there. Please open the door."

Oh God, she knew that voice. It was Charlie! How could she ever not recognize his voice? Had she become so panicky over a few background noises and some blood that she couldn't allow herself to recall the sound of Charlie's voice? Without thinking, she ran and opened the door, knowing deep inside that she should've looked through the peephole first. But it was Charlie's voice and so it just had to be Charlie.

"Hi, skinny," he said and smiled when she opened the door. "I'm sorry. I know I promised to stay away until tomorrow, but I couldn't. I missed you so."

Before she knew what was happening, she was in his arms, crying with all the hurt and tension she'd felt these past few days. And suddenly she was no longer worried about Phil, except that he might come back and start with Charlie. She had to get rid of Charlie and fast. And yet it had to be done in the best possible way, without breaking his heart.

But Charlie never gave her a chance to reject him. Before she could utter a word, he swept her up into his arms and started out the door. "What're you doing?" she asked, amazed by his actions but flattered nonetheless. "Where're you taking me?"

"Home! That's where I'm taking you. Back home with me where you belong. I can't stand anymore of this. You're in one place while I'm in another."

"But, Charlie. What about my clothing? What about my personal things: my jewelry, my furs—"

"I'll send my maid back to finish packing. You, skinny, are coming home with me now!"

"In a bathrobe? Let me at least get dressed!"

"My limo's waiting downstairs. Nobody'll even see you."

After he said that, Morgan felt warm inside and put her head on his shoulder. He was right, as always. Why not just leave and let his maid come back for her things? Why not? And if Phil started with the maid, she'd probably call the police and have him thrown in jail where he belonged.

But still Morgan wasn't completely at ease: her conscience was nagging at her. Phil had been bleeding and she really didn't know where he was or what condition he was in. What if he was hurt real bad, so bad that he was dying? But this was her chance to get out and escape his madness and she had to take it or be prepared to marry him in the morning. If she waited much longer, he might come back and stop her from leaving with Charlie.

"Okay, Charlie," she said and gave him a kiss on the cheek. "You wanna go home? Then let's go home."

"Right. And tomorrow we can start shopping for an engagement ring. And our wedding rings. A bridal gown, invitations. Boy, there's just so much to do."

"Yes, but don't forget we'll be doing it together. Oh, Charlie, I love you."

Asgar carried Phil Housner's lifeless body through several alleys before the truth came to him. He'd gone to Samantha's apartment to see her, only to find this human pig lying naked on her bed. And that enraged him. Samantha was his counterpart's whore!

And since he enjoyed screwing her as much as the human within him—although Sister June DeSoto was better and not as inhibited as Samantha—he went into a jealous rage and thought of nothing but killing the man in her bed. And for all he knew, the man was a priest! He had to be a priest! What other reason would he have for being in Bridge Gate Court, the church that was camouflaged to look like a normal building? So the bastard deserved to die.

Still, Asgar had to smile when he thought about how the little bastard fought for his life. And he was actually impressive: swinging his arms and his legs, punching Asgar the way he did. All for nothing, of course, because he was still dead. Asgar nearly ripped him to shreds: pulled his arms half out of their joints, broke one of his legs, then castrated him the hard way, by tearing his testicles off and stuffing them into his mouth.

Now Asgar was headed for those woods again with the body in tow. Satan had generously accepted his last offering of a full human body and perhaps he would this time as well. Perhaps he'd lift the curse and free Asgar from the bondage he was suffering by being a counterpart to a human.

And that was about where his mind had gotten

to when the truth came to him. He'd heard Samantha showering and had decided to leave without disturbing her, without feasting his eyes on her beautiful countenance. However, Samantha had gone away! The human in him knew this, but Asgar had forgotten up until now.

Therefore, the woman in the shower, if it was a woman, surely wasn't Samantha. And so, Asgar had allowed a perfectly choice specimen, with what probably would've been excellent body parts to escape unharmed. Damnit! Those body parts, along with the full body he was carrying, would've provided a more than fitting homage to his lord.

Unless she was as old as the chanter, the first woman he'd killed, the one he fooled into letting him in by telling her he was 'Uncle Max.' Her body parts were so old and useless he'd left them behind. So, if the bitch in the bathroom was anything like her, he'd wasted nothing by leaving her alive.

He was standing next to the human's car by this time, dumping the body into the back, laying it on the floor so it wouldn't be seen. It was a long drive to those woods, and since Asgar would've attracted too much unwanted attention behind the wheel, he bowed his head and yielded control to the human.

15

Ron Wheatley had seen Ramona Blattfield's death through the eyes of the killer, and it sickened him because he was looking into her face and listening to her cries of torment when her throat was torn out.

But it didn't stop there: the killer wasn't finished with her yet because he was extremely angry. In his opinion she was old, too old for anything usable to be taken from her body. And so, in his rage to get even, he carved her body with a knife; sliced the soft meat of her breasts as though he were carving a turkey, expanded her navel, and cut out her intestines, all while she was still alive, while she was still making gurgling noises and trying to stem the flow of blood from her throat.

After it was over, Ron dropped by the station to see if any report had been made, if anyone had found the body yet. Otherwise he had no business investigating the murder because he wouldn't have been able to explain how he knew she was dead. And even if he could explain it, even if he could put it into words and tell them he'd seen it happening through the eyes of the beast, nobody would've believed him.

So he had to wait for the normal flow of events that usually followed a killing. First somebody had to call and turn it in. Then the fabled crap would hit the fan because they had the wrong man in jail and the killer was still loose. And Ron would get the worst of it because he was the arresting officer on the case and had convinced his captain that all was safe in Bridge Gate Court. Oh yeah. He was in for it now.

Along with his partner, Candeles.

But only because Candeles had agreed with Ron about the Bridge Gate Killer being in jail. And Candeles told him about the alleged imitator in Samantha's apartment. Candeles was positive that any future murders would be committed by this so-called imitator.

And yet, Candeles had never suffered through the experiences Ron had, of being able to see the murders through the eyes of the killer. And Ron sure as hell wasn't looking through the eyes of an imitator when that woman, the one in her fifties, was killed a while back. So Candeles had no way of knowing the truth, and he'd go along with Ron.

Ron spent the night at the station, sitting behind his desk. He had no choice. If he wanted to leave and go home, he had to take his car. And when he came to the station house hours ago, he parked his car and ran, leaving it in the lot adjoining the building—

. . . without looking in the back.

After all, the demon had placed a man's body on the back floor of a car. Ron had watched him murder and mutilate this man right after the woman was killed. And while the man had been in Samantha's apartment, he wasn't Garrett Lang. He was obviously someone known to Samantha's roommate. And now that body was lying on the floor of a car somewhere, put there by the demon to be used in an exorcism.

Ron didn't know whose car it was because he hadn't seen it clearly, but he couldn't take the chance of finding out that it was his. So, when he woke up from his stupor, he didn't look at the floor in back because he didn't want to know if the body had been put into *his* car!

Once or twice during the night he considered calling J.J. Holiman at Garrett's house. He wanted to tell J.J. that he was right about the killer's background and had been all along. And that he, Ron, had been wrong and had made a terrible mistake in assuming the murders would stop when he arrested a prime suspect. The killer was a human harboring a demon, and not the caped degenerate they had in jail.

What's more, the demon was still loose, and he, Ron, needed help. Not much to ask from a man who'd already volunteered his services, a man who'd worked with the police in the past. And yet he was afraid to call J.J., afraid of what he might discover. For surely J.J. would find the human harboring the beast. And Ron Wheatley was afraid that the investigation the old man would conduct would lead back to his door. J.J. might prove that Ron Wheatley was harboring the beast.

He was afraid to call J.J. and afraid to search his car because the beast within him might become angry again.

Garrett Lang had also seen the murder through

the eyes of the beast. And, like Ron Wheatley, he was afraid to look at the floor in the back of *his* car, afraid of finding the body the beast had placed there as an offering to Satan.

So when Garrett came out of his stupor, he drove straight back to the Hamptons looking for someone to turn to, someone who could help provide the answers. But everyone was still asleep. In desperation he went to the kitchen to make coffee and sat down at the table, letting his mind wander back to that awful night ten years ago.

Closing his eyes, he allowed the memories to emerge and drifted back to a time when life was less complicated. He had little money and no corporate problems to struggle with. He was happier then, but he couldn't accept being poor, so he did what most fools do under those circumstances: he craved money and power with all that was in his soul.

In fact, he sold his soul, at a cheap price.

He was living at a cheap hotel with Ron Wheatley. They were roommates, best buddies, and they shared everything: money, food, women. Garrett smiled then when he thought back on the times when one of them would stumble in late at night with a broad on his arm and turn the evening into a three-partner orgy. Those were the days, all right.

He was carefree, completely without morals, and happy. Only he couldn't see it then, couldn't stop to think that because of his basic intelligence he would've eventually succeeded. He would've turned his brains and the knowledge gained from J.J. Holiman into a comfortable paying job. He could've joined a corporation—any corporation—

and would've wound up high on the corporate ladder, maybe even at the top.

But he couldn't see it because he made the mistake of evaluating his chances in terms of time. Time was the important factor. Most corporate heads were old by the time they achieved their status, and Garrett couldn't wait that long. He wanted it all while he was still young. And there was a way. . . .

J.J. Holiman had spent many hours teaching Garrett more than the business of economics and corporate structures. J.J. had taught him that there was a way of joining forces with the prince of darkness and achieving great wealth and power in an instant!

The only thing Garrett couldn't be assured of by joining forces with the master beast himself was everlasting life, or life after death. The prince of darkness didn't make any promises in that area, didn't give the same guarantees as the Lord God he'd been taught to worship. But then everlasting life didn't matter when you were young and hungry for material possessions.

He struggled within himself. He allowed the idea of instant wealth and power to eat at his insides until he could no longer hide it from Ron. His roommate knew there was something wrong. Especially when Garrett began turning down Ron's offers to share his dates, to form a one-night threesome with some blonde or redhead Ron had picked up in a bar. And Ron had questioned Garrett because he was concerned for his friend.

Garrett didn't tell him the truth at first. He couldn't. Ron might've left him cold. How could you tell someone that you were struggling within yourself, agonizing over the idea of joining sides with the most evil force in the universe? Eventually Garrett told Ron the truth.

Garrett smiled again despite his inner turmoil when he thought of Ron's reaction. Hell, Ron had a lust for the good life the same as Garrett. And Ron was amazed to think that Garrett knew of a way to insure the good life, but had been hesitant about making a pact with Satan. This was bullshit to him. Being good never got you anywhere, in Ron's opinion.

On the particular night that Ron talked Garrett into putting his plans into action, Ron came back to their room with a devastating blonde on one arm and a bottle of booze in the other. She was a hooker; not a pro but close enough. And despite his anxieties, Garrett couldn't resist this one. So he and Ron chipped in twenty bucks each and had the time of their lives.

They made love and drank, drank and made love until the blonde passed out around two in the morning. Then Ron turned to Garrett and mentioned something about being bored; he was still wide awake and hungry for some fun. "Too bad it's after midnight," he said, "Or we could do that experiment you talked about."

"What experiment?" Garrett wanted to know.

"The Satanism thing," Ron said. "The one where we get all that money." Then he glanced over at the blonde snoring on the sofa bed and smiled. "Then we could have women like this every night of the week. Maybe even have one move in permanently. Not to mention gettin' outta this dive!"

Garrett was drunk, just drunk enough and mellow enough to forget his inner turmoil and to respond by using the knowledge J.J. had taught him. "What does being after midnight have to do with anything?"

"The bewitching hour, man. You know, when all the ghosties and goblins start walking around—"

"Start *walking* around?"

Ron looked hurt because Garrett was being sarcastic and enjoying it. "Well then *flying* around or whatever the hell it is they do. Anyway we missed it."

"Three in the morning is the best time," Garrett said, knowing he shouldn't have. But he was drunk and in a wise-ass mood, so he continued. "Three is the hour of the beast." Then he had second thoughts about telling these things to Ron. And he wished he'd never mentioned anything about Satanic powers or what you supposedly gained from them. Ron hadn't stopped harping on the subject since Garrett had confessed all during a moment of weakness.

Well hell, no problem, Garrett. It's only a bit after two. How do we do this?"

"You mean tonight? Now?"

"Sure," Ron said, his face glowing with enthusiasm. "Why not tonight? Why wait?"

Garrett looked around for the bottle; he needed another drink. The conversation was sobering him up. But then he remembered Ron had dumped the bottle into the garbage because it was empty, bone dry. He sighed heavily, the strain of indecision marring his id. Ron wanted to do this thing and he didn't. But why not, he thought? Why not just try it once, and if the attempt fails, that's it! That would let Garrett off the hook as far as Ron was concerned, and it would help stem those inner conflicts Garrett had been suffering through.

"Help me move the table," Garrett said.

"Why, man?" Ron asked, staggering to his feet.

"Because I want to do this right! That's why! We need a pentagram, and if we move the damn table we might have enough room." Then he glanced over at the blonde on the sofa bed. "What about her? What if she wakes up?"

"We'll tell her it's a joke. We'll tell her we're just kidding around. Then we'll both stick it to her again and she'll sleep."

Garrett didn't like it, having her there. It was bad enough doing this when they were alone, but the blonde could complicate matters. After the table had been moved, Garrett realized he needed something to draw the pentagram with, and also the figures of the demons therein. Ron gave him a pen, a ballpoint. Garrett had a feeling, just from the way this was starting, that sure as hell something was about to go wrong.

But he went on with it anyway, knowing he couldn't stop because he'd already given his word. "Satan," he began to chant while completing the pentagram, "Lord of the winds from the four corners of the earth—Satan from the south, Lucifer from the east, Belial from the north, and Leviathan from the west. Hear us, oh mighty one, in our hour of need, and grant these our requests. Hail, Satan!"

"Hey, man," Ron said, "This is some heavy shit. You ain't just fooling are you?" He suddenly sounded as sober as Garrett, but he was still weaving when he moved. "You really do know what you're talking about. You weren't lying."

Garrett ignored him and continued, stepping

into the middle of the pentagram when it was finished while Ron remained outside, along the outer edges of its perimeter—a mistake Garrett would live to regret until the day he died. "Satan . . . I beseech thee. Come forth and hear our pleas. Hail, Satan."

This was no good. It wouldn't work. Most of the items Garrett needed were missing. He needed a sharp knife, candles, and an altar to put them on. He needed incense and human blood, the sacrifice of a body part. Then he made another grave mistake by informing Ron of their shortage of needed materials.

"Well hell, no problem," Ron said. "They got incense down the hall." Then, despite Garrett's objections, he left the apartment and went on down the hall to knock on somebody's door at two in the morning, returning moments later with the incense. "Guy's a hippy," he explained, holding up two sticks of frangipani for Garrett to use. "He burns this shit all the time. Didn't you ever smell it?"

He handed the incense to Garrett, reaching as far as he could without stepping into the pentagram and asked, "What's next?" Garrett was afraid to tell him about the blood, but he did mention the altar and the candles. Ron left the room again, returning about ten minutes later with two cardboard boxes and a handful of candles. "Stack the boxes," he told Garrett, "And you got an altar."

"Where did the candles come from?" Garrett wanted to know.

"The same place I got the boxes from. The storage room downstairs. I broke in."

"You did what? You wanna get us thrown out

on the street?''

"No one saw me. Besides, we needed them and they had plenty." Ron hesitated and started to speak again, but couldn't. Garrett knew he was agonizing over the blood part of it. They still had to have human blood to complete the ceremony. When he opened a drawer where they kept their silverware, Garrett felt his throat lump. Did Ron intend to cut himself?

But the answer soon became clear. As Garrett looked on in horror, Ron approached the blonde, took one of her hands and without thinking twice severed a finger below the second knuckle. She moaned yet never woke up. Garrett was in shock. He opened his mouth to protest, but nothing came out.

"I gave her something to make her happy," Ron said very matter of factly as though they were discussing the weather. "I dropped something in one of her drinks. Good thing I did. She didn't even feel the knife."

"You doped her up?"

"Sure." Ron said, and noticed that Garrett's expression never changed. He was still horrified. Ron narrowed his eyes and smiled, but it wasn't warm. "Look, man. She said twenty a piece for one lay. How else was I gonna get more out of her? So I gave her something to keep her happy and agreeable."

"I can't believe I'm actually witnessing this," Garrett said finally. "Doesn't it bother you? You disfigured that girl—"

"She's a whore! So don't waste any sympathy on her. Besides, after I get rich, I'll slip her a few bucks."

"Is that what this is all about? Getting rich?

Suddenly you've lost your morals.''

"Morals have nothing to do with it. So grow up! We gotta do this thing, and if it isn't done right— You know what I mean?''

Garrett knew; more than he cared to at the moment. "You better wrap her hand up. She's bleeding like hell." Walking to the edge of the pentagram, because Ron still wouldn't come inside, he took the finger and placed it on the makeshift altar. "Satan," he chanted once more, "Master of the Earth, lord of the princes of hell. Hear us, we beseech you—"

Garrett tried to finish, tried to say one more 'Hail, Satan,' but he couldn't. There was a man standing inside the pentagram with him, and it wasn't Ron. Garrett was frightened until he realized how normal and ordinary-looking the man was. And yet, he was different somehow. To begin with, he had the most handsome face Garrett had ever seen. And he was tall and stately, with coal black hair and eyes. And those eyes were what made him different; there was something disturbing about those eyes. One minute they were red, the next they were black again.

"You called?" he wanted to know, his voice a raging storm of violence.

When Garrett didn't answer right away, he looked at Ron who turned pale and pointed a finger at Garrett. "He called you!" was all Ron could manage to say.

Garrett realized then that he was face to face with the master beast himself and wished he was outside the pentagram with Ron, because if Garrett was outside he couldn't be touched. Neither Satan or his followers would dare cross the lines of the pentagram. So Garrett was trapped. Ron, it seemed, was the smart one.

The master beast smiled, baring teeth like spikes of steel. Then he opened his mouth and roared. Flames spewed forth from between his lips with such ferocity that Garrett was knocked to the ground. This was almost a comedy routine he remembered thinking at the time; this guy puking flames, him falling down.

"This guy?" Satan asked as though he'd read Garrett's mind. "Puking flames?" He stepped closer to Garrett's prone figure and extended his hand, his index finger aimed directly at Garrett's skull. "Tell me what's funny about this."

Lights exploded in a psychedelic burst of color. Then Garrett screamed in agony, grabbed his head and held on as pain seared his skull while pictures in the form of tiny vignettes of horror danced inside his brain. He saw hell, saw the many levels of torture, saw death and eternal damnation. And when at last it was over, when it had mercifully stopped, Garrett rose to his feet and faced the master beast head-on because he was different inside. Somehow he'd changed; his emotions had become hardened by the truth.

Satan smiled and spoke again, "I will grant your wishes. I will give you your power. I will give you great wealth. All that you desire is yours."

When he was finished speaking he continued to smile, but somehow the feelings behind it were twisted. Ron noticed it too. "What's the catch?" he asked. With the smile still frozen in place, the master beast turned to Ron, pointing his finger at him. Ron cringed and stepped further back, away from the outer rim of the pentagram. "No big thing, man," Ron said, his voice cracking. "All I wanted to know was what's the catch?"

"This!" Satan roared amidst a sudden puff of smoke. "This is the catch!"

Garrett felt his heart beating wildly. Cold spasms of fear shook his spinal column, for in the midst of the smoke was a creature so horrible, so very demonic in appearance he wanted to die. He ran to the edge of the pentagram and watched as Ron left through the front door. Ron was running out on him, leaving him there, abandoning him to the mercy of these creatures. And Garrett was almost there, had one foot on the other side of the rim when a hand—a skinless, fleshless, mutated talon of a hand—reached out and touched him—

But Garrett had fainted. When he woke up his head was spinning and he imagined it all had been a dream. He rose unsteadily to his feet and felt his heart pounding heavily. He spotted the pentagram. But they both had been so drunk, him and Ron, maybe he dreamed the rest. Maybe they hadn't performed the ceremony. His gaze wandered to the couch to see if Ron was there, sleeping with the blonde.

But Ron was gone, and so was the blonde. A crimson outline of her body stained the sheets where she had been lying. And Garrett knew it had really happened. And Ron had run out on him, had left him at the mercy of two of hell's foulest creatures. Damn him! And the blonde? Satan had taken her with him.

Garrett smiled then, because he remembered Satan's promises of great power and wealth. And when he stopped to think about his experience it hadn't really been so bad. At least he was still alive and unmarked. 'And hell, no problem, man,' as Ron would say. It had been easy. And to think that Garrett would be the rich one while Ron would remain a pauper because he hadn't stepped inside the pentagram, and because he ran when the going got a bit tough.

But now, as Garrett drifted from the past to the present, he realized that Ron was the lucky one. Ron wasn't rich, but then Ron wasn't the harborer of the beast, either. It was all too clear now. And Garrett also recalled how that feeling of being so very lucky had stayed with him for a long time. It was there when he achieved his goals, when he suddenly and irrevocably became the owner and president of The Garrett Lang Corporation Inc. Oh, yes, it was there for years . . .

Then he lost it, around the time that he first noticed the beast in him, when the beast emerged and started killing. Then he knew he'd never been lucky to begin with, and he also knew what that catch was that Ron had mentioned. Sharing his body with a demon, that was the catch!

And so, Samantha my love, he thought, the problem I have to solve before marrying you is to get rid of the beast. And time is growing short. The lord I've worshiped for ten years grows impatient for my soul. And since a bargain is a bargain, I may not be able to exorcise the demon within before the demon consumes me.

Garrett rose and went to his car to retrieve the body he knew he'd find in the back seat. After all, a whole body was a perfect gift, more than just fingers and toes, more than just an arm or a head. And since Satan had accepted the body of the punk rocker, maybe he would also accept this one and exorcise the demon from within his soul.

16

Jeffrey floated back sometime during the night, only half-expecting to see Uncle Max. Aunt Mona wasn't the best in the world at this, at the art of bringing people back from the 'other side,' and the day she snatched him from the garden of paradise he called home was either a mistake or a case of good luck.

So now Aunt Mona would either bring back the wrong person—someone she couldn't return as was the case with him—or she'd bring back nothing. Poor Aunt Mona, he thought, she tried so hard to please that sometimes she tried too hard, put too much effort into her chants and incantations and overshot her targets.

With this in mind he floated up to the front door and laid his ear against it, to eavesdrop in hopes of hearing Uncle Max's voice, when he noticed something particular: there was dead silence inside. Aunt Mona must've failed. But Jeffrey should've heard noises in there anyway. Aunt Mona generally had the television on when she was alone.

Not that she spent hours watching the soaps or quiz shows. It was more than that. The noise of the television in the background was good company. She felt as though she was never alone with so many voices in the house. And because of this she forgot her loneliness and was able to go about her business. She cleaned the house, baked her pastries, her cookies, her cakes, and did the laundry, all with the television on.

But then, Aunt Mona hadn't had the television on much since he came into the picture. He, Jeffrey, had filled a gap, had taken away the need for artificial stimulation. Then again, he wasn't home tonight. She'd sent him out because he didn't altogether agree with her attempts to bring Uncle Max there. So the television should've been on.

And if the television wasn't on, it was because someone had dropped by to visit. And yet he didn't hear her talking. In fact he didn't hear anything except the roar of silence, a loud, deathly-cold, silence, and it scared him. So did the dent in the door, the one that would've been at head level with Aunt Mona.

The door was part way open too, just a crack, but enough to allow the heavenly sweet aroma of spices and herbs to flow into the hallway. Jeffrey put an eye to the crack, but it was awkward. There was barely enough of an opening to see anything. And he wondered why he didn't just go on inside. It was his home too. He lived there. So why not just go on in?

Because the silence disturbed him. Made him afraid. Made him long for his quiet place, the one he'd found in death. Where there was sunshine all the time, and trees and flowers. And everything was peaceful and never scary or silent like this . . .

Putting his eye to the crack again, Jeffrey closed the other and concentrated all his energies on the art of focusing. And what he eventually saw made him scream inside. A crumpled figure lay on the floor. And it wasn't a sleepy kind of lying, or even a restful kind of lying. Rather it was a dead kind of a thing. And he knew at once that it was Aunt Mona and that she was dead.

She'd gone over to the other side. She'd entered his place of beauty, of eternal rest. She'd entered the same paradise that she had so unwittingly snatched him from, the place she couldn't send him back to. And now she was there, and he was here, and somehow he knew it would probably always remain that way—

"Jeffrey, I'm surprised at you."

He heard her voice coming from behind him and dared not hope. He was ready to charge it to his imagination until he turned and saw Aunt Mona floating up by the ceiling.

"Would I leave you? Would I desert you? I m surprised that you, of all people, could think such a thing."

"But Aunt Mona, I was scared. I figured you left because you had no choice. When you die you just close your eyes, and when you open them again, you're in this place. I mean, it's beyond your control—"

"No, it isn't. Nothing is beyond your control. Not when you want something badly enough. I just told those people up there, the ones in charge, I told them that I had no intention of leaving my Jeffrey behind. And here I am!"

Jeffrey turned back to the door for one instant, a

burning question searing at his brain. But before
he had a chance to ask it, Aunt Mona spoke,
explaining all.

"It was the Bridge Gate Killer. The original. They
have the wrong man in jail, you know." She
floated down beside him and planted a kiss on his
face. He was surprised that he could feel it for the
first time. Well, at least for the first time since he'd
died. "He—the killer—he heard me chanting and
listened at the door. Well, he gathered from what
I was saying that I was trying to conjure up Uncle
Max. He heard me use Max's name and used that
fact to trick me into letting him in so that he could
kill me."

"Oh God, Aunt Mona, I'm so sorry."

"Don't be. It was my own fault. If I hadn't been
fooling around with something I had no right
fooling around with, I'd be alive now. If I hadn't
been chanting in the first place, he never would've
had a chance to trick—"

"But you were doing it for me!"

"It doesn't matter who I was doing it for.
Anyway, let's not think about it anymore. What's
done is done. And now, let's get on with the rest
of our lives."

"Our what?"

"Our lives, Jeffrey." She put her arms around
him and kissed him again."

He sighed with relief. "I guess that means we're
going home. Back to our quiet place."

"Hell no. I wouldn't go back there if you paid
me. It's too quiet there. In fact, it's so quiet there
it gave me a headache. I spent my whole life
around noise. I couldn't survive in a place like
that."

Jeffrey couldn't believe he was hearing this.

"But, Aunt Mona. If we don't go back there, where else are we gonna go?"

She smiled and patted his face reassuringly. "Where will we go?" she asked, repeating his words. "I'll tell you where. To see the world, that's where!"

"To see the world?"

"Yes. I've spent my entire life in New York, even though I promised myself I'd see the world before I died. Well, it didn't happen that way. And now I'm dead. But just because I'm dead doesn't mean I have to give up, does it?"

Jeffrey wanted to run. She was talking crazy and he wanted to take her and run back to the safety of his quiet place. Maybe once he got her there she'd listen to reason. "Aunt Mona," he began, speaking as patiently as an adult would to a child. "How will we get around? You know, from one place to another. Would you consider that?"

"Oh hell, Jeffrey. Don't be such a stick-in-the-mud. Think! For God's sake, use your head and think. We'll travel on boats, on airplanes. I mean, who's gonna stop us? Nobody can even see us. We're just puffs of smoke. And it'll be wonderful. We'll get to see the world. We'll travel to Europe. We'll see Buckingham Palace and the changing of the guard. We'll see the ancient ruins in Egypt."

With that she grabbed his hand and headed for the elevator, but decided on the stairs instead. Since they could float, she said, it didn't matter which way they went, elevator or stairs. And besides, she had no patience to wait for elevators now when there was so much to do, so much to see.

"You know, Jeffrey, I saw a picture once called 'Auntie Mame' with Lucille Ball. In it, she took her

nephew off to see the world. I kind of feel like
Auntie Mame right this moment. And Jeffrey,
don't look so depressed. You'll love this, too, I
promise you will.''

It was Sunday, and J.J. Holiman decided to let
Garrett sleep while he went into the city to see
Ron Wheatley. At this point he still hadn't figured
what new thing or new exorcism to use on Ron
should he be the harborer of the beast. And since
this was only a fact-finding visit, to feel Ron out,
he left Garrett home.

This was what he told himself outwardly.

But inside he knew different.

He'd read something awful in those books of his
last night, something that made this more than a
fact-finding visit. And because of what he'd read,
he decided to leave Garrett out of it. After all,
there was still a way to exorcise the beast, but it
meant sudden death for J.J. It meant he wouldn't
survive this time.

Why, therefore, involve Garrett in this? And
Garrett would surely jump in if he saw that J.J.
was dying. And yet, J.J. didn't want to die and felt
that—

He should've burned that damned book before
he found the way!

Because now the choice was no longer his.
Asgar was a murdering machine who would stop
at nothing now that the rampage had started.

And J.J. was here for but one purpose now, to
stop the evil from gaining control. He was an
exorcist, wasn't he?

Sitting in the back seat of Garrett's chauffeured
limousine, J.J. tried to keep his mind on the task
ahead, on his meeting with Ron Wheatley, and at

the same time he tried to keep it from being influenced by the mark of the beast on his shoulder. It was very important at this point to stay in control of his faculties and not allow the beast in him to take over.

He tried to focus his attention on prayers to his Lord. But the beast—which he appropriately called the x factor, because he wasn't sure if it was another Asgar or not—the beast wasn't having any of this. He was there for a purpose; to keep J.J. on the straight and narrow, the straight and narrow road to hell.

J.J. fought his newly found primeval urges, the ones that had started days ago, with everything in him. He fought the urge to rip his clothes off and jiggle his dohickey out the window, in the faces of the old bitches riding in limos like his own. He fought the urge to punch a hole in the glass between him and the chauffeur and tell that lily-livered bastard what an ass-kisser he was. And he fought the urge to masturbate while screaming Samantha's name at the top of his lungs.

The only urge he couldn't fight was the urge to giggle, and giggle he did. It was low at first, something soft and silly coming up through his throat to leap between his lips and float in the air. Nothing big, nothing loud. But then it grew bolder, grew in volume, grew in intensity until J.J. looked up and saw the chauffeur staring at him through the rear view mirror, the muscles of his jaw twitching.

At that point J.J. decided it was time to resist the urge to giggle. So he clenched his teeth tightly together and tightened his jaw muscles. But it didn't help. The giggles managed to escape through the slight space in his front teeth.

Knowing it was useless to proceed with this, useless to try to stop the giggles, J.J. ignored the chauffeur and spent the rest of the trip staring at the world outside through a tinted pane of glass.

Ron Wheatley was about to leave the station house when the desk sergeant buzzed to tell him that J.J. Holiman wanted to see him. And suddenly he wasn't so anxious to leave: partly because of the body he feared was lying in the back seat of his car, and partly because he needed J.J.'s help. He was wrong about the man they had in jail, which meant that the real killer was still running loose.

J.J. looked awful, like someone had done a dipsy on his body. Ron surveyed the bruises, the welts, the marks on his neck and shuddered. But J.J. must've dismissed his wounds because he had this weird sort of smile on his face, and when he shook Ron's hand he giggled.

After exchanging pleasantries, after dragging out the hellos and the how-are-you-doings for all they were worth, they both just sat and stared at each other and didn't say another word for a long time. Ron was puzzled that J.J. would come to see him, make a trip from the Hamptons, merely to sit and stare. But then he, himself, should've said something. He wanted to. Hadn't he been tempted more than once to call J.J. and ask him for help?

"You look awful," Ron finally said, resigned to the fact that the truth had to be gotten out in the open, even if the truth was that he was the killer himself. Otherwise this thing between them would remain hidden, and that would be worse. Hidden things went unchecked; hidden things grew and festered like funguses. "What happened? Who beat you up?"

"Asgar. You have the wrong man in jail, you know—"

"Yes!"

And that was it, the essence of their conversation for a while. But Ron couldn't hold onto his silence, couldn't live with the thought of being the killer himself. "Am I the one?" he wanted to know. "Am I the harborer of the beast?"

J.J.'s mouth fell open. He looked shocked, as though this was the last question in the world he expected Ron to ask. "I think so," was all he could say.

"And I'm not psychic."

"I don't think so."

"How? When did it happen?" Ron suddenly wanted to leave, to run, to get as far away as he could and find a safe place to hide. Then he wouldn't have to face the truth about himself. Then he wouldn't have to think about the creature living in his body, and sometimes taking over his brain and holding onto him for all he was worth. Then he wouldn't have to think about how Asgar was a far worse disease than anything he could ever have imagined growing inside of him, worse even than cancer. "This creature . . . How did he get hold of me?"

J.J. sighed and raised a hand to his mouth. The hand covering the mouth wasn't part of the sigh; it appeared to Ron that he was trying to stifle himself, as though he was trying not to giggle. "I asked you a question before, about being involved in Satanism. At least I'm pretty sure I did . . . When you're as old as I am the mind plays tricks on you."

Ron thought back to his first meeting with J.J.

June DeSoto had been murdered and *beheaded* and *be-armed*. *Be-armed*? He thought about that, about how he'd just invented a word, and how it fit so perfectly. The killer had taken her arm, had be-armed her or disarmed her or whatever, and he wanted to giggle the same way J.J. was trying hard not to at the moment. "No," he said, "You never asked about Satanism. But you did ask me if anything had happened over the years . . . if anything had caused me to go into shock.

"Yes," J.J. said, his eyes lighting up as it came back to him. "I told you about how people sometimes become psychic after a violent shock." Then the old man trained his attention on Ron's face and Ron knew he wouldn't like what was coming next. "I only mentioned it because you told me you were seeing things through the eyes of the beast. And you're a cop. The last one I would ever suspect of being the harborer. So the next best answer was that you had to be psychic. Only now I don't think so. I don't think it's the case here."

Ron's brain screamed. He was hearing the truth and he couldn't live with it, couldn't live with knowing there was something malicious and evil and deadly sharing his body. His tortured mind searched for answers, searched elsewhere for a truth he could live with. "I did have an extremely shocking experience you know. So maybe you were right. Maybe I am just being psychic."

That's it, Ron thought after he'd said it. A much better answer. And one he should've accepted long ago, rather than doing what he did: disbelieving J.J.'s theory about him being psychic. Because by discarding J.J.'s theory, and still being able to see things through the eyes of the beast, there was only one other path open to him: the eventual acceptance of the fact that he, himself, was the harborer of the beast. And it was easier now to recall what he'd done to Debbie and imagine himself as being psychic as a result. Hell, there's a sound answer for everything, he thought, and it doesn't necessarily have to be a bad one.

"Maybe you are just being psychic," J.J. repeated, his eyes overcast, his voice dull. "But I don't really think so."

"But I shot my wife, in the back. By accident. That threw me into shock for years. I mean, I'm still not over it."

"Ron be truthful now. Have you ever been involved in Satanism?"

"Hell, no! What'dya think I am, a complete nut?"

"I'm not talking about something on a serious level. I mean, well, maybe years back. As a teenager, or a young adult, maybe you did something on a dare. Played with a Ouija Board. Performed a seance with your friends. You had to have done something in the line of Satanism or witchcraft to bring this beast forth."

"Oh, God!" He covered his eyes with his hands and wanted to die. 'What's the catch?' he'd asked old Satan that night in the room with Garrett. 'What's the catch?' And now he knew! This was the catch. Sharing his body with a demon was the catch. "Oh, God!" He bowed his head on his desk and began to cry as he never had before, except for the time when his mother died and the time he hurt Debbie.

"Ron! What is it?"

J.J. sounded alarmed and sounded like he

wanted to giggle, too. But Ron couldn't answer, not right away. This thing he'd done with Garrett, this had to be the answer. But it was too painful to face. He waited a few minutes, waited until he'd just about cried himself out, then he raised his head, turned his tortured eyes on J.J.'s face and told him the truth—how two very foolish young men had called forth the master beast himself. He told about their greed, their yearning for great wealth and power. And when his telling of the story ended, he felt as though something had been released inside him. That terrible anguish that had been festering and eating away at him for years had been released and couldn't gnaw away at him any longer.

J.J. sat for a long while, his hand covering his mouth, and said nothing. He seemed deep in thought, deeply engrossed in something that was too painful for him to face now. And when he was finally able to speak, his words loomed in the air and hung over them like some great vaporous beast waiting to consume them both. And again Ron wanted to die, but for different reasons this time.

"Garrett. Garrett is the one," he said very quietly as though he were now facing the death of his only son, as if his life were about to come to an end and he didn't care. Then he rose, stifled a giggle, and started to walk out without saying anything more. But Ron couldn't allow this, couldn't allow the man to leave with no further explanation.

J.J. had just relieved him of the burden of being a murderer. And now J.J. had to explain how he knew. J.J. turned and leaned against the frame of the door and told Ron how he knew. It took only a few minutes, but when the conversation was over, Ron knew the truth . . . Garrett was the one harboring the beast!

And now Garrett had Samantha out there in the Hamptons with him. But Garrett wasn't alone in his body. Asgar was in there with him. . . .

Without a word, Ron dug into his wallet and extracted a piece of paper with a phone number on it. "I'm going to call out there, to Garrett's. I have to warn Samantha, tell her to get out of there as fast as she can!"

He picked up the receiver, then stopped to listen when J.J. spoke again. "If you do this, do it in such a way that Garrett doesn't become suspicious. If he finds out the truth—that we know all about him and have told Samantha—he might kill her before either of us can stop him!"

Ron held onto the phone and realized his hands were shaking. Could he pull it off? Could he tell Samantha without alarming her? "Maybe I should call the police out there. Have Garrett picked up. Then we know she'll be safe—"

"And what would you tell them?" J.J. wanted to know. "What are your charges against him?"

"I'll tell them he's a prime suspect in a murder case. I'll tell them we've only now received evidence as to his guilt."

"Son, I'm afraid you're going to have to do better than that. Think about it. What if the police in another county called here and wanted you to pick up a suspect for them? Wouldn't you want complete answers before you stuck your neck out and arrested someone for somebody else's sake? Wouldn't you want all the facts before you got involved?" Ron nodded silently. "Well, then. What do you intend to tell the police out there?

That you know he's harboring a demon so he's a murderer? Think about it Ron!''

Ron hung up the receiver and jumped up, reaching for his jacket, lying over the back of his chair. ''Then I'm going out there—''

''You can't. You can't do anything at this point to make Garrett suspicious or angry until I've had a chance to perform my exorcism. And seeing you out there would accomplish both. He'd become suspicious and know that we were onto him. Then he'd get angry and use Asgar to kill us all. Not just Samantha.''

Ron sunk back into his seat, and felt as though he were sinking into hell. What could he do to help Samantha? Not much at this point. ''I still think I should make the call.''

''Yes. It's a good idea. But be careful of what you say!''

Samantha wasn't home when Ron called. Some stupid bitch of a maid had answered the phone and told him she'd gone for a walk. ''Is there any message?'' she wanted to know. And Ron, being the panicky individual he was, thought of telling her to relay this message: ''Tell her to get the fuck out of there as fast as she can!''

But he didn't say it for several reasons. First, there was the slight possibility that Samantha had taken her walk alone. He hadn't asked if Garrett was with her. He was afraid to. Because if Samantha was alone then Garrett could be in the house listening over an extention that very minute. And if that were so, then Garrett was in a jealous rage by now; jealous because Ron had called asking for Samantha.

And there was an echo on the line as it was, as

though someone were listening in on the call . . .

He dismissed it. Had to dismiss it. And went on to his second reason for not asking if Samantha was alone.

If Garrett had gone with her, then her life was in danger. Although Ron was aware of Garrett's love for Samantha, he also knew Garrett wasn't in complete control of his senses. Asgar was calling the shots now, and Asgar had no love for anybody. "No," he said to the maid, and felt his heart drop because he was so far from his Samantha and she was in grave danger. "No message."

He sat behind his desk for a moment and thought about the fix he was in. And he thought about Samantha being in danger. Or was she? Garrett had no reason thus far to be suspicious, and he also loved Samantha. Therefore Samantha was in no danger at present, and probably wouldn't be until J.J. Holiman started his exorcism.

Oh, God. J.J. was old and in no condition to take on Asgar by himself. He'd already been badly injured in a scuffle with that demon bastard. Ron jumped up and grabbed his jacket. No matter what J.J. Holiman said, he was going out there. And if God was on his side, he'd get there in time to do some good.

How much good he couldn't fathom at the moment; he was no exorcist. But maybe the fact of his presence would prove enough of a threat to cool Asgar's threats. Wiping sweat from his upper lip, he climbed behind the wheel of his car and considered using his siren and his hand-held flasher. This was a code three: a life-threatening emergency.

Then again, why didn't he just hire a brass band, or send up balloons and smoke signals? Why not call and tell Asgar himself he was on his way? Ron knew he could be an awful asshole at times. He decided against using his sirens or his flasher, and drove to the Queens Midtown Tunnel to get the fastest road out to the Hamptons.

Garrett turned away from his Telex to pick up the phone on the third ring, at exactly the same moment as the maid. A case of perfect timing. Ron Wheatley thought there was only one person listening to him. But no, Garrett was listening too.

And yet, when Garrett picked up the receiver, he had no thought of eavesdropping. It was simply a matter of the phone ringing for such a long time. One ring . . . Two rings . . . the damned thing was driving Garrett crazy with its persistence, distracting his attention from the messages he was sending, and making him think it might be an important call, even if it was Sunday.

And so he picked it up, and listened in.

And, being one with the beast on a more conscious level now, he was able to read into Ron Wheatley's thoughts. He was able to scan Ron's brain from a great distance and was able to know the truth!

Ron was onto him because J.J. Holiman had enlightened him. And now they both had intentions of telling Samantha! His Samantha! And of taking her away from him, of turning her against him.

He wanted revenge! . . . and knew he'd rather see Samantha dead than taken away from him, dead rather than turned against him, dead rather than in the arms of another.

Therefore, he'd kill Samantha first. Then old J.J., who was on his way back now, for telling Ron, for discovering the truth and spreading it like a cancer gone mad. And then he'd kill Ron Wheatley. Ron was on his way, too. Garrett had felt a terrible anxiety in the man when he scanned his brain, an awful fear picking at Ron's insides, one that said he could wait no longer. Samantha was in danger and he was coming out here on his white horse to save her.

Garrett had terrible, throbbing pains in his head. The beast wanted out. The beast wanted to be in charge of the massacre and the subsequence ceremony at which time both he and Garrett would offer three whole bodies to Satan, and not just a paltry token gift of some fingers and an arm. But Garrett was running this show. He was the one in charge now.

Besides, after being one with the beast for so long a time, he knew how to kill as well. How to kill and how to torture, and how to mutilate! And the center ring was his, along with the spotlight and the adoration of the crowd.

He would do it all himself. Then maybe let the beast take over. . . .

But first, Samantha, my love, one last lay for old times sake. And in a bed this time, not rolling around in the grass like dogs in heat! But Garrett dear, he thought to himself and smiled. She enjoyed her lay in the grass so much. And she was craving for more.

"Quiet, Asgar," he commanded the low soothing voice that had risen from somewhere inside of him. "Quiet! Your turn comes. But for now, patience, my friend, patience!"

* * *

Garrett was in his study sending calls over his Telex system to his offices overseas when Samantha decided to go for a walk. She was impressed because Garrett was wealthier and more important than she imagined. Still, she couldn't help but think about Ron Wheatley at times. About how Ron loved her and wanted her to marry him more than anything else in the world.

While Garrett only wanted her to live with him!

Ron had nobler intentions. But Ron was already married.

She walked into the woods to clear her head, the same as she'd done many times in the past, the only difference being that she was older now and more mature. And there was no rapist hiding in these woods, no one to tear her clothes off and do terrible things to her body.

Walking along a path that would take her deeper into the woods, she felt safe and wonderful in a place familiar to her, a place that granted the same sanctity as her woods back home. Pausing on the path for a moment before going on, she saw a spot where the grass had been flattended and knew this was the place where Garrett had taken her, where he'd made love to her and in such a way as to make her dream man seem pale in comparison.

Then she marveled that there had been no more dreams at night after that; no more sense of being in Dirk's arms, or Lance's. Garrett had erased her dreams forever because nothing in her sleep could ever take the place of reality with Garrett—

A twig cracked underfoot—but it wasn't under her foot . . .

Her mind went back to that awful day years ago

when she'd been walking through some woods and twigs cracked underfoot, under the rapist's foot! She felt suddenly frightened although she had no reason to. The rapist was dead. She'd killed him; she torched the bastard, which was a kind of poetic justice when she stopped to consider what he'd done to others. Besides, there was another reason to feel safe here: these woods belonged to Garrett!

Another twig cracked underfoot, and she realized where it was coming from.

Behind her, from the direction of the house . . .

So, if someone were coming toward her, it had to be Garrett. He realized she'd gone for a walk, and even though he'd been occupied with his Telex when she left the house, he missed her so that now he was looking for her.

Another twig cracked underfoot, closer this time . . .

With this in mind she decided to stay where she was and wait for her Garrett, the man in her life now. After all, she'd been waiting for him all her life—waiting and dreaming. And now she'd never let him go—

"There you are, my beautiful baby," Garrett said, stepping into the clearing. His voice sounded clipped and tight. But she ignored it.

"Oh Garrett, I knew it was you," she said, running to him, to embrace him, to let him feel her love. But strangely enough, she felt little coming from him. His body was cold and rigid, almost the same as his voice had seemed seconds ago. Probably a business deal gone bad, she surmised, and hugged him even tighter to show him she'd be there when he needed her.

"What say we go back to the house for some

lunch?'' he suggested, his body still an ungiving, unbending, unyielding force of rigidity.

Yes, she wanted to scream. Oh, Garrett yes! For lunch preceeded love-making in her dreams. And lunch now, here with Garrett, would surely mean the same. Putting his arm around her waist, he guided her back to the house.

17

J.J. Holiman had told the chauffeur to step on it. There were lives at stake here: Garrett's and Samantha's both. But why was he in such a damned hurry, he wondered, when he was only hurrying to his own death. And this wasn't only a possibility. The fact of his own impending death was definite, as was foretold in one of his books . . .

Clutching his hand to his mouth to keep from giggling, he tried to concentrate on the scenery outside and not think about how he was seeing it for the last time. He was breathing God's air and looking at the bounties of nature, the harvest of spring and would be able to enjoy it for another hour or however long it would take to get back to the Hamptons, and no longer.

He thought it over, considered the endless alternatives. He could run away and leave Asgar to others to worry about. Then he wondered about that: what others? Who knew him as well as J.J. who'd been fighting the bastard for years now? Running was out.

Well hell, then he could stop at a church, any church, and get a vial of holy water, and have himself and his Bible blessed. The holy water would burn Asgar's flesh; words from the Bible would sear his brain. But Asgar was wise to this and he knew J.J. was coming. Therefore, he'd run if J.J. stopped at a church, because he'd know that too. Asgar was constantly scanning his brain for answers. If J.J. wanted him to hang around, he'd have to face him head on. And therein lay the only answer and the assurance of death as well.

Ron Wheatley had also been stuck in traffic. J.J. Holiman had to be at least ten miles ahead of him and probably sitting still too. After all, the Long Island Expressway was often referred to as the world's longest parking lot.

With this in mind, he stuck his hand-held flasher out of the window and rode along the shoulder of the highway until he was ahead of the clog. He still didn't see J.J., but he knew he was up there, maybe five or six miles ahead of him by this time. And he hoped that one of them, either he or J.J., would get to Garrett's in time to save Samantha. And Garrett too.

The mere thought of Garrett's name caused a buckling sensation in his heart; he had palpitations. But it was only because of what he'd learned from J.J. that he felt pity for Garrett at this point, and a dark hatred for himself. After all, he was the one who'd talked Garrett into fooling with something he wasn't all that familiar with. And while it was true, Garrett could've refused, could've said no. He didn't because he was Ron's friend at the time and would've done anything for Ron.

So the blame was Ron's and sort of Garrett's too, because Garrett hadn't been paying attention when J.J. taught him about the other way to make money. And so Garrett had it all mixed up. And to think it started out in an innocent way: two young men, greedily eager for wealth and power, impatient to achieve it all, playing with something they really weren't sure of, or were sure would work.

As Ron narrowed the gap between him and the Hamptons, his mind went back to his earlier meeting with J.J. and he thought how J.J. had convinced him that Garrett was the one, the harborer of the beast. Ron had listened and understood, and now the guilt was Ron's.

"What are you trying to say?" he'd asked of J.J. "That if Garrett had been outside the pentagram with me he would've been safe? Is that it?"

"No," J.J. answered. "Garrett was safe where he was. He was safe inside the pentagram. And had he stayed there we wouldn't be going through this now. Asgar couldn't have touched him."

"I don't understand. Garrett said it was risky inside."

"Garrett had his information ass-backwards as usual."

"But," Ron said, persisting because he just had to have all the answers. "Garrett was in there, inside of the pentagram with Satan and Asgar. So he should've been safe according to what you're saying. And yet, Satan sent Asgar after Garrett—"

"Knowing Garrett would run. You see, Satan's a bluff artist and he's well acquainted with human nature. After all, he's been studying us since the beginning of time. He knew he couldn't touch Garrett while he was inside the pentagram. And hell, he wanted his revenge against Garrett for summoning him up to ask for money, and since he was mad at Asgar, what better way was there to get back at both of them than linking them together?

"And in order to accomplish his goal of revenge, he had to somehow force Garrett out of the safety of the rim of the pentagram. So, knowing human nature as well as he does, he put Asgar onto Garrett because he knew Garrett would run. I mean, wouldn't you run from a skinless horror like Asgar? When Garrett stepped over the rim of safety, he was doomed."

Ron shook his head silently because he couldn't believe what he was hearing. Then, "How come he didn't put Asgar onto me? I was outside and vulnerable."

"You didn't ask for anything. Satan had no quarrel with you, Ron."

Ron remembered holding his head in his hands at that point and speaking through his fingers. "So Garrett was linked with Asgar. And only because he was doing what I forced him into. Oh, God! More guilt to live with." He looked up at J.J. and saw his torment reflected in the old man's eyes. "But then, how come I see everything through the beast if he's living inside of Garrett?"

"That was your form of punishment. Probably for just being there."

My punishment, he thought. Oh yes. That was the catch he'd mentioned to old Satan. 'What's the catch?' he'd asked, making Satan aware of his presence. And old Satan showed Ron what the catch was. Satan fucked him twice. Garrett, although he was the harborer, got the wealth and power; Ron didn't. That was fuck number one.

And Satan fixed Ron so that while he wasn't linked with the beast he could still see the murders, the mutilations, through the eyes of the beast. That was fuck number two.

And now Ron had to live with the answers he'd gotten from J.J. for the rest of his life. He had to think and remember and recall for all time to come. Because as long as he lived, he'd never forgive himself for his part in Garrett's possession by Asgar.

In her dreams, lunch had always preceeded their love-making. And now, although those dreams were past and came to her no more, she was still reliving the best parts. Lying in bed, with Garrett on top of her, she moved to the rhythm of his body and thought how very lucky she was. Garrett, her Garrett, was the fulfillment of a lifetime of searching.

And her life with him was perfect. He was perfect; perfection personified, a dream come true. But there were doubts in her mind too, caused by her naive acceptance of things as they were.

For instance, Garrett looked exactly the same now as in her dreams. He spoke the same, walked the same, made love the same wonderful way. He took her to the same restaurant, and he owned a yacht, as she'd only recently discovered. And although she tried to keep her unruly mind from dwelling on these consistencies—because life had never imitated art as it was doing now—she was deeply troubled by them.

There were so many questions she wanted to ask, but dared not because Garrett didn't know about her dreams. And now she couldn't ask, out

of shame. How could you admit to the man you
loved with all your heart and soul that prior to
meeting him you lived in a dream world, a safe
place sealed in the privacy of sleep? A haven from
the hurts of the world, free from the fear of rape.
How could she tell Garrett that she'd never been
whole before she met him? That she'd been
nothing more than a shell buried in the sand—

"Samantha, please! How can I concentrate with
you carrying on so?"

Her eyes had been closed in passion, and
she kept them that way. Especially now when a
voice—not quite belonging to the man she loved—
echoed in her ears. What happened to his voice?
It was higher pitched than Garrett's, and softer.
The voice was softer; it didn't have that certain
roughness she admired so. And how did he know
what she was thinking, what had been going on in
the safe sanctity of her mind?

"I am legion. I know all things."

She lay still and tried not to think, to disturb the
act he was obviously engrossed in even though
the mood had been broken for her. But there was
something she couldn't ignore: it was the feel of
his body, all clammy and jelly-like in texture—

"Samantha, dearest. Does the feel of my body
really disturb you? Does the penetration disturb
you?" With that he gently thrust himself deeper
into her body and she could almost feel him
smiling when she moaned. "I thought not," he
said, then added, "Why don't you open your
eyes and look at my body? Why don't you revel in
my nakedness as you did before?"

Impossible, she thought. She was quite content
to lie here with her eyes closed and pretend that
nothing had happened to Garrett, that he hadn't

suddenly changed and that she wasn't frightened.
And as she lay there and tried to get back into the
love-making process, she knew it was over for
her. There would be no orgasm this time, no feeling of such complete release that she wanted,
at times, to scream at the top of her lungs.

So she lay quite still and was glad when his
body trembled because now she was no longer a
prisoner, trapped under a strange and foreign
body. Now she could be allowed the luxury of
escape.

"But there is no escape for you, my lovely
Samantha."

She listened to his words and knew her
questions had been answered. All along she'd
known there was a catch somewhere in the relationship, because Garrett had been so perfect,
almost too perfect. There had to be a catch somewhere.

"I'm everyone's catch lately, it seems. The
catch in the deal, the catch of the day, the catch
you've been waiting for."

She opened her eyes and choked back a
scream. The face looking down into hers wasn't
human. There was a network of spidery veins and
arteries, all pumping blood, laced throughout.
There were eyes brimming with madness, eyes
that were held in the head in such a way as to
reveal their entire being right straight back to the
source; the sockets, again with that same spidery
network of interlocking veins and arteries as the
face. And she found this to be strangely
fascinating as she'd never before seen an exposed
eye.

He smiled and she wanted to die. There were
huge teeth, jagged, dagger-like spokes. He had no

nose . . . This wasn't Garrett!

"You didn't enjoy it," he said, his breath stale and hot in her face. "Would you like me to do it again? I can, you know."

"Oh, that's all right," she said and smiled back. "I can wait for later." Her mind, she knew, had just caved in, had surrendered to the peaceful sanctity of madness. At least that's how she imagined it was because here she was smiling at a horror. At least she felt she was smiling. Her lips were drawn back into a smile or a reasonable facsimile thereof, weren't they? "Where is Garrett?" she wanted to know.

"Look into my eyes and you'll see him," he said, again assaulting her senses with his warm, rancid breath. And, like an obedient child, she listened and stared and saw Garrett, deep within the beast, his face echoing torment, his voice a howl of damnation. "Garrett's not entirely pleased with the situation. Garrett wanted to be the one fucking you. But I insisted on taking his place. After all, he's the one who continuously gets the girl. And what's fair is fair. Don't you agree?"

"Oh yes," she said and felt the skin on her face stretching back into a broader smile. "And now would you please get off me? I'd like to get up." She wanted to take a shower, and wondered for an instant if she'd shower with the beast as she had with Ron Wheatley and Garrett.

After he let her up, she stood back near the foot of the bed and surveyed him, and smiled again. This was only a dream, she'd gone back to those dreams again.

"I have to kill you, Samantha."

"I know." And somehow she did know.

"But it isn't the end," he said, rising from the bed, his body resembling Garrett's in height and build as well as the oversized penis dangling between his legs. "It's not the end," he repeated. "Rather, it's the beginning. I will take you over to the other side with me to spend an eternity as my mistress."

"Oh, but that's impossible. I'm going to heaven," she said, amazed at the little-girl texture of her own voice. "I've been a good girl and I'm going to heaven."

Just then someone came bursting into the room, making her wonder if this was to be the rescue part of her dream. And as she turned to stare at her knight in shining armor, she wasn't a bit surprised to see that it was that funny little man, J. J. Holiman.

"He's a bad man," she told J.J., pointing to Asgar. "He scared me."

Before turning his energies onto Asgar, J.J. stepped forward and gazed sadly into her eyes. "Dearest Samantha. You're quite mad. And that's good for now."

"Oh, but I'm not," she argued in her cutest little girl voice. "I'm not mad at anyone."

But J.J. wasn't listening. He was already on his way over to face the monster.

"What tricks have you brought today?" Asgar wanted to know.

"Read my mind, Asgar. And see the horrible fate that's in store for both of us. But, before you do, please release Garrett."

"Take him yourself!"

"I can't. You know it has to be done willingly on your part. The boy had nothing to do with this. He's just a pawn in the ongoing battle between you and me. Please, Asgar, release him.''

"FUCKING HOLD OFF, ASGAR!'' came a voice from within J.J. Samantha watched and listened and felt this was the best dream ever. J.J. was speaking in two voices and the effect was thrilling.

"In the name of the Lord—ISN'T HE AN ASSHOLE, ASGAR?''

The sound of laughter in the form of pure madness assaulted her senses. J.J. was laughing, the most awful sound coming from between his lips while he held a hand to his mouth. And Asgar, the beast who resembled Garrett in body only, the beast was laughing too. But then J.J. stopped laughing, or rather talked while he was laughing, and that confused her.

"Jesus, Lord,'' he said. "Please forgive my transgressions and allow me the luxury of victory over the beasts. Please, Lord—FUCK JESUS, LORD.''

Samantha wanted to tell him to make up his mind as to which voice he was going to use, but something happened then and she couldn't speak. A figure, one that was ethereal and smoky, floated from J.J.'s mouth and landed beside the beast. Then the two horrors faced one another, after which the one she'd had intercourse with—thinking it was Garrett—told the other one that he'd done his best and to go on home. Where was home, she wondered?

"You won that round, J.J.,'' Asgar said, "But you're still not getting Garrett back. He's lost forever, doomed to remain a part of my existence.''

"So be it.''

Samantha sat down on the floor, cross-legged in squaw-like fashion and listened intently to the ongoing conversation, her head bobbing back and forth from one to the other like a spectator at a tennis match. This was the best damn dream ever!

"You realize you're condemning yourself to an eternity of damnation and struggling? A battle without end?" the beast said.

"Yes," J.J. answered, exhaling the words in a breathy sigh.

"Well, then. Come on, old man—"

"Old man?" Samantha screamed, interrupting them both. "What's this old man stuff? Listen, you, we're following the Marquis of Queensbury rules here. There will be no name calling! You understand?"

Asgar and J.J. were both too dumbfounded to answer. But Samantha got them going again. Raising her hands high overhead like the flagman at a race, she hesitated a moment, then yelled, "Let the games continue!"

While she looked on, Asgar and J.J. squared off like Sumo wrestlers and to Samantha it was the funniest sight imaginable, what with J.J. and his scrawny legs and Asgar with his penis swinging in wide arcs. But she held onto what little was left of her dignity and suppressed the urge to laugh.

They moved around in a complete circle twice, each ready to grab the other, each hunched over, hands extended in front of them like claws, and Samantha thought this was bullshit. If you want to fight, do it and get it over with. She was almost ready to shout, to chastise them, when J.J. lunged forward and grabbed Asgar by the shoulders, while the beast imitated his movements.

And as their bodies met, she moved back and away from the sudden explosion that occurred; an arc of electricity emanated from the core of the struggling, writhing mass. And a band of white hot current encircled their bodies and then exploded, and suddenly there were two bands in place of the previous one. While she watched, the process was repeated over and over again until there were a dozen rings wrapping them together in a life-death struggle, and she knew they were doomed, both of them.

She moved back even further from the bodies when an arc of electricity—a rainbow of colors— shot from the mass and flew across the room, landing in the middle of the bed. Samantha clapped her hands and screamed with glee. What a wonderful dream this was!

But then something happened to spoil it for her. A bunch of people came bursting into the room and they were hollering and carrying on so she had trouble concentrating on the ongoing fight. One of them resembled Garrett's maid; another resembled his chauffeur; and still a third resembled . . . Oh, shit! Frigging Ron Wheatley! What the hell was he doing here, she wondered, and scowled at him when he tried pulling her to her feet.

"Samantha, we have to leave!" he shouted.

"Then leave! You hear me, Ron? Leave? Get the hell out of here," she yelled, slapping his hands away. "You want to leave, leave! I'm staying!" Hell, just when she was finally having a dream with the best special effects ever, he wanted her to leave.

"Samantha," he yelled again. "Everything's burning. You have to get out of here."

She looked in the direction he was pointing to and saw that the rainbow of electricity had landed in the middle of the bed in the form of a ball of fire. The flames had roared the length of the bed, crawling to devour the enormous wooden headboard, and then climbed the wall to consume the draperies lining the windows. She only half-fought Ron this time when he pulled her to her feet and carried her through the door to safety.

And as she went out of the room, she glanced over Ron's shoulder and saw the still struggling white-hot figures grappling in the middle of an electrical storm and she felt sad. J.J. Holiman was lost to her . . . And Garrett as well, because Garrett had been inside of the beast and the beast had refused to let him go. So Garrett was lost too . . .

And yet, as Ron carried her down the steps toward the main entrance, her fears over losing Garrett began to dissolve. After all, this was just another bad dream. And soon she'd awaken and find Garrett lying next to her in bed and things would be the same as before . . .

Wouldn't they?

18

Ron Wheatley drove along the road that would take him to Samantha, his mind boggled by the events that had led up to the here and now. He was experiencing a deep sense of loss, an open wound in his heart, and he knew it would take forever to heal.

And the whole thing was crazy, nothing made sense. How could all this have started with one awful night ten years ago? Two young men searching for wealth and power pulled a stunt that neither of them really imagined would work. And now, as a result Ron would have to live with the blame for each and every lost life, each and every lost soul for an eternity to come.

First he had to bear the guilt for the murders and mutilations committed by the demon, because he was directly responsible for Asgar's birth in Garrett's body. And that led to even more guilt.

He was responsible for the death of J.J. Holiman, if struggling against an evil force for all time to come could be termed death. But then he thought about it some more and realized that J.J.

was suffering through a fate worse than actual death. Death would've been a more natural release at this point. What J.J. had condemned himself to, by taking Asgar on hand-to-hand, was a living nightmare, one that would never end.

He was also responsible for the death of Garrett Lang. There was more than a temporary raw spot in his heart for Garrett. It was a hurt that had caused permanent damage, but only because he really liked Garrett in spite of the way he'd recently imagined he felt about his old friend. After all, Garrett had been the one with the basic hometown personality that set him aside from others, made him unique, made him a wondrously uncomplicated, unscheming, anxious to please, individual.

And Ron now took the blame for forcing him into doing something against his will. And when Garrett listened to Ron and fooled with Satanism, not knowing the proper methods to use, he became someone else; his innocence was destroyed.

There were no more words or thoughts to describe the rape of a personality. No more words to describe what Ron had done; he'd taken an immature, naïve boy who wasn't quite a man yet, and had corrupted him to the point where it eventually caused his . . . death? But then death would've been kind. Garrett had gone the same route as J.J. Holiman, locked in a deadly struggle for eternity. Such a long time.

And he was responsible for more than Garrett's untimely exit from this planet. He was also guilty of destroying his memory, for after Garrett was gone, and the fire put out, there was an extensive investigation. Ron was questioned himself. But his answers, the truth about Asgar and Garrett and J.J. Holiman, were unacceptable! Ron was laughed at and received an extended disability leave, until such time as he could either pull himself together or be willing to sit behind a desk where he would remain hidden from the public and the press.

And in seeking the truth, those in charge of the investigation decided to conduct a search of Garrett's office, of his apartment in the city, of the property surrounding his home in the Hamptons. For surely there was another reason why Garrett disappeared, why his body was never found. In carrying out their so-called searches, one of the investigators came across a clearing in the woods where Satanic ceremonies, or something resembling the same had been performed.

A rotted maggot-infested human head was found staked on a pole in the middle of a roughly fashioned pentagram. Two bodies were found also; the charred remains of a punk rocker and the corpse of Phil Housner, the father of Samantha's roommate, Morgan.

As a result of these findings, Garrett was termed a mental case. The newspapers played it up big. 'Millionaire Playboy Disappears in Satanic Ritual,' they said. Because if Garrett was involved in kinky shit, then the investigators concluded that this had led ultimately to his own death; very probably at the hands of his own coven. 'Poetic justice,' they called it, that someone who'd obviously murdered others in Satan's name had followed the same route; to be used as a human sacrifice for the glory of Satan.

Garrett had had his very own personal demon, thanks to Ron, but never his very own personal

coven! And so, not only was Garrett gone from
this Earth, but his reputation along with him.

And then there was Samantha, his Samantha,
his love. But Samantha wasn't dead, not yet
anyway. So there was still hope.

But how much? How long should he wait, how
long should he keep the faith? And yet, he'd
waited a lifetime for Samantha, for someone with
her basic personality, and her loving, giving,
unselfish frame of mind. Therefore he had to keep
hoping for as long as it took.

But an eternity was such a long time. . . .

Ron saw a sign that read 'Shady Rest' and
turned into a long driveway leading to high
wrought iron gates and a guard shack. The
building beyond was where they were keeping
Samantha. He slammed on his brakes when he
saw the building and wanted to die, wanted to
ignore the guard who'd just stepped from the
shack and was watching him suspiciously. The
hell with them all, he thought. He wanted to run.

The building was a good imitation of Bridge Gate
Court: fading white brick exterior, black wrought
iron gates covering the windows, gargoyles on the
upper ledges. And they were keeping Samantha
there. Samantha would never get better until she
was out and away from the memories.

"Can I help you, sir?" the guard shouted.

But no. They were, all of them, beyond help at
this point. He released the pressure on the brake
and rolled up to the guard, gave Samantha's
name and was admitted. But he should've been
committed, not admitted, because now he felt his
mind slipping.

The inside of the building also bore a close
resemblance to Bridge Gate Court. Tiled floors in

the hallways, dim bulbs, darkened corridors leading to—he didn't want to know where; couldn't even begin to guess. There might be demons lurking in the shadows of those corridors, and if so, he didn't care to know it.

A hawk-faced nurse dressed in an off-white uniform that was yellow with age led him down a long corridor lined on both sides with heavy doors that had those little cut-outs at eye level. The kind of cut-outs that were better termed peepholes, where you could peep at the patients without them knowing and hopefully without them peeping back. As he walked behind her, the smell of urine and antiseptic assaulted his nostrils, and voices—pleading, crying, wailing voices—assaulted his ears. And again he wanted to die, or to run, or to just close his eyes and blot it out because he was close to belonging here himself.

Samantha was in the one at the end, the padded cell on the far left. He saw her and called to her, but she didn't hear him. She was in her own little world now and no one was permitted to enter. No intruders, please!

So the best he could do was just to look at her, to study her, and try to remember Samantha as she had been: beautiful, voluptuous, eyes full of life. Because this person he was looking at now bore little resemblance to the old Samantha. He studied the blank stare; the mumbling, whispering lips, the wringing hands that he knew were never still. And the protruding abdomen!

"Is . . . is she. . . ?"

"Pregnant?" the nurse asked, completing the thought for him. "Yes, she's pregnant. We tried asking who the father was . . ."

"And?"

"Well, it's odd. She keeps saying the same thing over and over, all day long, even in her sleep at night. She keeps saying, 'Dear Lord, please let it be Ron's.' Do you know anyone with that first name, Mr. Wheatley?"

"No . . . I used to know a Ron once, but now I'm not so sure that I ever knew him." That was true, he'd never really looked at himself until it was too late. And he wanted to say more but couldn't. In his frustration, he turned back to Samantha and whispered to her silently, with his mind, so that not even the nurse could hear what he was thinking to himself. *'I'm sorry, Samantha,'* his tortured mind screamed inwardly. *'I'm not the father. I'm sterile. I told you that before, but you must've forgotten. It's Garrett's baby . . . or Asgar's. Either you've been injected with the seeds of a man harboring a beast, or worse yet, with the seeds of the beast itself!'*

Then he turned and went on down the hall, knowing Samantha was lost to him forever. Even if she came out of it, even if her tortured mind one day miraculously returned to the present, she'd lose it again as soon as that baby was born. They all would, in fact . . .